BETRAYED

JOSEPH LEWIS

Black Rose Writing | Texas

©2020 by Joseph Lewis
All rights reserved. No part of this book may be reproduced, stored in a retrieval system or transmitted in any form or by any means without the prior written permission of the publishers, except by a reviewer who may quote brief passages in a review to be printed in a newspaper, magazine or journal.

The author grants the final approval for this literary material.

First printing

This is a work of fiction. Names, characters, businesses, places, events, and incidents are either the products of the author's imagination or used in a fictitious manner. Any resemblance to actual persons, living or dead, or actual events is purely coincidental.

ISBN: 978-1-68433-572-5
PUBLISHED BY BLACK ROSE WRITING
www.blackrosewriting.com

Printed in the United States of America
Suggested Retail Price (SRP) $20.95

Betrayed is printed in Calluna

*As a planet-friendly publisher, Black Rose Writing does its best to eliminate unnecessary waste to reduce paper usage and energy costs, while never compromising the reading experience. As a result, the final word count vs. page count may not meet common expectations.

Being the second youngest of ten, I was fortunate to be born into a loving, caring family of brothers and sisters who also are my friends. I would not be the person I am without their influence, their love, and friendship.

Betrayed is dedicated to Donna Lewis Friedel (deceased); Judy Lewis Lesiecki; Mary Lewis Schad; Elizabeth Lewis Kriska (deceased); Joanne Lewis Rosenmeier (deceased); John "Jack" Lewis, Jr.; Kathy Lewis; Jim Lewis; and Jeff Lewis. Love you all!

ACKNOWLEDGEMENTS

A book the magnitude of *Betrayed* didn't happen without the help of talented and knowledgeable individuals who lent their time to my endless questions. A thank you goes to Andrea Schad for the information on the care of horses; to Brian Jorgenson for the information on hunting and everything associated with it; to Sharon King for all things medical and her eyes on the first draft; to Theresa Storke for reading through the manuscript and for being one of my biggest cheerleaders; to Reagan Rothe and the team at Black Rose Writing for giving me a home; to David King for a killer cover design. A special thank you to my wife and best friend, Kim, who puts up with the hours of writing and rewriting each night; and to my daughters Hannah and Emily for their love and support. I also want to thank you, the reader, for joining me on this journey.

BETRAYED

"You never know how strong you are
until being strong is your only choice."
~Bob Marley

"Courage doesn't mean you aren't afraid.
Courage means you don't let fear stop you."
~Svetlana M.

"In the solemnity of endings,
we find hope in new beginnings."
~Anne Scottlin

CHAPTER ONE

It was still. No breeze. The air, dead, smelled of red dirt and decay. A hawk circled overhead, cawed once, and glared at him. At least Brian thought it did. He wondered vaguely if it was an omen, a message from the spirit world George often talked about. A warning, perhaps. Fitting if it was, Brian thought. If they survived, he would ask him.

He lay prone in the dirt and glanced behind him. Brett was not visible. That was good. He wanted his brother safely behind the big boulder. Hidden.

Brian wasn't afraid to die. He just didn't *want* to die. Not yet, anyway. Fifteen was too young. However, he made a promise to watch over George and Brett, and that he would do. If it came to it, he would protect his two brothers any way he could, including sacrificing his own life.

The morning he made the promise, he didn't think much of it. George was independent. Always had been. Brett was stubborn. Yet, Brian said he would do what he could, and though it wasn't exactly a promise, he had given his word, and he had always kept his word.

On the long trek to the mesa, Brian had thought about life and death. It was not the first time death had crossed his mind. He had watched his twin brother die. Brad bled to death from multiple gunshot wounds and died in a stranger's arms. After his death, Brian's mother shot his father, and then shot herself.

Brian ended up alone. Alone, except for Jeremy, who took him in, and made him his son just as he did for five other boys.

He knew death. It didn't scare him. He never worried about it. If it happened, it happened.

However, he wasn't ready to die, and he didn't want to die.

At the same time, he had made up his mind that he would do everything in his power to make sure Brett and George would live.

No matter the cost.

CHAPTER TWO

Several Days Previous

They stood in the driveway of an expansive ranch home made of brick and glass that was out of place on Navajoland. When one had money, one could build whatever one wanted and as big as one wanted it. It was big and beautiful, almost obscene in comparison to the abject poverty most of the *Dine'* lived in. There were several of these monstrosities dotting the desert landscape, one competing with the next in size and expense. No matter. He had money and power and used both to his advantage. He liked what he had. His only disappointment was that he didn't have more.

"Have you found that kid yet?"

Two men looked at the red dirt and shuffled their dusty boots.

"Why the fuck not?" he shouted. His anger grew in proportion to their non-answers.

"We've been watching the girl and her old man hoping they would lead us to him."

"That isn't good enough, goddammit! For chrissakes, we need to find that kid. We don't have time to sit and watch."

He walked away from the two men. With his hands on his hips, he made two quick decisions. He was used to making quick decisions, and most of the time, they worked out to his advantage.

He viewed his small stature as a weakness, as something he couldn't control. It angered him, so his persona was that of a small, angry man. Wealthy and powerful, but small and angry.

"I want the two of you to make sure the *No Trespassing* sign is strung across the road leading to the abandoned ranch. When I swing by, I expect it to be posted."

"Yes, Sir. We will."

"Do it now!" he added.

He turned his back on them again, walked a few steps away and pulled out his cell. He turned back around and saw the two men still standing there.

"Didn't I just tell you what I wanted you to do?"

"Yes, Sir."

Both men turned and walked to the pickup they used.

"And find that boy!"

The man wasn't sure if he had wanted to keep these two nothings on his payroll. Others were more efficient, smarter, and dependable. Ruthless and lethal, if it came to that. They would know how to get answers. They would also know what to do with the boy, and anyone else, who got in their way.

He pushed the speed dial and without waiting for a hello, he said, "Do you have any leads on that kid?"

"Not yet. Still looking."

"There can't be that many places for him to hide."

"There are enough," the voice answered.

"Well find him. You know what to do with him."

He hung up abruptly and slid his cell into his coat pocket. He kicked a stone and stared off in the distance. The heat made the red desert floor shimmer.

He had a goal, and he wouldn't be denied.

CHAPTER THREE

"Would you at least think about it?" Brett asked.

The AC was not working, the overhead fan pushed around hot air, and the night was stifling. Covered in a fine sheen of sweat, George and Brett only wore boxers. The heat and humidity did not prevent Brett from sleeping up against George with their feet and legs tangled, nor did it prevent them from using a sheet to cover the lower halves of their bodies, though George had all but kicked it off.

It was far too early to get out of bed, and George was not ready to anyway, not that he had been in it much. He had spent more time in the bathroom watching over Billy than he did in bed.

Normally, George shared a room and a bed with Billy. However, the past night and the day before, Billy had spent more time in the bathroom kneeling over the toilet retching. Twice, Billy had to sit on the toilet with a bucket in his lap, because whatever had been in his stomach poured out both ends. George had held his breath and made sure Billy did not fall off his porcelain throne.

Randy, Billy's twin, had not fared much better in the bathroom at the other end of the hall. He had gotten sick a day earlier. Jeremy, the boys' dad, did for him what George did for Billy. Vicky, the boys' mom, worked her way between both bathrooms.

Brett, Brian, and Bobby had stayed away, and thankfully managed to escape whatever bug Randy and Billy had. So had George, though he did not know how after spending so much time with Billy.

"Please?" Brett asked with a poke to George's ribs.

George was exhausted. Maybe overly tired, which was why he had trouble sleeping. He yawned, scratched an armpit and his belly.

Brett rubbed his eyes, yawned again, rolled over onto his stomach and said, "It would be really cool if all of us played football."

"But we don't."

Brett rolled over onto his side, faced him, and said, "But wouldn't that be cool? Randy will be the quarterback for sure. Billy and I will be in the backfield. Bobby will be an H back or wide receiver, and even though Bri plays soccer, he'll be the kicker. His coach said he could. With your speed and hands, you could play wide receiver."

George rolled onto his back.

"I like running. I don't want to play football."

"But wouldn't it be cool? All of us would be on the same team. I don't think six brothers played football on the same team ever, anywhere."

"Brett . . ." George did not finish other than to shake his head.

He loved running. As a ninth grader, he had taken third at state in cross country. He finished first at the state in track in the 3200, and second in the 1600. George expected he would only get better in his sophomore year. By the time he was a senior, hopefully, he would earn a scholarship to Madison, major in Criminal Justice, and work for the FBI. His dream.

"Please think about it," Brett whispered.

Changing the subject, George asked, "I thought you were running cross country because you were worried about getting hurt for track?"

"Nah, I like football too much. Track is my favorite, and I think it's my best sport. Dad and I talked about it, and we decided that I can't live my life afraid of getting hurt. He said it would be going through life half-assed." Brett laughed, and said, "That's not exactly what he said, but that's what he meant."

"I like running. I like watching football, but I don't want to play it."

Brett sighed. He had known George's answer before he had asked, but he wanted to try. With a little over two weeks left before the first practice, he had time to work on him.

George checked the alarm clock. Three-twelve. In an hour and a half, he would get up, run, and then say his prayers to Father Sun as any traditional Navajo would.

He yawned again. Brett put an arm across George's chest, and his head on George's shoulder. Evidently the heat, the humidity, and the lack of air conditioning, did not bother Brett.

George smiled. He loved his family. He loved his brothers. He said, "Love you, Brett."

"You too."

They had shut their eyes, but before either of them could fall asleep, George's cell went off.

CHAPTER FOUR

George rolled over, grabbed his cell, and read the ID that came up with the number. He swung his feet over the side of the bed, stared at the phone. Something was wrong.

Brett leaned up on an elbow, and asked, "Who is it?"

"It's Rebecca," George whispered. He did a quick calculation. Three-fifteen meant two-fifteen in Navajoland. Did Navajoland follow Daylight Savings? He could not remember.

More than that, he pictured her bronze skin, her long silky black hair worn in traditional Navajo style. Her breasts, her beauty. His oldest friend from a lifetime ago.

"Answer it," Brett said, nudging him in the back.

George pushed the button, lifted the cell to his ear, and said, "Rebecca..."

Rebecca never got hysterical that George could remember, but she sounded close to it.

"Rebecca..." George repeated. He stood up and stared at Brett.

"George, it's Charles. He's missing."

"What do you mean Charles is missing?"

Brett jumped out of bed, hotfooted it out of the room, and down the hall.

"He's gone. He was watching the sheep. I went to take my turn, and he was gone. The sheep were everywhere. Some were dead. And Charles... he's gone."

Jeremy, Vicky, and Brett ran into the room. Brett flapped his arms and then ran back out. The big dog, Momma, soundlessly tiptoed into the room, head and tail low, not sure what was happening. Jasmine, George's dog, stood at attention at George's feet waiting for orders.

"How long?"

Almost as if she had not heard him, Rebecca said, *"He's gone. We don't know where he is. No one knows where he is. He's gone."*

Jeremy and Vicky stepped over to George, and Vicky slipped an arm around his bare shoulders.

"George, put her on speaker," Jeremy said.

Brett, Brian, and Bobby ran into the room led by Jasper, Brian's and Bobby's dog, followed by Randy and Billy, though the twins moved slower. They lay down on the bed crossways side by side and looked to be already asleep.

"Rebecca, my mother and father are here. I'm putting you on speaker."

"Okay, but George," and she dissolved into tears.

"Rebecca, this is Jeremy. Can you tell us what happened?"

It was slow and tedious with intermittent sobbing, but Rebecca told them.

Everything was fine when Charles left their hogan that morning at sunrise. He packed his lunch, grabbed his rifle and ammunition, and went out the door. Rebecca watched her older brother ride out of the stable on the tall dun he always rode.

When she rode out to their field in the early afternoon, she found six sheep shot dead, the rest scattered, and Charles missing.

Jeremy spoke again. "You said your sheep were dead."

"They were sh-shot," Rebecca answered with a sob.

Jeremy said, "Rebecca, about Charles not being there, has this happened before? I mean, maybe he went hunting and forgot to tell someone?"

George shook his head as Rebecca said, *"He wouldn't do that. Something happened."*

George whispered to Jeremy, "Charles would not do that."

"Rebecca, this is Vicky, George's mom." She paused, and said, "Tell us again, how long has he been missing?"

"Since this afternoon but we don't know for sure. Maybe sometime this morning. We don't know where he is," Rebecca sobbed. *"We need to find him."*

George did not say anything, but both Jeremy and Vicky read what he was thinking in his eyes.

Vicky said, "Rebecca. Jeremy, George, and I will discuss this, and call you first thing in the morning. Okay?"

It took time, but Rebecca said, *"Okay, but I'm afraid something bad has happened to him. Father rode out to look for him but couldn't find him. He's riding out in the morning to look again. He won't let me help. We're so scared."*

"Honey, I know. Let me talk it over with Jeremy and George, and I promise we will call you in the morning. Okay?"

"Yes, Ma'am. Okay." She sniffed, and said, *"Is George there?"*

"Yes, Becca, I'm here."

"I'm sorry I called so late. I didn't know who else to call," and Rebecca began crying again, not that she ever completely stopped.

"It is okay, Becca," George whispered. "Try to get some sleep. My dad, and mom, and I will figure something out. I promise."

CHAPTER FIVE

Billy and Randy walked back to their rooms. No one was sure if they would even remember being in Brett's room for the phone call.

George joined Jeremy and Vicky in their bedroom. Brett wanted to be with them but he decided to leave the three of them alone so he crawled back into bed to wait. George would fill him in anyway. Bobby went back to his bedroom and Brian to his with Jasper trailing. Momma laid down in front of his closed door, her head on her front paws facing the top of the stairs.

Brian slipped off his t-shirt, crawled into the bed, and covered his bottom-half with a sheet. He hoped Bobby would sneak in, shut the door, strip down, and climb into bed next to him. On previous nights, that is what Bobby would do. Except those nights had become fewer and fewer. Almost nonexistent.

He yawned and shook his head so he could concentrate on what he was doing.

Brian was pretty good with computers, but Bobby and Randy were the best. Instead of booting up his computer, he used his cell to look up flight information from Milwaukee to Albuquerque, and bus information from Albuquerque to Shiprock, Arizona. If he remembered correctly, he thought that was close to where George used to live.

He figured they could afford to spend no more than a week out there. Soccer and football began in ten days, and if they went for a week, they could get back and be ready for tryouts. George would probably know where to look for him, and hopefully, nothing bad happened to his friend.

Satisfied with what he found so far, Brian typed up a brief email explaining what he had done and why, and then sent it to his mom, dad, and George. That finished, he set his cell down on the nightstand, put both hands under his head, and stared at the ceiling fan.

George couldn't go by himself. Jeremy and Vicky wouldn't allow it. However, if the three of them went together, they could camp out and hunt after they found Charles.

Brian offered to use some money from his savings or his trust fund. He sat on a large pile of it, way more than the other guys because of the sale of the house after his biological parents had died. Between what his father had left him in insurance money, and what was in his mom's and dad's savings and checking accounts, he could afford it. More so than Jeremy and Vicky could.

He let his thoughts drift to Cat, his girlfriend. He was aroused and slipped a hand into his boxers to adjust himself. On the off-chance that Bobby would visit him, he didn't do anything other than that.

Then, just as quickly, his thoughts drifted to Bobby.

He loved Bobby. It was difficult to explain because he had never felt that way about any other boy. As close as he was to the twins and to Brett and George, it had never occurred to him to have sex with them. He liked girls. He liked what he and Cat did together. Just the thought of it made his head spin and his stomach tighten.

It was different with Bobby. Yes, they were brothers through adoption, but weren't related biologically. Brian thought that made a difference. Bobby wasn't so sure.

He wasn't sure when, but between the late hour and the hypnotizing effect of the ceiling fan, Brian fell asleep with hands under his head, legs barely covered, and without any dream that he would recall in the morning.

CHAPTER SIX

Neither Jeremy nor Vicky could sleep. Jeremy reread the email Brian had sent them. After Vicky read it, she handed the cell back to him. He set it aside, laid back with one arm holding Vicky, and stared at the ceiling.

"What are you thinking?" Vicky whispered. She dared not raise her voice because she did not know if one or more of the boys had their ears pressed against their door. It was fifty-fifty either way.

They had been married for two years. She was Brett's and Bobby's biological mother. The rest of the boys were all adopted by Jeremy at first and then by Vicky. They loved their boys- all of them. Each of the boys carried baggage from a previous life, and most of that baggage was battered and ugly. How the boys survived, neither Jeremy nor Vicky knew. But they adjusted and grew to be confident and happy. Love is magical that way.

Picking up on Vicky's quiet tone, Jeremy said, "Brian is right. George has to go, but he can't go by himself. At the same time, I don't feel good sending the three of them by themselves."

A high school counselor, he was in the middle of schedule changes and fixing course conflicts. It was one of the busiest times of the year with school starting in less than four weeks. Vicky would not be able to pick up and leave. She had just started a new job at Froedtert Hospital and Medical College. She was scheduled for two heart surgeries a day for the next four days. As head surgical nurse, she was tough to replace, especially in a new job.

Vicky rolled over on her side and whispered, "What if we ask Jamie or Pat to go with them? I mean, they're cops, so they would know how to find Charles."

Jeremy had been friends with them for a long time. Cops, one a detective with the police department, the other a detective with the sheriff department.

"They wouldn't have any jurisdiction, not that they would need it if all they're doing is searching for a missing kid."

"What if we contact Pete Kelliher? I read somewhere that the FBI has jurisdiction on Indian reservations. The FBI owes George for all he's done for them. Brett and Brian too for that matter."

Jeremy thought that over and shrugged. She was right. The FBI owed them. He said, "It wouldn't hurt to ask them."

The two of them were silent, though it was not comfortable. It was Vicky who broke it.

"Two summers ago." She stopped and shook her head. She sounded tired, and it wasn't just the late night and lack of sleep. "Then last fall, and then last winter. There has been so much death. The threats. The constant looking over our shoulder, wondering, waiting."

Jeremy sighed, and said, "And now George's oldest friend is missing."

Vicky shook her head and balled up her fists so tightly her fingernails left angry grooves in her palms. "When will this end? It's been one thing after another."

"Perhaps, Rebecca's brother went off somewhere. Hunting or something. Maybe he got hurt and couldn't make it back home. By the time the boys get out there, maybe her brother will be found, and they'll all go hunting together," Jeremy suggested.

"Do you really believe that?"

He shook his head. Even as he said it, he did not believe it.

"I thought this was all behind us," Vicky said as she stared at the ceiling fan. "When will it end, Jeremy?"

"I know," he answered, without answering her.

She kissed him and whispered, "I just want all of this behind us. For the sake of the boys. For our sake. All of this needs to end."

Jeremy smiled weakly and kissed her back. "I'll call Graff, O'Connor, and Kelliher in the morning. It'll work out okay."

Even as he said it, it crossed his mind that it might never be okay, and it might never end. Something would come up. Deep down, he knew it, and he was sure Vicky knew it too.

CHAPTER SEVEN

Rebecca Morning Star wanted to ride out and search for her brother, but her father would not let her.

"Take care of the sheep."

"But Father, I know Charles. I know where he hunts, and where he camps."

With his jaw set, he packed his saddlebags with a meager amount of food. He snatched his dirty and sweat-stained tan Stetson off the peg by the door and jammed it onto his head. He grabbed the double-barrel shotgun off the rack on the wall, pocketed a dozen shells, and walked out of their five-room hogan. He stopped at the pump and filled his canteen with water from the outdoor well.

Like his wife Rosetta, Franklin Morning Star was small. His two children towered over him, though at five-foot-six, it did not take much. His dark brown face resembled well-worn leather. His thick hands and fingers showed the calluses of a man who worked for a living. Real work that had begun in his preteens. His back was bent and his legs bowed from working horses and sheep. At night, when it was cold, his back did not speak nicely to him.

He was a stubborn man. He told Rebecca what she needed to do and where she needed to be, and he expected her to obey. Rebecca came by her own stubbornness honestly.

Her mother, Rose, as her father called her, watched the little scene in silence as she wiped away tears. She had spent the night sitting in a chair on the porch wrapped in a blanket, hoping her son would ride into their yard.

Rebecca packed what she needed. She grabbed a Winchester 30-30 Lever Action and threw her saddlebag over her shoulder. She pushed her black Stetson on her head of long silky black hair worn in a traditional Navajo style like George and stormed out the front door just in time to see her father leave the corral on the pinto.

"He hunts in the high country. Check the western slope of the Chuska Mountains," she yelled. When she was sure her father would not hear, she muttered, "That's where I would look. If I was *allowed* to." When George arrived, the two of them would ride out and find her brother.

Rebecca and Charles had known George since early elementary school. Their families were from different clans. Rebecca came from the *To'ahani* or the Near The Water Clan, while George was from the *'Azee'tsoh dine'e* which translated to The Big Medicine People Clan. Their ranches were within three miles of each other, and they had gone to the same school until George moved the summer his family was murdered.

Charles was one year older but the three of them, along with George's younger brother, William, had hunted together, rode together, camped together, and when possible and if there was a need, helped each other with their chores. All of that changed when George moved to Wisconsin.

Rebecca was a female mirror image of George. Bronze skin that turned dark brown in the desert sun. Both bore a near noble look, he handsome, she pretty. Both were nearly the same height and on the skinny side. Both were athletic, although Rebecca had never played on any team, nor had she found time for organized sports.

Lost in thought, she started to skirt past the dirt track that led to the burned down hogan that had been the Tokay home when she noticed it.

"Whoa," she said as she pulled on the reins.

Strung from two metal stakes across the road was a "No Trespassing" sign.

Rebecca frowned. It was not there yesterday that she remembered, so it had to have been hung sometime before sunrise. In any case, this land had belonged to George's mother and grandparents, so now it belonged to him.

Rebecca got down from her horse, took her rope from the saddle, tied it over the chain, and then looped the other end of the rope around her saddle horn. She hopped up onto her paint and used the heel of her boots to prod her horse forward. As the rope grew tight, the chain was ripped down.

"Whoa," she said as she pulled up on the reins.

She repeated the process with the two pipes. Once they were pulled up from the ground, she took the two pipes, the chain, and the "No Trespassing" sign, got on her horse, and rode down the dirt drive until she reached the burned down structures that had once been George's ranch. The barn, fence, outhouse, and hogan were nothing but blackened ruins. Time and the desert sun further weakened the charred remains.

She swung down from her horse, and carried her little bundle to what was left of the outhouse, and dropped them into the stinking hole.

Rebecca took her time walking the perimeter of the property. Ignoring the traditional Navajo belief to stay away from the hogan where people had died, she stood where the small living area had been. She could still make out the stone hearth, though much of it had fallen in on itself. Even though the early morning temperature tiptoed into the mid-seventies, she shivered, and as a response, hugged her thin, narrow self.

She backed out of the ruin, turned around, and walked quickly to her horse, mounted, and rode off.

It was not until she was in her own pasture, and among her own sheep, did she consider the chain, and the "No Trespassing" sign, and wonder who might have placed it there.

CHAPTER EIGHT

Before dawn, George had run six miles, and finished in time to greet Father Sun with his morning prayers. After, he practiced his knife exercises, perhaps with greater care and precision than he had since late winter. To those who did not know what he was doing, it looked like George practiced an Eastern art form like Tai Chi or Kung Fu.

Brian and Bobby did their sit-ups, pushups, and planks. That took Brian to eight o'clock. After a quick breakfast, he placed a call to Jeff and Danny Limbach, their neighbors and best friends, to let them know he would be shooting in the field behind the stable.

He took the three dogs, the three rifles, and the two handguns, and made sure each of the rifles were sighted in at two hundred yards. The two identical Glock 19s were good to twenty-five yards, but best to within twenty. He did not care for pistols, but Brett liked them and was good with them. Brett had teased Brian that he was a pistol snob.

Brett gathered up the boys' First Aid, CPR, and Hunter's Safety cards, and then packed. George and Brian met up in the stable. Together, they cleaned the stalls, fed, and watered the horses. The boys did not have time to take the horses out for a ride, but they did lead them to the pasture for sun and exercise. Jose, the Limbach's hired hand, would stable them later that afternoon.

The two boys and the three dogs walked the two hundred or so yards back to their house, using the path through the woods. There was a comfortable silence between them, as much friends as they were brothers through adoption, like the rest of their brothers.

Once there, George grabbed a glass from the cupboard, filled it with water from the dispenser in the refrigerator, and then raced up the stairs to shower, dress, and pack.

Brian walked to the family room where he broke down the rifles, and packed them into their metal cases, each individual part surrounded by thick foam. He locked all three and set the key aside. Fortunately, the same key worked on each case. He placed the Glocks in a separate metal case, locked it, and then picked up both keys. It was time to get himself ready.

Brian took the stairs two at a time, and before he reached the upstairs landing, he had already pulled off his t-shirt.

He found eight days clothes set neatly on his bed. In one row, there were two pair of jeans and two pair of shorts, three t-shirts and five button-down shirts, the kind Brian wore when he rode the horses. In a second row were socks and boxers. At the side of his bed were his cowboy boots and a pair of deck shoes.

Brian smiled. This was Bobby's way of packing and attacking life. Everything neat and orderly, and in stacks and rows.

He stripped down to his boxers, took a clean pair out of the dresser, and walked across to the bathroom to get ready for the trip. He had just finished brushing his teeth when Bobby knocked and entered, shutting the door behind him.

He grinned at Bobby and said, "Thanks for getting my clothes ready."

"I was waiting for you," Bobby said quietly. "I thought I'd help you pack."

He said, "I just got back from the stable so I don't smell very good."

"That's not what I meant. We need to talk," Bobby said with his chin on his chest.

Brian's stomach grew queasy. He leaned against the counter, while Bobby faced him.

"Bri, I have a bad feeling about this trip."

Brian smiled at him, shrugged, and reached for him.

"No, I don't want to do that." Then just as quickly, he said, "I mean, we need to talk."

Brian blushed. Caught off guard, he said, "George, Brett, and I have hunted lots of times. Graff and O'Connor are coming with us, and we're meeting some FBI agent in Albuquerque. We'll search for Charles and find him. Then we'll hunt and come home."

"You know what happened the last time any of us were in Arizona," Bobby said, his voice shaking. "George and dad almost died."

"That was two summers ago. Those people are either dead or in prison. It's over, Bobby."

"Promise you'll be careful and you'll come home," Bobby whispered.

"Of course. I love you too much not to." Brian caught something else in Bobby's eyes and said, "What?"

Bobby's eyes shifted to his hands. When he looked up, his chin quivered slightly.

"I think you and I need to stop . . . doing stuff." He shrugged again and lowered his eyes.

Brian opened his mouth to protest, but closed it instead. The silence sat between them unapproachable and forbidding.

Finally, Brian said, "Did someone say something?"

Bobby shook his head.

"Did mom or dad say something?" Brian tried again.

"No one said anything. I just think we need a break . . . to figure things out."

"I thought we already figured things out," Brian said. "We love each other."

"We do. I love you. I always will."

"So, what are we talking about?"

Bobby eyes searching Brian's face, begging to be understood.

"Bri, I love you more than anyone, but I'm not sure what we're doing . . . what we do, is good. We're brothers. I mean, if we keep . . . doing stuff . . ."

Brian shook his head. He didn't understand, and he didn't want to stop being with Bobby.

"Did I do something wrong?"

Chin on his chest, Bobby shook his head.

"We aren't related. We're adopted. We have girlfriends, Bobby. You know that."

Bobby wiped a tear from his eye and said, "I know that, but we're brothers, Brian."

Brian shook his head. This is not what he wanted before he left for a week. He didn't have enough time to fix this.

He stood in front of Bobby and took hold of both of his hands. The two boys put their foreheads together as they often did.

"Bobby, I love you more than anyone. Nothing will change that. And I think you love me the same way. I know you do."

"I do love you," Bobby said. He gripped Brian's hands tighter.

Brian leaned in and attempted to kiss Bobby, but Bobby turned his head.

Brett knocked on the door, barged in, and stopped, rooted to the spot. He saw the two boys holding hands, and when Brian glanced at him, he could not read Brett's expression.

Brett said, "We have about an hour and a half before Graff and O'Connor show up. Are you packed?"

"You need to knock," Bobby said, his voice cracking.

"I did." Brett took one last look, turned around, and left, shutting the door behind him.

The moment had vanished and there was no getting it back.

Bobby shook his hand free, and whispered, "Promise me you'll be careful."

Brian said, "I promise, Bobby."

Bobby walked to the door, didn't open it, but kept his hand on the doorknob.

In panic, Brian said, "Bobby, wait. Can you think about it? Please?"

Still with his back to Brian, Bobby said, "I have thought about it."

He opened the door, stepped out into the hallway, and shut the door behind him.

CHAPTER NINE

Brian pulled on a clean green polo that matched his eyes. With other shirts, his eyes were hazel. Cat liked how his eyes changed colors, and he smiled at the thought. Just as quickly, the smile vanished, and he sighed.

He stepped into his khaki shorts and finished with Dockers without socks. He had wanted to dress casually for the plane trip. He would change into jeans, his cowboy boots, and a cowboy hat when they landed.

His dark wavy hair was damp but he no longer smelled like a horse's stall. His step was slow and heavy. Normally, his life was good. He had always been even tempered, if not happy and upbeat. In actuality, his life had nowhere to go but up considering all that had happened before he had moved in with, and been adopted by, Jeremy. He had the best friends who happened to be his brothers, along with the best mom and dad any kid could ask for. Mostly, he belonged. That he fit.

However, the conversation with Bobby left him reeling. He didn't know how that might change his relationship with him, and if that changed, his relationship to the other guys might change, too. He tried to push that thought out of his head, but it wouldn't leave.

He was packed and ready, but he wasted time sitting on his bed by himself. Normally, he would be excited. After all, he was doing two of his favorite things in life: hunting and camping. If someone were to throw in fishing, soccer, or basketball, he would have thought he had gone to heaven. But the conversation with Bobby hung like a cloud and any excitement, any joy he might have felt had vanished. He kept thinking that someone must have said something.

He picked up his duffle bag and his backpack and walked to the doorway and right into Vicky.

Her long brown hair hung on her shoulders. Her hips were small, and her waist, smaller. Bobby and Brett had a similar build. Broad on top, narrow on the bottom, except that Bobby's and Brett's thighs were thick and muscled from their workouts and lifting. Their complexion matched hers: an olive tone that grew dark brown in summer. Brian had only met their biological father, or "Tom" as Brett referred to him, twice. Though he was a handsome man, it was clear that the two boys got their looks from their mom and her side of the family.

"Oops, sorry, Brian."

Brian smiled weakly and said, "It's okay."

Vicky tilted her head, lifted Brian's chin and said, "Is everything okay?"

Brian couldn't make eye contact even though Vicky gently tilted his chin upwards.

"I'm just tired."

Vicky had every mother's antenna, and it was working just fine. "You sure? Is something wrong?"

"I'm fine."

She frowned, and said, "Something is wrong."

Brian sighed and said, "I don't want to talk about it."

Vicky nodded and said, "Okay."

He tried walking past her, but she held him back, taking hold of his shoulder gently.

"May I talk with you for a minute?"

Normally, he and Vicky talked often. School. Sports. Girls. Everyday stuff. He could talk to Jeremy too. It had always been easy with them. However, not so on this morning. Brian was afraid he'd break down in front of her and he didn't want that.

He decided to go with a partial truth. "I'm worried about Bobby. He's more nervous about us going than Randy is. When he plays his guitar, that's his happy place. Piano too, I guess. Don't let him be by himself too much. If you hear 'Tin Man' or 'Like A Cowboy' or 'Over You' . . . well, he's sad."

Vicky smiled at Brian, and said, "You've got a good heart, Bri. Like your dad."

Brian blushed, and said to the floor, "I love him, Mom."

Vicky kissed his forehead, gave him a hug, and said, "Anyone who sees the two of you together knows that you love each other. You do understand why your dad and I made the two of you move into separate rooms, right?"

Brian, stared at the wall, and blurted out, "I don't want to talk about that." To soften it, he added, "Please."

Vicky was smart enough to figure out what was bothering Brian. She nodded and said, "Okay." She hugged him even though Brian didn't hug her back.

Brian blushed, shrugged, and wanted to change the subject so he said, "Just don't let Bobby be by himself too much."

Vicky said, "I'll keep an eye on Bobby and the twins. I promise."

Brian relaxed.

"You know your dad and I love you, right?"

Brian nodded unenthusiastically.

She held his chin, and said, "I need you to do something for me. Just between us."

"What?" he asked.

"Normally George is tuned into what is around him. His Navajo thing, as Dad calls it. But George is worried about his friend. That is what he's concentrating on, so he won't be tuned into anything else. Indian country will be new for Brett. You too. But Brett can be impulsive. Normally, he thinks clearly but you know him. If one of you is in trouble, Brett will risk everything to protect you."

Brian nodded.

"So, I'm asking you to keep an eye on both of them. Kind of think for them. You've always shown good judgment. You're careful. You tend to go slowly and not rush into things. I'm hoping that when you get out there, George's friend will have already come back from wherever he is, and the three of you can just relax and have fun."

"Me too."

"But if he's still missing, and if Graff, O'Connor, and the FBI agent can't figure out what happened to him or who killed their sheep, I'm asking you to watch over George and Brett, and think for them. Be careful and make sure they're careful too. I'm not asking you to do anything risky. I just need you to anticipate for them. Keep them out of trouble."

Vicky noticed Brian's frown.

"Are you okay with that?"

"Brett's always been the leader."

"He listens to you. I watched the two of you during basketball season. He relied on you. You gave him confidence. You steady him, so he might need that. Both George and Brett might need that."

Brian said, "I think I can do that."

Vicky kissed his cheek, and said, "That's all I can ask. Do your best."

"I will."

Brett yelled from somewhere down the hall, "Bri, we have to go. Pat and Jamie are here."

Brian walked ahead of Vicky, who followed him frowning. Something happened to change Brian's mood. She didn't know what it was, but she'd find out.

George and Brett said goodbye to Bobby, Billy, and Randy, saving Jeremy and Vicky for last. Brian worked in reverse of that. He said goodbye to Jeremy and Vicky, and then the twins.

Bobby waited for Brian's goodbye, but Brian barely looked at him. Instead he loaded his duffle and his backpack into O'Connor's trunk, shut it, and then climbed into the backseat next to George and Brett without saying a word to Bobby.

Out of the corner of his eye, he saw Bobby push his hands into the pockets of his Nike sweatpants and take a step back. Randy and Billy stepped up on either side of him. Brian lifted a hand and half-heartedly waved goodbye to his brothers as O'Connor pulled out of the driveway.

Puzzled, Brett pursed his lips as he studied Brian. Brett had a million questions he wanted to ask, but he held his tongue. George stared straight ahead. He had as many questions as Brett, but kept his expression neutral. Now and then O'Connor would glance at him using the rearview mirror.

Once or twice Graff glanced over his shoulder at him. He tried to make small talk, but only George and Brett took part. When asked a direct question, Brian answered in one or two words or not at all. Mostly, it was not at all.

Brian shut his eyes and leaned his head on the window. It seemed to him that everyone was left wondering what had happened. He didn't care. He just wanted to get away. Far away. Maybe the trip to Arizona would do him good. Do everyone some good.

CHAPTER TEN

There was one brief layover in Chicago, enough for a pit stop and to buy bottles of water. Brett added an orange that he peeled and ate in the waiting area. Finally, they boarded the plane for the last leg of their journey to Albuquerque.

The boys sat together. Brett asked for the aisle seat because the window and middle seats were too confining. George took the middle and promptly fell asleep using Brian's shoulder as a pillow. He would twitch and jerk, but remained asleep not even hearing the flight attendant offer peanuts and a drink. Neither Brett nor Brian accepted, content with their bottles of water.

Pat and Jamie sat across from them, and after watching George, Jamie asked, "Is he okay?"

Brett stared at George, shrugged, and said, "About what you'd expect."

It was silent the rest of the way. Brian shut his eyes but did not sleep. Now and then, he would glance out the window and guess where they were by the changing landscape. Brett reclined his seat and shut his eyes but did not come close to sleeping even though if a bed were handy, he would plop down and end up comatose in seconds.

George woke up as the plane began its descent. He looked around, remembered where he was, and sat up straight.

"You good?" Brett asked him.

George nodded once.

It took another twenty minutes to land but to George it seemed to take hours. After the plane taxied to the gate, the five of them grabbed their bags from the overhead bin. The three boys followed Graff and O'Connor down the aisle, through the moveable tunnel, and into the terminal.

Graff pointed at the signs, and said, "Baggage claim is this way," and the group followed him.

George checked his phone, and there was a voicemail from Rebecca.

"Charles is still missing. Meet at your ranch. Text or call when you get there."

Graff led the group to the baggage claim, and as they waited for their bags and guns, his cell rang.

He answered, "Graff."

"This is FBI Agent Ronaldo Reyna. I'm driving a black Suburban with New Mexico plates, and I'm waiting at the curb just outside the baggage claim."

"Okay, thanks. Should be there shortly."

O'Connor got a porter with a cart, and the boys loaded up the cases with their rifles, pistols, and the bigger bags. The rest were carried out either on their backs or by hand.

They found Reyna leaning against the passenger door of the Suburban. He wore a brown sport coat over a white-buttoned down shirt. A bolo tie with a turquoise gem hung from his neck. He wore jeans topped off with a sizeable silver and turquoise buckle. On his feet were boots, and on his head was a black cowboy hat. He stood a narrow five-eleven with thick arms. His bright white teeth competed for attention with the dimple in his left cheek, and gave him a little boy look, though he was probably in his early to mid-thirties. Graff could not tell.

"Hi, I'm Ronaldo Reyna. Call me Ron." He shook hands with the group as each identified himself. He continued, "We'll load up, and then we're driving to an airfield just north of here. We'll hop on a small jet that will take us to Four Corners Regional Airport in Farmington. It's a short flight but faster than the three hours it would take to drive there."

George considered that Gallup might have been closer and wondered why they were taking a longer route.

"Agent Kelliher said we're supposed to treat you as our guests and to give you guys any help we can."

They loaded up the back of the Suburban with their luggage. O'Connor took the passenger seat because of his long legs. Brett and Brian sat in the very back even though they were taller than George. Brett figured it was George's trip and everyone else were tag-alongs. Jamie sat behind O'Connor, and George sat behind Reyna.

As Reyna pulled away from the curb, he asked, "I know George grew up here but have any of you ever visited this area?"

There were some no's and shakes of heads. Brian said, "When I was little, my family took a trip to the Grand Canyon but I don't remember much of it."

"You're still little," Brett said with a smack on Brian's thigh.

Brian mouthed an "ouch" but said, "I'm taller than you are."

"But I'm smarter and better looking."

"In your dreams." Brian's mood lightened some.

Reyna laughed, and said, "I try to get there once or twice a year. It's as peaceful as it is beautiful. A nice place to center yourself."

"Excuse me but have you heard anything about Charles?" George asked.

Reyna glanced at him using the rearview mirror, and said, "Nothing you don't already know. Once we get on the jet, we'll talk."

Reyna's comment did not do anything to reassure George.

CHAPTER ELEVEN

Graff, O'Connor, Reyna, and George were already dressed in clothes more fitting for an Arizona desert that was filled with the heat and surrounded by dust and dirt. Brian finished changing his clothes in the jet's bathroom. Both he and George wore their cowboy boots. Brett wore an older pair of basketball shoes. He did not like cowboy hats, so he wore a Wisconsin Badgers snapback.

The jet was small, sleek, and spacious. There was a galley of sorts with a small sink and a refrigerator. Reyna passed out bottles of water. The seats were soft leather and faced each other rather than the front of the plane. A small table sat between each grouping. George, Graff, and Reyna sat on one side with Brian, Brett, and Pat on the other.

George alternately glanced at his watch and then at his cell, willing time to go faster, hoping for a message from Rebecca. Graff reached over, gripped George's forearm, and whispered something to him, to which George nodded.

"As I said, we don't know much more than you do. We know your friend, Charles, disappeared. However, unless he somehow had an accident he could not recover from, we think he's alive. We just don't know where he is," Reyna said.

"Or why he disappeared," O'Connor added.

"That's true. We also know there was at least one other ranch where sheep were shot and killed."

"The same way? All shot?" O'Connor asked.

"Yes," Reyna answered.

"What would make him leave the sheep and leave his family without telling them why or where he was going?" Graff asked. "I met him briefly during that . . . summer, but from what I remember, and from what George told us, it isn't like him."

"Why would someone shoot his sheep or shoot the sheep at another ranch?" O'Connor asked.

Reyna leaned forward, his forearms resting on his knees, his fingers laced.

"There have been odd things taking place in *Diné Bikéyah* ever since the election. I'm sure you've seen intolerance where you live, but here it is dramatic. It's out in the open, especially towards indigenous people. Anyone of color, actually. It's been a while since you've been back, George, but you will feel it. Our people are nervous."

Surprised, Graff said, "You're Navajo?" Graff thought he was Mexican or some flavor of Latino.

"I am *Dine'* from my mother. I belong to the *Shash dine'é* or the Bear Clan People. We are in the same clan group as George's family, the *'Azee'tsoh dine'é,* the Big Medicine People."

"What's your story? How did you get into the FBI?" Graff asked.

"My mom and I were poor. She made jewelry, wove blankets, and cleaned rooms at the Navajo Inn. None of that amounted to much. I worked on two ranches tending sheep and cattle. The two of us were happy, but life was tough."

"No father?" O'Connor asked.

O'Connor had a similar story, and Reyna's story sounded like a chapter from the same book. O'Connor had two older brothers who took turns beating him up. They ended up in prison on drugs and weapons charges. When O'Connor had become a cop, it had been O'Connor who had arrested them and read them their rights.

"As soon as my mom told my father she was pregnant, he took off. She never saw him again, and I never met him. Didn't care to. My story is common among my people."

"How did you get from there to the FBI?" Brian asked.

"My grades were good enough to get into West Point. I graduated, served two tours in the Middle East, and when I got out, I was recruited by the FBI."

"How did you end up here?" Graff asked.

Reyna shrugged, and said, "This is my home. I was posted in Philly, and then Detroit working gangs and weapons." He shrugged again, and said, "I did some undercover work because I am part Mexican and fluent in Spanish. When Albuquerque opened, I applied for a transfer and got it."

"Why were you assigned to help us?" Brett asked.

"I know the area as well as anyone. As well as George, and I'm good at what I do. I think being Navajo will help."

"I do too," Graff said with a smile. "If Pete Kelliher has faith in you, that says something."

Reyna smiled back at him, and said, "He told me a little about each of you." He turned to O'Connor and said, "Pete said you're one of the best investigators he's ever known."

Reyna had noticed glances, a hand on a shoulder here, a small hug there. All of it told Reyna that O'Connor cared about the three boys as an older brother might.

He turned to Graff, and said, "You and Pete worked several cases together, and he called you a perfect partner."

"Brett, he said you not only saved his life in Chicago, but you saved the lives of about a dozen kids, and almost died doing it."

Brett's answer was a level stare.

In a softer voice, Ronaldo said, "George, my brother, Pete said you put your own life on the line for your family without thinking about it. Pete said that even if you had thought about it, you still would have done it."

George's expression was unreadable to the three men. Brett and Brian knew exactly what George was thinking. George was not proud of taking lives. Nine lives. It caused him pain, and it caused him to question whether he was worthy of being *Dine'*. Mostly, it caused him to doubt being worthy in the eyes of his grandfather.

"And Brian, Pete said that you took on a serial killer, and made two shots in a freezing whiteout at night and at forty some yards out. He tells that story to trainees. You shot him not once, but twice."

"Yup. Two great ass shots," Brett laughed, and the adults broke up.

To Graff and O'Connor, Brian said, "I didn't want to kill him because I figured you'd want to question him."

"Yeah, but in both butt cheeks?" Brett said, and everyone laughed again and everyone laughed along with him.

There was no way Brian would ever live it down, so he shrugged and hung his head. It annoyed him, but at the same time, and faced with the same decision, he would not change a thing.

"So, how are we doing this?" O'Connor asked.

"Pete and I talked about it, and he had some ideas."

Reyna reached for a large brown envelope, opened it, and took out sealed business envelopes, each with names printed on a small label.

"Brian, this is yours. Brett, and George," handing them one each. "You'll find five hundred dollars to spend, but I need receipts. You'll also find drivers licenses and hunting permits."

"Drivers licenses?" Brian asked.

"We're not sixteen yet," Brett said.

"In Pete's eyes, I guess, you are. At least until you leave Arizona," Reyna said.

"How much driving will they be doing?" Graff asked, his concern showing.

Reyna's eyes twinkled and his dimple took center stage as he smiled broadly. "They'll need to get around some."

O'Connor and Graff glanced at each other. Brett and Brian stared at Reyna not believing what he had said. George gave no hint of what he was thinking.

Ignoring them for the time being, Reyna added, "Each of you have both an open and a concealed carry permit. Pat and Jamie, here are your envelopes. I'll need receipts."

Jamie and Pat took their envelopes but did not open them.

"Pat, Pete said you like to work alone. Jamie and I have rooms at the Holiday Inn Canyon De Chelly in Chinle. I have a room for you at the Thunderbird Lodge in Chinle." He turned to the three boys, and said, "I figured the three of you might want to camp out."

"I'm okay with that," Brett said as he elbowed Brian.

"George?" Brian said.

"Rebecca and I will try to find Charles. He has to be up in the Chuskas. That's where he likes to hunt, and he knows that area better than anyone."

"What are Brett and I going to do?" Brian asked.

"Hunt," George answered.

He took Reyna's map of Navajoland and spread it out on the table. George drew a triangle in pencil connecting Teec Nos Pos, Round Rock, and Chinle. He placed three dots within the triangle, and labeled them "Tokay Ranch," "Morning Star Ranch," and "Swimming Pond."

"In this area, just beyond the two ranches, you'll find antelope, elk, and deer. They might be on the slopes leading to the Chuskas, but usually, they will stay in the Chinle Valley near Round Rock. If you harvest elk or deer, take it to the trading post in Round Rock. Jonathon Laidley is the owner. He will know a butcher and take care of sending it back home. You have to make sure you give some to the Morning Star family. They will need it now that Charles is missing. At night, go to the pond and camp there. The water is clean and clear, and it will feel good after the heat of the day."

"Are you and Rebecca camping with us?" Brett asked.

He shook his head, and said, "If we find Charles or his sign, we will camp near in case we are followed. If the four of us travel together, he might not show himself."

Brett nodded. Brian remained thoughtful, and asked, "Who would follow you, and why?"

George shrugged, and said, "Someone caused Charles to run away and we know someone shot his sheep."

"Is it safe letting Brian and Brett roam the country by themselves?" O'Connor asked. "How will we know where they are?"

"Guys, you need to check in with us. Once in the morning, once in the afternoon, and once in the evening," Jamie said. "If there is any kind of trouble or if you need anything, you need to get in touch with one of us right away. That understood?"

The two boys nodded, and then they glanced at George.

George said, "Father and Mother Morning Star will help you if you need it. So will Mr. Laidley. They know me, and my family. Tell them who you are, and they will know what to do."

"Pat, what are you going to do?" Graff asked.

O'Connor looked at Reyna, and said, "You have any ideas?"

Reyna nodded, and said, "A few." He looked at Jamie and Pat, and said, "Jamie and I will find out what we can from the Navajo Nation Police in Shiprock. See what you can find out from listening to the locals in Round Rock. Mostly listen to the folks on the other side of the Chuska Mountains in Red Rock, possibly in Many Farms. With your long hair and tan, if you put on some cowboy boots and a baseball cap, or better yet, a cowboy hat, some might think you're a Ute."

"Ute?" Pat asked.

"The Ute are like cousins to the Navajo. There are some living in Navajoland."

"Just like the boys, check in with Ron and me when you hear something or if you need anything," Graff said.

George placed an X on the map near the Tokay ranch.

"This is the mesa where my grandfather and I said our morning prayers."

"*Chaha'oh* Mesa," Reyna said.

"What?" Graff said.

"Navajo for Shadow Mesa. Named by the Navajo after George," Reyna explained. "George, correct me if I'm wrong, but your grandfather was a *Haatalii*."

George nodded.

To the others, he explained, "A *Haatalii* is a medicine man or shaman of the Navajo people. George's grandfather was well-respected."

George nodded, a little embarrassed but at the same time, proud. A whole lifetime ago, as the sun peeked over the red dirt of Navajoland, or *Diné Bikéyah*, the two of them would stand side by side and say their prayers to father sun, their voices echoing across the valley which is how the mesa received its name among the locals on the reservation. Those days had ended when his grandfather had died along with each member of George's Navajo family.

George turned to Brett and Brian, and said, "If Rebecca and I do not show up at the swimming pond in two days, go to the Morning Star ranch, and tell them you are going to Shadow Mesa. I will meet you there."

"What about Rebecca?" Brett asked.

"In two days, if the three of us are on Shadow Mesa, it will be because we are in trouble," George said.

Brian and Brett gawked at him.

Graff and O'Connor stared at Reyna.

Reyna said, "Before that ever happens, one of you has to promise that you'll give one of us a call. You have to promise us that."

"That's an order," Graff said with emphasis.

Brett and Brian nodded. Their faces betrayed their anxiety. George's expression never changed.

"What kind of trouble are we talking about?" O'Connor asked.

"The kind of trouble that made Charles hide," Reyna answered.

CHAPTER TWELVE

"This is a sweet ride!" Brett exclaimed from the passenger seat of the two-year-old Avalanche with Arizona plates. It was black with silver trim and had been in impound after it was taken from an LA drug dealer. It sat four passengers in soft leather bucket seats with a console separating each set of two. There was a premium, satellite sound system with Bluetooth, and an up-to-date navigation system in the center dash.

He ran his hands over the faux-wood door, the leather armrest, and the padded dash. For the second time he opened the glove box that was empty except for two items. There was the bulky vehicle manual enclosed in a black case with a snap clasp that came with any car. The other item was an envelope that contained the vehicle registration and insurance information made out in Peter Gallagher's name. It was fictitious and would lead to someone in the FBI field office in Albuquerque who would vouch for it if checked. In the same envelope was a notarized statement from Peter Gallagher giving George Tokay, Brett McGovern, and Brian Evans permission to use the vehicle for as long as they needed it. The boys were instructed to tell anyone who asked that Gallagher was a family friend.

Brian laughed, and said, "Did you see the beater O'Connor got? It's worse than his old Ford." He and Brett laughed.

"He is going undercover, so it fits," George said from the driver's seat. He had not taken his eyes off the road except to check his rearview and side mirrors.

Whenever George spoke in more formal sentences and phrases, he was all business. Or sometimes when he had something on his mind, or both. Both boys knew what was on George's mind.

Brett laughed, and said, "True. Pat seemed happy with it."

George did not exceed sixty miles per hour, though the speed limit in some stretches moved up to sixty-five. When it dropped to fifty-five, George drove fifty, not wanting to draw any undue attention. The road was two-lane macadam, pitted with broken asphalt, and dotted with potholes. They headed almost straight west into the blistering sun, causing the boys to squint. Their air-conditioner worked just fine and was almost too chilly for George's taste. Brett was in charge of it, along with the music. Brett had it tuned to a classical rock station. He had adopted Jeremy's musical tastes.

They had not encountered more than a handful of vehicles since leaving Farmington. George drove because he knew the roads and where they were headed. From the backseat, Brian took careful note of the road numbers and names, checking Reyna's map George had drawn on.

"We'll need sunglasses," Brian suggested.

"Definitely," Brett said. To George, he asked, "So, where are we going?"

George had considered stopping in Shiprock at the Navajo Tribal Police station but decided against it. Reyna and Graff were already going there, and he did not want to interfere with what they were doing.

"We are going to Teec Nos Pos where my grandfather and I would bring the wool from our sheep. We will pick up some bigger stuff like camping supplies, blankets, a cooler, and some food."

"Why there and not the trading post in Round Rock you told us about?" Brian asked.

"Mr. Laidley's post is smaller and not as well stocked. It is good for essentials, and he has been good to our family so we will stop there too."

What George did not say was that he wanted to see for himself how things had changed since he had left. Not that he had doubted Reyna, he just needed to see and feel it for himself. Most importantly, he wanted word to get around that he was back in the area in hopes that Charles might hear the news. By stopping at both posts, word would spread. Nothing travels faster than the Navajo pipeline.

Brett had been on his cell, and was still looking at it when he said, "Would we have time to see the Four Corners area, and some ruins? Canyon De Chelly is close by, right?"

George nodded and said, "We might have time after we find Charles."

Brian leaned forward, and said, "Will you be okay, you know, with Rebecca?"

Both George and Brett knew what Brian meant, and the three of them had been thinking about it separately since Jeremy and Vicky gave them permission to fly to Arizona.

Brett looked up from his cell at George, who nodded. George's jaw was set and his eyes were narrowed. Brian did not push any further.

West of Shiprock, they traveled through Becklabito, a little blip on the map that had a rundown diner and a gas station. The houses, if one could call them that, were nothing more than a patchwork of corrugated tin and wood, and did not look to be any bigger than one or two rooms.

Little kids, barebacked and shoeless, some wearing sandals, played in the dirt of their front yards along with a smattering of chickens and a rooster or two. The kids were skinny. Most wore their black hair long like George. A few were in braids. Adults sat on the porch in ancient wooden rockers or what looked like kitchen chairs. Most smoked, drank, or spit brown tobacco juice into cups, buckets, or over the railing into the dirt.

There were rusted cars and trucks on cinderblocks. Most had broken or cracked windows and had weeds or some sort of plant overtaking them. There were a few dogs and cats with their rib cages showing.

Brett licked his lips, glanced at George, but dared not stare too long because he recognized that at one time, George might have been only one or two rungs higher on the economic ladder.

"George, you okay?" Brian asked tentatively.

George looked away out of the side window and never answered. Perhaps that was his answer, Brian considered.

They reached Teec Nos Pos which was only a little bigger than Becklabito, and there was a lot more similar than not. The largest structure was the Trading Post. It also seemed to be the center point with everything else built around it.

Parked in the front dirt lot and in the larger side lot, were a dozen or so pickups of various ages, predominately Chevy. Most were older models wearing rust and sporting scrapes, dents, and dings. There were also four horses and a mule with their reigns tied around a one-log fence like the old west. To Brian and Brett, it was like a foreign country. By far, their Avalanche stood out, and those leaning against bumpers and doors stopped their conversations to stare.

"This isn't uncomfortable," Brett muttered sarcastically.

"They are curious," George said as he put the truck in park and shut off the engine. "Let's go," he ordered.

Brett glanced over at him thinking George was angry, but Brett was not sure why he would be.

"I made a list but I'm not sure what you want to get here, and what you want to get at the other trading post," Brian said.

George took Brian's cell, glanced at the list, and handed it back without comment.

George's demeanor had changed.

Normally relaxed and easy-going, he had become hypersensitive and tense, and it was the second time Brett considered that George acted as if he was angry.

Brian smiled or nodded at the onlookers, but more or less kept his head down and his mouth shut, content to let George lead. Brett was a little more obvious as he defiantly offered nothing more than a blank stare.

"Don't you think you should lock the truck?" Brian asked. "We have the rifles and handguns and our stuff in there."

George reached into his front pocket, pulled out the key fob, aimed it towards the truck, and pushed the button. Brian waited for the audible click.

George led with Brian and Brett following. They climbed the wooden steps and pushed through the door. Brett and Brian had to blink to get their eyes accustomed to the dark and shadows. The wood floors creaked with their steps, and it smelled pleasantly of tobacco and leather.

One wall had saddles, bridles, and all things dealing with critters. In the back were boots, belts, buckles, and cowboy hats along with an assortment of sandals, and tennis shoes. Towards the back but more centered was a small and bland selection of Western short and long-sleeved shirts and jeans, and skirts, blouses, and casual dresses. There were colorful blankets of various thicknesses, some soft, some coarse. The other side of the store was the grocery side. The trading post was not like a Festival Foods or Giant, but it had a good variety.

George ignored them, so Brian nudged Brett, grabbed a cart, and wandered off to the grocery side leaving George on his own. As they did, Brian grabbed his cell, clicked the memo app, and silently read over his list with Brett looking over his shoulder.

George wandered around the trading post taking in all the merchandise as well as treasuring the memories that came bubbling to the surface. Memories that he had pushed away or beaten down. While the memories were mostly good and sometimes amusing, they nudged him towards melancholy, and he found himself flirting with sadness.

He glanced at a variety of knives, some long and heavy, others small and light. None of them like the knife he wore on his hip in a leather sheath. The shaft of his knife was eight inches long, and the handle was an extra four inches made of elk bone bound to the shaft with leather. George kept the blade shiny and sharp, because not only was it a gift from his grandfather for his twelfth birthday, it kept him one with his grandfather. Unconsciously, he gripped the handle as if it would send him a message. It did not. He moved deeper into the store.

"*Yá'át'ééh.*"

George turned at the sound of the voice, and came face to face with an old man, shorter than George, and with his gray hair in two long braids. The old man was not smiling, nor was he frowning. Rather, he regarded George as a professor who might stare at a student who had asked an interesting question.

"*Yá'át'ééh, Hosteen* Ngo," George answered through a smile. George did not particularly care for him, because he never thought his grandfather cared for the elder.

"You look like him."

George nodded.

The old man continued, "I thought you moved away . . . with *Biligaana.*"

In Navajo, George said, "I did, *Hosteen* Ngo. I am back for a visit in *Diné Bikéyah.*"

The old man nodded, and with hooded eyes said, "You have not lost our language."

George was not sure if Ngo was surprised or critical. He let it pass, and said, "I still speak it."

"Difficult when living with *Biligaana.*"

"I am *Diné*. My blood is that of *Diné*. My heart and my soul will always be *Diné*.'"

Ngo cocked his head, and said, "Soul? That is a *Biligaana* belief."

"My grandfather believed in the spirit world. The *Biligaana* believe the soul dwells within each of us but comes from the spirit world. I believe my grandfather's teachings, and I have come to believe in a soul."

Ngo folded his arms across his chest and frowned. George stared impassively at the old man, his expression neutral.

Ngo was one of the six tribal elders. He did not always see eye to eye with George's grandfather. Their disagreements had always been civil, and there had been a mutual respect given from his grandfather towards Ngo. However, that respect was not always reciprocated. At least, not publicly.

"Excuse me, George, can Brett and I have the keys to the truck?"

George had heard him, but he kept his eyes fixed on the old man.

Ngo frowned at Brian, and when Brian glanced back at George, it looked as if George's face had reddened.

Unsure of what to say or do, Brian smiled at the old man, stuck out his hand, and said, "Hi, I'm Brian, George's brother. This is our other brother, Brett."

Brett did not smile or nod. In his mind both George and the old man were rude.

Ngo never shook Brian's hand. He said to George, "*Yá'át'ééh*," turned, and walked away.

"What the hell?" Brett asked.

"Have we done something wrong?" Brian asked.

Just great, Brian thought. *First Bobby, and now George is pissed. What else can go wrong?*

George dug the key fob out of his pocket, handed it to Brian, and then turned around and walked deeper into the store leaving both Brett and Brian staring at his back.

"Well, that's great," Brett muttered. "Fun times in the old west."

CHAPTER THIRTEEN

At one time, they were known as the Navajo Tribal Police, but the name had changed to the Navajo Nation Police. A Chief of Police, six Police Captains, and eight Police Lieutenants formed a pyramid of control. They were responsible for seven districts: Chinle, Crownpoint, Dilkon, Kayenta, Shiprock, Tuba City, and Window Rock. There were 210 sworn police officers, and of that, 134 were patrol officers, and twenty-eight were criminal investigators. The difficulty was that there were approximately only 1.9% police officers per 1,000 people, and any one officer was responsible for patrolling seventy square miles of reservation land. A lot of space to cover effectively.

Reyna had given Graff the information, trying to help him gain some perspective. He and Graff had also discussed the pros and cons of who should take the lead. Graff finally told Reyna that the young FBI agent was in charge, and that he would follow along.

They walked through the glass entrance, and into the red brick station. There was one rather sleepy looking officer sitting at a desk behind a counter wearing a dark green uniform. It was a little tight at the buttons which had nothing to do with the protective vest he wore under his shirt. His dark hair was cut in a bowl style, and his dark round face matched his girth.

Two other officers tipped their hats and walked out past them. Another, a young slender woman with her long dark hair in a single braid down her back, nodded at them and disappeared down a hallway. Graff and Reyna heard laughter coming from somewhere in the back.

The two men walked up to the counter. Reyna smiled, and said, "*Yá'át'ééh.*"

The police officer did not smile, but he repeated the traditional Navajo greeting, and added, "How can I help you?"

Reyna flashed his creds, and said, "We would like to speak to the officer investigating a missing Navajo boy of sixteen, Charles Morning Star?"

The officer shuffled through some papers while shaking his head, and said, "We looked into it but couldn't find him. It's not an active case."

"What do you mean it's not active?" Graff asked.

The officer glared at him, and asked, "Why is the FBI interested in one missing Navajo boy?"

Reyna smiled, and said, "He's a friend of a friend, and we were asked to help find him. Can we speak to the officer who did the investigation?"

"He's out on patrol. I can radio him and have him meet you somewhere."

"That would be great," Reyna said with a smile. "Can we have a copy of the file you have on the investigation?"

"File?"

"Yes. We'd like to get caught up."

The officer smiled, and said, "File."

Reyna and Graff waited.

"There isn't a file but I can give you a copy of what we have. There is a report, and there might be some notes, but no actual file."

Graff's impatience got the better of him, and he asked, "He's a sixteen-year-old boy. Why isn't there more action than this?"

The officer said, "Are you FBI too? You act like it."

Before Graff could answer or climb over the counter and choke the shit out of the officer, Reyna said, "We'd be happy with a copy of the report and any other notes you might have. This boy has been missing for twenty-four hours or more. We'd like to get started as soon as we can."

If the officer moved any slower, he might have moved in reverse. Eventually, he ran off a copy of the report, along with some notes, both fitting on one-half of an eight-by-eleven piece of lined paper. That was the extent of the report on Charles Morning Star.

Reyna pulled out a card, used a pen from the counter to write his cell number on it, and said, "Please have your dispatcher contact the officer who filed this report, and have him call me. We'll meet him when he's available."

"Sure."

"We understand that some sheep on the Morning Star ranch were shot. Can you tell us if other ranchers had similar circumstances?" Graff asked.

Puzzled, the officer hesitated, and asked, "Do you think this is related to the missing kid?"

Graff glared at the officer, but kept his mouth shut. He couldn't understand why the missing boy and the dead sheep weren't connected or at least investigated simultaneously.

"We aren't sure. Yet. But . . . perhaps," Reyna said.

"Well, we have reports on sheep being killed on four other ranches."

Graff took one step forward towards the counter. "Four other ranches? Couple that with a missing kid? You don't see a possible pattern?" Graff asked.

Reyna cut in, pulled out a map, spread it out on the counter, and asked, "Can you indicate where the other ranches are in relation to the ones shot on the Morning Star ranch?"

"And their names, please?" Graff added.

The officer glared at Graff. It seemed to Graff that the officer had any number of things he had wanted to say.

Eventually, he turned around, opened another file drawer, pulled out another file, and as he looked through it, he placed a dot in pencil on the map, and under it, wrote the names of the owners of the ranches where sheep were shot and killed.

It bothered Graff that there was a larger file on sheep than there was on a boy but he kept his thoughts to himself.

Graff glanced at Reyna to see if he noticed the pattern. It was not difficult. The small cluster of dots were east of Round Rock, west of the Chuska Mountains, and north of Highway 12.

"The Tokay Ranch is in this area, isn't it?" Reyna asked.

The officer nodded, and said, "Since the family . . . *died*, and *Hosteen* Tokay moved away, the ranch had been abandoned."

"*Hosteen* Tokay? You mean the grandfather?" Reyna asked.

The officer shook his head, and said, "The *Dine'* believe that the boy, George Tokay, had become a *Haatalii* like his grandfather."

Graff turned to the officer, and asked, "When you say *abandoned*, it still belongs to George, right?"

"Technically, yes. There are some who might invoke eminent domain, or at least, squatter's rights."

"If I'm not mistaken, squatter's rights can only be invoked after two years. It hasn't been that long since George was last here," Reyna said.

The officer said, "You're correct. It's close, but it hasn't been two years."

"I want to thank you for your help, Officer," Reyna bent a little to read the name tag, and said, "Thompson."

"You're welcome. If you have any more questions, give me a holler." He pulled a business card from a drawer and wrote his cell on it.

Reyna turned, walked towards the door, opened it, and held it open for Graff who had not moved.

The officer looked up, and said, "Yes?"

"A sixteen-year-old kid has been missing for twenty-four hours. I was just wondering why there isn't more . . . activity. Just a question, not an accusation."

The officer stood up, hiked up his pants but they were not even close to covering his bulging belly. He walked over to a file cabinet, opened it, took out a large folder, and placed it on the counter in front of Graff.

"We have several missing kids in *Diné Bikéyah*, along with a lot of drugs, alcohol, and every sort of shit you have anywhere. Our force is small but we care. We are all *Diné*."

"At least they keep track of missing kids," Reyna said as he walked back to Graff and the officer. "Did you know that there is no statistic for missing Indigenous women?"

"What?"

"Not one."

"How is that possible?" Graff asked.

Reyna shrugged. Graff turned to the officer behind the counter, and he shrugged.

"I don't understand."

"The government doesn't think the statistic is important," Reyna answered.

"Or our women," the officer mumbled.

Graff's mouth hung open but he could not help it. How was this possible? It could not be true, could it?

He shook his head and said, "I'm sorry. I didn't mean to offend you. I'm not from here, so I don't fully understand . . . any of this. I just know this young man. He helped save some friends of mine when I was here last, and I'd like to help find him if I can."

The officer remembered the shoot out on the mesa. He took his time to answer but when he did, he said, "Understood. I'll have Officer Mills get in touch with you."

Graff shook the officer's hand and said, "Thank you. It's appreciated, and I'm sorry if I was disrespectful. I didn't mean to be."

The two men left the station and got into black Chevy Blazer. Before Reyna started it up, Graff sighed, and said, "Shit! How will we find him if they can't?"

"I think we have more information now than when we started," Reyna answered. "Can you call O'Connor and let him know what we found out? Send him a picture of the map. It might be helpful."

"We should get a hold of George and the boys. Let them know there were other ranchers with dead sheep. Someone means business."

Reyna thought for a moment, and said, "Someone is intimidating ranchers. We need to let him know about his ranch. That could be important." he added with a shrug.

Graff nodded, and said, "My gut tells me it is."

CHAPTER FOURTEEN

O'Connor clicked off his cell and pulled over onto the side of a sometimes dirt, sometimes gravel road labeled "Highway 13." At Shiprock, he had traveled south on 491, and decided to cut over to Red Rock on this track that hardly qualified as a road, much less a highway. It was more than desolate. It was lonely, empty, and miles upon miles of red dirt and scrub with the backside of the Chuskas in his face.

He was not worried about traffic. He had not encountered anyone since he turned onto this nothing of a road.

O'Connor studied the map and thought about the information Graff had relayed to him. His first thought was to contact the three boys. He wanted to know where they were and what their plans were. More than Reyna and perhaps more than Graff, O'Connor worried about Brett, Brian, and George.

In many respects, Pat had developed an equal dose of respect and love for them forged through battles during the summer of death, and through their hunting and fishing trips. He watched the boys compete in sporting events. George was a state contender in both cross country and track. Brett made all-conference in football and basketball, and was a state champion in track. Brian made all-conference in both basketball and soccer. Those three boys, more so than the twins or Bobby, were his buddies.

O'Connor checked to see if there was any traffic headed his way, and as he suspected, there was not. He pulled back onto the highway and drove the short distance into Red Rock.

It was no more than a dot on a map. There were a cluster of broken-down houses with older model vehicles, mostly pickups, parked in front of them. Trucks and a few cars that were in no shape to be driven had been ditched behind them. Dogs and kids ran wild in the dirt.

O'Connor reflected that at least the kids looked happy, probably because they didn't know any better. Chances were they had never traveled more than fifty miles out of the area. Chances were even greater that they would never leave the reservation unless God Almighty sent a modern-day Moses to lead them to a new and better life. That wouldn't happen. At least, not with the current occupant in the White House.

The only glimpse he had into the Navajo lifestyle or belief system was gained from conversations he had had with George. More often than not, those conversations occurred along with Brett and Brian, sometimes with Graff and another cop, Earl Coffey. They would sit by the fire late at night after spending a day hunting or fishing. They would roast marshmallows, watch stars, and enjoy a peaceful moment as the campfire dwindled to red embers.

Hopefully, there would be time for that after they found the Morning Star boy.

O'Connor had learned that the key to undercover work was to hide in plain sight and blend in. The problem was that in such a small town as Red Rock, where if you fart everyone smells it, no matter how hard he would try, he would stick out. There would be curious looks by the cautious and questions by the bold.

He stepped out of the truck and pushed his long brown hair back under his newly purchased cowboy hat. While it was new, he made sure it did not look new. He took the time to rub dirt into it and had run over it twice. It had taken on the weathered, aged look he had hoped for. His boots, also new, were likewise beaten into submission, and suffered the same fate as the hat.

He locked the truck, not wanting anyone to find the Beretta Semi-Automatic Pistol. One would wonder why a drifter might have a piece with 17 rounds and a night sight.

He didn't look at anything in particular. Nonetheless, he saw everyone and everything. O'Connor walked a little hunched over up three wooden steps to the door. He bent over to scratch a mutt, part yellow lab, part whatever, and pushed open the door. He was greeted by a smell of beer, cigarette smoke, and body odor, not necessarily in that order.

He stopped just inside to let his eyes adjust to the dark. There were two middle-aged Navajo men wearing jeans, shirts, and vests with boots, and topped off with ever-present cowboy hats at the bar sitting one stool apart but looked to be together. There was one elderly person, a Navajo, sitting in the corner of the bar but separate from the two men. It took O'Connor a little time to determine that the elderly person was female. There was a middle-aged man and woman, also Navajo, sitting in a booth, and another couple sitting at a table. Of course, they were Navajo too, and all of them dressed similarly. They had a hardened, aged, and weathered look that alcohol and tobacco enhanced. Aged by coke, oxy, and weed. At least one or two had that look. O'Connor suspected that the drugs were obtained as liberally as the beer and whiskey, and he guessed the bartender sold them along with the booze.

Most of the conversations stopped in mid-sentence. Heads did not turn but eyes shifted sideways. O'Connor ignored them, walked to the bar, and leaned on it with his forearms until the bartender came over.

He was Caucasian or at least a mix, but heavy on the white side. He had long black, graying hair, seventies-style sideburns, and an Adam's apple that competed with his nose for prominence. Like the patrons, it was hard for O'Connor to determine how old he was.

"What will you have?" he asked in a gravelly voice that gave away the fact that he must have smoked three packs a day. O'Connor wagered that with the amount of alcohol he consumed along with the cigarettes, the man might live to see three more birthdays, if he was lucky.

"Something wet," O'Connor drawled.

The barkeep grabbed a mug that did not look quite clean, held it under the tap, and filled it with amber liquid the color of piss. He set it down in front of Pat and waited until O'Connor slid his wallet out of his back pocket, lifted out a five, and laid both on the bar. Satisfied, the bartender walked back to the two men. With each step, out came a thick wet cough.

The three of them bent forward and spoke together. The other conversations started up again. The couple in the booth laughed about something. O'Connor listened to the simultaneous conversations but concentrated more on the bartender and the two men. He did not get anything of value, and he did not expect to.

Pat put on a bit of a show, taking off his hat, pushing back his hair, and rubbing his eyes. He did not, however, take more than a swallow or two from the mug of beer, not because he was on duty, but because he did not trust the fact that he might catch something he would not be able to shake without a heavy dose of antibiotics.

He was about to call it quits when a Navajo boy with long black hair in traditional style came out of the back. O'Connor guessed he was twelve or thirteen. He looked like a young George. Dark skin, handsome, narrow face. He wore a stained t-shirt, dirty jeans, dusty beat up boots, and an even dirtier apron. He carried a case of beer from the back and walked behind the bar.

The boy looked O'Connor up and down not so subtly, and only as a kid might do. He stopped long enough to restock the old refrigerator. He turned around, smiled at O'Connor, and hesitated before he walked back through the door to what Pat figured was the storeroom. Before he disappeared altogether, he glanced back at O'Connor again.

"Taking a break," he said to the bartender while his eyes were on O'Connor. The barkeep didn't even look in his direction and waved a hand dismissively as he coughed into his sleeve. The boy's voice was deeper than O'Connor had expected.

Pat waited what he thought was a fair amount of time, left the five-dollar bill on the bar and stuffed his wallet into his back pocket. He half-waved, half-saluted the bartender, and left. He noticed that the conversations had stopped the moment he moved away from the bar.

He pushed open the door, stepped outside onto the porch, and scratched the pooch behind the ear. He walked not more than ten or twelve steps along the porch and leaned against the corner of the building. Even though he did not smoke, he pulled out a cigarette, lit it up, and sucked on it. Thankfully, he managed to keep from coughing. He kept his eyes on the dirt street, and the kids playing in their yards beyond it, and at their parents sitting on their porches.

"What's up?" O'Connor asked quietly with his lips hardly moving.

"Not here."

O'Connor dropped the cigarette and crushed it under a boot.

"When and where?"

The boy hesitated. Finally, he said, "In an hour. Meet me one mile west of town. Go towards Cove. There's a bend in the road. I'll be there."

Then he disappeared as quickly and as silently as he appeared.

CHAPTER FIFTEEN

O'Connor had one hour to kill but because of the kid, he had already come up with a plan, though he had not yet fleshed it out. First, he would have to have a conversation and see how that went, but he trusted his gut, and his gut told him he might be onto something.

He walked across to what looked like a trading post. It was small but not rundown like the bar. O'Connor was surprised upon entering that it held more than he actually thought it might.

He spied a small section that displayed electronics. He found what he hoped he would, tapped on the glass cabinet, and said, "I'd like to pick up a phone."

The clerk came around the side, opened it, and O'Connor picked out the one he wanted. He walked over to the cooler and grabbed four bottles of water.

Pat placed everything on the counter, and asked, "How fresh is the jerky?"

The old man behind the counter, and whom O'Connor suspected was the proprietor, studied the lanky man with long brown hair under a cowboy hat. He said, "The missus made it fresh this morning."

O'Connor nodded and said, "I'll take two pounds."

As the old man weighed the jerky, he glanced at O'Connor again, smirked, and said, "You're not from around here."

Pat smiled, sighed, and said, "Guess not."

Either the old man coughed or chuckled- O'Connor was not sure- and said, "You're a cop."

O'Connor laughed. He asked, "Will this phone work out here in the desert?"

The old man nodded, and said, "There are cell towers, so it should. Just fill out the paperwork and leave it with me. What carrier do you use?"

"Verizon."

"Can you hear me now?" the old man laughed.

That particular ad for Verizon had long ago been discontinued, and the pitchman had signed on to a rival network. Perhaps the news might have been slow getting to the reservation.

"I sure to hell hope so," O'Connor said as he laughed along with him.

After O'Connor filled out the paperwork on the phone and paid for his merchandise, they shook hands. Pat grabbed the paper sack and walked out to his pickup. He got in, programmed the phone's speed dial buttons with his number and name, Graff's number and name, Reyna's number and name, and then followed those with George's, Brett's, and Brian's.

Satisfied, O'Connor slammed down one of the waters to rinse the insipid beer taste out of his mouth. He started up the truck and drove west out-of-town watching the odometer closely. At one mile plus a tenth, he came to a bend in the road with a near-natural turnout. O'Connor did not slow down but instead drove past it for another mile. Nothing out of the ordinary, and there was no one around. More importantly, no one had followed him.

He made a U-turn and drove back to the turnout. He took it and drove over a little hill far enough so the truck would be out of site. He pushed open the door and stepped out into the heat.

"Fuck dry heat!" O'Connor muttered to himself as he took off his hat. He smoothed his long hair back and used a sleeve to wipe off his face. "Jesus!"

"Took you long enough."

Pat blinked once, twice. The boy stood fifteen yards away with his rifle in his right hand. From that distance, he could have been George Tokay when O'Connor had first met him. A twin. It had a dizzying effect on him as the image sucked him back to the summer of death.

Regaining his composure, Pat walked towards him carrying his sack from the little store.

The boy took a step back and held the rifle at the ready.

Pat stopped and regarded the boy. He had cleaned up. He wore an open leather vest, but no shirt, just as O'Connor had seen George similarly dressed. The boy had on a clean pair of jeans, and his face looked scrubbed.

Eyeing the rifle, Pat said, "You wanted to meet me, remember?"

Uncertain, the boy licked his lips, and said, "I have weed, pills, and coke. What do you want?"

Bewildered, Pat shook his head, sighed, and said, "That's what you wanted to meet about? You thought I was looking for drugs?"

The boy shifted his weight from his left to his right and gripped the rifle a little tighter.

O'Connor had to laugh at the absurdity of it. Selling drugs and holding a rifle like a life preserver.

He stuck his chin out, and said defiantly, "What?"

Pat laughed, and asked, "Kid, what's your name?"

The boy hesitated, and said, "Michael. Michael Two Feathers."

He was overly tired, but he laughed again, and said, "Kid . . . Michael, I'm not interested in drugs."

The boy shifted from foot to foot and bit his lower lip, afraid that perhaps O'Connor wanted something else.

"All I want to do is talk. What would that cost?"

The boy licked his lips, and said, "Ten, no twenty. Twenty dollars."

O'Connor decided to chance it. He shifted the sack of merchandise to his right arm, and with his left, pulled out his wallet, and tossed it to the boy who caught it without bobbling it.

"Take out a twenty, and we'll sit down on the blanket and have a conversation."

O'Connor walked forward, set the paper sack on the blanket, and sat down. He reached into it and pulled out the sack of jerky and the bottles of water. He left the burner phone inside for the time being.

"You just want to talk?"

O'Connor thought the boy sounded relieved.

"Just talk. I'm not into drugs or alcohol." He gave it a bit of thought and said, "I'm not interested in anything else, if that's what you're thinking. Okay?"

The boy did not waste any time. He took out a twenty and handed the billfold back to O'Connor. He sat down next to the skinny cop. He drew his knees up to his chest and hugged them.

Gently, O'Connor said, "It's okay, Michael."

The boy lowered his head and said nothing.

"How old are you?"

The boy glanced at O'Connor, and warily answered, "Thirteen."

"The bartender, what's his name?"

"Lou. Feldcamp."

"He put you up to this?"

The boy shrugged.

"What about your parents? You have a mom and a dad?"

The boy shook his head. His chin quivered, but he did not cry.

"Brothers or sisters? Any family?"

The boy shook his head again.

"You live with Feldcamp?"

The boy shrugged, and said, "I work there. He pays me. He feeds me."

"And in return . . ."

The boy turned his head and shrugged.

When he looked back, his chin quivered but still there were no tears. "He doesn't hurt me."

O'Connor slipped an arm around the boy, gave his shoulder a squeeze, and said, "You don't always measure hurt with bruises, broken bones, or blood. Sometimes there is hurt you don't see. And sometimes, it's the hurt you don't see that you end up feeling the most."

The boy nodded.

"The drugs . . . Feldcamp sells them out of the bar."

Two Feathers nodded. "He has a stash in some barrels in the storeroom."

O'Connor let the silence roll. It was Michael who broke it.

"You're a cop." It was a statement, not a question.

"Yeah, I am."

"Are you going to bust me?" Michael asked as tears dripped down his cheek, and side of his nose.

O'Connor playfully pushed Michael's cowboy hat over his eyes, and said, "That hadn't occurred to me."

"Lou?"

"Yes. Not me, exactly, but a friend."

"What will happen to me? I won't have any place to go," Michael said in a panic. "That's the only . . ." he did not finish.

"I might have an idea about that. If you can trust me, that is."

Two Feathers looked up at O'Connor, the hope in the boy's eyes visible.

"Do you think you can trust me?"

The boy hesitated and then gave O'Connor a tentative nod.

"From this point on, though, you can't go back there. He'll be dangerous if he gets out on bail, and we don't know what will happen to the bar."

The boy looked off in the distance, but tears had welled up for another run.

Changing the topic, O'Connor asked, "I have a question for you, Michael. How well do you know the reservation?"

The boy made a face, and said, "I live here." He wiped his eyes with his hand and then wiped his hand on his jeans.

O'Connor pulled out his cell, brought up a copy of the map, and showed it to Two Feathers.

"Do you know this area west of these mountains?" The boy was sitting so close to him, O'Connor could smell the faint smell of soap and the stronger smell of deodorant.

"The Chuskas. The valley to the west is where I hunt," Michael said as he pointed to the map.

It occurred like this. Something would happen. A glimpse, a moment, a word, a look. Nothing extraordinary. To an ordinary soul, a moment like this would be overlooked and soon forgotten. Perhaps never even noticed in the first place.

O'Connor was not ordinary, and that was how he had survived undercover. Facing all manner of threats, his life could be taken in less than a tick of a moment. He lied to save his life, and at times, he lied to save the lives of others. A lie in order to find the truth or to right a wrong.

The moral dilemma facing O'Connor was not that he would be facing danger necessarily. The real dilemma was that this boy might. A boy he had just met, and who at the young age of thirteen, did not have a place to sleep or a steady meal or someone to care for him. O'Connor never liked putting anyone in danger, but he never liked putting kids in harm's way.

O'Connor stared at the handsome, bronze-skinned boy with dark eyes that matched his long hair. Skinny, but Pat had the impression that the kid was deceptively strong. Perhaps stronger where it counted the most. There was nothing much to call his own except for a rifle he clutched tightly.

He had two horses, though O'Connor was not sure if they were his or if they belonged to Feldcamp. One, the big dappled gray had a beat-up saddle on it. The other had a tarp strapped to its back along with sacks containing all of his earthly wealth. Whatever else he had was at the bar, the one to which he could no longer return.

It was his reservation, and even though he spent more time in the desert than he did under a roof, he was, after all, still a boy.

O'Connor had a decision to make, and with that decision, a promise he would have to make to himself and to the boy.

"I want you to tell me the truth."

Michael stared at him with an expression O'Connor could not read. It was the same look George would fix on him from time to time. Must be a Navajo thing.

"If you spend some time out in the desert on your own, will your parents worry about you?"

"I already told you, I don't have parents. I don't have brothers, or sisters, or anyone. Except Lou, and now . . ."

"Okay, okay. I'm sorry. I get it." O'Connor put an arm around the boy's shoulders and gave him a squeeze. "So, if I asked you to spend a week out there," Pat waved his arm towards the mountains, "where you said you hunt, can you do that? Safely, I mean?"

The boy said, "I do it all the time."

"Truth?"

"Truth."

"Okay, here's the deal. I came here with another cop . . . he's a friend. There are three boys. We came to help find a missing Navajo boy. One of the boys, George Tokay, and this missing Navajo boy have been friends forever. George is from here so he knows the area and knows how to take care of himself."

"I have heard of George Tokay."

O'Connor nodded and continued. "His two brothers have never been here and don't know the area. Both are good hunters though. Here's the problem. Until we find that missing boy, those two boys will be on their own."

"What do you want?"

"I would like to hire you. We will be here for one week. I'll pay you a hundred dollars a day to keep an eye on them."

Puzzled, Two Feathers asked, "But what do you want me to do?"

"I would like you to prevent anything from happening to them. The trick is, I would rather not have them know you are watching over them."

Two Feathers made a face, and said, "You want me to baby-sit?"

O'Connor laughed, and said, "Not really. Brian and Brett are pretty self-sufficient. It's just that they don't know their way around, and I don't want them lost or hurt."

"So, I'm baby-sitting."

O'Connor sighed, and said, "Think of it like you're a guide. Kind of."

"How old are they?"

"They're both fifteen, almost sixteen."

"They won't care that a kid like me is watching over them?" Michael asked as he squinted at O'Connor.

"Not if they don't know they're being watched over, right?" O'Connor asked with a smile.

"These two guys," the boy asked. "Who are they to you?"

O'Connor had thought about this question a lot, actually. There was no blood tie. They were not his kids but, in some respects, they were as important to him as they were to Jeremy and Vicky. Especially Brett and Brian.

"I love them as if they were my own sons, Michael. Those boys have been through a lot. I don't want them to go through any more."

Michael looked off in the distance. He took off his hat, and swept his long hair back, and reset the hat back onto his head, brim low just above his eyes.

"Okay."

"Okay?"

The boy nodded, and said, "Okay."

"I'm not asking you to put yourself in danger. I don't want that. So, if it looks like something bad might happen," O'Connor reached into the paper sack, and pulled out the cell, "call me. Do you know how to use one of these?"

"I'm not stupid."

O'Connor laughed, elbowed him, and said, "No, I think you're a pretty smart young man."

Michael grinned and elbowed him back.

"I already programmed it."

He showed him how it worked, just to be on the safe side. He showed him how to use speed dial and gave him the names associated with the numbers.

"I have a charger, but you might not have an opportunity to use it, so you'll have to be careful."

Michael nodded.

O'Connor picked up his wallet, opened it, and handed the boy five twenties. Then he thought about the fact that he might need more clothes and supplies, so he pulled out another five twenties.

"This will get you started. At the end of the week, I'll give you a five-hundred-dollar bonus."

"I don't need that much," Michael said quietly.

O'Connor studied him, and said, "What's wrong?"

"You said you'd be here a week."

O'Connor nodded.

"What will happen to me when you leave?"

"I'm asking you to trust me, Michael. I know that might be hard because we just met, but I keep my word."

It was the boy's turn to study O'Connor. He wanted to trust him. He just did not know if he could bring himself to.

"When I make a promise, I keep it. I can't let you go back to Feldcamp, but I will find you a home."

"Where?"

"Give me a week. You take care of Brett and Brian, and I will take care of you."

The boy pursed his lips, took a deep breath, and nodded. "Okay."

"Do you know where Chinle is?"

"I told you, I know my land. I am *Dine'*."

O'Connor smiled. George might have answered the same way.

He said, "Of course. Well, I'm staying at the Thunderbird Lodge in Chinle. Graff and Reyna are staying at the Holiday Inn. If you need a place to stay for any reason, get yourself to Chinle or call one of us, and we'll come get you. Same for the boys. If it looks like they need something or if there is some sort of danger that you think you or they can't handle, call me immediately. I'll come running. If you can't reach me, call Graff or Reyna."

The boy looked puzzled. "We'll just be in the desert hunting. There isn't much that can go wrong."

O'Connor hoped Michael was right.

CHAPTER SIXTEEN

The boys reached Red Mesa, another dot on a map that was no bigger than Becklabito. It had the same sad and tired look and feel. Like a town hoping for a steady, strong wind to blow it away and end its misery.

George turned south on 35, which was sometimes graveled and sometimes dirt. Brian, now sitting in the passenger seat with Brett in the back behind him, turned around, and watched the dust trail obliterate any visibility behind them.

"Doesn't rain much, does it?" Brian asked.

"No."

George did not offer any other commentary. Brian glanced over at him, shrugged, turned his head and stared out the passenger window.

To rescue Brian, Brett said, "Bri, at the trading post, did you see all those guys packing guns, and all the rifles in racks in the pickups?"

"Yeah. Not used to seeing that. Kind of eerie."

Brett's and Brian's cell buzzed. Brian was the first to reach for it. He had placed it in the armrest on the door. He said, "It's Bobby, Randy, and Billy."

They had captured funny-looking faces with funnier-looking poses. Under any other circumstances, Brian would have done his part to answer them. He set his cell back in the armrest.

Brett held his cell out in front of him, made a face, and took his picture, sending it to his three brothers with the caption, 'Traveling in the desert.' He received a text back from Bobby that said, 'Send pictures!'

Still smiling, Brett put his phone back in the armrest, and stared out the front and side window.

Brian said, "There's a lot of nothing but it's pretty."

"It's so different from Wisconsin. Everything there is green. Here, everything is red," Brett said. "A lot of dirt and not much else."

"And you can see forever," Brian said. "I like the hills."

"Mesas and plateaus. The Chuskas are off to the left," George said.

"It's cool to think that wind carved them like that," Brian said. "It looks like a broken crown."

"You're sounding like a Brainiac," Brett laughed.

Brian smiled. George never changed expression.

After bouncing around in the dirt, the boys drove past Sweetwater, another dot on the map that was the same as all the other dots on a map. Place one set of kids and parents from one dot on a map and substitute it with another set from another dot, and no one would know the difference. Everything would be the same, but everything would be different.

Brett and Brian said nothing. Their only reaction was to offer a shake of their head, not so much in disgust as it was in dismay. They had so much. Even before they were adopted by Jeremy.

In Brett's case, he and Bobby lived comfortably in an Indianapolis suburb before moving to Waukesha, Wisconsin during the summer of death. Vicky was a surgical nurse. Their father, Tom, was an English professor at Butler University. Music lessons for Bobby, travel basketball, football, and track for Brett.

They had nice clothes and a nice home. They were comfortable with little to care or worry about. All that ended when Brett was abducted off his bike as he peddled to a pickup basketball game. He had been set up by his uncle, Tony, and was forced into a brothel catering to perverts. During the time Brett was missing, this same uncle, along with a few of his pervert friends, had molested Bobby. Once freed, he, Bobby, and Vicky had to move away. There was no other choice. They needed a fresh start.

Brian's twin brother, Brad, was shot during a soccer game in that same summer of death, and he had died along with other men, women, and children. His parents had never recovered. To a lesser extent, neither had Brian. Brian made an effort to go on living, reaching out to Jeremy, and then Vicky. His parents, on the other hand, existed like extras in the "Walking Dead."

After his mother shot his father, and then committed suicide, Brian went to live with Jeremy, Vicky, and the five other boys. It was the happiest he had been since the summer of death. Still was. Until that morning, anyway.

The three boys made it to Round Rock, no bigger and no different looking than any of the other towns. Laidley's Trading Post was not as big as the one in Teec Nos Pos, but it was kept up, and it contained almost everything one might need.

Jonathon Laidley stood behind the counter ringing up a sale from two Navajo girls. He glanced at the three boys and did a double take when he recognized George. He smiled and nodded in his direction. He counted out change, handed it to the two preteen girls, and told them to help themselves to some candy off the shelf.

They did, waved, and skipped out of the store.

"Look who's back in town," Laidley said reaching out to shake George's hand.

"Hello, Mr. Laidley."

"How have you been, George? I hadn't had the opportunity to tell you how sorry I am about your family."

Laidley had a thick head of wavy black hair, a narrow face that was pleasant to look at, and a tanned and weathered complexion with a perpetual five o'clock shadow. His typical expression was a smile, his green eyes shining under long lashes. He was on the small side, a little taller than Brian or Brett. He was thin like George, and was given to wearing jeans with a plaid shirt of some sort, with cowboy boots or work boots.

George smiled, but kept his head down. He had been on edge all day and had almost lost it. Like the trading post in Teec Nos Pos, Laidley's Trading Post, as it was named, brought back a flood of memories. Most of them were warm, but the cloud of his dead grandparents, his mother, and his brothers and sister turned the warm memories dark and cold.

Brett and Brian stood behind George and to the side, waiting for their brother to introduce them.

"Um... Mr. Laidley, do you know anything about Charles Morning Star? Have you heard anything?"

Laidley shook his head, and said, "I know he's missing, but that's all I know."

George nodded and sighed. "Have you heard anything about ranchers having their sheep killed?"

Laidley's dark eyebrows knit together and helped form the frown on his face. He said, "You think the two are related?"

"I am not sure. Rebecca told me that when she went to the field to take over for Charles, she found him missing, and some of her sheep dead. They had been shot. There were other ranchers who had reported dead sheep."

"I had heard that, but I guess I hadn't put the two together."

"Rebecca and I will ride out to look for him."

"I hope you have better luck than Franklin," he answered shaking his head. "Is there anything I can get you? Do you need anything?"

"I think we are good on most things."

Brian spoke up, and said, "Excuse me, I'm Brian, and this is Brett. We're George's brothers. I would like to purchase 180 drain bullets for a 30-06 and some 9mm for Glock 19s if you have them."

"Happy to meet you, Brian. You too, Brett. Yes, towards the back of the store in a case. I'll bring my keys and you can pick out what you need."

He came out from behind the counter with a fistful of keys and led the boys to the back of the store.

"Elk hunting?" he asked as he opened up a case.

"Yes, Sir," Brian answered. "Maybe deer."

Laidley pointed to the boxes of 180 drain bullets, and said, "Take what you need."

Brian took one box.

"George, you need any?" Brian asked.

George reached into the cabinet and took out two boxes of Remington 30-06 Sprg 170gr Pointed Soft Point shells. "This is all I need."

Laidley locked up the case. He opened another containing smaller caliber ammunition that would work with the Glock 19s, and Brian took one of those.

"You boys need anything else? Canteens?" He looked at Brian and Brett closely, and said to Brian, "You're not as dark as your brothers, so you need suntan lotion and some aloe after you get burned."

Brett laughed, and said, "He is a white boy."

Laidley laughed along with Brett. Brian smiled. George did neither.

"I'd like to get a holster for a Glock 19, if you have them," Brett said.

"Hmm . . . let's see what might work for you," Laidley said as he locked up the glass, and barred cabinets.

He walked to the side of the store where the leather products were and pointed out several holsters.

"Why do you need a holster?" George asked Brett.

"Because I don't want to haul out the metal case when I want to use them," Brett explained.

"Why do you think you will use them?"

Annoyed, Brett said, "Snakes and coyotes." He paused, and said, "Not that I'd ever shoot a coyote. I'll just scare them off."

George shrugged and moved back to the front of the store.

"I think we'll need some rope and two Bungie cords," Brian added.

"What for?" George asked.

"If we harvest an elk, it will make it easier to carry if we tie up the carcass, and strap it to the truck," Brian said.

"Or horse if we use Rebecca's horses," Brett said. "Like you said we could."

The three of them hunted together plenty of times, and Brian had used this system each time. He wondered why George questioned him.

The boys carried their merchandise to the counter, and Laidley rang it up.

"If we harvest an elk, can we get it butchered here, and sent back home?" Brian asked.

"I can help with that. I won't do it myself, because I'm not a butcher. I know someone who will, and I can send it wherever you want. Just be sure when you field dress it, you keep the genitalia intact. That's the law here."

"I read that," Brett said. "We'll make sure we do."

"Do you have proper identification and hunting permits? The Navajo Nation Police do spot checks."

"Yessir, we have everything we need," Brian answered.

"Except the elk," Brett added with a smile.

Laidley laughed. "Hey," he called as they said their goodbyes and headed for the door.

"Yes, Sir?" Brett said.

"You three be careful out there. Some crazy stuff is going on. You need anything, let me know."

The boys nodded and walked out the door. Laidley placed both hands on the counter, frowned, and shook his head.

61

CHAPTER SEVENTEEN

There were a number of twisting, turning dirt roads, and one or two switchbacks. At one point, the road, if you could call it that, laced itself up one side of a hill and down the other. From a distance, it looked like a lanyard. Brian did his best to remember all the roads and turns as he checked the map Reyna had given them, and the one George had drawn on. He found it difficult as they were jostled by the bumps and dips in the road, but he was fairly certain he knew where they were.

The black Avalanche was covered in red dust kicked up from the road. The windshield so much so, it was difficult to see out of it. George had not used the windshield washer with wipers fearing that would only make a muddy mess.

"We're heading to your property?" Brian asked as he looked at the map.

George nodded. His jaw was set. Brian decided he would stop attempting to make conversation, because George was not having any of it.

Brett frowned. He understood that George was nervous about his friend. He understood that George might be anxious about seeing Rebecca. He understood about being nostalgic and all, but he did not understand why George was rude, almost cold towards them, especially Brian.

As he drove, George had peculiar memories. Even as a boy, he was given to visions and dreams, which he and his grandfather believed to be from the spirit world. The problem was that he could not distinguish between what might be a vision and what might be memories of his homeland, his beloved, *Diné Bikéyah*.

He took a wide turn that ran along a deep crevice, an arroyo, and was whisked back in time, dizzy with Deja vu.

He was the age of twelve. He had ridden Nochero, his big black stallion in a driving rain late at night chasing two sheep rustlers in a beat-up pickup. He shot at the tire and hit it, causing the pickup to roll into the same arroyo he rode parallel to. The two men suffered bumps, bruises, and broken bones. Several of the sheep had jumped to safety but one of the lambs had been hurt and died the following morning.

George remembered the conversation he had had with his grandfather after he had ridden out to tend to the sheep the following day. He had not slept. After all, the two thieves suffered broken bones, a damaged truck, and the little lamb had died. All because of him.

The two of them had sat side by side on the piney ridge that overlooked the area where their sheep grazed. George had asked his grandfather if he was disappointed in him, and his grandfather had assured him that his reasoning was sound, and that his actions were the result of good intentions. Then the conversation shifted as it often did with his grandfather.

"What is greater, the life of a lamb or the life of a man?"

Without hesitation, George said, "The life of a man."

His grandfather stared out at the sheep and at Nochero, and then said, "Life is life. All life is important." He reached down into the sand and picked up several ants. *"From the smallest ant to Nochero. From a lamb to a man. All life is important."*

George had reflected on that conversation often. He had discussed it with Jeremy, and with Pastor Schwab at St. William's, the Catholic Church they attended as a family. In two short years, he had killed nine men, and the guilt was overwhelming. It consumed him, threatening to eat him alive. No one had been able to convince him that even though he had acted in self-defense and out of protection for his family, that it was necessary and just. In George's mind, but mostly in his heart, it was not, nor would it be if he had to do it again.

George shook his head at the memory and pulled the truck to a stop in front the road that doubled as the driveway to his ranch house. Blocking the way was a chain attached to two smallish metal posts with a sign on the chain that said, "No Trespassing."

Neither Brett nor Brian said anything. George let the truck idle as he gripped the wheel and stared at the sign. Brett finally spoke.

"If this is your land, we need to take that chain and sign down. You're not trespassing."

Brian didn't comment. George did not acknowledge that he had even heard him. Instead, he sat and stared for the longest time.

Finally, George drove down into the ditch, around the metal post, and then back onto the road. He backed up the truck, turned off the engine, and jumped out. George walked to the back of the truck, opened the heavy rubber Tonneau lid, and took out the rope. He attached one end to the bumper, and the other to the chain. He got back into the truck and drove down the road until the chain strung across his road snapped. Then he backed up. He repeated the process with the two metal posts and left them in a pile in the ditch.

He got back into the truck and drove down the road but stopped about twenty yards in front of the charred rubble that had once been his home.

Brian said nothing but glanced nervously at George after taking in the destruction. Brett leaned forward.

"Jesus!" he said.

Nothing Randy or Billy had told them had prepared them for what sat in front of them. Sure, time and the elements added to the scene, but the charred, dilapidated remains sat in front of them. Brett wondered how wind hadn't knocked them over a long time ago.

George got out of the truck and at first, stood by the door. Then he walked to the front and squatted down. The boys suspected he was asking *chindi* for permission to come closer.

"Why would he have to ask for permission if he lived here?" Brett asked.

Brian shook his head, and said, "As I understand it, a *chindi* is a spirit left by those who were killed or murdered. The spirit hangs around until there is justice."

"But this was George's family, so I don't think they'd be angry with him," Brett reasoned. "Besides, everyone responsible for this," he gestured at the ruins, "and for murdering his family was either killed or caught, and put in prison. So, there shouldn't be any *chindi* hanging around, right?"

Brian shrugged, and said, "Shit, I don't know." He turned around, faced his brother and said, "Is this why George has been acting . . ."

"Like an ass? Probably," Brett answered for him.

Brian didn't argue with that, but George was certainly not acting like himself. Brian thought back to the night he, George, and Jeremy found his parents.

He turned back around, and said, "When, you know . . . when my parents . . ." He did not know how to say it, so he said, "Did I act like this?"

Brett leaned further forward, pulled Brian towards him, pushed his cowboy hat up on his head, kissed his forehead, and said, "You acted like a butt. Not as bad as George, but you were a butt."

"Sorry."

Brett smiled, leaned further into the front seat, hugged him, kissed his forehead again, and said, "It's already forgotten, Bri. We love you. I love you."

Brian nodded. Both boys got out of the truck and reverently shut their doors so as not to disturb the quiet. An odd mixture of sage, dust, and burnt wood hit them. Brett winced and Brian blinked.

The scene reminded Brian of church. He was annoyed at how people whispered or spoke out loud. He always sat between Brett and Billy, and one or the other would whisper to him during the service. It bothered him because church was sacred. He never told them that, but he never whispered back either. Standing on this ground in front of the blackened ruins, it looked and felt like church, and in his mind, there should not be any talking. They should not even be here, but he was not about to say that to George.

He stuffed his hands into his front pockets and shivered.

Brett walked up and stood next to George, but said nothing as George brushed tears off his face.

CHAPTER EIGHTEEN

Reyna and Graff did not have a productive day. After receiving the call from O'Connor, Reyna arranged for a raid on the diner in Red Rock using a combination of Navajo Nation Police and FBI. They had a search warrant for the premises where they found twenty pounds of weed in brick form, ten pounds of coke, and a variety of pills, mostly Oxy. The cops on site knew there had to be someone up the food chain who supplied the bar owner, and that would be used as a bargaining chip for Feldcamp.

They exercised another warrant for anything electronic, including video tapes, CDs, DVDs, and his cellphone, computer, and anything else that ran on electricity. They were sure they would find something worthwhile, or so Graff had hoped.

After the raid, Reyna and Graff visited two of the four ranches where sheep had been shot. Their mission was three-fold: find out if anyone knew where Charles Morning Star was; find out if anyone else was missing; and find out if someone saw anyone shooting their sheep. They figured the fourth goal was a lost cause and beyond their immediate reach: find the why. Of course, they would try, but they wouldn't snag anything substantial.

The ranches were on the small side for the reservation. They were certainly smaller than most any dairy farm in Wisconsin, the type that Graff was more familiar with. One of the ranches ran seventy-five head of sheep while the other ran ninety. While there were a few of the bigger ranches that might have propane tanks for electricity and such, these two ranches were like most of the ranches on the Navajo res. Neither had electricity nor running water. Both had outhouses and wells with a pump. There were outbuildings that held horses and sheep-shearing equipment. The larger of the two ranches had a twelve-year-old dented blue Chevy pickup and the smaller one had a seventeen-year-old dark green Ford that looked like it was a refugee from Afghanistan.

The first ranch had three sheep killed in the early evening just after sundown. If the family knew anything, they didn't share it. The middle-aged man who was part-Navajo-part-Mexican, Jesus Megena, had shrugged, smiled, and had told them he didn't know who had shot his sheep.

At the second ranch, it was much of the same except that five sheep had been killed shortly before midnight and again, no one saw anything. Delbert Yazzie at first claimed not to have heard anything, but recanted when Reyna suggested that a shotgun blast, and five of them at that, were hard to disguise. His eyes had shifted nervously from Reyna to Graff and then back to Reyna. Mostly, he had stared at his own beat up boots. His shoulders had been hunched and his fingers had never left his front pockets.

"So, what do we have exactly?" Graff asked as the two of them drove down Yazzie's driveway away from the small ranch.

"Not much more than not a helluva lot," Reyna muttered. "The thing is, they know who did it. What would make them so afraid to say anything?"

Graff thought about that for a moment and said, "It's not what, it's who? Who would wield that much power to cause them to button up?"

"And why?" Reyna added.

The two men drove in silence towards the third of the four ranches when Graff turned to Reyna and said, "You know we'll get the same pile of shit that we got from Megena and . . . who is the other guy?"

"Delbert Yazzie," Reyna said. "That's about as Navajo as you can get."

"Well, okay, him too. If we get the same crap we got from Megena and Yazzie, I think we go at them directly. Why are you afraid? Who has that much power over you to keep you quiet while your sheep are shot dead?"

He glanced over at Reyna and saw him frowning.

"Or not," Graff said.

"Hmmm, I'm FBI. The *Dine'* don't deal well with FBI. I wonder if that's part of why we're getting the responses we've been getting."

"I'm a white cop with no juice. If we were back in Wisconsin, our roles would be reversed. I'm not much help to you out here."

The two men were silent, and it was not long when they ended up staring at one another as they came to the same conclusion.

"The only one who might get something from them would be George. They might talk to him because of his name and reputation," Reyna said.

"That makes sense," Graff said as he stared out the window at the Chuskas. "Let's hold off on the other two ranchers. Give George and Rebecca a day to look for Charles. I'll call him, pitch the idea and see what he says."

Reyna nodded and said, "We won't lose much time if we wait. We'll meet up with O'Connor and see what he found out, if anything."

"I'm guessing not much more than we did."

"I was thinking that," Reyna said. "Let's head to Chinle. I want to get Quantico on this. I want to know who has power, real or perceived, on the res."

That was when Reyna's cell buzzed. When Reyna answered, the voice on the other end said, "This is Deputy Ned Mills. I heard you were looking for me."

CHAPTER NINETEEN

They met in Lukachukai off Highway 13 and near the junction of Highway 12 out of Round Rock. O'Connor had to backtrack three miles, but fortunately, he had not stopped at the beaten down town, but buzzed on through. If he had, folks might wonder why he left only to return. Most people don't forget strangers. It's the ones they see every day that become invisible. Still, he hoped that no one would remember the beater of the pickup he drove.

The diner had been converted from what had been a gas station. Reyna and Graff sat at one table towards the back. Graff shook his head, made a face, and decided he would stick to chips and salsa with a Diet Coke even though he was starving. Reyna ordered three chicken tacos swearing that this eatery was one of the best in Navajoland. Graff wondered what the worst was, but didn't ask out loud.

O'Connor had a thing about having his back to the door, so he was able to sit by himself two tables away facing not only the door but also Reyna and Graff. Neither man looked in his direction. They planned it that way. Pat could keep an eye on the other patrons, especially those who might pay a little too much attention to Graff's table.

Deputy Ned Mills walked into the diner, stood in the doorway for just enough time to find the two least likely patrons. He walked over and sat down.

Leaning slightly forward and reaching for a glass of ice water, Mills said in as low a voice as he dared, "We'll eat and then we'll talk." His eyes flitted left and right. "Too many ears."

"We ordered," Reyna said cheerfully as he toasted Mills. "Jamie doesn't believe me this is one of the best diners on the res."

"Don't know what you're missing," Mills said to Graff, "but suit yourself."

Graff thought the cop looked more Caucasian than Navajo. He could not have been a day over thirty, and his big deep voice did not match the slightly built man. He had bronze skin and short black hair that matched the color of his eyes. Crow's feet gave him a tired, if not weathered look that may have contributed to giving him an older appearance.

Two men at an adjacent table took interest though they pretended they weren't. O'Connor noticed it. Reyna, Graff and Mills picked up on it, so their conversation remained innocuous.

When was the last time it rained? Is it always like this? – Graff.

Able to get out and hunt much? – Reyna.

Elk is always a good bet. Some deer. Plenty in the valley. – Mills.

The desert does not come alive until after sunset, so the best hunting is just before daybreak. – Mills.

Graff smiled. He had hunted with them so he knew the boys understood that. Not for the first time, he wondered how they were managing.

The food showed up and as Reyna and Mills dug in, Graff's stomach growled. He snagged the waitress and ordered three chicken soft-shelled tacos and waited impatiently as the other two men ate. To bide his time, he drained another basket of chips along with a dish of salsa.

The two men at the nearby table glanced over intermittently, but decided that nothing important would be said. Still, they were more than a little curious and their impatience showed.

The shorter, older of the two squinted at them over the longneck he drank from. Despite the desert heat, the Mexican wore a jean jacket over a button-down shirt, jeans with a big silver buckle and dusty boots. He wore his cowboy hat so low, it nearly covered his eyes. His friend or partner, O'Connor couldn't decide, was about the same height as Graff, and thickly built like Reyna. Big, calloused hands. What looked like a scar from a knife ran in a straight line just above his jawline.

Their meal had ended, their dishes had been taken away, and the older of the two had paid the bill, but instead of leaving, the two sat there nursing a beer apiece. At least their third. O'Connor had noticed.

Graff, Reyna, and Mills finished eating. Reyna paid the bill and asked for a receipt. After, the three men stood up, pushed in their chairs, and walked out of the diner. The two men at the nearby table waited a beat and then followed. O'Connor waited a short minute or two and followed the two men. No one had followed him out of the diner.

When O'Connor stepped out into the late afternoon sun, he found Mills leaning against the front of his Jeep Liberty with Graff and Reyna facing him.

The two men from the nearby table sat in a newer green Ford F150 facing them from about fifteen yards away. The younger of the two sat in the driver's seat. The older man had his window down and he leaned out making no secret that he was trying to listen in.

O'Connor took out his cell phone, pretended to scroll through messages, but instead, snapped two pictures. One was of the truck and in particular, the license plate. The other was a close up of the two men in the truck. Using the email app on his cell, he sent the pictures off to Pete Kelliher who was stationed at the FBI Academy in Quantico, Virginia, and to his own partner, Sheriff Detective Paul Eiselmann back in Waukesha, Wisconsin. Eiselmann was a wiz at the computer. He offered an explanation and requested any ID they could provide. Then he texted the pictures to Graff and Reyna.

As he strolled to his truck, he wondered who they worked for and why they were interested in the three cops. At the back of his mind, he wondered how, not *if*, they figured into the missing Navajo boy and dead sheep.

CHAPTER TWENTY

She had ridden out of the sunset, at first a silhouette. She was obscured by the golden sun and her image shimmered and danced on the desert floor. The closer she came, the more into focus she got. In equal measure, Brett's and Brian's eyes widened.

When she pulled up, Rebecca jumped down from her horse and ran to George, who scooped her up into his arms. At first, they embraced, clinging tightly to each other. George buried his face in her hair.

He pulled back and pushed her hair to the side with his thumbs to scrutinize her more closely. There were dark circles under her bloodshot eyes and there were worry lines on her forehead. Her dark eyes had a haunted, frightened look, and her chin trembled.

As tears spilled down her cheeks, George answered with his own. He buried his face in her long, black hair again, and then they pulled back a little and kissed. Urgently, passionately, and long. It was only then when Brian and Brett turned away. The two boys shuffled their feet and studied the terrain beyond the horizon.

"I'm going to get a bottle of water," Brian said in a low voice just above a whisper. "Want one?"

"Sure," Brett said. "A cold shower too."

Trying not to laugh out loud, Brian walked to the back of the truck, lifted the Tonneau lid and pulled two bottles of water out of the cooler.

"George? Rebecca? You guys want a bottle of water?" Brian called.

"Yes, please," George answered. He asked Rebecca, "Do you want one?"

"Yes, please. Thank you."

Brian pulled out two more bottles, walked back, and passed one to Brett, and then to Rebecca and George.

"Hi. I'm Brian. That's Brett."

Rebecca smiled and studied Brian closely.

"What?" he asked.

She shook her and turned away towards the burned down ranch house. Brian offered George a questioning look that went unanswered.

"Any sign of your brother?" Brett asked.

Rebecca shook her head once.

"You and George will find him," Brett offered with a smile.

Rebecca turned to him. Brett recognized the hope, if not the desperation she felt. He smiled at her.

"George described you as a leader," she said.

Brett blushed. He was in some cases, maybe a lot of the time, but he only saw himself as an equal, as a brother and a friend who sometimes took charge when charge needed to be taken. He smiled and shrugged.

"You have a brother," she said. "Bobby?"

"Yes, but we're all brothers."

She turned to Brian and said, "You and Bobby like each other? You are . . . involved?"

Brian took a step back and stared at her and at George as one might watch a tennis match. He didn't know how to respond or if he should respond. He pushed his cowboy hat up on his head and then down low just above his eyes. He turned towards Brett and then George.

Brett gave George a *What the hell?* look, but said nothing.

"I mean . . . I don't . . ." Rebecca stammered.

Brian sort of flapped his arms and walked away behind the truck. He pulled out his 30-06 and slung it over his shoulder. Not sure why, he grabbed extra shells and pushed them into his front shirt pocket. He slung his binoculars around his neck, drained his bottle of water, and placed the empty into a plastic sack on the bed of the truck. Then without a word or a glance back, Brian began a slow trek up the hill towards a stand of pine trees.

All eyes were on him but he kept walking. He didn't stop or turn around when Brett and George called to him. He felt let down, betrayed. An ugly ending to an ugly day that was supposed to be a great time with his two brothers who were two of his best friends.

Given the conversation with Bobby earlier that morning, he didn't think he and Bobby were involved any longer. Besides, it was no one's business except his and Bobby's.

Rebecca turned to George who grimaced. Brett caught the look and kicked a rock with his toe sending it a few feet away.

Brian had disappeared into the stand of pines at the top of the hill when Brett said, "You don't even know him."

"I didn't mean . . ."

"What exactly didn't you mean?"

"I wasn't judging." Rebecca said. It had just tumbled out of her mouth. She had hurt Brian and didn't know how she could fix it.

"You weren't *judging*? Then why would you say something like that?"

He turned to George who had his hands stuffed into his front pockets. George looked back at the ground.

"Feel free to jump in, George." When George didn't, Brett said, "What, nothing? He is our brother. You know him. He would give you the shirt off his back if you needed it. You know that."

"I'm sorry," Rebecca said. "I am!"

"Brian and Bobby both have girlfriends, but yeah, they love each other. *Really* love each other. Anyone who sees the two of them together knows that. I would kill to have someone love me like Brian loves Bobby."

"I'm sorry. Should I go talk to him?" Rebecca asked. She brushed fresh tears off her face.

"I'm Bobby's biological brother, and if it's okay with me that Brian and Bobby love each other or are *involved*. . . you know what, why don't you two just go?" Brett said. He turned to George and said, "You didn't want us to be here anyway, so leave."

George started to object but Brett cut him off.

He laughed and said, "You know something? This was Brian's idea. He even offered to pay for all of it."

Brett pointed at George and said, "He did this because he didn't want you to be alone. He wanted to make sure someone had your back." Brett laughed again. "And you can't even defend him?"

Ashamed, George said nothing. Brett was right. George had abandoned Brian, and Brian didn't deserve that. George knew he had more to do with this than Rebecca. He had been mistreating both of them, especially Brian, ever since they had landed, but he didn't understand why.

He turned and stared up at the stand of pines and said, "I will go and talk to Brian."

Before he could, a black Escalade barreled up the driveway in a cloud of red dust.

74

CHAPTER TWENTY-ONE

Michael Two Feathers picked his way up the eastern side of the Chuskas taking the familiar pass that led to the valley on the west side. He still had a long way to go and his goal was to be on the western slope by nightfall. Once there, he would pitch his camp and look for other campfires. It was good to know who was out in the desert with him, friendly or not- as the case may be.

Two Feathers had enough water to last until morning when he would replenish from the waterfall that fed the mountain stream. It was cold, pure, and sweet. Just thinking of it made him thirsty, so he reached behind and into his saddlebag, and pulled out his beat-up canteen and took a swallow.

He had more than enough ammunition for the Model 94 Winchester in the scabbard attached to the saddle, certainly enough for a hunt or two, since he seldom needed more than two shots. The jerky O'Connor gave him would last several days. He had only three fresh carrots and two apples, so he would have to purchase more at the trading post in Round Rock for his two horses, along with a small amount of oats.

Michael was curious about O'Connor. He was good at recognizing con artists when he ran into them. After all, he knew what Feldcamp had wanted the moment the man asked him if he needed a place to stay and if he wanted a job. Michael agreed because it was a roof over his head, food to eat, and money in his pocket. More importantly, he had nowhere else to go. However, Michael couldn't figure out O'Connor.

The tall, skinny cop with long hair seemed like the real deal.

In the six or seven months he had lived with Lou above the bar, Michael only tolerated the man and did what he needed to in order to survive. It was convenience.

Now, however, Michael could never go back to Red Rock. Other than the desert, he didn't have anywhere to stay.

Michael shivered, and the mare swung her head around. Michael patted her neck and then wiped tears from his face. He did not like crying and he did not like being scared. He would have to see what happened at the end of

75

the week. Maybe O'Connor would find him somewhere to stay. Just in case, he had decided to save most of the two hundred dollars he had been given.

The boy sighed, took off his hat, and mopped his brow with his bare hand. He held the reins loosely, giving his dappled mare her lead because she knew where they were headed. They had been on this trail hundreds of times. They had been together a long time and were best friends. Maybe she was his only friend.

He glanced at the sun. He would have to pick up his pace in order to reach the western slope before nightfall.

Michael made a clucking sound and gently used his heels to the old mare's belly to speed her up.

He scanned the mountains and the pass in front of him. Coyotes were skittish and wolves stayed mostly to themselves despite what people thought. Yes, if they ran out of food, they might go after sheep. They were good hunters and could live on their own. Like him.

What he was most concerned about were mountain lions. They would sneak up silently on their padded paws, claws ready, head low, their eyes shiny yellow-gold. They were not particularly big, but they were fast and dangerous. He would have to be on alert.

Charles Morning Star.

If Michael knew where the good caves were, Morning Star would too. Perhaps he was hiding in one of them, but from what? From who? He would have to think about that.

Michael had spent time in caves when it rained. He would much rather be out in the open. He liked to sleep under the stars near a fire and covered only with a blanket. He liked the expanse of the desert, the smell of it. More than anything, it was home. It filled his soul and gave him peace.

What of the two boys he was supposed to babysit? O'Connor said they could hunt and were good at it. They were older than he was. Would they care if he watched over them? He was not sure why he was needed or exactly what he was supposed to do. He would play that by ear.

CHAPTER TWENTY-TWO

George stood in the middle with Brett on his right and Rebecca on his left. Their arms hung at their sides, and while they appeared to be relaxed, they were anything but. Brett had his right hand near his Glock 19, but did not dare touch it.

The Escalade pulled to a stop amid a swirl of red dust and at first, it sat there as if it were glaring at them. Then the driver's door popped open and the back-passenger door did the same. Two modern day cowboys dressed in black and wearing Wayfarers stepped out. The driver kept his hand on the butt of a holstered handgun. The passenger from the back held a Mossberg 500 in one hand as he opened the door on the front passenger side. Then he stepped back and held the shotgun out, but not pointed directly at anyone.

A short man wearing fancy silver-framed sunglasses, dressed in a dark suit with a black shirt, and a silver and turquoise bolo tie smoothed out an invisible wrinkle on his sport coat. He stepped forward and sighed.

Brett could smell his after shave. It was so strong Brett wondered if he had bathed in it.

"The three of you are on my property."

Brett glanced at George but chose to not to speak. This was George's show, not his.

George cocked his head, and said, "Your property."

The man smiled. It was oily and cold. "Yes, my property. You have less than five minutes to get off of it."

Unable to contain himself, Brett said, "This is my brother's property. It belonged to his family . . . his grandfather and his mother, and now it's his."

The man smiled again, and said, "I think you just used up a minute."

"The *Dine'* believe the land belongs to Mother Earth."

The man did not smile, but even behind the sunglasses, the three kids could see his dark eyes narrow to a squint.

"So, you are *Hosteen* Tokay's grandson, the new *Haatalii*. Funny, you look like any other skinny Navajo kid who moved off the reservation."

"This is George's land. We're not trespassing, you are. Get back in your caddy and leave," Brett said.

"You sound like a smartass."

"You look like a dumbass."

Ignoring Brett's bait, the man focused on Rebecca. He smiled, and said, "Your brother is still missing."

Rebecca lifted her chin defiantly but said nothing.

The man chucked, and said, "We've wasted enough time. Get off my property. Now!"

"What makes this your property?" George asked quietly.

The short round man with the black mustache and two-day-old beard lifted his shotgun a little. The other man gripped the butt of the handgun, but did not pull it out of his holster.

"That's none of your business. The only thing you need to know is that it is now mine. However, I am a fair man. I'll pay you for it."

"It is not for sale," George said.

The man pulled back his sport coat revealing a shoulder holster, and the driver lifted the revolver out of his holster. The short round man with the shotgun pointed it at Rebecca.

CHAPTER TWENTY-THREE

Unknowingly, Brian sat on the same rock George had used when he watched sheep as a boy. The same rock George's brother and grandfather used. Not five feet from where he sat was where George's brother, William, was cut down by a high-powered rifle.

The small outcropping was shaped like a chair. It allowed Brian to stretch his legs and sit at a slight decline just enough to relax. In the heat of the day and in the shade of the pines, the rock chair might coax one to nap. Brian had no interest in napping.

He stared out into the distance, but he did not take in the rugged beauty. The sun-splotched valley below was rimmed with a broken crown of red rock mesas and buttes, chipped and craggy like a homeless man's teeth. It was at once beautiful and lonely. Lonesome.

Brian wanted to go home. The trip stopped being fun the moment they had landed, when Reyna, Graff, and O'Connor left the boys on their own. The thrill of hunting elk had vanished.

George must have told Rebecca, and Brian wondered what else he might have said, what other thoughts George might hold. Rebecca left the statement hanging. The meaning was there, the implication. *He and Bobby are gay.*

He and Bobby wondered and worried a little about that. They loved each other in ways other boys did not.

Worse than George saying ... *whatever* he said to Rebecca, and in doing so betraying him, and worse than what George might think or feel, about him and Bobby, was that Brian did nothing to defend himself and Bobby. His silence was worse than anything George might have said, worse than anything George might feel.

He did not stand up for himself, and he did not stand up for Bobby. If he really loved Bobby, and he knew that he did, he should have said something, anything.

What could he say, though, that would not be an admission, an indictment that he actually might be gay? No matter what he said, even if he had used Cat as a shield against the threat or thought of being gay, it would still cast doubt.

Brian leaned forward, placed both hands on his face, and wept. He was scared for perhaps the first time in his life. He was uncomfortable and lonely. Worse than when his brother Brad was shot and killed, and worse than when his mom shot his dad.

Bobby had abandoned him, and now George. Who else might abandon him?

What if Jeremy harbored doubts about him? What if Jeremy and Vicky were disgusted about what, or who, he and Bobby were . . . might be? They had already made him and Bobby sleep in different bedrooms. What if Jeremy and Vicky weren't truthful about how they felt? Brian could not live with that.

He stared at his rifle. He flicked the safety off and wrestled with dark and dangerous thoughts. He moved it upside-down and stared down the barrel. As much as he wanted to, he hesitated. While it seemed like a long time, it was only a moment or two before he flicked the safety back on, but the thoughts were there like an ugly monster residing just below the surface.

Brian attempted to dry his face on the sleeve of his shirt but the tears would not stop. He pulled out his cell and dialed.

"Hey, Bri. Are you guys having fun?" Jeremy sounded cheery.

Brian could not bring himself to speak.

"Bri, are you there?"

Silence

"Brian! Hello!"

Brian held the phone in one hand, while the other covered his eyes and wept.

"Bri, are you okay? Is that you crying? Brian, answer me!"

Brian wept.

Jeremy frantic. *"Brian, what's wrong? What happened?"*

Brian could not answer. He dared not answer because he didn't know what might spill out. He held the phone away while his dad spoke to him, pleaded with him.

At last, Brian pushed the button to end the call.

When his cell vibrated, he ignored it. He wiped off his face again, took off his cowboy hat, and wiped down his hair. He repositioned it back on his head the way he normally wore it. He sighed, lifted his chin, and resolved that no matter what, he was not about to talk to George or Rebecca the rest of the trip. Maybe ever. He hoped that when he got back to the burned-out ranch, they would be gone.

He reached the edge of the stand of pine and saw what was happening down below. His mouth went dry, his knees almost gave way, and his hands shook as he reached for the binoculars around his neck.

He had made a promise to his mom that he would keep George and Brett safe. It was not long before he knelt in a shooter's stance.

CHAPTER TWENTY-FOUR

Brett's cell vibrated.

"My cell just went off. I'm answering it."

He lifted his right hand in the air because the Glock 19 sat on his right hip and he did not want them to think he was reaching for it. With his left hand, he reached into his back pocket and pulled out his cell, pushed a button, and put it to his ear.

"What's up?"

The two men on either side of the short man in the suit hesitated, lowered their weapons, and waited to be told what to do.

"What the fuck, Brett! Who are they?" Brian whispered, not sure if his voice would carry.

"They think we're trespassing on George's land."

"I need Rebecca and George to take two steps back and kneel down. They're in my line of sight."

"Okay, just a minute," Brett said. To George and Rebecca, he said, "We need to take two steps back and kneel down."

"What?" the man asked. "No! Stay where you are!"

"Rebecca, George, take two steps back and kneel down. Now," Brett said.

George did as he was asked. Rebecca hesitated, but followed George's lead. The last to step back and kneel down was Brett.

To Brian, he said, "That good?"

"Yes."

"Okay, take a picture. This should look good in case anything happens. Us kneeling and these three assholes pointing their guns at us."

"Who are you talking to?" the man in the black suit demanded.

"A Guardian Angel," Brett answered with a smile. To Brian he said, "Did you get the picture?"

"Yes, three."

"Three pictures. Good." Brett thought for a second and said, "Hold on a minute."

He turned his cell around and snapped four pictures- one of each man and one of the Escalade's license plate.

"Okay, got 'em. They weren't smiling, and they didn't seem happy, but who gives a shit, right?" Brett said with a smile.

"Put it down! *Now!*" the man ordered.

"Got to go, Bud. Do what you do best," Brett said.

George turned and shook his head slightly.

The guy raised his Mossberg and pointed it at Rebecca. The man with the handgun could not decide whether to aim it at George or Brett, so he waved it at both almost like he was reciting the kiddies' jingle, "Eenie meenie miney mo . . ."

Brian's 30-06 barked, and the bullet struck the Mossberg's barrel before the report was heard. It flew out of his hands. Stunned, the three men took a step back, unsure of where to go or what to do.

The man bent down to retrieve his shotgun, and Brian slammed two shots into it, one into the firing mechanism, and one cutting the stock in two. The man backed off and raised his hands.

The sidekick with the handgun aimed at Brett and said, "Tell him to stop!"

Brian blew the gun out of his hand, perhaps with a finger or two. Brian could not tell.

The man screamed and bent over, holding his hand to his belly to stop the flow of blood.

Brett took the opportunity to pull his Glock from his holster and point it at the man in the suit.

"Get back into your Caddie and drive your sorry ass outta here. This is George's land. It is not for sale. You're trespassing."

"You committed a felony," the man said menacingly. "Next time, we'll be ready."

"Whatever, Fuckhead."

The man took one step at Brett, and Brian's 30-06 barked once more, blowing the black cowboy hat off his head. The bullet traveled onward into the Escalade's windshield.

The man ducked, and both hands flew to the top of his head.

"*You Fucker!*"

Brian, who had reloaded, placed another bullet through the windshield, one into the rearview mirror, took off the driver's side mirror, and blew out one of the headlights.

"Better leave before he takes the mole off the left side of your butt-ugly face," Brett said with a smile.

"This isn't the end. We'll report this to the Navajo police," the man yelled.

"You do that. We'll show them the pictures of us kneeling down on George's property as you point your weapons at us. A picture is worth a thousand words, right?"

Knowing he had been bettered, the man turned three shades of red, holstered his sidearm, and reached for his hat. Brian blasted it again. The man jumped, turned around, and got into the passenger side of the vehicle. The man holding his bloody hand managed to climb into the backseat, and the man whose shotgun was now useless, walked around the front of the big SUV with his hands raised. He got in the driver's seat, started it up, and backed up ten yards before he turned it around. They drove off down the driveway.

Brett was the first to stand up, but he held his Glock at the ready. George helped Rebecca to her feet.

"Who were they?" Brett asked.

George shook his head and then looked over at Rebecca who shrugged.

"I . . . we do not know," he said quietly staring at the red dust kicked up by the departing Escalade. "I do not know," he repeated almost in a whisper.

CHAPTER TWENTY-FIVE

Strangely enough, the heat of the desert dried whatever sweat that ran down his neck, back and armpits. Something he had never experienced before. The sun's rays bounced up from the hard-packed earth. He could feel the heat on his arms and face. His feet burned through his boots.

Brian walked down from the stand of pines. He glanced furtively at George and Rebecca, not willing to make direct eye contact. He busied himself behind the truck reloading his rifle. He pocketed more shells into the breast pocket of his shirt. He snatched a bottle of water out of the cooler and gulped it down, spilling a little down his chin and neck. He wiped himself off with his sleeve. He snagged another bottle and placed it next to his rifle.

He needed to cool off, so he rolled up his sleeves and adjusted his cowboy hat on his sweaty tangle of hair. He was sure it was matted down, but he did not bother to finger comb it. No matter what he did, it would become matted down in the perfect shape of his hat. He did not care.

He put the empty bottle in the plastic sack, slung his rifle over his shoulder, and walked up to Brett.

George and Rebecca stood back a step.

"Nice shooting, Bri," Brett said. "I thought it was going to get a helluva lot worse."

"How bad was his hand? I didn't mean to hit it but I had to get him to drop the gun," Brian said. "Did I screw things up?"

Brett looked over at George and Rebecca, then back to Brian, and said, "You saved our lives. That counts for something. Who gives a shit about his hand? He was aiming at both George and me."

"You don't know who they were?" He kept talking directly to Brett as if George and Rebecca were not there.

"No, and George and Rebecca don't know either."

"We should leave in case they come back. Are you sending the pictures to Jamie and Pat? They'll want to know." Brian remembered the three pictures he had taken and pulled out his cell.

"Don't," Brett said as he put his hand over it. "Wait. Please."

Brian could not comprehend why Brett hesitated. They had almost been killed, and they should tell someone.

Brett glanced at George, who was equally puzzled, and at Rebecca, who folded her arms across her chest. She was curious.

"I think we'll be safe for at least a day. We can tell them tomorrow."

Brian's jaw hung. "Tomorrow?"

"The way I look at it, those three guys won't touch us for a while. They know we have pictures, and they know we'll use them. If we go to Jamie and Pat now, George and Rebecca won't be able to search for Charles because Graff and O'Connor will make sure we're tucked away at some motel. Hell, they might even ship us home. You know how they are."

"But Brett . . ." Brian said as he shook his head.

"Just a day. That gives us one night to camp out and one day to hunt. We'll see what happens after that. We need to give George and Rebecca time to look for Charles. They're his best chance."

Brian looked directly at George, and said, "You're okay with not telling O'Connor or Graff about this?"

"Rebecca and I need to look for Charles." It was all he said, but it sounded like George agreed with Brett.

Brian shook his head.

Rebecca said, "Thank you for what you did. You saved us."

What Brian wanted to say was, *'Not bad for a gay guy, huh?'* Instead, he ignored Rebecca, turned to Brett and said, "I'm walking down the driveway."

"Why?"

"To make sure they're gone. If you load up, we can leave when I get back. I don't think we should stay here any longer than we need to. They could come back or they could send others. I think you're wrong about not letting Jamie or Pat know about this."

"We'll tell them tomorrow after we camp out tonight, and after we hunt in the morning. By then, George and Rebecca will be up in the mountains, and Pat and Jamie won't be able to get in touch with them."

Brian shook his head as he took off down the dirt road.

"Brian, wait up," George called to him. He jogged up to join him.

Brian quickened his pace but George stayed with him.

"Wait, please!"

Brian kept walking as if he hadn't heard him.

When they were a safe distance away, George said, "She didn't mean anything, Brian. She's not like that."

Brian glared at him but said nothing.

"She's not. I am not."

Brian stopped, jabbed a finger on George's chest, and said, "You're supposed to be my friend, George. My brother. Why did you tell her Bobby and I were gay? It's no one's business. No one's!"

"It wasn't like that," George said quietly.

Brian placed a hand on George's chest and shoved him.

"So, tell me, how exactly did that random piece of information come up?"

George started and stammered, "I . . . we were talking, and Rebecca asked me who was coming with me."

"Oh, I see. You said something like, 'My brother Brett and my gay brother Brian.' Something like that?" Brian placed both hands on George's chest and shoved him again. "Fuck you! Leave me alone."

When George didn't move, Brian said, "Just fucking go. You didn't want us to come, anyway. We're in the way. I get it. So, leave. This whole trip is fucked up. Everything is fucked up! Don't worry about Brett and me. We'll hunt, spend the night by the pond, and then we'll go to Chinle or wherever the fuck we want but we'll be out of your hair. We won't bother you anymore. I won't bother you anymore. You won't have to babysit us because we won't be tagging along."

Still George didn't move.

The pained expression on George's face got to Brian. They were friends, he, Brett and George. He was close to each of his brothers. They were his friends, and he loved them. They loved each other. But he, Brett, and George were the most alike. Brett and George were his buddies.

It hurt Brian to look at George, and he was angry with himself for causing George pain regardless of what he did or said. Add it to the conversation he had with Bobby. Everything was fucked up. Vicky had asked him to take care of his brothers and he had failed.

All the steam left him. Defeated, Brian said, "Just go. I want to be left alone."

George didn't move.

"Please leave me alone," Brian pleaded. "I don't want to talk to you. Not now. Not for a long time."

Brian turned and continued walking down the driveway. The toe of his boot caught a rock. He stumbled but caught himself before he fell.

George wanted to walk with him, to give him a hug, and tell him that he was sorry for everything.

George had not acted the way he should have. Yes, Charles was missing, and Charles had been a friend longer than any of his brothers. But his grandfather would not have approved. Jeremy would not have approved. He, himself, did not approve.

Somehow, he would make it up to Brian. And Brett. He had to. He owed it to them and he owed it to himself.

CHAPTER TWENTY-SIX

Reyna and Graff pulled over onto the west side of the road south of Lukachukai about halfway to Tsaile on the backside of Canyon de Chelly National Monument. They connected with O'Connor using Graff's cell. Graff used the speaker function so the two cops could tag-team the conversation. O'Connor did not stop, but continued on his drive to Chinle.

"The green Ford F150 belongs to the driver, Henry Stone of Phoenix, Arizona. He works for a private security firm out of Phoenix," Reyna said as he read from his notes. "Quantico did a little more digging and found that Desert Security is mostly made up of ex-military. They have been used in a variety of international situations mostly in Afghanistan or Iraq. They also worked domestically supporting law enforcement. They helped during the mining disaster that took place in West Virginia two or three years ago, and again after hurricane Katrina."

"What West Virginia mining disaster?" O'Connor asked.

"You mean which one, right?" Graff laughed.

Reyna laughed, and said, "According to Wikipedia," he read right from his cell, "The Gosa Mine disaster was a coal mine explosion in February 2017. The blast and collapse trapped 17 miners for nearly three days. No one survived."

"What did they do?" O'Connor asked.

Reyna scratched his cheek. "That's sketchy. Ostensibly, they served as a sort of extension of the National Guard. The Guard was brought in for crowd control. That's the official line."

"What's the unofficial line?" Graff asked.

"A goon squad that used scare tactics and intimidation to keep the public in line."

O'Connor frowned. "Law enforcement and National Guard weren't enough, so they brought in Desert Security to work behind the scenes. The question is, why? Who was hiding what?"

Reyna and Graff exchanged a look, and Graff said, "Good question."

"What are they doing in Arizona on the Navajo reservation?" O'Connor asked more to himself than to Reyna and Graff.

"And why were they so interested in us?" Graff asked.

"If they're based out of Phoenix, that's not far away," Reyna said. "Coincidence?" Even though he said it, he didn't believe it.

"No such thing," O'Connor said.

Graff stared off at the red-gold horizon. The sun hung low. Shadows were already spreading across the desert floor.

He turned to Reyna, and said, "We need to know why they're here, in this area of Arizona."

Reyna pulled out his cell, hit Google, did a quick search, and said, "We're about 360 miles away from Phoenix. That's what, a six-hour drive?"

"They're not on vacation or seeing the sites," O'Connor said.

"What's the draw?" Graff said as he turned to Reyna. "We need to find that out."

"You think they had something to do with that boy's disappearance and dead sheep?" Reyna asked.

"Don't know," Graff said. "But they're here and they took an interest in us for a reason."

"I'll have Quantico dig some more and find out what projects they're currently working on, and what companies are involved," Reyna said as he composed an email from his cell.

"What did Deputy Mills have to say?" O'Connor asked.

"Nothing that we didn't already know," Graff said. "He approached four ranchers who claimed to know nothing."

"No one heard anything, even though a shotgun was used on the sheep," Reyna answered.

"Anything on George's friend?" O'Connor asked.

"Nothing. He hasn't been seen or heard from," Reyna answered.

Deep in thought, O'Connor said, "Here's what we need to find out. What is the connection between a missing kid, dead sheep, ranchers too afraid to say anything, and armed goons running around the reservation?"

"If we can find a connection between two of those, the others will fall into place," Graff said.

"Assuming each is related to the other," Reyna said.

"They're related . . . somehow," Graff answered.

"Have to be," O'Connor explained. "There's no such thing as a coincidence."

CHAPTER TWENTY-SEVEN

George rode the horse Rebecca had brought with her, and he took the lead in their trek across the valley though essentially, they rode side by side. They scanned the horizon, but not obviously in case they were being watched. George was interested in any telltale flashes of light, glints from the sun that might catch on a lens, like someone with binoculars. So far, he had not seen anything. It did not necessarily mean they were alone, though.

They had a tougher time searching behind them, so they took turns. First, George would ease himself ahead so he had to turn around to talk to Rebecca, though his eyes were everywhere but on her, and then Rebecca would pull ahead so she would have to turn around to talk to George. Again, so far, there was no sign they had been followed.

In the vast red desert with the sun at their back, it looked like they were chasing their own shadows across the valley floor. The two of them traveled at a leisurely pace, but quickly enough for them to cross the valley, get up on the hillside, and set up camp before dark. Charles had to be up there somewhere.

"Did your father look in the Chuskas?" he asked her in a faraway tone.

Rebecca shook her head, and said, "No. He didn't go out too far and not up in the hills at all. He thought Charles would be somewhere in the valley."

"Didn't you tell him where he hunted?" George asked.

"Of course, I did. He didn't listen," Rebecca said defensively.

George caught the tone of her voice, turned, and said, "I wasn't accusing you, Rebecca. I am sorry."

Rebecca nodded curtly, turned her head slightly, and kept riding.

"I think we need to pick up our pace to get into the mountains before it gets dark," he suggested. "That way, it will still be light when we set up camp."

Rebecca's response was to use the heel of her boot, a clicking noise with her tongue, and a flap of the reins to speed up her horse.

It was awkward being around her. He did not understand girls. He could not comprehend their thinking. To be sure, he was interested. He just didn't understand them.

Not only was Rebecca his oldest friend, they had been intimate, sharing a blanket in the stand of pines above the small pasture where his sheep had grazed. She knew him best, even better than Brett and Brian, Randy, Billy, and Bobby. Second to Jeremy, who had an uncanny ability to see right into the heart of his boys.

With Rebecca, there was . . . *something* between the two of them still, even after the two years they had been separated. Even after the intimate relationship she had had with Billy.

It was frustrating and not for the first time he had wished he was as quick-witted and smooth as Billy was. For as good as he was with horses and hunting, and as confident as he was when he raced in cross country or track, he was hesitant and shy when it came to girls. He was awkward. He stumbled over his words.

"I am sorry for hurting your brother," Rebecca said. "I don't know why I said what I did."

George shook his head, and said, "Brian has a gentle heart. He is quick to forgive. It is his way."

Rebecca wasn't so sure.

"If I call him and apologize, would that help?"

George squinted up at the rolling hills that led to the mountainside, and said, "Wait until morning. Give him time."

His answer stung.

"Time will give Brett a chance to talk to him. Brian does well with time, and Brett knows how to talk to him better than any of us," George added. He almost said, *'Except for Bobby,'* but didn't.

Rebecca pulled her horse up, and he stopped alongside her. She stared further up at the hill. George followed the line of her gaze.

"There is a campfire near the spring," Rebecca whispered.

Indeed, there was. It looked as though someone had taken pains to bank it in such a way as to hide it from view.

CHAPTER TWENTY-EIGHT

"Dad wants to know how you're doing," Brett said as the two boys waded into the pond.

Naked, neither boy rushed to dive in. Brian and Brett wanted to get used to the water gradually as they always did.

Changing the subject, Brian said, "You don't see anyone watching us, do you?"

Brett spread his arms out, turned in a slow three-sixty and said, "No one's around."

Brian looked down at himself but the major parts were underwater. He said, "Just seems like someone's watching us."

Brett laughed. "You're paranoid."

Brian shrugged.

Brett waited, and said, "So what happened with Dad? What did you say to him?"

Brian bent over, splashed water on his arms and chest, and said, "Nothing."

"Must have said something."

"It must have been a butt dial."

He dove into the water to end the conversation. His bare white butt and his feet were the last to disappear. Under water, he used breaststroke-like pulls and fluttered his feet to carry him further away.

He reached the middle of the pond and had to tread water to keep his head above the surface. With one hand, he whisked water out of his eyes and out of his nose. He shook his head first one way and then the other to get water out of his ears. Brett was nowhere to be seen.

He came up behind Brian, placed both hands on his shoulders, and dunked him.

Brian came up sputtering.

"Dork!" and then turned around and did the same to Brett.

Brett had a mouthful of water ready, and as he broke surface, spit it into Brian's face with a laugh. Brian dunked Brett again, and was ready when

Brett surfaced, catching him in the face with his own mouthful of water before Brett fired off another. The two of them ended up laughing.

The cool water refreshed them. While it washed away the sweat, along with the dirt, dust, and grime, it didn't do much to wash away the mood that held a death grip on Brian's heart.

"I want to climb on your back," Brett announced.

"Too deep. I can't touch bottom."

"Okay, come back to shore until you can."

Brian did as he was told. He found the sandy bottom, but had to stand at an incline.

"Man, it gets deep in the middle," he said.

Brett laughed, took Brian by the shoulders, and said, "Turn around."

Brett climbed onto Brian's back. Brian held him under his knees, and said, "You look heavy, but you're kinda light."

"I have massive muscles," he said with a laugh, and then he ordered, "Mush!"

Brian ferried him deeper to the point where he had to swim. Brett still clung to Brian's back, laughing, though he did help Brian by stroking with one arm.

"You're making it difficult to swim," Brian managed before his head went under once, and then twice.

He shook Brett off him, turned around, and said, "Okay, you carry me."

Brett laughed, dunked Brian, and then headed to shore where he waited for Brian to get onto his back.

"Damn, you're heavy! Your legs are like tree trunks."

Brian laughed, and said, "I have soccer legs."

"And a soccer tan!" Brett said with a laugh.

"It's not that bad," Brian said, though when he looked down at himself, his shins were pale, while his thighs were tan.

"Have you seen yourself?" Brett laughed.

"Dork!" Brian found himself smiling as the dark clouds around his heart let in a bit of sunshine. He loved his family and his brothers.

They did this back and forth before they finally walked out of the water shoulder to shoulder.

"I'm going to air dry," Brett announced. "We can save the towels until we need them. Tonight, let's share two blankets, one under us, and one on top. That way, we can save the other two if it rains."

It was the tail end of twilight, more dark than light. They stood shoulder to shoulder looking off into the horizon. The pond was at the foot of the Chuskas across the valley from where they would hunt. From their position, they could look both up into the dark mountains, and across the western horizon where the valley was, though the darkening landscape made any visual into the distance difficult. Brian counted two campfires on the mountainside not far from one another. One was dim.

"Where do you think they are?" Brian asked as he studied the mountainside.

"Up there looking down here and wondering where we are."

"They know where we are," Brian muttered.

He didn't care because he didn't believe either George or Rebecca cared. The anger faded away to hurt, just as the daylight had faded behind the curtain leaving darkness to stand center stage.

Brett caught his mood, smacked Brian's arm gently, and said, "I'm hungry."

He turned, slipped his feet into Nike slides, and walked to the three horses tethered to metal stakes. They had borrowed the horses from Rebecca's ranch at her suggestion, leaving their truck behind the barn out of the way. There was only one saddle, so Brian had ridden bareback because he was the more experienced rider.

From the pack horse, Brett pulled out two blankets, and carried them over to the bank where Brian stood staring up at the mountain.

"Here okay?" Brett asked.

Brian turned around and said, "Back a little further from the water."

Brett followed Brian's suggestion.

"You want to build a fire?" Brett asked.

"Yeah, sure. A small one. We don't need much."

"One big enough to cook elk burgers and baked potatoes, and big enough to keep wolves and coyotes away."

"Good idea."

He threw on a pair of shorts and his slides and gathered dry twigs and sticks. Brett slipped on a pair of shorts and began preparing their dinner.

By the time Brett finished cooking, the night had turned black as tar, and the desert was silent. Between mouthfuls of burger and baked potato, they contented themselves with small talk- the upcoming school year, classes they were signed up for, and of course, football and soccer. Brett brought up hunting, and Brian described how they might go about it.

Brett listened. While he was pretty good, Brian was more experienced. Every hunting trip he, Brian, and George had taken, Brian had always bagged some critter. George did most of the time, and Brett only some of the time. Not often at that.

The fire burned hungrily. Brian fed it twigs and sticks to keep it satisfied. The two of them sat side by side on the blanket, their stomachs full, and their greasy fingers clean, having washed them off in the pond along with their faces.

"You want s'mores?" Brett asked.

"Later. I'm stuffed."

"Yeah, me too," though Brett sounded disappointed.

He elbowed Brian and said, "So . . . what did you say to Dad?"

Brian sighed. "I told you. Nothing. It must have been a butt dial."

He ended up shaking his head, and he turned away so Brett could not see his expression. He didn't like lying to anyone in his family.

Brett studied him in silence. To rescue him he said, "You'll need to call him tomorrow. The night is pretty. We ate well because I'm a great cook," Brett said with a laugh. "And, we're camping. This is the best."

Brian smiled weakly. He laid down on the blanket, placed both hands under his head, and stared up at the sky.

"Put your left arm out straight," Brett ordered.

Brian did as he was told, and Brett laid down on top of it, almost on top of Brian, using Brian's shoulder as a pillow. Brian laughed and brought his arm around Brett's stomach. His fingertips giving Brett goosebumps.

"Do you know the constellations?" Brett asked.

"Not really. The Dippers and the North Star. That's about it."

"Same for me."

"You know most if not all of those stars are already dead? We still receive light from them though. Weird, huh?"

Brett laughed, and said, "Yes, and so are you."

Brian poked Brett in his bare ribs causing Brett to laugh, and squirm.

"If you poke me, I'll poke you." He turned his head slightly, and said, "And not your ribs."

Brian smiled but said nothing. A million and one thoughts ran through his mind randomly and all at once, each screaming for attention. From dead or dying stars, to God, and if He was watching them and if He was disappointed in him, to wondering if any wolves or coyotes were around, to wondering what Bobby, Randy, and Billy were up to, especially Bobby.

He missed him. He missed being around him, talking with him, and even being silent with him. He wondered how their relationship might change, knowing that it would. He wondered how that might change his relationship with the others in his family.

Finally, he wondered how worried Jeremy might be. He didn't mean to make him worry. He had needed to ask him one question. The question that most haunted and tormented him.

"What are you thinking about?" Brett asked.

"Stuff."

There was quiet laughter and talk about this or that. A satellite scooted above them, and from the east traveling to the west, they spotted a shooting star. The tail of it glowed in the dark night sky.

"That's so cool!" Brian said. "I've never seen one before."

"Did you make a wish?" Brett asked.

Brian nodded. "You?"

"Yup. What did you wish for?"

"If I tell you, it won't come true," Brian said quietly.

"It was about Bobby," Brett said.

Brian caught a tone in Brett's voice. He glanced at him.

It was frustrating that Brett knew him so well. Each of his brothers were like that. So was Jeremy and Vicky. Nothing was private in their family.

A coyote or wolf howled off in the distance. Both boys sat up.

"Where?" Brett whispered.

Brian held up a hand and listened. The wolf howled once more, and both boys stared up at the mountainside. Echoes made it difficult to pinpoint the location.

Brian whispered. "I think up to the right two or three hundred yards." He paused, licked his lips, and said, "Give or take."

"Near that campfire?"

Brian squinted up at the mountainside. "Maybe"

"Are we safe?"

Brian pulled his lower lip, but didn't take his eyes off the dim campfire. Whoever was there might be in more danger than they were.

"Don't know. Keep your Glock handy. My rifle is loaded and I have it right here," he said as he touched it reassuringly.

"Best we can do, since we left the truck at Rebecca's house and rode the horses out here. What the hell were we thinking?"

Brian nodded and laid back down but did not take his eyes off the mountain.

"Move your arm," Brett said.

Brian did, and Brett resumed his previous position.

"Scared?"

Brian shook his head. "I don't get scared."

The two sat up once more, hearing it at the same time. It was not the howl of a wolf or coyote, but the purr of a vehicle. Its headlights bouncing in the distance below as it came straight up the dirt path directly at them.

CHAPTER TWENTY-NINE

Instead of heading to Chinle, O'Connor drove back into the valley to do some recon near the ranches where sheep were killed. Something was happening, and he needed to know why. The way O'Connor liked to do that was to stir up some shit and see what stunk.

There were five ranches, so he could not cover them all. He would have to choose. He decided to go with Delbert Yazzie, who had five sheep killed. Reyna and Graff both said he was too afraid to talk. He would push him a little further towards the edge.

He called Graff. "I want to stir some things up."

There was a pause, and then Jamie asked, "Like what, exactly?"

"Don't know yet. Probably stake out the Yazzie ranch."

"What will that get us?" Reyna asked.

"Maybe something, maybe nothing. If I see something happening before anyone sees me, then that will be something. If nothing happens but Yazzie spots me, he might freak out and lead us somewhere or to someone, and that will be something. Can't lose either way."

Graff and Reyna shrugged at each other, and Jamie said, "Be careful."

O'Connor clicked off without a response. With or without their blessing, he would do it. Working undercover as he did most often, he found that being careful might be the smart thing to do, but playing it smart would not necessarily be productive. Mostly, it was not in his nature to be cautious. Not that he was ever needlessly reckless, just that he would rather dance on the edge.

The roads, if one could call them that, were nothing more than one lane dirt tracks covered in ruts like veins or arteries that crisscrossed the land. It took him a little over an hour as he looped around the bottom edge of the Chuskas. Because he did not want to tip anyone off, he drove the last ten miles by moonlight and this caused him to slow down.

As he approached the ranch, O'Connor saw two dim lights he took for lanterns. George had told him that it was not possible to have electricity out in the middle of nowhere unless the ranch had propane. Few of the Navajo were wealthy enough for that luxury.

He cut to his right and drove into a copse of pinons, junipers, and pine all tangled haphazardly in a way only Mother Nature could create. It provided adequate cover and an excellent vantage point to watch the comings and goings in or around the area. Though he was not worried about being seen, O'Connor was confident that if spotted, he could simply drive off leaving Yazzie frightened at being watched.

O'Connor chuckled. Yes, Delbert Yazzie was being watched. As quickly as that thought came, the chuckle died in his throat.

What if O'Connor wasn't the only one watching Yazzie?

CHAPTER THIRTY

She should not have been watching them but she could not help it. They were laughing, and they were naked. They built a fire, ate, and were now laying on a blanket looking at stars. With the binoculars, she was close enough to reach out and touch them.

She wanted to ride her horse down to the pond and apologize to Brian. She didn't want to wait until morning. She needed to make amends and do that sooner rather than later.

Rebecca sat on a blanket next to George. She had been watching Brett and Brian ever since George had set down their blankets and started their fire.

She had begun by searching the side of the mountains for any sign of her brother but she didn't see anything that might indicate he was around. No movement. No fire. No smoke. She never thought she would. If Charles didn't want to be found, he wouldn't. She and George would have better luck in daylight looking for a sign.

They had discussed it and had come to the conclusion that Charles would leave a trail like breadcrumbs in a children's fairy tale. They would be the only two that would be able to follow the trail because they knew him better than anyone else. However, they would have to pay attention to subtleties, concentrate on what would appear to be normal and ordinary to anyone else.

After setting up their camp and starting their fire, George had crept off, leaving her alone as he circled higher up the mountain. He had wanted to see who belonged to the campfire by the waterfall. It took him a half an hour because he traveled on foot, wanting to blend into the background. Riding his horse would not allow him to do that.

He returned and saw Rebecca staring down at the pond.

"They are laying on a blanket looking at stars."

As was George. Something he used to do with his youngest brother, Robert, before Robert and the rest of his family were murdered. That memory drove him further into the dark recesses where he rarely traveled.

Rebecca tried again. "You said it was a younger boy camping by the waterfall?"

"Yes. He had two horses, and it looked like he was hunting."

"Something the four of us would do. You, your brother William, Charles, and me."

George turned his head to her and whispered, "William liked you."

"I know."

"That is what kept the two of us apart," George whispered. "He resented my relationship with you."

Rebecca rolled over onto her side and placed her head on George's chest. She unbuttoned George's shirt and ran her fingertips across his chest and stomach.

"I loved you. Deep down, I think I had always loved you."

"What about Billy?"

She raised her head, pushed her long hair behind her ears, and stared deeply into George's eyes.

"Yes, I loved Billy. But deep down, I always loved you."

She kissed George lightly.

"I always loved you, Rebecca. Never anyone else."

She undid his belt, unzipped his jeans, and kissed him again as her fingers found him ready. He unbuttoned her shirt and gently caressed her breast.

Rebecca slipped her shirt all the way off and with George's help, slid out of her jeans and panties. George kissed her stomach, and then she helped George out of his jeans and boxers. The two of them were naked with her laying on top of him. They kissed deeply and passionately as she straddled him. Without effort or thought, she guided him inside her. They took up a slow, familiar rhythm.

At their climax, Rebecca leaned back and quickened her pace as she moaned. George clung to her even after he had emptied himself, making sure she was satisfied. It was his way, their way. After, she fell into his arms, her face buried into his neck. She nibbled on his ear playfully.

"I missed that . . . you," George said.

She raised her head and smiled down at him.

"You had many girls since you and I . . . dated."

George shook his head. "No one."

Surprised, Rebecca said, "No one?"

"No one."

A wolf howled at the moon. It came from above them and to their left. It had to have been close to the boy near the waterfall.

Rebecca looked up from George's chest and bit her lip.

"Will that kid be safe?"

"It looked like he's been out here before. His horses will warn him if it gets too close."

"What about your brothers?"

George thought for a minute, reached for his cell but before he could use it, he saw the headlights in the distance.

CHAPTER THIRTY-ONE

Wondering if whomever drove up on them might be part of the group who had threatened them at George's ranch, Brett grabbed his Glock and darted toward the horses. He crouched down and waited as he held the reins in his left hand. Brian grabbed his rifle, fled in the other direction, and knelt on one knee in a shooting position. Both boys hid in the shadows away from the headlights.

The jeep stopped ten or so yards from the campfire, and only one person stepped out. Brian didn't think there was anyone else in the vehicle.

"Hello the fire!" a voice called out. "Detective O'Connor asked me to check on you."

Neither boy moved nor said anything but both noticed the handgun on the man's hip. He had not touched it, and it didn't look like he would.

"I'm Deputy Ned Mills with the Navajo Nation Police."

"How do we know?" Brett called out, knowing that by doing so, he had given up his position.

"Good question," Mills laughed.

He tugged on his shirt and displayed the badge pinned to his chest.

"Other than this, you'll have to take my word for it."

He squatted by the fire warming his hands though the temperature was anything but cold. He tossed some twigs and sticks into it and watched the flames flare up.

Brian was the first to step out of the shadow. With his rifle at ease, he cautiously walked forward but didn't get too close. That prompted Brett. He re-tied the reigns on their pegs and crept closer but from the other side of the fire.

Mills smiled and said, "O'Connor said you two were smart. Good thinking to separate yourselves like that." He chuckled and pointed up at the mountainside. "George and Rebecca up there?"

"Yes, Sir," Brian answered.

"Who belongs to the other campfire?"

"We don't know," Brett answered. "Whoever it is isn't with us."

"Are you boys okay? Did you eat?"

"Yes, Sir. We're fine." Brian answered.

"Good. What are your plans for tomorrow?"

Brett smiled at Brian, and said, "Hunting."

Mills nodded. "You'll want to get to the valley before sun up. The desert is nocturnal. More activity takes place in the dark than in the sun because of the heat. There should be a good-sized herd of elk and deer about two miles to the west of here, give or take. Set yourselves up on a hillside, and stay downwind. Don't try to get closer than a hundred yards or you'll spook 'em."

"Thank you. We'll do that," Brian said.

"If you manage to harvest one, where will you take it?"

Brett said, "We made arrangements with the guy at the trading post in Round Rock. He said he knows a butcher, and he said he'd send it back home for us."

"Laidley's a good man."

"I have a question," Brian said. "We heard a wolf howling. Is there anything special we need to do? I mean . . . are we safe?"

Mills pursed his lips, and said, "Wolves can be tricky. They're bolder than coyotes but for the most part, with a good fire, they'll stay away." He glanced around at their camp and said, "You've policed your site pretty well. Keep your food packed up as best you can. Stay close to the fire. Keep your rifle and your handgun close by. You should be safe."

"We'll do that," Brett said.

"About hunting tomorrow," Brian said. "If I use the alarm on my cell, what time should I set it for?"

"Four-ish. Still dark enough for critters to be out, and if you head back the way I came, you'll come up on a little rise. Shoot from there. It will be off to your right as you face the valley."

"I think we saw that when we rode here," Brett said.

"Stay safe and stay together." Mills reached into his shirt pocket and pulled out two business cards. He handed one to Brett and one to Brian. "If you need anything, call me. Anytime, day or night."

"Yes, Sir," Brian answered. "Thank you."

Brian considered telling the officer about the encounter at George's ranch, but decided against it. He'd contact Pat and Jamie at some point in the morning for sure.

They shook hands and Mills left the two boys alone.

CHAPTER THIRTY-TWO

Michael Two Feathers took in the scene with his binoculars. He swung them over to his right in the direction of George's and Rebecca's fire, and saw George watching the scene by the pond as well. Rebecca gripped a rifle.

He swung his binoculars back down to the pond and watched the cop drive away. The two boys settled in on the blanket after one of them threw some sticks and twigs on the fire.

Michael watched as one boy laid down next to the other with his head on the other boy's shoulder, and loneliness swept over him. There was no one remotely close to him that he could call a friend.

Sad and anxious, he didn't know what would become of him at the end of the week. One way or the other, he would survive. He always did.

He kicked off his boots and set them near his left hand but off the bedroll. He stripped out of his vest, jeans and socks and set them on the other side of the blanket. He set his rifle to his right, but on the blanket because he wanted it handy.

Michael was curious why George had not said hello when he snuck over to his campfire. Odd, because they were both *Dine'* just as Rebecca was. Michael considered that George must have had his reasons.

CHAPTER THIRTY-THREE

A light Indian blanket with bright shades of red, blue, and black stripes covered their shins and feet. They wore only shorts because the evening was still warm. The stars bright like diamonds spilled out on a black velvet sky. The moon, bright amber like a single teardrop earing.

Brian was unusually quiet. Off and on, he had wrestled with a thought ever since the night in the woods during the snow storm. He had shot the psycho in the ass. Twice. Both shots were nonlethal and purposeful. Still. He had been bothered by the fact that he had shot someone. He felt the same when he shot the pistol out of the hand of the man at George's ranch.

But ever since the conversation that morning with Bobby, and after shooting the man at George's ranch, and shooting the serial killer that winter evening, it was what the serial killer had said to him that touched both his head and his heart.

He dared not look at Brett, but instead stared up at the dark starry night, when he said, "Brett, do you think when I moved into our family . . . do you think, you know, I ruined it? Our family, I mean?"

Brett scrunched his face up wondering where that had come from.

"What do you mean? How?"

Brian shrugged. He tried to keep his voice from breaking and covered it with a whisper. "Do you think I screwed up the family when I moved in?" He shrugged again and said, "I mean, I screwed things up with Bobby and now he's pissed or something. George is pissed. I think mom and dad are pissed that Bobby and I did stuff." He shrugged again and said, "Everyone might be better off if . . . I moved somewhere else."

Brett rolled to his side and propped him up on his elbow and stared at Brian, shaking his head. Brian dared not to look at him.

"Where did that come from, Bri?"

Brian didn't know how to put it in words. The best he could do was to repeat what the psycho had said.

"He said George and I ruined the family. That he and I didn't belong in it."

"Who said that?" Brett demanded.

"That guy, the psycho guy," Brian whispered. "That night after I shot him."

"Shit, Brian, that guy was nuts! Kelliher, O'Connor, Graff all said that. The guy was fucking nuts!"

Brian glanced at Brett and said, "But he was a shrink."

Brett placed a hand on Brian's cheek and turned Brian's face towards him. Keeping his hand on Brian's cheek, he bent down and kissed Brian's forehead and then rubbed his nose with Brian's.

In a whisper, Brett said, "Bri, he is nuts. He's seriously fucked up. You can't let him get inside your head." Brett kissed his forehead again.

"But . . ."

Brett placed a thumb on Brian's lips and said, "Shhh. Stop. Bri, the guy is a psycho asshole. He's fucked up. Besides, you belong in our family, so you aren't going anywhere."

Tears streamed down Brian's cheeks and he struggled with what he wanted to say. All he managed was, "But George . . . Bobby."

Brett reached over and hugged his brother and held him while Brian cried into his neck. Now and then, he'd run his lips in Brian's hair or he'd kiss the side of his head.

It took a little time, Brian quieted down. He wiped the tears off his face, and the emotional storm ended with a sigh.

"You're not going anywhere. Dad adopted you. You live with us because you belong with us."

Brian didn't fight him. He still wondered. He still doubted. He decided that a part of him always would.

"Hey," Brett said as he smiled at him.

Brian didn't answer.

"We're a family. There will always be fights. Well, not actually fights, but you know what I mean. We're family. Bri, I love you. Seriously. I love you. Our family wouldn't be the same without you. *I* wouldn't be the same without you. None of us would."

"But . . ."

"Haven't you been listening?" Brett hugged him fiercely and held him. "I love you."

At last the two boys broke about apart, but Brett placed his arm across Brian's chest. Brian looked over at Brett and saw him struggling.

"What?"

"When I saw you and Bobby this morning, I got jealous."

"Why?" Brian asked.

Brett glanced up at Brian and then rested his head back on Brian's shoulder.

"Because no one loves me like you love Bobby." He paused, and then said, "Sometimes, I don't think anyone ever will."

"Of course, someone will. I do," Brian protested. "I love you."

Brett said nothing, so Brian tried again.

"You have lots of friends, and I can think of three or four girls who would go out with you."

"Having friends and going out with someone doesn't mean they love you," Brett countered.

Brian said as he took hold of Brett's hand, "I love you."

"But not like you love Bobby."

Brian did not know how to respond. In some respects, Brian loved Brett as much or more than Bobby. He and Brett had more in common than he and Bobby did. However, Bobby was special.

"Something happened between you and Bobby," Brett whispered. "What was it?"

Brian sighed and said, "I don't want to talk about it."

"Tell me." Then he added, "Please."

Brian didn't know if he was more embarrassed or ashamed. Maybe both.

"He said that he didn't want to do . . . stuff with me anymore."

"Did he say why?"

Brian glanced at Brett, but couldn't make full eye contact with him. "He said he didn't think it was right."

Brett shrugged, and ran his hand over Brian's chest and stomach, using his fingertips. Goosebumps popped up on Brian's skin.

"Bobby and I hardly do anything anymore. Now, we probably won't."

After a bit of silence, Brian said, "You did stuff with guys. I know you had to. But, did you ever think you might be gay?"

Brett paused. He kept his hand on Brian's lower belly and said, "Not really. I mean, I always liked girls. Sometimes, I miss . . . you know . . . stuff."

Brian shifted subjects. He asked, "When you were in Chicago, did you ever worry about dying?"

Brett resumed tickling Brian's chest and stomach.

"All the time. We never knew how long we'd live."

He rolled onto his back. "We pretty much figured that as soon as we had hair on our balls, our time was up. Tim, Johnny, Ian, and I lasted the longest, I think, because we brought in the most money."

He rolled back over onto his side and asked, "Are you worried about dying?"

Brian frowned, thought over the question, and answered, "Not really."

Brett smoothed the bangs off Brian's forehead and then rested his hand on Brian's chest.

Brian asked, "Besides what you did in Chicago, have you done anything with any other guy?"

Brett pursed his lips. He thought about lying, but didn't. "Yeah, a couple of times."

That did not surprise Brian. Brett had always been physical. He liked to wrestle around. He was never shy about hugging or touching a shoulder or an arm when he talked to someone.

Brian had noticed that other than hugs among the brothers, and except for him and Bobby, no one kissed anyone anymore. It was like they had outgrown it or something. This was the first time in a long time Brett had kissed him.

Brian turned his head, and said, "Bobby was the first guy who did anything to me. Besides Bobby, no guy ever touched me there."

Brett took a gentle hold of Brian's face, turned it to him so that they could look into each other's eyes, even though it was dark, even with the dying fire.

"I'm going to say something to you and I want you to listen, okay?"

Brian nodded.

"Dad and I talk . . . about me mostly, but about all of us. About you and Bobby, too. Dad said that if you love someone, really love someone, then having sex is okay. Dad said that sex is like expressing your love when there aren't words. He just wants us to wait until we're older."

Brian blinked. "They made us sleep in different bedrooms and told us they don't want us to do stuff."

"They think you're too young. And, you guys are brothers, adopted or not."

That answer didn't satisfy Brian. While he understood that they shouldn't because they were brothers, age shouldn't matter.

"Just because you and Bobby do stuff doesn't mean you're gay. It means that you love each other so much, words can't express it."

He paused, rubbed his nose with Brian's. "That's what I said, not dad. All of us know you and Bobby love each other. What I'm saying is that when you have sex with Bobby or some guy, it doesn't mean you're gay. It just means you love each other more than words can express."

Then he added with a chuckle, "Or you feel horny."

Brian flashed back to a conversation he had had with Sean about guys doing stuff with each other.

"Well, tell that to Bobby."

Brett smiled and said, "Maybe I will." He poked Brian's belly. "Maybe I won't."

Brett had never done anything to him. He had never suggested or hinted that he had wanted to do anything with him, at least that he could recall. He didn't know what, if any, signal Brett might be sending. It both excited him and terrified him.

Brett was silent a long time, but he finally whispered, "How come you and I never did anything?"

Brian glanced over at him but didn't answer.

"I mean, we had plenty of opportunities. We even slept naked but we never even touched each other."

"Why didn't you ever do anything to me?" Brian asked.

Brett was quiet for a bit and then said, "I'm not gay, Bri. And I don't think you or Bobby are either. Sometimes, I just want someone to hold me. Sometimes, I want to do stuff." He shrugged and added, "You know."

Brian said, "The thing is, I never did anything with any guy. *Ever*. Bobby was the only guy I ever did anything with. It's not like I see some guy and think, 'Hmmm, I want him' or anything." He stared at Brett, who didn't even blink. "But Brett, I . . ." He didn't finish because he didn't know what to say.

"So, if I would have started things," Brett whispered, "you wouldn't have minded?"

"I . . . I . . . I mean, no, I don't think so. I mean . . . you know what I mean."

Again, there was a long stretch of silence. An owl screeched off in the distance. The fire low, but persistent, snapped and popped.

"I'm jealous of Bobby."

Brian blinked. He had a quick-wit but not like Billy or Randy. He had to think things through, and it infuriated him that he would come up with a good response after the fact. It was no different this time, and this was not the time for that to happen.

Brett flipped over onto his back.

Brian rolled to his side, placed a hand on Brett's stomach. He said, "Brett, you know I love you, right? You're my best friend. Honest."

Brett smiled, but it was a sad smile. He brushed away tears, and said, "Yeah, but not like Bobby."

He rolled over and turned his back to Brian, though he remained up against him, his feet and legs still tangled with Brian's.

Brian rolled over onto his side in a spoon position with Brett, put his arms around Brett, and held him, his cheek against Brett's neck.

"Brett . . ." Brian said as he gently shook him.

Brett didn't answer, and Brian heard him weeping quietly.

"Brett," Brian said again.

"Stop, Bri. Please," Brett whispered.

"Brett, I do love you. You're my best friend."

Brett shrugged, and whispered, "I know, Bri. I'm just not Bobby."

Brian wept. He kissed Brett's neck, and finally said, "I'm sorry, Brett. I'm really sorry," though he wasn't sure what he was sorry for.

CHAPTER THIRTY-FOUR

O'Connor kept his head facing forward, but his eyes searched everywhere. Using his mirrors, he looked for any movement in any direction, for something that seemed cautious or slow like someone working hard to not be seen. He tried to ferret out any out-of-the-ordinary sound that did not fit with the quiet evening. The trouble was that this part of the country was foreign to him, so he had to rely on his instincts, his gut. And, his gut never failed him. Yet.

Casually, he reached over, popped the glove box, and withdrew his 9mm Beretta. He did not hold it, but set in on his thigh where his right hand could grab it quickly. He placed his left elbow on the window frame, his hand casual as he scratched his chin.

He had been sitting in the copse of trees for over an hour. Normally, O'Connor was as patient as he needed to be. He had learned that impatience killed the lives of undercover cops faster than any bullet.

He was spooked. He wasn't sure why or from whom, but he was spooked. O'Connor never spooked easily.

He noticed a coin on the floorboard on the passenger side of the truck. A quarter. O'Connor wasn't sure why he did it, but he leaned over and bent down to pick it up. As he did, he heard the *spit* of a silenced weapon.

It slammed into the dashboard and a second poked a hole in the windshield.

O'Connor scrambled over the seat and out the passenger door as fast as his lanky body could move.

He crouched low and listened, but heard nothing. The two shots had come from the driver's side of the truck. He also had a thought that whoever shot at him had not meant to kill him, but warn him.

O'Connor heard a vehicle's engine start up and the telltale crunch of dirt under tires told him that whomever shot at him was done for the night. To be certain, he crept around the back of the pickup, gun pointing out with his finger covering the trigger. He was not about to take any unnecessary chances so he stayed low and focused.

He saw taillights disappearing over the little rise in the road, so he relaxed a little. He thought about chasing them down, but he did not know how many there were or what their firepower might be.

O'Connor walked back to the driver's side. As he pulled open the door, he noticed old man Yazzie standing in the doorway of the ranch home. *Hogan*, as George would call it.

The two men stared at each other briefly, but long enough.

As O'Connor started up the engine, he flicked the safety on his Beretta, and placed it on the seat next to him. He took his cell out of his breast pocket, speed-dialed Graff and said, "Somebody shot at me. Twice."

CHAPTER THIRTY-FIVE

"Was it Yazzie?" Graff asked.

He had been in bed half-asleep. He sat up and swung both feet over the side of his bed ready to speed-dress if he needed to.

Reyna was in a room next door that adjoined his by an inner door. Graff walked into Reyna's room and shook the detective awake. Ron sat up with his .45 in his hand. It had been under the pillow on the other side of the bed.

Graff switched to the speaker so Reyna could listen in. He explained, "It's Pat. He was shot at."

"Is he okay?"

"I'm fine. Either he was a shitty shot, or he wasn't trying to hit me. Put one in the dashboard and one through the windshield."

"Sounds like you were made," Reyna said.

"And if Pat was, we might have been," Graff added.

"You might want to take a peek out the window and see who might be watching you. That is *if* someone is watching you. I'm guessing someone is," O'Connor suggested.

Graff moved to the side of the window and peered out. He was careful not to move the curtain too much. He had a fair view of the parking lot. It was full, and it was bound to be. Chinle was a tourist attraction with the Indian ruins nearby.

He didn't see anyone sitting in any cars or trucks but that didn't mean anything. If they were out there, and he was sure someone was, they would be good. Ex-military and all, if he was correct in his assumption.

Graff turned back to Reyna, shook his head and said, "I don't see anyone."

"Just keep your head on a swivel, guys," O'Connor said. "And a thought just occurred to me. Might want to sweep for bugs. There could be a tracking device on your truck. That's what I might do if I were them."

"Will do. Where are you headed now?" Reyna asked.

"Chinle. I'm beat. Say, anyone hear from the boys, how they're doing?"

Graff said, "I checked in with them earlier. Brett and Brian are camped out at a little pond. They're going hunting in the morning. George and Rebecca are up in the mountains. They plan to search for Charles at daybreak."

"I had Officer Mills check on Brett and Brian. He said they're good," O'Connor said. "He also saw two campfires. One was George and Rebecca. I think the other is the kid I told you about."

"With you getting shot at and with all that's going on, do you think the boys are safe?" Graff asked.

It was Reyna who answered. "Let's give them tomorrow. George might pick up the Morning Star boy's tail. Brett and Brian will get to do some hunting. We'll see what happens and bring them in tomorrow night. We'll need George and Rebecca to make a run at Yazzie, anyway."

Graff stared at the window and the night beyond. The cell's speaker picked up O'Connor's truck engine. Reyna gave them space and time to consider his suggestion.

"Okay, but we need to check in on them a little more frequently," Graff said.

"I'll check in with Michael and get his assessment." O'Connor chuckled and added, "I kinda like that kid. He's a combination of George and Brett with a touch of Brian. Hell, he's the spittin' image of George when he was twelve."

"Have you thought about what you might do with him at the end of the week?" Graff asked.

"Been thinking about it. Need to make a phone call or two."

"If you're thinking what I'm thinking, it might take more than one or two phone calls," Graff said.

"Who says you're thinking what I'm thinking?"

Graff laughed, and Reyna smiled and said, "Listen, it's late. We have a big day ahead of us. Pat, watch your six. If there's any sign of trouble, call. I hope to get some answers from Quantico in the morning."

"Will do."

Pat checked the review mirror, and all was dark behind him. Same as in front of him. Only he didn't know if that was good or bad. He liked to know what he was facing.

CHAPTER THIRTY-SIX

Brian woke up first and turned off the alarm on his phone before it buzzed. He had not been asleep for most of the night. It did not happen often but he couldn't turn off his head as he replayed the conversation with Brett, wondering if he should have or could have said or done anything differently. His back and legs were stiff from cradling Brett all night.

Brett had slept fitfully. He had wept long into the night, and no matter what Brian had tried to say to him, Brett ignored him. Brian had never seen Brett that hurt.

"Brett, we have to get up if we're going hunting," Brian whispered as he gave Brett's shoulder a gentle shake.

Brett rolled over onto his back, almost on top of Brian. He stretched, yawned, and wiped the gunk out of his eyes.

"Can we talk?" Brian asked.

"Gotta get going," Brett said as he tried to sit up. Brian held onto him.

"Brett, please?"

"Not much to say." He did, however, lay back down, although he didn't make eye contact.

"I just want to make sure you understand that I love you. You are my best friend. I mean that."

Brett glanced at him but quickly looked away. He stared up at the gray sky with his left hand under his head. His right rested on his stomach.

"I felt that way the first time I met you. The morning in the hotel after Brad was killed. We talked, and you listened, and ever since, we just seemed to . . . be friends. At least I thought we were. I want us to be."

A tear ran down the side of Brett's face just as tears ran down Brian's. While Brett did nothing with his, Brian wiped his off, and then placed his hand on Brett's, and laced his fingers with his.

"I'm sorry, Brett. I love you. I mean that."

Brett finally wiped his own tears away and nodded slightly.

Brian wondered if Brett believed him. He felt hurt and lost. Like swimming in an ocean without a lifejacket.

Brett shook his head again but just slightly as if he was considering something.

"I love you. Honest."

He gave up. It was not going the way he had hoped, although he had no idea what might happen or what he had wanted. Brian lay back down. He was not sure if he was afraid of losing Brett's friendship or if he had already lost it. He had already lost Bobby, and now George. He couldn't afford to lose Brett.

The problem was that he did not know what he felt- about Brett, Bobby, or even himself. Mostly, he was scared, and he did not like being afraid, especially if he didn't know what he was afraid of.

Finally, Brett rolled over, kissed Brian's forehead, and brushed his lips in Brian's hair. He held him and the two boys clung to each other.

"I'm sorry, Brett. I'm sorry."

Brett's response was to kiss his forehead and then his nose, and say, "I know. Me too."

CHAPTER THIRTY-SEVEN

Michael took the time to bathe in the waterfall, even though it was ice cold. He had to get moving in order to get to the valley at least at the same time as the two boys. He wanted to help them spot the herd.

Goosebumps broke out all over his body and he shivered. He had done this any number of times when he camped and hunted, so he did not let the cold bother him.

He stood nearly under the waterfall and washed himself quickly but thoroughly. When that task was finished, he filled his battered canteen and took several swallows before he refilled it again. He set it on the dry ground near his rifle.

Knee deep in the small pool created by the force of the waterfall, he stepped away to avoid the splashing water so he could use his hands to squeegee his long hair. That done, he picked up the rifle and canteen, and walked out of the pool at the base of the fall. It was then he had noticed George and Rebecca on their horses watching him. The noise of the waterfall had covered their approach.

Michael stood facing them, his rifle in one hand and his canteen in the other. He was as naked as he could be but he didn't flinch. He didn't turn away, and he didn't attempt to cover himself.

George spoke. *"Yá'át'ééh."*

Michael nodded, and said, *"Yá'át'ééh."*

"I am George Tokay. My clan is the *'Azee'tsoh dine'é*. This is Rebecca Morning Star of the *To'ahani."*

Michael should have properly introduced himself but he couldn't. He did not know his clan information. He turned red.

The pause was awkward and when Michael said nothing further, George said, "We were wondering if you saw a boy near here. He would be a little older than us."

Michael regarded them. Rebecca had made no pretext of looking away but stared at him. Michael had the impression that she was hopeful for any word on her brother and not checking him out.

"I have not seen Charles Morning Star, and I have not seen any sign of him," Michael said calmly.

Surprised, George tilted his head, and said, "How did you know we were looking for Charles?"

"Pat O'Connor told me. I met him on the other side of the mountain. He told me the story."

George nodded, and said, "Where did you come from?"

Michael explained, "I come from Red Rock, east of the Chuskas. O'Connor stopped there on his way to Chinle, told me about Charles, and asked if I had seen him. I have not."

Both George and Rebecca seemed disappointed.

"He gave me a cell phone. I told him I would call if I saw him."

"Oh."

Michael added, "He gave me your number." To Rebecca he said, "Yours as well."

"Good," George said. "My two brothers are down below at the pond."

"Yes, Brett and Brian. I have their numbers."

"Oh. Good. Thank you."

Michael nodded.

"Yá'át'ééh."

"Yá'át'ééh."

They turned their horses around and rode off to the north and a little higher in the mountains. He watched both of them looking more at the ground than off in the distance, and he knew they were searching for sign. When they turned and headed up a trail, he walked back to his bedroll, set his canteen and rifle down, and got himself dressed.

He stuffed the previous day's dirty clothes into a plastic grocery sack and then stuffed the sack into one of his duffle bags. It was hot, so like the day before, he dressed in his jeans, boots, and his leather vest with no shirt.

After, he pulled out his binoculars and stared down at Brett and Brian, who were packing up, and getting ready for their hunt. It was time he did the same.

He noticed that much of their gear was stowed snugly and securely at the pond, so the boys were planning to return.

Michael waited until they were a distance off in the horizon before he descended the mountain. He stashed some extra gear near the pond but away from Brett's and Brian's. He took with him his rifle, extra ammunition, water, and his other horse.

He skirted the pond in order to come up on the other side of the valley across from where Brett and Brian would end up. He figured they would take the nearside of the valley rim, since they were not familiar with the area. It had a good vantage point and one he had favored.

Michael glanced up at the sun winking at him over the crust of mesa and butte. The black of night dimming to the gray of morning. He reset his hat and smiled. It was a good morning for a hunt.

CHAPTER THIRTY-EIGHT

The silence was awkward, so different from any experience the two boys normally had with each other. They had not spoken other than to decide what they would leave at the campsite and what they would take with them. For Brian, it was a moldy cherry on top of the shit sundae the trip had become.

They took plenty of water along with extra ammunition, the tarp, Bungie cords, and some rope. They had their rifles equipped with scopes, and they took their knives. Brett holstered one of the Glocks on his hip. What they left at the campsite, they bundled up tightly to discourage any critters from raiding it.

Neither had eaten breakfast other than a few pieces of jerky washed down by lukewarm water. They had not bathed or swam because they didn't have time. Brett thought that after they hunted and took the carcasses to Laidley's Trading Post, they could spend time at the pond, and then visit some of the ancient sites. Neither had used deodorant because they did not want to take the chance that elk or deer might pick up their scent. Besides, it was an unspoken ritual of hunting in the Northwoods of Wisconsin they had merely transferred to their hunt for elk and deer in Arizona. At last, they took one last look around and mounted up.

Brian did not want to look at Brett, afraid that if he did, it might give the appearance of an invitation for conversation. However, like a passenger in a car passing an accident, he could not take his eyes from him, though he kept it to intermittent glances.

In truth, if Brian could have ridden off in the other direction, he would have. He felt as alone as he ever felt in his life, as lost and alone as he felt when his twin had died. When Brad had died, he did not have anyone to turn to, just like he didn't have anyone to turn to now.

Brian owed his dad a phone call and an explanation. The problem was that he did not know what to say.

Brian could not talk to him about Brett or any feelings they might have. If they even *had* feelings for each other. He never thought of Brett in the same way as he thought of Bobby. Worst of all, he did not know how any of this would affect his relationship with Bobby, if he still had a relationship with him.

Though they rode side by side, they may as well have been on opposite sides of the valley.

Following the directions Mills had given them the night before, they came to a gentle rise that looked out over the valley below. It wasn't that steep but Brian knew they would have to adjust their targets to account for the distance and the downward slope.

They pinned their horses, a pinto, a buckskin, and a bay behind them a distance away so the shots wouldn't startle them. They grabbed their rifles and extra ammunition. They would have one shot, perhaps two to harvest an elk or a deer.

They crept forward and lay side by side on their bellies looking out at the valley below. It was bathed in darkness. The little rise was hard-packed sand, baked by the brutal unrelenting sun. The mixed herd of twenty or thirty elk, and a smaller number of deer grazed down the hill in the valley amongst the sparse grass and scrub.

Normally, Brian would be in his element, but the hunting excursion did not evoke anything other than function and formality. There was no excitement or joy. Only an emptiness like the surrounding desert. An emptiness that consumed him from the inside. An emptiness that threatened to suffocate him.

He whispered, "On the edge near us, there are two elk. Female, I think."

"I see 'em," Brett whispered back.

Brian judged the distance to be a hundred and fifty yards, give or take. Their bullets were chambered in their spring-loaded semi-automatic 30-06s. Even though the two rifles were equipped with scopes, the dim light on the floor of the Arizona desert, and the way the valley waved and shimmered made sighting on the targets difficult.

Brian explained that when Brett pulled the trigger, the bullet would rise, but then gravity and the earth's rotation would pull the bullet downward.

"Make sure you hold the cross-hairs right behind the front shoulder, centered from the top of the back to the belly to get a double lung pass through shot," Brian whispered. "If she quarters away, you might get a lung and the heart. Either way, it's a kill shot."

Brett licked his lips and sighted. Brian was better with rifles than he was. Even better than George.

"I don't know."

"You've got this," Brian said. "Don't hold your breath. Exhale and pull the trigger. I'll shoot if it doesn't fall, but mostly I'll aim at the one behind."

If pressed, Brett might not be able to explain his mixed emotions nor would he want to. The elk grazed peacefully in the valley below. It didn't seem like a fair shot. It wasn't moving. It was stationary and eating what little grass that grew here and there like hair on a chemo patient. It sensed nothing of the two hunters on the rim above.

Then there was the ugly two-year-old memory of him shooting two of the pervert guards in Chicago. He still sported the scar as a token '*thank you*' from the shot in the shoulder that traveled into his armpit and lodged in his bicep. The shot that had nearly killed him.

Then there was the ever so unpleasant memory of him shooting his pervert uncle that same summer. Brett had never intended to kill him, but his uncle ended up confined to a wheelchair during rehab. Eventually, he was able to walk with haltered steps with the use of a walker because of the bullets Brett placed in both knees. The pervert had to pee through a catheter into a bag because Brett had shot off most of his dick and one of his balls.

Even though his uncle, Tony Dominico, had molested him and had been responsible for his captivity and the two years of forced prostitution, Brett was always remorseful for that shooting. In his mind, one or two shots would have been enough.

"You take it, Bri," Brett said in a voice just above a whisper.

Brian took his eye away from the scope, stared at his brother for a beat and said, "You sure? It's easy."

"You take it," Brett repeated.

Brian stared at Brett, sighed and then set his site on the front elk, counted down silently, *3 . . . 2 . . . 1*, exhaled and pulled the trigger. The elk dropped right where she stood. He sighted again and dropped the trailing elk as it began to sprint away. The rest of the herd took off down the canyon.

The two boys slung their rifles across their backs and dusted off their shirts and jeans and got their horses.

They were half-way down to the dead elk when Brett said, "Nice shots."

Still puzzled as to why Brett hadn't taken the shot, Brian only said, "Thanks."

"We're being watched," Brett said as he rode up next to Brian.

Brian rode the big bay with just a blanket under him and led the buckskin as the pack horse behind him. "I noticed."

"Who do you think he is?"

Brian had wondered that himself. "Another hunter."

Brett stretched his back first one way and then the other and whispered, "I think he's our age. Maybe a little younger."

"I think so too." Brian touching the barrel of his rifle slung on his back. "We have another set of eyes. On our right half-way up the hill."

Brett glanced and then stared. "Is that a coyote, dog, or wolf?"

"Legs aren't long enough for coyote. More wolf or dog, I think. Sorta looks like Momma, but bigger."

"Do we need to worry?" Brett asked.

Brian stared at the big animal. It had a mix of colors- brown, white and black. Beautiful. A lot like Jasper, his and Bobby's dog, only bigger.

"I don't think so. Just hungry."

They reached the two elk where flies had hovered. Brian shooed them away with his white Stetson, Brett with his red Wisconsin Badgers snapback. Bri took out his Buck 192 Vanguard knife and field-dressed the first cow and then the other. He couldn't remember when he had gotten over the smell, the blood, and the guts. It was to the point where he didn't think about it other than to get it right.

The worst was the slime that caked on his hands and under his nails. Brian had a thing about his fingers and hands being clean. He was known to go through a dozen napkins eating a hamburger or a slice of pizza, and his brothers had teased him about his obsession with clean fingers and hands during every meal.

Brian had hunted with his father and twin brother, Brad, ever since he was ten. He bagged a deer that first hunt and he had field dressed it with the help of his father. Each time, he had gotten better.

"Where did the Indian kid go?" Brett said quietly as he squatted down next to Brian.

"Not sure. He disappeared before we got down here."

"Did you notice how much he looked like George?" Brett asked.

"Yeah, I thought so too."

Brett stood and did a slow three-sixty as he stretched, stood with his hands on his hips and whispered, "George or Rebecca might know him."

Brian stood up, wiped his knife on a rag and placed the rag into the tarp with the elk carcass. "The wolf is closer."

He cut off a fair-sized chunk of meat, held it out in front of him as he walked slowly towards the large wolf. The wolf lowered its head but didn't move. Brian took that as a sign that it wasn't interested in harming him or Brett. It was only hungry.

He continued his slow walk holding the meat out in front of him like a priest holding a chalice of consecrated hosts. He stopped about thirty yards from the wolf, squatted down without taking his eyes off the animal, and set the meat down on the ground. Then he backed away six or seven steps, squatted down and waited.

"Bri?" Brett called softly.

Brian ignored him and stared at the wolf. The wolf stared at Brian, but then stood up, head low, tail hanging down. It crept forward towards the chunk of elk. It never took its eyes off Brian, but picked up the meat in its big muzzle, turned, and ran off about twenty yards. Then it stopped, turned around and stared at Brian, and took off over the rim and disappeared.

Brian smiled. He turned around at Brett and grinned.

"The dog whisperer," Brett laughed.

Brian smiled wider, cleaned his hands off with sand, cleaned off his knife again, and then together with Brett, wrapped up the two elk carcasses in the tarp and secured it with Bungie cords. The two boys laughed as they struggled to mount the bundle on the packhorse. It was the friendliest they had been since the night before.

"Are we riding all the way to Round Rock?" Brett asked.

Brian shook his head and said, "I thought we'd go to Rebecca's ranch, let her mother pick out how much she wants, and then drive the rest to the trading post. Faster that way."

"Then we can get something to eat and go back to the pond and get cleaned up."

"Sounds like a plan."

Brett smiled and said, "I'd like to see some ruins."

Brian smiled at him and said, "Yeah, lets."

CHAPTER THIRTY-NINE

Graff and Reyna ate the complimentary breakfast buffet in the dining area of the Holiday Inn. Graff had finished and sipped his second cup of coffee just like he did at home. The only thing missing was the *Milwaukee Journal Sentinel* he usually read.

A youngish man and woman wearing the same smile and green blazer manned the check in-check, check-out desk. Families or couples left for day excursions or to get breakfast somewhere else. One or two couples checked out. Jamie saw these scenes in most any city in any hotel.

Sitting in the back and facing the door, he and Reyna had a clear view of everyone who entered, ate, and left. There didn't seem to be anyone out of the ordinary or any likely suspects who didn't fit in, but if O'Connor was correct, a GPS locator attached to Reyna's truck would be all that was needed to keep track of them.

"Have you heard anything from Quantico?"

Reyna worked on the results of his second trip through the food line and had his mouth full of eggs and sausage, so he put up his hand, finished chewing and swallowing, and said, "A little, but not much. Two possibilities. One, there is a mining interest on the reservation. For uranium. Coal, possibly. That would fit with Desert Security being in the area given the history they have in West Virginia." He stopped and shrugged.

"That's something. What's the other possibility?" Graff asked.

Reyna frowned. The trouble with his frown was that his dimple showed, and he looked like a kid playing a practical joke.

He twirled his fork loaded with what was left of his seventh or eighth sausage and said, "There is a construction company owned by a Navajo. He wants to build a resort."

Graff had not seen anything that would be a draw to the reservation. "Seriously? Here?"

Reyna laughed and said, "Apparently, this guy, Archer Goodnight, has been lobbying the tribal elders to allow him to build a resort with individual cottages and a swimming pool out in the valley for people to hunt, ride horses, hike, and explore."

"This is the same valley where the four or five ranchers live and had their sheep slaughtered?"

"The same," Reyna answered. He picked up his cup of coffee and sipped it, grimacing at the taste.

"Motive?"

"Possibly."

Puzzled, Graff said, "Only possibly?"

"The tribal elders haven't agreed. One in particular, Daniel Ngo, is not in favor of it."

"If the others agree, wouldn't the majority rule?"

Reyna shook his head, "It doesn't work that way. For something this big, all of them have to agree."

Graff shrugged. He didn't pretend to understand tribal politics. George tried to explain it, but Jamie failed to grasp it.

"That's what Quantico came up with," Reyna said shoveling food into his mouth.

"Doesn't leave us with much."

Reyna said, "Maybe, maybe not. Mining could take place in the valley or in the mountains. So, there is a possibility of mining being the motive."

"Two possible motives."

Reyna shrugged and said, "Maybe three."

"Three?"

"This one is simple." He flashed those white teeth and dimple and said, "Somebody wants all the sheep and the land on which they graze."

Graff frowned. "Can't be that simple, can it?"

"Sheep is the number one industry on the reservation."

Frustrated, Graff said, "Okay. All possible I guess, but how does mining, a resort, or sheep have anything to do with a missing sixteen-year-old kid?"

Reyna pushed his plate away, wiped his mouth off with a paper napkin, and said, "The kid could be the result of the three, but a ranch takeover might be the most logical." He paused, shrugged, and said, "We don't know yet, and neither does Quantico."

"Whoever shot at O'Connor last night is a part of it." Graff waggled his head from side to side and amended, "Possibly."

"That's what I'm thinking," Reyna said as he sipped some more coffee. "Damn, this tastes like horse piss."

"Didn't know you drank horse piss."

"Never did, but if I did, it would taste like this."

Graff laughed. He liked Reyna. He was all personality. Friendly, smart. Kind of a big kid in an adult body.

"So, what are we doing today?"

"Been thinking about that."

Graff laughed and said, "And? I mean, besides the sixteen trips you made through the buffet line."

Reyna laughed, and said, "I think we go talk to the tribal elder, Ngo. Then, we should check out the construction guy. But first, we need to check the truck for a GPS tracker."

"I don't know much about the technology, but is there a way to backtrack the GPS to see where it came from or who is behind it?"

Reyna thought for a moment and said, "I can check with Quantico. We'll get the serial number or whatever before I stick it on a jackrabbit to screw with whoever stuck it on the truck."

Graff belly-laughed and said, "I like the way you think." He pulled out his phone and said, "I almost forgot. Brett sent this to me."

He held out his cell and showed Reyna the selfie Brett took of him and Brian kneeling over two dead elk. While Brett sported a grin, Brian looked tired.

"Cool, huh?"

Reyna smiled and said, "I can see why you like those kids. Brett is quite the character."

"He is. Smart as hell, and one of the best athletes anyone has come across."

Graff looked at the picture for the sixth or seventh time, wishing he was out there hunting with them.

"Looks like they're having fun," Reyna added. "Brian looks a little tired."

Graff nodded and bit the inside of his cheek. He wondered about Brian. A lot going on inside of his head.

He said, "Looks like it. I haven't heard anything from George."

Reyna frowned and said, "Depending upon where they are, he might not have a signal."

Given the remoteness of the reservation, and if George and Rebecca were up in the Chuska Mountains like they said they would be, Graff figured that might be the case. Still, Graff had hoped to hear from him. It was one of the stipulations he had placed on the three boys. They were to check in three times a day. More, if there was any hint of trouble.

Yes, it could be something as simple as reception. He hoped that was all it was.

"What?" Reyna asked as he watched Graff puzzle it out.

"Not sure."

CHAPTER FORTY

O'Connor laid around in bed. He did not sleep but an hour or two. However, that was common when he was on the job.

Once in Chinle, he did not drive right to the hotel. Instead, he made several stops. A diner for coffee and a piece of cherry pie, though he left it except for one or two bites. A 7-Eleven for some bottled water, two apples, two bananas, and a protein bar. After, he drove to a gas station to fill up his truck. It was there where he found a tracking device when he went to put air into tires that did not need any air.

Mounted up in the wheel well was a black box with a small antenna and a green light. He knew all about them as both someone who put them on vehicles for surveillance, and who, from time to time, found them on vehicles he had driven. For the time being, he decided to leave it alone, but it was important to warn Reyna and Graff.

He lay in bed trying to piece the puzzle together. A missing kid. Dead sheep. Ranchers who would not talk. Someone shoots at him, intending to miss. *Maybe* intending to miss. A para-military security outfit roaming the reservation. It was one hell of a puzzle.

It wouldn't necessarily have to be Desert Security who placed the tracker on his truck. This particular device could be found at Walmart for $130. That was where he had purchased them when he needed one. As an undercover cop, there was always a need. Anyone could have placed it on his truck at any number of stops he had made throughout the day.

Perhaps the shots into his truck were a distraction. Perhaps while the shooting was taking place, a partner planted the tracker.

He did not know who or why. If he discovered the answer to one of the other questions, he would solve the puzzle.

CHAPTER FORTY-ONE

George was in a hurry, but he made sure his horse moved slowly. He picked his way up and across the mountain trail made of scrabble and hard-packed dirt. At this altitude, the sun was up, but the valley had a dark veil over it. The air was still, dry, and hot. As the day drew on, it would get toasty. He and Rebecca had water and both of them knew where they could get more.

Rebecca was impatient and anxious. He and she both knew that the longer Charles went missing, the chances were that Charles was dead.

Charles had always been deliberate about everything he did, and that was the frustrating part of it. However, everything about this lacked any semblance of what Charles might have done. He would never leave their sheep untended. He would never ride off without asking permission to do so.

There had not been any trail and had not been any sign large or small that Charles had left intentionally or unintentionally. He and Rebecca had already searched two caves. There had been no hoof prints or footprints. Nothing.

George led them to one of Charles' favorite open-air campsites. At first, he searched from the saddle, but he had wanted to get a closer look. He swung down, handed the reins to Rebecca, and walked in a spiral inside to outside. There had not been any sign Charles had been there. No sign that anyone else had been there either. No footprints. No sign of a horse. No campfire remnants.

George picked up a pebble, threw it sideways, and sighed. He dipped his head, lifted up his hat, ran his fingers through his hair, and reset the hat back on his head. As he stood up, he saw a glint of light.

It was brief, only a moment. Just a flash, but he saw it nonetheless.

He knew better than to stare in the direction it had come from, so he smiled up at Rebecca.

"What?" she whispered.

"Let's eat something."

Rebecca tilted her head.

"It's... we haven't..."

"Let's eat something," George repeated.

Rebecca regained her composure and dismounted. George held her around the waist and she placed her arms around her neck, their faces inches apart.

"What is it?" Rebecca whispered.

George kissed her, and whispered through a false smile, "We're being watched."

CHAPTER FORTY-TWO

The stable was dark with sunlight peeking through rickety wooden slats, some of which were falling off. The rest of the light shown through the open door. The sun's rays caught dust floating like tiny astronauts in golden shafts highlighting Brian in a golden halo. He had his shirt off, his hat on, and sweat dripped off his arms, chest, and back.

As George had requested, the two boys had delivered half an elk to Rose Morning Star who thanked them with hugs and kisses, and with fresh, warm fry bread and honey. As they left the small room that served as a kitchen, she again thanked them with kisses and hugs. Brian wanted to take care of the horses and tidy up the stable before they left for Round Rock and the trading post.

"Do we have time? I mean, it's hot. Won't the meat spoil?" Brett asked.

"We need to make time. The meat will keep. With Rebecca and Charles gone, someone has to help clean up the stable," Brian answered as he took the bridle and saddle off Brett's horse, and the bridle off his horse.

Like George had taught him, he rinsed each horse off at a rickety wash rack using the halter and lead rope, putting each horse in crossties, one after the other until all three were clean. After each had been washed, he used a squeegee with a sweat scraper. Lastly, he worked on their hooves, picking rocks and debris with a hoof pick.

"Can you wipe down the saddle and bridles?" he said bending down to begin the process on the last horse.

Unsure of what to do, Brett said, "What do I do with them after I wipe them down?"

"Hang the saddle on the railing over in the corner, and hang the bridles on the peg by the door," Brian answered from somewhere under the horse.

Brett did as Brian asked him. He had never done this kind of work. It had always been George and Brian. George and Brian used the stable the most, even though it belonged to their friends and neighbors, Jeff Limbach and his son, Danny.

Brett sat down on the bales of hay and took four pictures of Brian. The first was of Brian leaning on the wooden stall whispering and cooing to the animal's delight. The second was a near silhouette of him leaning on the pitchfork, one foot firmly on the ground while the other rested on the toe of his boot. The third was of him readjusting his cowboy hat with his head tilted back. The fourth picture was of Brian scratching an itch on his side with a thumb while he held onto the pitchfork. In each picture, Brian looked faraway and more than a little sad.

The last task was feeding and watering each horse. Brian used the pitchfork to shovel hay into each stall. Then he gave each horse a bucket of water he drew from the pump in the yard.

The horses were taken care of and the rundown stable was as clean as Brian could make it, so he wandered over to the short stack of hay and lay down with his right hand under his head and his left flung back over his head. The heat, the lack of sleep, and even less food had caught up with him.

Brett slid over closer to Brian, bounced his finger on Brian's pec and said, "Put your arm out straight."

"I smell and I'm sweaty," Brian said.

"That makes two of us," Brett said with a laugh.

Brian did as he was asked. Just like the night before, Brett laid down using Brian's arm as a pillow. If he was bothered by Brian's sweat or odor, he didn't show it. Besides, as Brett said, he was just as sweaty and just as smelly.

"You know I'm taking Photo One this year, right?"

Brian mumbled, "Yeah."

"I have to have five pictures ready for the first class. I've chosen these so far. They're some of my best, I think."

He turned on his side and showed Brian the pictures he took of him. He watched Brian's expression closely. As he did, he placed his hand on Brian's chest.

Brian shook his head and said, "I didn't know I looked like that."

Brett laughed again and said, "Look like what?"

"I don't know," he answered shaking his head. "I didn't realize I was this big."

"Shit, Bri. You and Bobby do planks, pushups, and sit-ups every morning. You lift weights with us three times a week. You run for cardio, and you play soccer every minute of every day. What did you think would happen?" Brett laughed again.

"I just . . ." he said shaking his head again.

Brett took the phone away and flipped to the picture of Brian leaning on the pitchfork with a sad, faraway look on his face.

"I like this picture the most. What were you thinking?"

Without any hesitation Brian said, "That this trip sucks and that I wish I was home."

Brett lowered the phone, and said, "It's not that bad."

Brian didn't answer but stared at the ceiling.

"We need to talk."

Brian held his breath and waited. He shut his eyes wishing it had never happened and if it did happen, he wished it would remain at the side of the pond in the desert where the sun and wind would wipe it off the face of the earth.

"I'm sorry for everything I said last night. I should have kept things to myself. It put you in an awkward position, and I'm sorry."

Brian opened his eyes, glanced at Brett, and nodded.

Brett continued, "You love Bobby and I'm cool with that. I know you love me. I love you too. We *are* best friends. I talk to you about everything. You don't judge. You're pure, Bri, and there aren't many people I can say that about. The thing is, I put you in a shitty situation. You want to be in a relationship with Bobby. I respect that."

Looking straight up at the ceiling, Brian said, "Last night . . . did you mean what you said?"

Brett placed his hand on Brian's face and turned it towards him.

"Yes, Bri, I meant everything I said."

Brett took his phone, opened the Gallery app, and thumbed through the pictures until he found what he was searching for. He studied it, sighed, and turned the camera so Brian could see it.

"I've never showed this picture to anyone, because I wanted it to be mine. Alone. It's my favorite."

It was a picture of Brian and Bobby watching TV. Bobby sat between Brian's legs, his head against Brian's chest. Brian had his arms around Bobby, and Bobby had his fingers laced with Brian's. Brian had his cheek resting in

Bobby's brown hair. They watched a movie or something on TV, and the two of them looked natural and content. Happy and at ease.

Brian stared at the picture and then glanced at Brett. Both boys had tears in their eyes.

"I want what Bobby has . . . or what he had. Someday, with someone. I would kill for that. The thing is, I wanted that someone to be you. I can't think of anyone else I'd trust that much. I know it can't happen for a while. Possibly never. But I want that with you."

Brett shrugged and then wiped the tears out of his eyes.

Brian started to say something, shut his mouth, and tried again.

Brett watched him struggle, and he smiled.

"It's okay, Bri. I know we're best friends, and I know we love each other. Sometime . . . you know."

Brian's words left him. He searched and couldn't find anything to say. Nothing.

Brett stared at Brian and said, "I don't want charity, and I don't want sympathy." He showed Brian the picture again. "I want it to be like this. I want it to be like you and Bobby."

Brett smiled sadly as he studied the picture. He tucked his cell into his back pocket and said, "Someday, maybe."

CHAPTER FORTY-THREE

They sat in the dirt yard in front of a small hogan. The angry sun beat down on them and, like most of the reservation, there wasn't any shade. He was parched. It had crossed Graff's mind more than once that the reservation, if not all of Arizona, was the lobby of hell.

The small ranch house was built of wood and bricks fashioned out of the red dirt of the reservation. Corrugated steel served as the roof. A fire pit had been dug in the dirt in the front of the house that served as a kitchen hearth in good weather. Graff had learned that from George. A rusty metal pump stood close by. Not one animal was visible, not even a dog or cat, but that didn't mean there weren't any. There was a barn in the back, but there were no animal noises Graff could hear. An outhouse that tilted to the left stood between the barn and the hogan.

Reyna sat gingerly on a table chair that tottered and threatened to break. Graff sat on a boulder that might have been placed purposely in the yard by *Hosteen* Ngo for those who might visit him. Ngo sat on a tattered floral print chair one might have found in a fancy parlor a hundred years ago.

Reyna came at him from a different angle.

"We have a missing boy, ranchers with dead sheep, and a group called Desert Security on the reservation, but nothing seems to make sense. There's got to be a connection, but we can't find it."

Ngo had his arms folded on his chest and the only time they weren't was when one hand shifted his pipe from one side of his mouth to the other. Then the arms went right back to their original position. Other than that, he puffed on his pipe and didn't answer any question. Instead, he studied them, mostly Reyna, with hooded eyes like an annoyed professor studying one of his students.

Reyna shifted to the Navajo language to see if that might elicit a response.

"*Hosteen* Ngo, you are not in favor of the proposed resort that Archer Goodnight wants to build. Can you tell me why?"

Ngo's eyes widened, perhaps at Reyna's use of Navajo, perhaps at the question itself. Graff couldn't tell but he was sure Ron noticed the reaction too.

"Navajo land is sacred. Even young Tokay knows this. It is not for sale."

His answer didn't surprise either Graff and Reyna, except for his reference to George. Neither of them knew what it meant, though both believed there was meaning attached to his statement.

Reyna let it pass, but he would circle back to it. He frowned and asked, "Would you have any reason to believe that this man, Archer Goodnight, had something to do with Charles Morning Star's disappearance or the sheep that had been killed?"

Ngo's eyes narrowed as he said, "Greed is an infection that darkens a heart."

Still using Navajo even though Ngo had reverted to English, Reyna said, "Could it be that Goodnight is a businessman with a money-making idea?"

While his expression resembled the stone figures sitting on Mt. Rushmore, Ngo said, "Many times ideas rise from a dark heart."

Reyna nodded, shifted back to English, and said, "Would you know anything about Desert Security and what they might be doing on our land?"

Ngo cocked his head, removed his pipe, and said, "*Our* land?"

Reyna smiled broadly, bowed his head, and said, "Perhaps I should have properly introduced myself. Please forgive me, Father. I am *Dine'* from my mother. I belong to the *Shash dine'é*, the Bear Clan People. I was born on this land."

Ngo nodded. His eyes were hooded, and he took time with his answer.

"You moved away to live with the *Biligaana*. You no longer live among the *Dine'*."

Reyna's boyish smile glowed, his dimple as prominent as his white teeth. "We were poor. I went to West Point and served my country. I still serve my country in the FBI. The first opportunity I had, I moved home so I can serve my people, the *Dine'* as well as *Biligaana*."

Without warning or provocation, Ngo turned to Graff and said, "Why are you here in *Diné Bikéyah*?"

Up until then and just as he and Reyna had planned, Graff had remained silent, content to listen and watch.

"George Tokay and his brothers, Brett and Brian, are friends of mine. I care about them. They are the adopted sons of my friend, Jeremy Evans. I came to keep an eye on them, and to make sure they are safe."

"But you aren't with them. I saw the three of them at Teec Nos Pos, but I did not see you."

"No, I was not there. They know how to find me and we keep in contact."

"And this Jeremy Evans . . . he is not their father."

"Not by blood, but by love," Graff answered, a little annoyed at the old man. "Sometimes love is stronger than blood."

Ngo stared at Graff, but Graff did not flinch nor did he look away. It seemed to Graff that Ngo was sizing him up.

Reyna repeated a version of his previous question. "Father, do you know why Desert Security is in Navajoland?"

Ngo stood up signaling the end of the interview.

Reyna stood but held his hand up for Ngo to wait. "You mentioned George and that he knew that our land is sacred. Why?"

Ngo had the faintest of smiles that dissolved as quickly as he flashed it. Instead of answering, he tapped his pipe on the side of the house and emptied its contents. Then he stepped on the ash to make sure it was out.

Reyna fished a card out of his pocket and handed it to the tribal elder who took it, and shoved it into his front pocket without even looking at it. Graff suppressed a smile. Ngo did not want anyone to see Reyna pass him the card.

"I thank you for your time, *Hosteen* Ngo. I hope we didn't bother you with our questions. We want to find Charles Morning Star and uncover the reason for his disappearance. If you can think of anything further, we are staying in Chinle at the Holiday Inn."

Graff thought he saw Ngo nod, but he wasn't sure. It was so slight and nonchalant, he couldn't tell. However, Graff thought Ngo never did anything with nonchalance.

Graff said, "Thank you, Sir. I appreciate your time and patience."

Ngo regarded Graff silently for a beat and then turned and walked back into his hogan.

In the vehicle, Reyna kept his head and his eyes forward, and barely moved his lips as he said, "He knows more than he's saying."

"Why did he mention George? What did he mean about George knowing his land is sacred?"

"Not sure," Reyna said as he glanced out the side and rearview mirrors. "Knowing George's reputation, of course he knows the land is sacred."

"He's being watched," Graff said. "I think Ngo knows it, and I think he wanted us to know it."

"I think Ngo might be in danger, but I don't know from who."

CHAPTER FORTY-FOUR

Rebecca wanted to separate in order to split them up.

"Chances are no better than fifty-fifty that your plan will work," George argued. "They could stay together and go after either of us."

Rebecca could handle herself, unless she was taken by surprise. She could use a rifle, and could ride better than anyone he knew. Still, it was Rebecca, and Rebecca was special, even after all this time.

"Trust me," Rebecca said as she rode off, pretending to stare up at the mountain trails.

George frowned. Of course, he trusted her. With his life. With his heart. With his love.

Rebecca had been his best friend. Besides Billy, she still was. They had grown up together. Together they had tasted first love. While there had been no promises, there had been the hope of a promise. He had believed Rebecca held onto that same bit of hope.

He moved to Wisconsin but had to come back that same summer to tie up loose ends. Three corrupt, pervert cops high up on his mesa died by his hand.

While he was protecting his family, George had arranged for Billy to be protected by Rebecca at the pond. The two of them had a torrid two days, a declaration of love or what Billy thought was love, and then when absence made the heart grow less fond, they broke up. Mutually, if not satisfactorily. Now, George and Rebecca were back together, at least at the moment.

George hid his horse behind an outcropping of rock and shrubs. He exchanged his boots for his moccasins so he could move faster and with less noise. He took with him both his knife and his rifle. It was the first time he had wished he had one of the Glocks that Brett had favored.

George found a barely visible animal track to make his way to the backside of whom ever it was with the binoculars. His jeans and shirt snagged on brambles. Thorns ripped and stung the backs of his hands and on his arms. He bloodied the palm of his left hand when he stumbled and caught himself on the edge of a rock. He dodged a pissed off rattle snake and startled a jackrabbit. He came across wolf sign. Regardless, George was intent and focused on one thing: get to whoever had his eyes behind the binoculars.

George was patient when he needed to be, and this was a time he needed to be. It was slow going because he had to circle north along the mountain and then west to get behind the spot where the binoculars flashed. Yet, he had to hurry in case Rebecca's plan did work.

It took him twenty minutes to get to the area where he had seen the flash of light. He spied one horse, dark brown with a black mane, tied on a bush. As he neared it, the horse snorted and stamped a hoof.

George dropped to a knee on the lookout for who might be close by. Just yards east of the horse and in a scattering of scrub brush, a jackrabbit hopped out and sped away, flushed out by a middle-aged man, older than George's father, with the binoculars in his right hand. A Winchester, much like the one Rebecca carried, slung over his shoulder. George remained hidden, still as the cactus in front of him. He waited, hoping the man would turn back around and face the mountain.

The man, Mexican from the look of him, stared at the horse, and then his head darted to the left and right, but not in George's direction. The man's brow furrowed but the many lines and creases in the man's face made frown lines hard to distinguish from the others.

He had several day's growth of black-gray beard. His dark eyebrows were thick and bushy. He stood, five-seven or-eight, about the same height as George. Whoever it was had carried more weight and was not in as good of shape as George, judging by the paunch and double-chin. Finally, the man turned back around and stared up the mountain.

George shut his eyes and controlled his breathing. As anxious as he was, he needed to focus. He had only one opportunity.

George crept forward until he stood less than five yards away. The man stood hunched over and from his movements with his head and binoculars, it was clear that he was searching for George, not Rebecca.

George slung his rifle over his shoulder, shifted his knife to his left hand, and picked up a baseball-sized rock. He covered the last few steps quickly and swung the rock down on the man's head before the man knew anyone was behind him.

The man fell hard, face first, dazed, but conscious.

George moved quickly. He pulled the rifle away from the man and tossed it a short distance toward the horse. He aimed his own rifle at the man.

"Don't move. Keep your hands out in front of you. I have my 30-06 aimed at the back of your head."

The man shook his head to clear some cobwebs, but he involuntarily placed a hand on the spot where George clocked him with the rock.

"I said, keep your hands above your head and remain on your stomach."

Ignoring George, the man started to push himself up. George took a foot and shoved the man back onto his stomach. For good measure, George shoved the barrel of his rifle into the back of the man's head very near where it bled from the rock.

The man grunted, but gave up and moved no further, his arms out over his head imitating a swimmer diving into water.

"Who are you and why are you following us?"

"Fuck you! You don't know who you're dealing with."

"Tell me who I am dealing with," George said.

"Fuck you and your friend."

"I asked you a question. Why are you following us?"

"Fuck you!"

George aimed just to the left of the man's head and inches from his ear and sent a bullet into the dirt.

"*Jesus Christ! What the fuck?*" the man screamed as he grabbed his ear.

George had to act quickly now because the shot would alert the man's partner.

"Put your arms over your head and answer my question or the next shot will take off your ear."

"Okay, okay! *Jesus!*"

"Answer my question," George said quietly.

"We were told to follow the Morning Star girl. That's all."

"Why?"

"Because we knew she was looking for her brother."

"Why are you interested in finding Charles?"

"I don't know. We were just told to follow her because she would lead us to him. That's all. That's what we were told to do."

"By who? Who told you to follow Rebecca?"

The man glanced back but then stared straight ahead. He said nothing further.

George repeated the question. "Who told you to follow her?"

"I'm not sayin' nothing more. Fuck you!"

George considered his next course of action and came up empty. He was out of time and this man wasn't cooperating.

"I suggest you head back to wherever you came from. The next time we meet, you will get more than a bump on the head."

"Where's my rifle?" the man asked.

George backed up, picked up the man's rifle and emptied the chamber. Cartridges littered the ground. Then George swung it hard against a boulder. The stock broke off. For good measure, George swung the rifle as a club and bent the barrel.

"You can pick it up on your way to your horse."

"You bastard! Next time, we'll be ready."

"Next time, the bullet will not be in the dirt," George said as he backed away.

CHAPTER FORTY-FIVE

O'Connor sat down to breakfast at The Junction Restaurant in Chinle, choosing not to eat at the Thunderbird. He picked at his eggs, bacon, and lightly buttered wheat toast. Given the choice, he would have preferred one of the fruit smoothies he normally ate for breakfast back in Wisconsin. If there was one appliance O'Connor could not do without, it was his blender.

He flagged his waitress, asked for his check, and pulled fifteen dollars from his billfold. It was enough to cover his bill and leave her a nice tip. He shoved his chair back, reached for his hat at the back of the table and began to stand. A hand on his shoulder prevented him from doing so. Two men sat down, while a third stood behind and to O'Connor's right side. Smart, Pat thought. That was his dominant hand.

"You didn't eat very much."

O'Connor chose not to respond.

The speaker smiled, but it was cold. O'Connor judged him to be six-foot-one or two and about two hundred-thirty pounds. Every inch and every pound of him muscle. His black hair was cut short, but it receded at his temples. His dark eyes were small and narrow.

O'Connor figured his partner to be about the same height but looked bigger. A blockhead covered with short-cropped blond hair. Both men wore a black cotton sport coat with a telltale bulge indicating shoulder holsters. He did not get a good look at the third man standing behind him. Perhaps that was by design.

"What are you doing in Arizona, specifically on the reservation?" Again, he smiled, but it was cold as steel.

O'Connor said nothing.

"My friend asked a question and he would like an answer," his partner said.

"I didn't realize I needed to check in or out with anyone. Who are you and why should I answer?" O'Connor said. He kept his hands in plain sight so as not to provoke an unwanted response.

"Let's just say we're curious why you're traveling around the reservation by yourself. You have a Midwestern accent. Perhaps you want to cut your visit short and go back home."

O'Connor shook his head and said, "I have a couple more days left, and there are some sites I want to see. I think I'll stick around."

"That might not be the wisest choice. This is a big, wide-open country. Accidents happen. I would hate for anything to happen to you or anyone else you might be traveling with."

That got O'Connor's heart racing, though Pat was too experienced to show it.

He frowned, looked at dark-hair and then at blondie, and said, "Who says I'm traveling with anyone?"

Both men smiled.

"Let's just say it might be unwise for you or any of your friends, young or old, to be out here. There's so much that can happen. Hunting accidents. A nasty fall during a hike. A fall from a horse. An auto accident."

Blondie added, "Especially for kids camping on their own, don't you think?"

O'Connor gave them a *not sure what you mean* shrug.

Dark-hair stood first, blondie followed, but leaned over so his face was so close, O'Connor could smell stale cigarettes. He said, "You've been warned. Whatever happens is on your head." He sneered and said, "Maybe it will be your head."

The man standing behind O'Connor gave Pat's head a shove as he trailed the other two out the door. The third man was shorter, more slightly built, but O'Connor had the impression he was every bit as strong as the other two, and just as lethal.

Pat waited as long as he dared. Just long enough to make certain all three men were out the door with no chance of them coming back into the restaurant. He pulled out his cell and speed-dialed Graff.

Without waiting for a hello, O'Connor said, "I was visited by three goons, ex-military. I was told to leave, and they threatened me if I didn't. They all but mentioned the boys, warning that accidents happen out here all the time."

Stunned, Graff remained silent.

"Has anyone heard from George? From Brian or Brett?" O'Connor asked.

"Brett sent a picture. He and Brian went hunting and got two elk," Graff said. "Haven't heard from George."

"We need to bring them in, Jamie."

"Could it be a bluff?" Graff asked tentatively.

"You want to take that chance?"

O'Connor pictured Graff thinking, knowing that there was only one solution.

"I'll get in touch with them right away. George will be more problematic because he's in the mountains somewhere. Cell reception sucks up there."

"Is Reyna there?" O'Connor asked.

"Yeah, just a minute." Graff pushed the speaker function and overheard him bringing Reyna up to speed. "Okay, he's on."

"Ron, can you get FBI in Phoenix to check on Desert Security? You know, put some pressure on them? That way, they might lay off the boys. I don't give a shit what they do to me, but nothing can happen to those boys. And have them check the security cameras for The Junction Restaurant in Chinle. Those three assholes should be on it. Two big, one smaller. Dark short hair. One blond. The third wore a baseball cap."

"I'll make a call."

"Jamie, give Kelliher a call and let him know what's happening. Make sure he has my number, and if he needs to get a hold of me, tell him to do it. This is spinning out of control and we're nowhere near where we need to be to wrap this up."

CHAPTER FORTY-SIX

Before they had left the Morning Star ranch, they cleaned up at the pump in the yard. They took turns pumping water from the well as they washed their hair, faces, neck, and upper torso. As a result, they smelled like soap. No deodorant, but still much better on everyone's senses.

They drove to Round Rock in silence. The last words exchanged were before they had left the Morning Star ranch when Brett told Brian he could drive. Brian would have preferred sitting in the passenger seat so he could take a nap.

The sun sat low above the Chuskas and at their backs, and the boys chased diminishing shadows across the valley in a never-ending, never-winning battle. Fry bread was a start, but not an end, and their stomachs protested.

It was a relatively short drive, but Brian made it a little longer by driving past the Tokay ranch. He slowed down as he came to the driveway. He had wanted to see if the *No Trespassing* sign was back up, but it was not. Satisfied, Brian drove on.

As Brett fiddled with the stereo system, he said, "What would you have done if they were waiting for us?"

Brian had not thought of that. Brett carried the Glock on his hip, but the rifles were in the back and not accessible in a hurry with one and a half dead elk sitting on top of the hood wrapped in a tarp and strapped down with rope and Bungie cords.

"I guess I would have kept driving," he said.

Brett chuckled and said, "Great plan."

Brian glanced at him, frowned, and did what he himself suggested. He kept driving.

Round Rock appeared over the rise. Uncomfortable with the gulf of silence between them, Brett reached over and took hold of Brian's forearm.

"Are we good? You and me?"

As tired as he was, and still unsure of where he stood with Brett, Brian managed a nod and a smile, along with, "We're good."

It didn't sound like it was very sincere and it hurt. He let go of Brian's arm and looked out the side window at rundown houses, barebacked kids, and skinny dogs and cats.

He did not know why he had unloaded on Brian the way he did the night before. Brett did not mean to make it about sex, because sex was not all he had wanted or needed. What he wanted was the intimacy of the kind of relationship that Brian and Bobby had with each other. He wanted the same comfortableness. That was what he was trying to tell Brian, but it came out twisted. He wanted the relationship Bobby had with Brian. It was that simple, but it was also that complicated.

He had feelings for Brian, but had tamped them down because he was unwilling to admit it. Maybe afraid to admit it. In any case, he couldn't because of Brian's relationship with Bobby. Still, he thought that, perhaps, the friendship he and Brian had would be enough. Little by little, and as hard as he had fought against them, they bubbled to the surface as most feelings do.

Over the past year, Brett had sent vague signals to Brian testing the waters. Brian had never responded. The closest they came was the night at the pond. Worse, at least in Brett's mind, their friendship had suffered some damage. Just how much, he didn't know.

Brian said, "How come you don't want to drive?"

He shrugged, "I don't mind sitting and watching."

The boys got out of the car and Brian clicked the lock on the key fob.

"Before we take the elk off the back, we should go see where Mr. Laidley wants us to put them," Brett suggested.

The two boys walked in and spotted Laidley wearing an apron over a plaid shirt, jeans and work boots, and pushing a broom around the wooden floor. A country song played over the speaker. A Luke Bryan song, Brian thought, one that Bobby liked. The store smelled of freshly brewed coffee and . . . cinnamon, mixed in with the smell of leather. It was warm and friendly.

Laidley looked up and smiled.

"You two are here early. Did you guys get lucky?"

Brett said, "No luck needed. Brian shot twice and dropped two right where they stood." He nudged Brian, who shoved his fingertips into his front pockets. Brian blushed deep red and gave a sincere *aw-shucks* shrug.

Laidley stopped sweeping and said, "Two shots, two . . . what? Elk?"

Brett did all the talking, and that was okay with Brian.

"Yup, two cows. Where do you want them?"

"Are they out in front?"

"Yup. On the back of our truck."

Laidley set the broom against the counter and followed the boys out to the Avalanche. He checked the tarp, loosened the Bungie cords and rope, and peeked at the two harvested critters. He placed his hands on his hips and nodded.

"You guys know what you're doing, all right. Nicely done."

"Thanks," Brett said with a smile.

Brian's phone buzzed in his back pocket. He pulled it out and read the caller ID.

His shoulders sagged and his mouth went dry. He pushed his hat back on his head and then set it low over his eyes. He said, "It's Dad. I better take this."

He walked over to the edge of the porch and sat down on the stoop.

Brett watched him sit down and wanted to sit by his side. But Brian had to have this conversation with Dad by himself.

"Hi Dad. Did you get the picture Brett and I sent?"

"Yes, I did. I forwarded it to Mom and the boys." He paused and said, "Bri, you called yesterday and it sounded like you were crying. Is everything okay?"

Brian sighed and said, "I think it was a butt dial. It was breezy and that might be what you heard. I'm just tired, that's all."

"Bri, you and I have a better relationship than that. We trust one another, right?"

Brian nodded even though Jeremy couldn't see it. "Yes, I'm sorry."

"So, tell me. What's going on?"

"George told Rebecca that Bobby and I are in a relationship. I don't know why or what the context was, but he said something." He paused and said, "It's nobody's business about Bobby and me. Maybe your business and mom's business. Maybe the guys, but nobody else's business."

"Bri, all mom and I want, all we ever want for you and Bobby and for all the guys is for you to be happy and successful. That's all, Brian."

"Dad, I'm sorry for everything. I never meant for any of this to happen. I'm sorry."

"Brian Evans, there is nothing to be sorry for. Nothing. Now stop that." Jeremy softened and said, "Please."

Brian wept, nodded, and said, "I love you, Dad." He wanted to tell him how screwed up he was, but he didn't.

"Hell, Brian, I know that. I love you too." Then he added, "Where are you and George with this?"

Brian shrugged. A kid who looked like George rode into Round Rock leading a pack horse. He wore the same kind of clothes George had worn in a photograph from the summer of hell. A leather vest with no shirt, long black hair the way George wore his, jeans, boots and topped off with a dirty cowboy hat. Brian thought he might be the same kid who had watched them during the early morning hunt. The boy looked long at the Avalanche and at Brian and then nodded. Brian lifted a hand in hello.

"He and Rebecca went off to find Charles yesterday and we haven't seen or talked to him since. They're up in the mountains and cell service sucks."

Jeremy said, "Brian, you and George need to figure this out. We're family, and you two are not only brothers, you're friends."

Brian sighed. He didn't much want to talk to George. He couldn't tell anyone about Brett and him. Not even Bobby. But Dad was right. He and George would have to fix things.

"I'll fix it as soon as I can. Promise."

Jeremy said, "Good. Bobby had a conversation with his mother and me. He told us about the conversation the two of you had."

"I don't want to talk about it."

Jeremy let the silence drift, and then he said, "The two of you love each other. Only the two of you can figure things out."

"Dad, please, I don't want to talk about it," Brian said. Besides, he didn't think there was anything to figure out. Now on top of everything, there was Brett.

"Okay, that can wait. For now, at least, but I want you to promise me something."

"What?"

"You and Brett go have fun. Do some more hunting. Go sightseeing. Then come back and be yourself. That's what I want. Can you do that?"

Brian's cell flashed a low battery light indicating he had only five percent battery life.

"Yes, I can do that. Dad, my cell is dying so I have to cut this short."

"Okay, but Bobby and Randy have some exciting news to share. Hang on and I'll get them. And Bri? Just know I love you so damn much, I don't even know how to say it," Jeremy said.

Brian wiped away some tears.

"Just a minute." Then, Jeremy said, *'Bobby, Randy quickly. Brian doesn't have much battery left.'* "Okay, here's Bobby and Randy. You're on speaker."

"Hey, Bri," it was Bobby. "We have news!"

"I don't have much time," Brian said, not willing to speak to him yet.

Randy said, "Remember when Danny sent six songs to Tim McGraw? Well, he took three of them! He has an option on them and they might end up on his next album!"

"No way!"

"Yeah," Bobby said laughing. "Isn't that cool?"

"Seriously?"

"Yup," Randy said. "He has an option on *So Goes Love, Side By Side,* and *That Man.*"

"Wow! What happens next?"

"We wait and see if he records them. He faxed a contract to Danny's dad's literary agent. He's looking it over for us and then we sign it," Randy said.

"Isn't that cool?" Bobby asked.

"Wow!"

Brian's cell flashed another warning.

"My cell is dying. I have to go."

"Wait!" Bobby said. "You know our two songs *Empty Chair* and *That's Not Love*? He said they're too good for anyone to record but us. He said that."

"Isn't that cool?" Randy added.

"Seriously?"

Bobby laughed and said, "Yeah, seriously!"

"Listen, my phone is almost dead. I have to go."

"Okay, charge it and give us a call back," Randy said.

"Wait, can I talk to Brian, just me, really quickly? Before his battery dies?"

Brian didn't know if he was being asked or if Randy or Jeremy were being asked. There was some noise on the other end that Brian couldn't identify, and then Bobby said, "Okay, you're off speaker. It's just me."

He didn't want to talk to him. Without knowing it, he shook his head and said, "I have to go."

"But . . ."

"Bye," and Brian clicked off.

CHAPTER FORTY-SEVEN

O'Connor looked at the map and thought that if he took 64 East skirting around the north side of Canyon de Chelly to Tsaile and then head north on 12, it would be the fastest route to Round Rock. He wanted to get to Brett and Brian as quickly as he could. They had not answered any of his texts, and all of his calls went straight to voicemail. Remembering the visit from the three goons, he was doubly worried.

He pushed the old truck as fast as he dared. Intent on the road ahead, O'Connor did not notice the black truck behind him. At first.

O'Connor didn't know if it was following him as a tail or if by chance the two vehicles shared the same stretch of road. He kept his speed constant and checked the rearview and side mirrors as much as he stared at the road stretching out in front of him. As far as he could tell, he and the truck behind him were the only two vehicles traveling on the road in either direction.

The little hairs on the back of his head straightened up at attention as the truck drew closer. He reached for his cell and hit the speed-dial for Graff, who picked up on the first ring.

"What's up?"

"I'm being followed. Black truck. Newer model Dodge Ram. Arizona plates. Driver and a passenger. Maybe a third guy. Can't tell for sure."

"Where are you?"

"Traveling east on sixty-four, about two or three miles away from Tsaile."

"It will take us a half-hour to reach you, but that's a guess."

"I'm hanging up. The truck is closing the gap," and O'Connor punched off and gripped the wheel.

The black truck crept closer. Twenty yards, fifteen. O'Connor could hear the roar of the Dodge Hemi.

One car length.

O'Connor could clearly see the driver. It was the blond blockhead from the diner. The passenger was the black-haired dude who did most of the talking. Just like in the diner, O'Connor only caught a glimpse of the third man.

Five yards and closing.

O'Connor damn near pushed the pedal through the floorboard. The Dodge nudged his truck from behind, causing O'Connor's head to slam back into the headrest. Again, and then again.

O'Connor wrestled with the wheel as the truck slid first right and then left. He managed to steady his truck and fought for any last bit of speed he could muster. The old Ford shimmied left, then right, and skidded left.

The Dodge gave O'Connor's Ford a final nudge sending Pat off the road and into the ravine where the truck rolled once, twice, and a third time, finally ending upside-down in a cloud of red dirt and dust.

The men in the Dodge stopped to take a closer look.

The blond block head said, "The asshole said he wanted to see some ruins."

With a laugh, the black-haired dude said, "Now he's in one."

None of the three got out, but instead, sped off towards Round Rock leaving O'Connor strapped in his seatbelt. As far as they could tell, he was either unconscious or dead.

CHAPTER FORTY-EIGHT

"You don't know who they were? He didn't tell you? What about Charles? Did he say anything about him?" Rebecca, tired and frustrated with the lack of progress in their search for Charles, peppered questions at him as she leaned over the saddle and her horse's head.

"He did not say much, Becca. The only thing he said that made sense was that they were watching us, but he did not say who told them to."

George stood with his hands on his narrow hips and stared at the dust clouds caused by the two men as they rode down the mountain towards the valley below.

"I think we should do what Detective Jamie asked us to do. Go visit *Hosteen* Ngo and Delbert Yazzie. See if they will talk to us."

"What about Charles?"

"They might know something about Charles and what happened to him."

Rebecca turned her horse and with a "ha" and a jab at her horse's ribs with her boot heels, started back up the mountain.

"Where are you going?" George asked.

"There are places we haven't looked."

"Becca," George said as he shook his head. She didn't bother to look back or stop, and George didn't bother to stop her.

An hour later having checked the last of the caves Charles favored and not seeing any sign of him, Rebecca hopped down from her horse and yelled, "Charles! Charles! Where are you?" and broke down completely. Shoulders hunched, face buried in her hands, sobbing.

George tried to comfort her, but she shrugged him off and walked several steps away. He watched her not knowing what he could say or do, so he squatted down, picked up a pebble and tossed it. He would not push her.

At last, Becca dried her eyes and wiped the tears from her face with her sleeve. She took a deep breath and said, "What now?"

George hesitated, then stood and said, "We should go see Yazzie. After, we go see *Hosteen* Ngo. We talk to them. We see if they know anything about Charles. After that, we will decide what to do next."

"And if they don't want to talk to us? What if they don't know where Charles is?"

George took Rebecca into his arms and held her tightly. He whispered into her hair, "We will find him, Becca. We won't stop looking."

CHAPTER FORTY-NINE

Michael Two Feathers fed his horses two carrots and one apple each, along with a handful of oats. He and his horses were across and down the street from the trading post where Brett and Brian were.

He saw the truck as it rolled into Round Rock. It stopped across from the trading post and then pulled in next to the vehicle the two boys drove.

Three men, tall, and thick. Two wore sports coats, and all three carried handguns. Two of the men looked into the Avalanche. One of the men tried the door, and it was locked, as was the cover on the back.

A man on either side of the vehicle pressed their faces against the side windows using their hands to shield them from the sun in order to get a better look inside. Upon stepping back, they shook their heads at the other man.

A big man with a head of black hair led the way, followed by a blond-haired man and another who had a shaved head under an Arizona Sun Devil baseball cap. They took the steps leading up to the trading post and entered, shutting the door behind them. One of the men turned the sign from open to closed.

Michael side-stepped across the street, but not so quickly to cause any undue attention. As he did, he took his knife from the leather pouch on his hip and first hid behind the Avalanche, peering into the trading post window to see if any of the three were watching the street. They weren't, so hunched over, he duck-walked to the rear passenger tire of their truck and cut off the air nozzle. He could hear the air hiss as the tire flattened. Moving fast, he reached the driver's side rear tire and did the same thing, achieving the same result.

He straightened up and crossed the street to his horses where he retrieved his rifle. He made certain it was loaded, but pocketed extra shells.

With his knife securely back in its leather sheath on his hip, he crossed the street to the trading post looking for a back entrance. One had to have existed. Michael wasn't particularly nervous, certainly not scared, at least for himself.

He had made a promise to O'Connor to look out for the two boys and he wouldn't fail.

CHAPTER FIFTY

Once conscious, he had a hell of a time escaping from the seatbelt and shoulder harness. He was upside down and the pressure on the system worked against him. He couldn't prevent the awkward fall to the crumpled roof of the truck, and he cut his hand on glass. His shoulder stung.

O'Connor shut his eyes and laid amid broken glass and bent metal taking stock of himself. His head throbbed. The last thing he remembered was his truck being hit from behind and knocked from the road. Nothing after that.

While he was bruised and scraped up, he didn't think he had suffered any broken bones. He could breathe fairly easily and though sore, he didn't think there were any broken ribs. Both his arms and his legs worked, but were stiff and sore.

All in all, he was in fair shape. Miraculously so.

There were some cuts and gashes, some deeper than others, some still dripping, others dry. Each singing loudly off key.

O'Connor pulled himself through the broken driver's side window, tearing his shirt and picking up another deep cut on his shoulder blade.

He sat against a red boulder and stretched out his long legs cautiously. Nothing broken, though he was plenty stiff and sore. It would only get worse.

"Fuck!" he muttered out loud.

O'Connor needed to get a hold of the boys, Graff and Reyna–in that order–but his cell was either somewhere in his truck or was strewn in the dirt within a what, a twenty- or thirty-yard radius? So was his gun.

If whoever did this came back to see if he was alive, he had nothing to protect himself with.

O'Connor looked around and other than the boulder and some sort of short shrub, there was nowhere to hide. The way his head hurt, maybe them coming back and finishing him off might be the lesser of the two evils.

"Fuck it!" he muttered again.

He pushed himself up onto his two feet. He weaved like a drunken boxer and staggered to the truck. He lowered himself back down to the driver's side window by bracing himself on the dented door.

O'Connor had to shut his eyes to stave off the overwhelming sense of nausea. Once that ebbed, he peered inside the truck. He couldn't see either his cell or his handgun. He grimaced as he worked his way on all fours to the passenger side window. From that angle, he saw his cell wedged between the seat and the door.

He reached up and retrieved it, rolled onto his back, held it to his chest, and passed out.

O'Connor woke up, head pounding and body aching. Waves of nausea surged through him. He kept his eyes closed, fighting the urge to lose the breakfast that fought to climb up from his belly.

It was then he heard car doors slam and shoes crunching on gravel. He was defenseless. His revolver was somewhere in the truck or in the dirt between the road and the truck, unless it was thrown further into the desert.

"Fuck it," he whispered. "A shitty place to die."

CHAPTER FIFTY-ONE

Brett watched the three men enter the trading post. His suspicion intensified as one of the men turned the sign on the door from open to closed. Quietly and smoothly, he took the Glock 19 from his holster and placed in on the table within easy reach.

"Brett, no," Brian whispered.

Brett ignored him and remained focused on the three men.

"I want to see your permit for that," one of the men said. He had a head of blond hair and had thick lips. With a face like that, Brett didn't think he could ever smile.

"I have one, but unless you're a cop, I don't have to show it to you."

The man sized him up. He said, "You have a smart mouth."

Before Brett could answer, Laidley came out from the back with two plates of eggs, sausage, and toast. He stopped mid-way, then kept walking, and said, "Can I help you gentlemen?"

He placed the food on the table in front of Brett and Brian, wiped his hands on his apron, and casually walked behind the counter towards the cash register.

"Stay where you are and keep your hands where I can see them," the man wearing a University of Arizona baseball cap said. He stood nearest the counter.

"I don't want any trouble. Get what you need and I'll ring you up," Laidley said evenly.

Ignoring him, the men moved to three abreast with the one nearest the counter facing Laidley. He never took his eyes off the proprietor. He was a tad smaller than the other two, but solid. Bald with dark narrow eyes and a black mustache.

The other two men faced Brett and Brian. Neither boy touched their food nor did they take their eyes off the three men.

The three men were carbon-copies of each other minus the differences in clothes, though all three seemed to prefer the color black except for jeans.

Big, muscled, and tan. Only one wore a hat, and he was bald under it. All of them packed handguns in shoulder holsters.

"Where's the Indian kid?" The man with dark hair stood slightly ahead of the others.

"When we walked in here, there were about a half-dozen Navajo kids playing outside," Brett said. "Take your pick."

Brian sighed. Brett was trying to piss him off.

Jaw clenched, face reddened, the dark-haired man started forward. Brett picked up the Glock and pointed it at the man. That stopped him.

The man laughed, and said, "I suppose you think you can shoot all of us?"

Brett cocked his head, smiled, and said, "Nah, just the biggest asshole with the biggest mouth. Maybe one other. I'm quick."

Michael stepped out from the back of the store and said, "And I'll shoot whoever he doesn't. Between the two of us, I think we have you covered."

The man wasn't expecting that. He took a step backward. Momentarily flustered, he regained his composure quickly.

"You're smaller than we were told."

"And you're a bigger piece of shit than anyone expected," Michael said.

Brett chuckled. Brian's mouth went dry.

The bell dinged and in walked Deputy Ned Mills, who sensed the tense atmosphere. The hair on the back of his neck stood on end. He had to decide whether to run, duck, or kiss his ass goodbye.

In a casual, almost friendly manner, he asked, "So, how's everyone doing?"

Mills stood by the front door, but a little to the side to provide a pathway for the men to leave. He hoped they would take it.

The blond-haired man half-turned to see who was talking. He said, "Good morning, Deputy."

To the boys, Mills asked, "Boys, are you okay?"

"Brian and I were eating breakfast, but I think we lost our appetites," Brett said pushing his plate away. "Brian, can you put a twenty on the table?"

"No need, boys. I'll keep a tab for you. Come back any time," Laidley said, lifting his shotgun from the shelf below the counter.

"Brett and Brian, come this way," Michael said, still aiming his rifle at the three men. "Walk backwards just in case."

"Shit, they're stupid, but not stupid enough to shoot us in the back. A deputy is watching them," Brett said, carrying his Glock casually at his side. He wasn't about to put it back into his holster.

"Everyone, let's put the rifles and guns down," Mills said. He added, "Before someone gets hurt."

Brian raised his hands waist high showing everyone they were empty. He said, "Mr. Laidley, sorry about breakfast"

"No worries, Brian. We'll see you again soon."

Brian and Brett walked towards Michael glancing over their shoulders. They made sure Michael had a clear line of sight on the three men. The boys walked past him, but Michael waited until they were safely out the backdoor. Only then did he back out.

"Who the fuck were they?" Brian asked.

"Not sure," Brett answered. To Michael, he said, "Do you know?"

"We'll talk about it at your campsite. I bought us some time by flattening their tires, but you have to get out of here fast!"

"What about you?" Brian asked.

Michael said, "I know how to hide if I have to. Easier with two horses than with that fancy SUV you're driving. Now go! Don't waste time. You have to move before they leave the store."

They rounded the side of the small trading post and quick-walked, almost ran to the Avalanche. Brian clicked the unlock button on the key fob and jumped into the driver's seat. Brett stood in back of the black truck and snapped two pictures with his cell. Then he hopped into the passenger seat.

Brian had it started and was in the process of backing up as Michael ran across the street to his horses. Brian sped away as Michael mounted up.

Michael waited until the Avalanche was nothing but a cloud of red dirt. Then with a "Haw!" and a flap of the reigns, Michael took off between two houses and up into the hills perpendicular to the road into town.

Michael looked over his shoulder. No one had left the trading post. That was okay with him. But he didn't know what, if anything, might happen to the cop and to the owner.

CHAPTER FIFTY-TWO

"Jesus!" Jamie said.

Reyna pulled to a stop on the opposite side of the road. Graff got out of the truck as a cloud of red dirt swirled around him. He stared in all directions with his gun drawn. Reyna did the same. They didn't see any oncoming traffic nor did they see anyone following them. Still, they weren't taking chances.

They climbed down the dirt and scrabble embankment and jumped over a ravine. As they crept towards Pat's truck, they saw broken glass, twisted metal, and a part of a bumper. They wondered if they'd find him in as many pieces as the truck. Graff shivered.

"Here's his Beretta," Jamie said. "It must have been thrown from the truck when it rolled."

"Pat! You okay?" Reyna sounded more hopeful than doubtful.

No response.

Jamie pointed at Reyna, indicated for him to go around the back of the truck. He would take the front. Both moved in a crouch, heads turning, guns out front at the ready.

Graff sucked in his breath and held it as he rounded the front to the passenger side. The first thing he saw was Pat's long legs stretched out in front. O'Connor had leaned himself up against the metal door and window frame. He listed to the side, chin on his chest, and clutching his cell phone in his right hand.

"Hoss, you okay?" Jamie said as he moved to him quickly, knowing that Reyna would cover them.

O'Connor didn't answer, perhaps couldn't answer. Graff wasn't sure which.

Graff holstered his gun and shoved O'Connor's Beretta into his belt on his back after he made certain the safety was on. He checked Pat's carotid artery for a pulse and found it beating.

"Ron, can you get a bottle of water?" Jamie asked.

"Fuckin' place to die," Pat said. "Shit. A fuckin' place to live."

Graff ran his hand over O'Connor's arms and legs looking for broken bones. There weren't any that he could tell. At the least, Pat didn't jerk or protest at any point.

"Touch my dick and I'm tellin' Kelli," O'Connor said.

Graff laughed and decided that other than a concussion, some cuts, scrapes, and bruises, Pat was in good shape. He looked at the truck and wondered how that was possible.

"You want to lay down?"

"Not sure. My head might explode."

Reyna came back on a jog with three bottles of water, handing one to Graff. He unscrewed the cap of another and held it to O'Connor's lips.

"Take a sip or two, but go slow," Reyna said. To Graff, he said, "I called for an ambulance."

O'Connor coughed after two sips.

"God damn head!" O'Connor said, wincing at the pain. He brought up his hand to his brow, then ran it over his face.

"Can you tell us what happened?" Reyna asked.

At first, O'Connor shook his head, winced, and stopped. Moving his head was not a good idea. He fought off another wave of nausea, not wanting to puke in front of them.

"Can't remember much."

Reyna stepped away to call the deputy and must have gotten his voicemail because all Jamie heard was a one-sided conversation of Ron telling Mills what had happened and asking him to view restaurant security footage.

"Didn't answer," Reyna said as he came back. "Left him a message."

"Call your office and let them know what we have. I'll call Kelliher. I think we've found ourselves in a mess and we need some help."

Reyna said, "On it."

Both men stepped away to make their calls. Graff hoped reception was okay. As they did, Pat's cell buzzed. His head hurt too much for him to bother looking at it. In fact, he turned it off and shoved it into his back pocket.

CHAPTER FIFTY-THREE

Neither boy spoke. Brian drove as fast as he dared to get to the Morning Star ranch before anyone went looking for them or before anyone saw them. He sure as hell didn't want those men to find them.

Brett sighed. His cell sat at seven percent, and Brian's was toast.

As quickly as he could, he forwarded the pictures he had taken of the black truck and the license plate to O'Connor along with a short message telling him what had happened. His cell registered five percent. Jaw set and fingers flying, he forwarded O'Connor the pictures taken at George's ranch, explaining what had happened the day before. He noted that the vehicles were not the same, and neither were the individuals involved.

His cell managed to function just long enough for him to get the pictures and the messages sent before it died.

Brett stared out the passenger window and then at Brian.

"I'm sorry for everything. I should have listened to you and we should have told Pat and Jamie what happened at George's ranch. I screwed up last night and today. I'm sorry. For everything. I know you blame George for this shitty trip, but I'm as much to blame as he is. I'm sorry."

Brian didn't say anything, but frowned at the road in front of him.

"Honestly, Brian, I am."

Brett took Brian's silence for anger. He decided to give up before Brian threw him out of the truck.

Finally, Brian said, "Who were they?"

Brett hoped Brian was just preoccupied with what had happened at the trading post and that he wasn't angry with him.

"I don't know," he answered.

"Do you think whoever was at George's ranch hired them to come after us?" Brian asked.

Brett shook his head. "Maybe they were looking for two kids." Then he amended his statement, "Three kids, if you count the Indian kid who they thought was George."

"That doesn't seem right. Three guys just happened to come to the same trading post where we were, looking for us and George? No way."

"Then I don't know who they were."

After a bit of silence, Brian asked, "What now?"

"What do you mean?"

Brian said, "That kid is expecting us at the pond. He knew where we camped last night. Maybe those guys know we camped there, too. So, do we drive there in this or do we use the horses?"

Brett thought it over. The Avalanche would provide speed, but the men in the trading post knew what they drove. The kid said he knew how to hide with a horse. He shrugged and told Brian what he was thinking.

Brian pursed his lips, sucked on the inside of his cheek, and said, "Horses. It will be slower than the SUV, but that kid, whoever he is, knows the area. He must know a back way to Chinle. That's where O'Connor and Graff are."

Brett nodded. "About as good a plan as any." He was worried though because he didn't ride horses well. At least not as well as Brian or George or that Navajo kid. "We've got to get our phones charged."

"We'll take our chargers with us. We have to take water and the guns," Brian said. "And ammunition." He wasn't going to take any chances.

"What about food?"

"Quick stuff. We won't have time for big meals until we get to Chinle."

Brett was hungry and Brian was too. He thought about the eggs, sausage, and toast Laidley had made them, and his stomach growled. He didn't know how long it would take to get to Chinle from the pond, and it would be awhile to get to the Morning Star ranch and then to the pond. But damn, he was hungry.

He sniffed his armpit. It wasn't too bad. The quick wash at the Morning Star ranch hadn't worn off. He said, "Will we have time to clean up?"

Brian sniffed his own under arm. "It will have to be quick."

"It will take time for that kid to get there, anyway."

Brian said, "We hide the truck behind their barn next to the other truck. We take two horses, not three. I'll saddle them up while you pack."

"George said that if anything happened, we should tell Rebecca's parents we're heading to the Mesa."

Brian frowned. What happened if the men from the trading post knew about Rebecca and her family? They had asked about George, so it was fifty-fifty. If they did, and if he and Brett told the Morning Stars where they were heading, those men from the trading post would know where they were.

"We'll go to the pond and talk it over with that kid. Chinle is our best bet."

They drove on in silence. As the Morning Star ranch appeared below them, Brett said, "I know we have to warn George and Rebecca." He held up his dead cell phone, and said, "But how do we do that?"

CHAPTER FIFTY-FOUR

George and Rebecca stopped at the top of the long dirt driveway leading to the Yazzie ranch. From a distance, it looked quiet, almost sleepy. It was mid-morning and there should have been some activity.

George thought back to his own home a lifetime ago. Robert might be racing around the yard with his sister, Mary. William might be in the barn working with the horses. His mom and grandmother would be hanging laundry or cooking a meal.

However, there was no laundry hanging on the line. There were no kids playing in the yard. There was no smoke coming from the chimney, and there was no fire in the outdoor stove.

Maybe no one was home. Maybe they were in Round Rock at the trading post.

Impatient, Rebecca flapped her reigns and made a clicking noise getting her horse to move forward. George followed at first, but as they neared the ranch, he sped up next to her.

He whispered, "Rebecca, wait. Something is wrong."

She pulled on the reins to stop her horse. She turned, stared at him, and whispered, "What?"

George frowned and shook his head. "Stay back."

Rebecca reached for her rifle and laid it across her lap. George's rifle was within reach, but he kept his right hand on his knife.

"Hello, the ranch. Mr. and Mrs. Yazzie?" He and Rebecca waited, but no one responded, nor did anyone appear in the doorway.

George was at once patient and impatient. He wanted to give the Yazzies time to respond, but something was wrong. His "Navajo thing." A sixth sense sort of thing. Many times, his grandfather would speak to him, sometimes appear to him. Always warning, counseling, or guiding him.

One more time George yelled, "Hello the ranch! Mr. and Mrs. Yazzie!"

Nothing.

George dismounted, handed his reins to Rebecca, took his rifle out of the scabbard and held it like a sentry, his finger above the trigger, not on it.

The smell. In three short years, he had experienced this same smell. Nothing like it. Stronger in the hot desert air, and not at all pleasant.

He held a hand up to Rebecca, though he didn't need to. She hadn't moved.

George knelt down, bowed his head and shut his eyes, and asked whatever *chindi* might be present for permission to advance. He promised to find out the truth of what he suspected had taken place, and to bring their spirits justice as well as peace.

He opened his eyes and instinctively searched the ground. He found tire impressions in the dirt, as well as footprints in at least three different sizes. A shell casing- large caliber. Then another, and another. On the left side of the driveway, there were small caliber casings.

Hard to do in cowboy boots, but he tip-toed into the front yard avoiding any footprints he saw. He would mark and take pictures of them later. The closer he got, the pock marks caused by bullet holes became more noticeable. So were the broken windows.

And the smell. Dark, thick, and wet.

George flashed back to his own ranch home, and he imagined his grandparents, his mother, his little brother and sister huddled together in the driveway. He pictured his brother William on the slope watching over the sheep. His cousin had described the two scenes to him, and as he did, George knew his cousin had purposely held things back.

He pictured Brian's home. The mess of blood, bone and tissue that covered the desk and computer in the office. The dark wet stain in the hallway. Though he had never seen what was behind the bedroom door, he knew who was in there and he suspected- correctly, according to Graff- what had happened.

Just like he knew what had taken place inside the Yazzie home as he stood in the doorway. Wanting to go into the house, but not wanting to. Knowing what he would find and not wanting to find it.

George turned to Rebecca who looked anxious. He shook his head. Rebecca's response was to grip her rifle tighter.

Cautiously, George took one step inside and held his breath. His second step took him into the kitchen.

Mrs. Yazzie lay on her back on the floor. Blood had pooled on either side of her like angel wings. George touched it and found it tacky, not wet, but not dry. Her death was recent. Further back in the room towards the hallway were a teenage boy and a preteen girl. The boy lay on his stomach with his arms outstretched overhead, the back of his shirt ripped open and bloody. George counted at least four bullet holes. A bloody trail led to the girl. Bullet holes had shredded her blouse leaving the back of her shirt bloody. It looked to George as though she had not died right away, but had tried to crawl to safety.

The only person George didn't see was the old man.

Staying close to the wall, George moved further down the hallway and peered into the nearest bedroom. Pock-marked walls and shattered glass blown in from a window. George surmised that the shooters moved around the house and fired indiscriminately into the ranch home.

The second and last bedroom appeared in the same condition.

The old man was not in the house, and there weren't many other places to look for him.

George left the house, held up a hand to Rebecca to stay put. He patted his knife once to reassure himself and then crept around the side of the house towards the barn. He stayed close to the walls, but had to cross an open area to reach the barn. He took a deep breath, hunched over, and sprinted to its side.

Staying low, George took off his cowboy hat and peered into the barn from a crack between two broken boards. He set his hat on the ground behind him and tiptoed to the doorway. He peered into the barn, first just one eye. Then he stood up and entered.

He wasn't surprised at what he first saw. However, further back in the corner in a small corral, he saw something he didn't expect to find.

CHAPTER FIFTY-FIVE

O'Connor's head pounded. It wasn't like a migraine where it hurt in one area. Rather, it was a dull ache that hurt all over. It was constant with no let up.

He had thrown up once, but managed to fight off a second round. He sat on the back end of an ambulance with his feet above the ever-present red dirt. He wore a thick white cervical collar and a blood pressure cuff, along with various bandages and gauze taped to scrapes, cuts and abrasions. One of the EMTs listened to his heart through a stethoscope. The other read numbers from a portable monitor connected to electrodes and EKG cables that ran from his chest and side.

Tired, Pat only wanted to lay down in bed in a quiet room with an air-conditioner cranked up high. Unenthusiastically, he answered a third round of questions, this time from a Navajo Nation detective. He repeated what he had told Graff and Reyna, and what he had told Mills.

Through the retelling, there was something important, something that sat on the tip of his tongue that he couldn't remember. He tried to shake the cobwebs out of his beat-up head, but that set off a round of cannon-fire behind his eyes and between his ears. He held his head in both hands, shut his eyes, to fight the pain but was unsuccessful. He tried to think, but whatever it was never broke surface.

"Pat, I'm sending you to a hospital," Graff said. "You've got a concussion and what little you have in the way of brains are scrambled. You need to get checked out."

O'Connor wanted to object. But Graff was right. He wasn't good to anyone in the condition he was in.

Reyna reached for O'Connor's cell, but Pat stuck it into his back pocket not willing to give it up. He wasn't sure why, but the cell was important to him. Maybe it was related to what it was he couldn't remember. Besides, it was his, and he wasn't about to give it up.

The heavier of the two EMTs said, "He ready for transport?"

Mills shrugged, and Reyna let Graff answer. Jamie said, "Take him. But I want to know where he is, and I want an armed guard outside his room."

Reyna said, "I've already called Albuquerque and they're sending a couple more agents. I'll make another call and have someone contact Chinle and have a cop stationed outside his room with orders that no one except medical personnel are allowed in."

O'Connor stood on wobbly legs and weaved left and then right. The two EMTs caught him before he fell. They stood on either side, each taking an arm, guiding him to the gurney. O'Connor laid down and was strapped in. One EMT hooked up an IV of saline and the heavy guy got behind the wheel. Mills shut the door, banged on it, and the ambulance took off with lights flashing and siren blaring.

"Now what?" Mills asked as he turned around and faced Graff and Reyna.

"We need to backtrack. We need to check the video from the restaurant he had eaten in," Graff said. He turned to Mills and said, "He called us and said a black Dodge Ram was following him. He said it was getting closer, so he ended the call. My guess is that they ran him off the road. Would there be a way to tap into any street or traffic cameras," he shook his head and raised his hands waist high, "ATMs and stuff to see if we can spot a Dodge Ram?"

As if he hadn't heard him, Mills frowned, and said, "O'Connor said it was a black Dodge Ram?"

"That's what he said."

Reyna asked, "Why?"

"Did he say how many men were in it?" Mills asked.

Graff and Reyna exchanged a look, and frowning at Mills, Graff said, "Two for sure, but he thought there was a third. Why?"

"Because earlier this morning, I stopped at the trading post in Round Rock to check on the boys. There was a black Dodge Ram parked out front. Inside were three men. They were carrying sidearms in shoulder holsters."

"Where were the boys?" Graff asked.

"They sat at a table with their breakfast in front of them. Laidley was behind the counter. I'm not sure of the purpose of their visit, but it had to do with the two boys."

Graff was pissed. He didn't understand why Mills waited this long to tell them about this. "What happened?" Reyna asked.

"Brett had his handgun, Glock, I think, on the table. An Indian kid came out the back with a rifle and told the boys to follow him. They did."

"It wasn't George. He is with Rebecca," Reyna said to Graff.

"This kid was younger than Brian or Brett. Smaller."

Through clenched teeth, Graff said, "It was the boy, Michael What's-His-Name that O'Connor asked to watch over Brian and Brett. Where did they go and what did the three men do?"

Mills shook his head and said, "The boys left by the back door. They stayed long enough to slit the tires on the truck. I talked to the men, but they refused give me any information. I warned them to stay away. They said they were only talking to them and didn't give me any other explanation or what they wanted to talk to them about. The trading post owner, Laidley, hadn't seen them before."

"You let them go?" Graff asked.

"They didn't give me any cause not to," Mills said defensively.

Graff walked away and pulled out his cell and speed-dialed Brian. It went straight to voicemail. The same thing happened when he called Brett. "Shit."

Graff stormed back to Reyna and Mills, "We have to find those boys and bring them in." He dialed again and said, "I need to get a hold of George. Shit!"

CHAPTER FIFTY-SIX

Brian sprinted from one horse to the other prepping them to ride. He led both out of the barn to the back of the Avalanche where Brett had packed supplies into bags that would fit on the backs of their horses.

"Did you pack water?" Brian asked.

"Yup. Water and some light food."

"Your Glock?"

Brett nodded, "Yes, and ammunition for both. Only the one box we bought, but I think it will be enough." He shrugged and added, "I think."

"I think we bring the whole box for the rifles."

Brett wished he had more. "I hope that's all we'll need."

Brian puffed out his cheeks, shrugged, and said, "It's not like we're at war or anything."

"Right."

"I hope not, anyway."

He finished packing and then locked the hood and then clicked the lock on the truck.

"Where should I put the key fob?"

Brian thought for a moment and said, "Driver's side tire. I think there's a ledge you can set it on it."

Brett ran around to the front of the car, knelt down, and looked up. Sure enough, there was a small metal ledge that framed the tire well. He snaked his arm up and set it there. He brought his hand away slowly just in case it might not stay, but it did. He straightened up, dusted off his knees and then his hands.

"You ready?"

Brian looked around and said, "Yeah. Let's get going. I want to get to the pond as fast as we can without killing the horses."

"I know I said this already, but at some point, we have to recharge our phones. We've got to get in touch with Graff and O'Connor."

As Brian hopped up on the big horse, he said, "And George. We need to warn him. Those three men came looking for him."

CHAPTER FIFTY-SEVEN

"What is Charles' horse doing here?" Rebecca asked.

She ignored old man Yazzie bent backwards over a bale of hay. There were at least three shots to his chest and stomach. The hay bale was soaked in his blood. His arms were spread out to either side and his head tilted back at an improbable angle. Yazzie's eyes were still open and the expression on his face registered shock, not pain.

Without taking his eyes off of the old man, George shook his head, and said, "I do not know."

Not believing what she saw and wanting to make certain it was Charles' horse, Rebecca walked over to the small corral. The horse's nostrils flared and its eyes showed white. It stamped, whinnied, and reared up before backing away as Rebecca neared it.

"Shhh, it's okay. It's me, Rebecca," she said, the palms of her hands showing. She moved as patiently as she could manage. "Shhh, it's okay," she repeated.

The thought crossed her mind to take it out of the corral, but she was afraid it would bolt. It took time, but it finally settled down enough for her to pat and stroke its neck. The horse stamped once or twice, but otherwise calmed down.

"If his horse is here, Charles has to be nearby."

George wasn't so sure. Charles could have used another horse or left in a truck or other vehicle. He did not want to think that whoever shot the Yazzie family might have taken Charles, or worse, left him somewhere to die.

As if reading his mind, Rebecca said, "I'm looking for him."

"Where?" George panicked. He did not know if the ones responsible for murdering the Yazzie family were still in the area.

"I'll look for any tracks or sign and I'll ride in that direction. If I don't find him that way, I'll circle the ranch."

"Just do not go too far. I will work the scene like Agent Skip taught me, and then I will send pictures to Detective Jamie and Detective Pat."

Reluctantly, she walked away from Charles' horse. With one last glance at George, she left the barn, got on her horse, and rode away to begin her slow, methodical search of the property and beyond.

George was torn. He wanted to be with her in case she did find him, especially if she found him dead. At the same time, he needed to get pictures to Graff and O'Connor and tell them what he and Rebecca had found.

Careful not to touch or disturb anything, he took several pictures of Yazzie from different angles. He left the barn and just as he had done before, he worked the scene. George took pictures of shell casings. Using his own boot to compare sizes, he took pictures of the three other footprints he had found, leaving the tire tread for last.

George hesitated, took a deep breath, and made his way back into the small home. He took pictures of each of the victims, capturing each scene from various angles. He wanted to show as much of the destruction as he could.

He left the house and stood in the yard as he sent the pictures and a short message to both O'Connor and Graff. He finished by letting them know they had found Charles' horse in the Yazzie barn, and that Rebecca was out searching for him.

It wasn't a minute later when his cell buzzed.

Graff.

"George, are you and Rebecca okay? Are you safe?"

"Yes, Detective Jamie. We are fine."

"Listen, I need you and Rebecca to get to Chinle or the nearest Navajo Police Station right away." Graff went on to tell him what had happened to O'Connor and about the three men from Desert Security. "I don't want to take any chances. I need you, Brett, and Brian safe."

George frowned, looked off into the horizon wondering where Rebecca was, and what, if anything, she may have found.

"George, did you hear me?"

"Yes, Detective Jamie. But I cannot do that. I have to help Rebecca find Charles. He might be nearby and if he is nearby, I do not believe he is . . . in good shape."

"George, please!" Jamie didn't mean to shout, so he regained his composure and said, "Please, George. I need you three boys safe."

"There was an . . . incident at my family's ranch. Brian wanted to tell you, but we convinced him not to. You would have made us come in. That would have prevented me from helping Rebecca search for her brother."

"What incident? What happened?"

"It doesn't matter now."

Without raising his voice, Jamie said, "I'm pissed at the three of you. More than that, I'm worried. Your dad is my best friend and if something happens to one of you, I won't be able to face him. Now, find your two brothers and get your asses to Chinle or to the nearest police station. That's not a request. That's an order."

"Detective Jamie, I do not know where Brett or Brian are for sure. They might be at the pond. Rebecca and I will look for Charles and then we will go to the pond. The four of us will be safe."

Exasperated and out of his mind with worry, Graff tried to reason with him. "George, you know I respect you and the boys. The three of you mean a lot to me. This is serious. Pat's already in the hospital and I don't want the three of you to end up there too. Or worse."

"Detective Jamie, we will be careful. Rebecca and I will look for Charles and then meet up with Brett and Brian at the pond. We will then go to Chinle."

Graff started to object once more when George said, "I have to go now. I will be in touch."

CHAPTER FIFTY-EIGHT

Brian cleaned himself up in the lake while Brett kept watch. Every so often, Brian would find Brett watching him instead of searching out across the valley. He was seldom, if ever, self-conscious around other guys, but he felt uncomfortable standing knee deep in the pond.

The other unsettling thing was that when the two boys rode up to the pond, they spied another bundle of belongings. The two boys decided that because it was public land, anyone could use the pond whenever one wished. Both boys ignored it, but they kept close watch just in case.

Brian finished washing and trudged up to the blanket he and Brett had set down.

Brett walked over and said, "You're sunburned."

He touched Brian's shoulders and his back, then his upper arms and his chest. As he did, he left a white hand- or finger-print.

"The thing is, I don't know if I should use suntan lotion or aloe."

Brian looked down at himself. Even though he had a fairly decent tan, he wasn't close to being as dark as Brett, Bobby or George. He wasn't even as tan as the twins.

"I don't feel burnt."

Brett smiled and said, "But you are and it will only get worse. So, do I put suntan lotion on you or do I put the aloe on you?"

"I don't know. Use whatever you think will work best."

Brett settled on the lotion and spread it thickly on Brian's back and his arms, working it in until it was semi-dry.

"Spread your legs a little."

Brian did as he was told. Brett worked the lotion up and down each leg.

"Okay, turn around."

Brian followed orders.

"Shut your eyes and hold your hair off your forehead."

Careful not to get it in Brian's eyes, Brett worked it into his forehead and eyebrows, his ears, nose and cheeks, and then his neck.

"Hold your arms out to the side while I get your chest and stomach and your sides."

Brett stopped below his belly and just above Brian's privates, but then continued down each leg and the tops of his feet.

"There, that should hold you. Wherever we end up, I should put aloe on you."

"Thanks."

Brett said, "Your turn to watch while I wash up."

As Brian layered on deodorant and dressed, Brett undressed. He took the soap and shampoo and walked into the pond.

Brian grabbed his rifle, the binoculars, a bag of jerky, and a bottle of water, and walked away from their camp towards the valley. He found a rock to sit on, placed his rifle across lap, and took up his watch. As he did, Brian did some thinking.

It was probably the same questions Brett had thought about. Where was George and was he okay? Who were the men in the trading post and were they connected to the three men who had threatened them at George's ranch? Who was the Indian kid, and why did he help them? The overall looming question that hung over him was how safe were they?

Along with the questions came the doubts and worry. How badly did he screw up by shooting at the three men at George's ranch? How badly did he wound the man holding the revolver? He thought of his dad and his caution that he and George had to make up before they got home. He thought of Bobby. That triggered thoughts of Brett and the conversation they had.

He mumbled, "Fucked up."

Brian lowered the binoculars to sip some water and noticed he had a visitor. He didn't know when the visitor had arrived. There had been no sound and little, if any, detectable movement, at least none that Brian had noticed.

The large, four-legged visitor looked remarkably like Jasper, his and Bobby's dog. The large wolf-dog had laid down not three arm's length from Brian and stared at him with his head resting on his front paws.

The two stared at each other. At first Brian didn't move. He wasn't particularly scared or worried, but he also didn't know if he needed to be. He had fed it that morning, so maybe he came back for more.

Brian reached into the bag of jerky and tossed a piece to the big wolf-dog, who caught it mid-air and swallowed it with minimal chewing.

Brian smiled.

He reached into the bag once more, but this time held it out towards the big animal.

The beautiful animal stared at Brian and didn't move.

Finally, head low, tail swishing from side to side, the wolf-dog crept forward and stopped a foot away. Keeping its eyes on Brian, it took the jerky, chewed it, and swallowed. Then it did something Brian didn't expect. It laid down at Brian's feet with its massive head resting on its front paws.

Brian decided it was more dog than wolf. Tentatively, Brian reached down and ran his hand over and into the dog's fur.

"What are you doing out here by yourself, huh, boy? You don't belong to anyone do you?"

"He might belong to you now," Brett said.

He stood a short distance away wearing his Nike slides and a pair of shorts, holding the suntan lotion.

"No, I think he belongs to the desert."

Brett tiptoed quietly and stood behind Brian. The big dog raised his head, decided Brett was no more of a threat than Brian was, and put his head back down on its front paws.

"Will he let you put lotion on me?"

"Yeah, I think so."

Brian set his rifle down, pet the big dog again, fed him a piece of jerky, and stood up. Curious, the dog looked up, and watched Brian take the lotion from Brett.

Brett pushed his shorts down and he stepped out of them and turned his back to Brian.

It took under five minutes to coat Brett front and back, top and bottom, just as Brett had done for him. Brian noticed large red blisters on the insides of Brett's legs near and above his knees.

He touched one lightly, glanced up at Brett and said, "These hurt?"

Brett made a face and said, "Just uncomfortable."

On one knee, Brian ran his hand over both legs as he stared up at Brett. Brett never changed expression.

"Remind me to adjust your stirrups. I'm wondering if we should pad these before they get worse and bleed."

Brett shrugged. "Do we have gauze and tape?"

"If not, we'll come up with something," Brian said.

Done, Brett held his shorts in one hand and said, "Will he let me pet him?"

"I think so. Go slowly."

Brett handed Brian his shorts, squatted down, and stroked the big dog's head. The dog didn't move.

"Is he coming back with us?" Brett asked as he scratched the dog behind the ear.

"Do you think mom and dad would mind?"

Brett made a face and shrugged. "No. I think he's yours now, anyway. We can't just leave him here."

Brian smiled. He squatted down next to Brett to pet the dog.

"What should we call you, huh? How about 'Papa'?"

Brett chuckled and said, "We have Momma, so Papa makes sense. Not very original, but it makes sense."

The two boys laughed.

"'Papa', it is," Brian said.

The two boys stood up and Brett took Brian by the shoulders, and said, "Bri, I love you. You know that, right?"

Brian nodded and said, "I love you, too, Brett. Always have, always will." He smiled at him and said with emphasis, "Always."

The two boys embraced, and as they did so often, rested their foreheads together.

"I've always loved you, Bri. From the very beginning when I first met you at the hotel. There was . . . *is* something about you that's special."

"I think deep down, I loved you. We just connected from that first day."

The two boys turned and stood side by side as they looked out over the valley. Nothing moved. No hawks or other birds. No antelope, elk, or deer. No jackrabbits. Nothing. Not even a dust devil because there wasn't even a breeze. Just endless expanse of red dirt, sage, scrub, and cactus. Some boulders and outgrowth in haphazard patterns. Some sort of tree, pine, Brian thought, grew in irregular patterns like hair on a balding man's head.

Beyond and behind them sat hills, buttes, and mesas as if they were judging all who dared to trespass.

"Kelliher said that George found a kid out here somewhere. George watched the kid get executed." Brett turned to Brian briefly and then back out towards the valley. "I knew the two men who killed him." He shook his head in disgust.

It was during the summer of death, and it was how George had helped solve the case of missing kids, Brett being one of them.

"Kelliher, he's the FBI guy with the flattop?"

Brett smiled and nodded. "I met him in Chicago when he, Graff, and Skip came to rescue Stephen and Mikey."

"You saved his life," Brian said as he ran a hand, then a thumb over the scar on Brett's shoulder and in his armpit.

Brett lifted his arm to take a better look, something he did most mornings just to make sure it was still there or hoping the scar had disappeared while he slept.

Brett sighed. "Not very pretty is it?"

"Makes you look tough," Brian said with a smile. "Besides, no one notices it anymore."

Brett put an arm around Brian's shoulders and said, "It's pretty out here but lonely."

Brian slipped his arm around Brett's waist, and said, "You know that story about George watching that kid get shot? Makes me wonder how many others died out here. Out there somewhere." He paused and added, "Forgotten."

"Kelliher told me he had found kids in remote areas all over the country." He waved an arm towards the valley and said, "I mean, between the sun and the sand, someone can die out here and no one would ever know."

Brian shivered and said, "That's an ugly thought."

Brett raised his eyebrows and said, "It's the truth."

"You're not thinking it could happen to us, are you?"

Brett said, "Hope not. But we have to get somewhere safe. I think we need to get to Chinle."

"Agreed."

Still looking out over the valley, Brian said, "Before we left, mom and I were talking. She and dad had hoped that Charles would have been found before we even got here and we could just hunt and stuff."

"Honestly, I don't know if George and Rebecca will find him. They know the area, but he could be anywhere."

Brian turned to him and asked, "Do you think he's still alive?"

Brett shrugged and then kissed Brian's forehead.

"It depends upon why he left and why he's missing. He would have a better chance than you and I would out here, that's for sure. But he's been gone a long time."

Brian sighed.

Brett gave Brian's shoulder a squeeze, bent down to pet the big dog, and slipped his shorts on. "When that kid gets here, we'll decide what to do. But we need to get somewhere safe."

CHAPTER FIFTY-NINE

They divvied up the duties. Because Mills knew where the boys were, he went after Brett and Brian to get them to Chinle where they would be under protective eyes. Reyna and Graff would do a quick check on the crime scene at the Yazzie ranch. Navajo police had been dispatched to the scene, but the two officers wanted to see it for themselves.

More of an urgent need was to check on Jesus Megena, the other rancher with dead sheep, and then Ngo, the Navajo elder. They wondered out loud if one or both might have suffered the same fate as Yazzie.

As they drove to the Yazzie ranch, Graff called Brett, and then Brian, but each call went to voicemail. The alarm in the back of Graff's mind was loud and urgent. He was tempted to go with Mills, but the Navajo policeman had promised to call Graff as soon as he reached the pond.

Reyna pushed their truck faster than he should have. It still took too long to reach the Yazzie ranch for Graff and played into his panic. Graff couldn't remember a time when he had felt this anxious.

They pulled into the driveway of the Yazzie ranch.

"We need to check on Henry Stone and Desert Security," Graff suggested almost as if he was thinking it, not meaning to say it out loud. "But he and they are in Phoenix."

"Kelliher said he's sending Phoenix FBI to their office. He also has some cyber guys on them. He made it sound like he's sending an army to scare them off . . . if they're involved."

Graff looked at him somewhat surprised. The way he said it was puzzling. He said, "You don't think they are? You think some construction guy ran Pat off the road?"

Reyna shook his head and said, "I didn't say that. We have too many variables and not enough of us to check them out."

"At some point, sooner rather than later, we need to check out Goodnight to see what he has to do with any of this. I still find it hard to believe he wants to build a resort out here and is scaring off sheep ranchers to get it done."

"We'll have to check it out, but I'm thinking that the Navajo police might have a better shot at him than we might."

Graff frowned and said, "Why?"

"He's Navajo. His company is Navajo. He lives on the reservation."

Graff scratched his cheek and said, "So we get Mills or someone to check him out?"

"I think he's our best bet. I don't want to bring too many more into this."

Graff cocked his head and said, "Are you having trust issues?"

"I didn't say that."

"What are you saying?" Graff asked.

Reyna paused before he said, "Besides you, me, and Mills, we don't know anyone. George has connections, but we don't know where he is or what he's up to."

Graff knew that it was a Navajo policeman- George's cousin- who had betrayed George and set him up to be killed along with Jeremy. Maybe Reyna was right to be cautious.

"Right now, Mills is going after the boys to get them to Chinle." Reyna paused and looked squarely at Graff. "That has to be the first thing he does. Then, he can check out Goodnight. We do a quick check on the Yazzie ranch," he said nodding at the ranch house, "and then we get to Megena and Ngo."

"I wish O'Connor wasn't in the hospital. We could use another hand and a pair of eyes."

"And another gun."

CHAPTER SIXTY

There was a cluster of Navajo police vehicles- one Tahoe, and two jeeps on site. Joining them in the now crowded driveway were two ambulances from the same hospital where O'Connor had been transported.

Reyna flashed his creds and asked for an update.

A round-faced, dark-skinned officer said, "Three dead in the house. An older woman and two kids. One dead in the barn. A lot of shell casings and footprints. They left us some nice tire tread we can make prints from."

Reyna turned to Graff and said, "About what George told us."

Graff asked for the officer's cell number so he could forward George's pictures and email. After Graff did, the officer thumbed through them and read the email twice.

"Who took these?"

"George Tokay," Reyna said. "We had asked him to stop by to see if Yazzie would talk to him." He nodded at Graff and said, "Jamie and I didn't have much luck, but we knew he wasn't telling us everything. I am FBI and Jamie is an unknown. We thought George might have better luck." He shrugged and said, "Evidently, George arrived too late."

The officer squinted at Reyna, then at Graff, and said, "You asked *Hosteen* Tokay, a boy of what . . . fifteen or sixteen to interview Old Man Yazzie?"

"I'm Navajo, but I'm FBI. Graff is white."

"Yes, I see that," the officer said staring pointedly at Graff.

He glanced through the pictures and reread the email. At last he looked up and said, "Unusual, don't you think? Even for *Hosteen* Tokay to be this thorough? It looks like the work of a crime scene specialist."

Graff sighed and said, "You don't know the half of it."

It wasn't George's first crime scene. There was the scene somewhere out here where a boy was shot and killed. George walked through the scene with Kelliher and his partner, Summer Storm. There was a scene in Northern Wisconsin where another boy and two perpetrators were shot and killed. There was the scene outside Jeremy's and the twin's first house where

George killed a man intent on killing his soon to be adopted family. There were other crime scenes, not to mention the eight or nine men he had killed to protect himself and his family. Far too much killing for a teenage boy. Far too many crime scenes he had walked through. Far too many for anyone, for that matter.

"I'll send these to the crime scene tech and the detective assigned to this case, but at some point, we will need to speak to *Hosteen* Tokay."

Reyna said, "Right now, he and Rebecca Morning Star are searching for her missing brother. When we catch up to them, we'll let him know. Deputy Mills is aware as well."

They gave the officer cards with their contact information. Before they left, Reyna turned and said, "There should be two or three other FBI agents in the area."

"Great," the officer said unenthusiastically.

"They will check in at a police station to let you know."

"Of course, they will," the officer muttered as he turned and walked towards two officers inspecting footprints and shell casings.

"I don't think he was impressed with you or the FBI," Graff said.

"No, not very. Typical, though," Reyna said.

The two men left and drove the short distance to Jesus Megena's ranch. Both had expected the worst.

At first, they sat in the truck with the windows down and with elbows on armrests, considering why Yazzie and his family were murdered, and not Jesus Megena and his family.

"Huh," Graff muttered.

"Hadn't gotten here yet?" Reyna asked.

"Or they might not have been after Yazzie necessarily. Charles Morning Star's horse was in the Yazzie barn."

Reyna screwed up his face in thought, turned to Graff and said, "Why would someone go after a sixteen- or seventeen-year-old boy with heavy weapons?"

Graff shook his head. It was one of many questions he wrestled with.

"Let's go see what he has to say," Reyna said as he pushed open his door.

The two men walked into the front yard as Doli Megena pushed her children towards the house. She turned to face the Graff and Reyna with her hands wrapped in her apron and barely able to look them in the eye.

Two round brown faces appeared in the window. Graff smiled and waved at them, causing the middle-aged woman to turn around and wave them away with the back of her hand. She turned back around and faced the two lawmen.

"Hi, Mrs. Megena," Reyna said with a smile. "I'm not sure if you remember us, but we stopped by yesterday to ask your husband some questions."

She gave no indication if she remembered them or not. A perfect poker player. Graff had seen that same look on George's face. Must be bred into all Navajo people like their bronze skin and black hair.

Reyna tried again. "Is your husband around? We would like to speak with him?"

With hesitation, Doli answered, "He is with the sheep." She pointed to the west and said, "About a mile."

Then she turned around, walked into the house and shut the door behind her.

"That was friendly," Graff said. "Is it like this all the time?"

Reyna sucked on the inside of his cheek and said, "It can be, but it's more pronounced for whatever the hell reason. I think it has something to do with everything happening on the reservation."

"And everyone who is not Navajo on the reservation," Graff added. He had begun to feel he was more of a hinderance than a help.

They got back into the truck and as Reyna eased the vehicle into a three-point turn, Graff read over the notes from their first interview.

He frowned and said, "Her name is Doli?"

Reyna nodded and said, "A traditional Navajo name that means, Blue bird."

"Pretty."

"His name is Jesus," Graff said as he closed the folder.

Reyna laughed and said, "Glad you pronounced it as it should and not as the Man on the cross."

Graff laughed and said, "I don't know Spanish, but I know that much."

Still smiling as he drove the truck over a little rise, Reyna pulled to a stop behind a beaten up, older model, Chevy pickup.

Megena sat on the hood of the vehicle watching his sheep and sipping from a plastic jug that looked like water to Graff. It had to be so warm, it tasted like plastic. Graff winced at the thought.

Megena turned around, stared at them, and then turned back around. His shoulders sagged.

"Let's go straight at him," Reyna suggested. "Tag team him. Gloves off."

"Lead with what happened to Yazzie and his family. That might shake him up enough to get him to talk," Graff said.

They got out of the truck and walked up to Megena.

Reyna stuck out his hand without smiling. He nodded curtly and said, "Mr. Megena, we just came from the Yazzie ranch. Delbert Yazzie, his wife and two children were murdered. From the looks of it, high-powered weapons were used. His wife was on her back in the kitchen. His son and daughter died in a hallway, and Delbert was found in the barn. All dead."

"It was a bloody mess. Looked like they were attacked by at least three men," Graff said.

"The house was shot up. They didn't stand a chance," Reyna added.

"And Charles Morning Star's horse was in the barn."

They let that sink in, and the fear registered on Megena's face.

"Before they come after you and your beautiful family, tell us what you know."

Graff said, "About your dead sheep. About Charles Morning Star, and who came to threaten you."

Megena stared at the ground. If his shoulders sagged any further, they'd be below his waist. He gripped the water jug in both hands. Graff suspected they had gotten to him.

He looked up and said, "Three men. The rich man wanted my land. He offered to buy it, but I said no." His expression begged to be understood. "This is my land. My family's land. I told him it was not for sale. He warned me that if I did not sell it, there would be consequences. Later that night, they came back and shot some of my sheep. They warned me that if I reported it, my wife and children would be next."

"You said they had a shotgun," Graff said squinting at him. "Did you see any other weapons?"

Megena shrugged and said, "The rich man and the other guy had fancy pistols."

"No semi-automatic weapons?" Reyna asked.

Megena shook his head and said, "I did not see any."

Graff and Reyna exchanged a look, and defensively, Megena said, "I am telling you the truth."

Reyna shook his head and said, "We don't doubt you. It's just that the Yazzie family was gunned down by high-caliber semi-automatic weapons."

Graff took another tack. "Has anyone else been around asking questions? Anyone you might not know?"

Megena frowned and shook his head. "No, no one."

"Did you know the three men who came and wanted to buy your land?" Reyna asked.

Megena hesitated a beat too long before he said, "No, not really."

Graff cocked his head and repeated, "Not really?"

Megena clammed up. He was done talking.

"One last question, Mr. Megena, and this is important. Do you know anything about Charles Morning Star and why he's missing?" Reyna asked.

"The thing is, if you know something and don't tell us, and if something happens to the boy, you could be held just as responsible as those who caused him to run away," Graff said. "That would be a felony and prison. That would be tough on your family, don't you think?"

"And if those same men who murdered the Yazzie family come after you and your family . . ." Reyna let it hang there. It was enough.

Panic lit up Megena's face like a billboard. His eyes darted from Reyna to Graff like a pinball.

He shook his head and said, "Yazzie did not say much. Delbert said the Morning Star boy was running from someone. He thought it was the same men who wanted our ranches, but we did not know for sure. Morning Star showed up and asked Delbert to hide him, so he did."

Graff asked, "Why didn't you go to the Navajo Police or the FBI?"

Megena shrugged and said, "We did not know who to trust. Neither did the boy."

And, so it seemed, neither did they.

CHAPTER SIXTY-ONE

There was little, if any breeze. Rebecca followed a trail of footprints deep into the valley like a bloodhound. The trouble was that the footprints were intermittent, as if someone deliberately tried to erase them. At one point, the footprints had double-backed and then veered east.

That puzzled George. He wondered why Charles, if it was Charles, wandered north, then back south, only to turn East. It was as if he was trying to lose someone. Perhaps Charles was just confused. George didn't know how much water Charles had with him. Traveling on foot in the desert without water could only have one end.

He lifted his binoculars from the saddlebag and scanned East, but came up empty. Nothing remotely human. It was the wrong time of day for an animal, large or small. As he set the binoculars back down around his neck, another thought occurred to him. Perhaps Charles changed direction because he decided where he was running to. There were two possibilities.

Rebecca had not talked to him, nor had she responded when he tried to talk to her. He could tell she was weeping because she wiped her eyes off either on her sleeve or her hands.

"Do you need any water? Are you thirsty?" George asked.

No answer.

She would lean over studying the hard-packed and sunbaked earth, first on one side of the horse and then on the other. Never looking up at the horizon. Only concentrating on the ground beneath her.

George had tied Charles' horse to his own using rope over its head and neck, tying the end of it to his horse's saddle horn. The horse came willingly, perhaps because it had nowhere else to go.

He reached around and took one of the water bottles from the saddlebag, opened it, and took a long pull. His cellphone was off. Graff had wanted him in Chinle, but Rebecca would never agree to it, and he didn't want to leave her out here alone with Yazzie's killers on the loose.

George felt guilty about O'Connor. Both O'Connor and Graff were only here because of him, and he had never intended on anyone getting hurt. He was concerned about Brett and Brian being alone. He just hoped they were safe. George hoped that if things went sideways, they would remember to go to the mesa.

He patted the saddlebag where the cellphone was, but that was as near as he got to calling either Graff or Brett. He wouldn't call Brian. Not without first having a face-to-face conversation.

Once more, he lifted the binoculars and scanned the horizon in all directions, but mostly towards the East where the Chuskas loomed in the distance. Nothing but scrub and cacti dancing in shimmering heat waves. Nothing that didn't fit the typical desert topography. If his hunch was correct, George knew where Charles was. Or at least, where he was headed.

Rebecca pulled up, hunched her shoulders and wept. Her dusty hands covered her face. Dirt had gotten under her nails. When George pulled up next to her, he saw the tracks of her tears that ran through the dust and dirt on her face. Self-consciously, he wiped his own face off leaving his sleeve streaked with reddish-gray grime.

He didn't know what to say to Rebecca. He had never been good comforting her or anyone else. Not even his brothers. As gifted as he was with hunting and riding, with working a crime scene or running, George was lacking when it came to dealing with tears. Not that he didn't want to help. He didn't know how.

"I think . . . if it is Charles, I know where he is going."

Rebecca wiped her face first with one sleeve and then with the other. She blinked back fresh tears and squinted at George.

He pointed at the footprints in the dirt and then pointed further back, and said, "It looked like he was doubling-back on purpose. At first, I thought that he was followed, and he tried to lose them."

Rebecca looked doubtful. There wasn't any cover for Charles to hide. Doubling-back wouldn't matter because no matter where he walked, he'd be seen for almost a mile.

As if he read Rebecca's mind, he shrugged and blushed.

"I think he doubled-back because he decided where he was going," he said. "I know who lives in that direction."

Rebecca shook her head, but didn't answer. Then her face registered understanding.

She used the heels of her boots to nudge her horse onward. George sighed and dutifully followed her. He resolved to see it through to the end, whatever end that would be. He didn't know if he should contact Graff. He decided to wait until he and Rebecca were sure.

CHAPTER SIXTY-TWO

After what had happened at the trading post, they were not taking any chances. The longer they waited, the more anxious they became. Neither could understand what was taking the Indian boy so long.

With the wolf-dog, Papa, by his side, Brian stood on an outcropping of rock and behind a copse of scrub pine and cactus searching the valley below with binoculars glued to his eyes, his rifle slung on his back and his knife on his hip. He had made sure there were five bullets loaded in the 30.06 with another ten in his shirt pocket. Unconsciously, Brian would pat his knife, though he didn't want to get too close to anyone to have to use it.

Brett stayed back at the pond and paced from one side to the other, searching the mountainside for any movement. Both boys had decided that while it was unlikely anyone would approach them from the mountainside, they didn't want to take a chance that someone might. Like Brian, he had his binoculars, his knife, and had five bullets loaded in the rifle slung on his back with extra ammunition in his shirt pocket. Both Glocks were fully loaded, but only one sat on his hip. The other was securely locked in the metal case with the rest of their gear at their camp.

Brett never saw or heard him.

"See anything up there?" Michael asked him as he stood a step or two behind him.

Brett jumped, spun around, stumbled and fell on his ass. He crab-walked backwards away from the voice until Brett saw who it was. Michael tried not to laugh, but couldn't help himself.

"*JESUS Christ!* You scared the shit out of me! Seriously, Dude! Don't do that!"

Michael doubled over and laughed harder. He grabbed his belly and then sat down in the dirt and laughed more.

"Where did you come from?"

Michael pointed off to the North, still laughing.

"How did I not hear you?"

Michael raised both arms and shrugged.

"Shit! Don't do that again!" As his heart quit racing, Brett smiled and then he laughed along with Michael.

"Gotcha!" Michael said.

Brian heard the laughter and walked over to investigate.

"Could you two make any more noise?" Brian asked.

Brett pointed at Michael and said, "He snuck up and scared the shit out of me!"

"You should've seen him jump," Michael said with a laugh. "His face..." He tried to mimic the face Brett had made, but ended up laughing.

Brett took off his binoculars and rifle, and playfully wrestled Michael, putting him in a cradle hold.

"Say you're sorry!" he said with a laugh.

That only made Michael laugh harder.

"Say you're sorry and that you promise never to do that again!"

"Better check your shorts," Michael laughed. "I smell somethin'."

Brett let him go and said with a laugh, "You're a little shit!"

"Where did you come from?" Brian asked.

Brett stood up and gave a hand to Michael, helping him to his feet.

"From the North. I took the long way around. I had to skirt the valley because I didn't want to draw them to the pond," Michael said as he beat dirt from the backside of his jeans. He took off his vest and beat the dirt from it.

"Do you think they know where we are?" Brett asked.

"Maybe, maybe not," Michael said. "We shouldn't take any chances."

"Who are you?" Brian asked.

"I'm Michael Two Feathers," Michael said with a broad smile.

"How did you know about us? You didn't just show up at the Trading Post, did you?" Brett said.

Michael shook his head and said, "I met Pat O'Connor yesterday. He told me about you guys and asked if I could show you around and stuff."

"That was you on the ridge this morning," Brian said.

Michael smiled, and said, "Helluva shot!"

Brian blushed. "Thanks."

"Did you know those guys at the Trading Post?" Brett asked.

Michael shook his head. "Never saw them before. I was across the street when they drove into town. They looked into your truck and checked the doors. I figured they weren't friends of yours."

"Thanks for coming in when you did," Brian said. "It could have gotten ugly."

Michael smiled, took off his hat, and ran his hand through his long black hair.

"We have another brother," Brett said. "Four others, actually. But you look just like our brother, George."

"George Tokay," Michael said with a nod. "O'Connor mentioned it yesterday when we talked. This morning, I met him and Morning Star's sister."

"Are they okay? George and Rebecca?" Brett asked.

"Seemed fine to me."

"So, what's next? Any ideas?" Brian asked. "We were thinking on heading to Chinle. We think that's where we'd be the safest."

Michael took one knee to pet the big wolf-dog. He pushed his face into the dog's fur and said, "You kinda stink." It didn't stop him from burying his face into the big dog's fur again.

"Is he yours?" Brian asked cautiously, almost sadly.

Michael shook his head and said, "Nope. I've seen him around though. Mostly when I hunt."

Brian sighed in relief, and Brett nodded at him.

Michael stood about a half a head shorter than Brian and Brett. Certainly, thinner and more compact. The boys noticed his ribs, but also the muscle definition in his arms and shoulders. Natural definition, not weight-training definition like they had. Like George and Brian, his hands were calloused from rugged work, his fingers long and thick. He had bronze skin, and looking at the younger boy, Brett and Brian marveled at the similarity between him and George.

"What?" Michael asked.

Brett shook his head and said, "You look like George."

Michael shrugged and said, "I'm cleaning up and then I'll make us some breakfast."

"Wait," Brian said. "What do you think about Chinle? Wouldn't that be the safest place?"

Michael took one knee and drew in the dirt.

"We're here. The mountains are here. Chinle is south of here. A long trip by a horse with some open country in between. If someone was looking for us, and if I'm that someone, I would look for us along that route."

"Yeah, but that's where Graff and O'Connor are," Brett said.

"And that's where they said we should go if there's any trouble," added Brian.

Michael stood up and said, "All I'm saying is that we'd have to be careful. Travel at night. We would have to stay off the main roads because if I was looking for someone, that's where I'd be. If we go to Chinle, it won't be an easy trip."

Mike and Brian stared at each other. Brett who muttered, "Shit!"

Michael shrugged and said, "Sorry."

Brian turned around and looked towards the valley, but from his position, he couldn't see it. What he was thinking was that if they could make their way across the valley to the Morning Star ranch, they could get the truck and drive to Chinle. But if Michael was correct, they'd be watching the roads, so that wouldn't work either. He sighed.

He turned back around and said, "We have a little time, so we can think about it."

Michael smiled at them and then turned and walked towards his pile of stuff under the tied-down tarp.

"We wondered whose stuff that was," Brian said.

"I dropped it off this morning before I went to the other side of the valley."

Brian gathered some dry wood and kindling and added it to the stack they already had.

"We'll need to bank the fire because I don't want anyone seeing it. If somebody's looking for us, that is," Michael explained as he walked over to the other side of the pond with Brett.

He showed them how to do it, placing the sticks in such a way as to minimize smoke.

"See?" he asked smiling at his work. "You guys want pancakes and bacon, or eggs and bacon?"

"Anything," Brian said.

"We're not fussy. We could eat a skunk's ass if one was around," Brett said.

"Speak for yourself," Brian muttered. "Regular food would be good. Need help?"

"Nah, I got it," Michael said with a laugh.

He ran back across the pond, took out his mixing bowl, a fry pan, and a large spoon from his supplies. He fished around and brought out some eggs, flour, some oil, and bacon, and carried everything back to the fire.

"Hey, I never asked. Which one is Brett and who is Brian?"

The two boys introduced themselves.

"You guys don't look like brothers."

It had always rankled them, but Brett and Bobby had been told from little on that they looked like Tom Brady without the cleft chin. Being from Indiana, they were Peyton Manning fans, though both had come to like and admire Aaron Rodgers. Both boys had chestnut-colored hair and eyes.

Jeremy had teased Brian that he could be one of the Beatles with his longish dark wavy hair. His eyes changed from hazel to green depending upon what he wore.

All six boys were handsome.

"We're adopted," Brett said. "I have a biological brother, Bobby."

"He looks exactly like Brett," Brian interjected.

"Bobby's eighteen months younger than me. And Randy and Billy are twins, but all of us are adopted."

Brett didn't bother to explain about him and Bobby not being adopted. It was a complicated story he'd save for another time. Besides, he wasn't ready to even think about Tom, his biological father.

"Brett's and Bobby's mom married, Jeremy, our dad," Brian added. "Eight of us all together. Mom and Dad and six boys. All of us are the same age, except for Bobby."

"And three dogs, now four counting Papa, and a bunch of horses," Brett said.

"We live out in the country," Brian said. "Our friends, Jeff and Danny live down a path near us."

"Jeff is like an uncle, and Danny is like a little brother or cousin. You'd like them."

Michael listened and couldn't help feeling sad. Their family and their life reminded him that he had no one and nowhere to go. No one to belong to.

Brett sensed the change of mood, but kept it to himself.

Halfway through the cooking, Papa appeared in front of Brian and danced from one side to the other, and then forward and back, growling low. Brian watched him closely. At last, Papa took Brian's forearm in his massive mouth and pulled him towards the valley.

"Okay, okay!" Brian said as he struggled to keep his arm attached to his body. Both Michael and Brett trailed behind.

Together they reached a position from where they could look down into the valley. The three boys didn't like what they saw.

To be certain, Brian used his binoculars. He said, "We've got no time."

Brett muttered, "Fuck me!"

CHAPTER SIXTY-THREE

Though Graff worked hard to hide it, the clenched jaw, the folded arms, and the lack of eye contact were dead giveaways to his frustration. He had the feeling Ngo enjoyed all of it, and that pissed him off even more.

Reyna was patient. Smiling, congenial, speaking in Navajo and sometimes in Spanish, doing everything he could to get Ngo to give them any information he had.

It was like water torture.

Reyna sighed. "Father, the Yazzie family is dead. They were shot in cold blood. The old man, his wife, his son, and his daughter. All dead. Nothing has happened to the Megena family. Yet. So far, nothing has happened to you and your wife. We want to find out who is doing this and why, before anyone else is murdered."

Ngo stared at him, his eyes nothing more than slits.

"The last time we were here, you were being watched," Graff said. "I'm assuming you still are."

Ngo turned from Reyna, faced Graff. With as little of facial movement as possible, he said, "Yes."

"Do you know who they are?" Graff asked.

Ngo nodded ever so slightly.

"Do they have something to do with whom murdered the Yazzie family?" Reyna asked.

"Perhaps, but not at this moment."

Graff and Reyna exchanged a *What the hell does that mean?* glance.

Reyna nodded and said, "The dead sheep."

"Yes."

There was silence, but it seemed to both lawmen that Ngo was content to play twenty questions.

"We're dealing with two different groups, aren't we?" Graff asked. "One wants to move ranchers off their land, and other who ran our friend off the road and murdered the Yazzie family."

"Yes."

Reyna and Graff tried to read each other's thoughts. Ngo stood in silence.

"Do you know what the other group wants?" Reyna asked.

Ngo whispered, "The *Diné* see our land as holy and sacred. Others, the *Biligaana*, not."

"Sir, what can we do for you?" Graff asked. "You and your wife are isolated out here. Can we take you somewhere? A friend? Family? Can we offer you protection?"

Ngo's face softened. For many years, he had distrusted the *Biligaana*. They didn't belong in *Diné Bikéyah*. However, he recognized the sincerity in Graff's words.

He smiled and said, "We are *Diné*. This is our land. We will stay."

"Can we do anything for you?" Graff asked.

"You have a good heart. Perhaps you might be *Diné* after all," he said with a small smile.

Graff smiled back.

"Father, how much danger are you in?" Reyna asked.

Ngo smiled again, shrugged and said, "Danger is around us. But we are old. We've had a good life and I look forward to the next. I do not think we will leave this world anytime soon."

"That is good to hear, Father."

"Sir, if you need to get a hold of us, do you have a way?"

Ngo nodded and said, "I will leave word at the trading post in Teec Nos Pos."

Graff looked at Reyna, who nodded, and said, "That is fine."

He put out his hand. Ngo shook it.

"If you need anything at all," Graff said.

Ngo and Graff shook hands, and then the two men walked to their truck, got in, and left.

They drove down the driveway, and the last time Graff glanced out the side window, Ngo stood exactly where they had left him. Neither of them felt good about it. In fact, both experienced a sense of dread.

CHAPTER SIXTY-FOUR

O'Connor hated hospitals. The bells, the PA announcements, the blood pressure sleeve tightening and releasing, the nurse checking the monitor with the probes and wires and crap attached to him, and asking *'How are you doing?'.*

At some point he must have dozed off. How that was possible, he didn't know.

The room was bathed in dim light. They gave him sunglasses, but he refused to wear them. The curtains were drawn. He didn't know how long he had been in the hospital, and he barely remembered how he got there. He couldn't remember details of the accident. But what bothered him the most was that he couldn't tell if it was day or night.

His head throbbed. It was better with his eyes shut, but it still felt like an icepick had been jabbed inside his head. He hadn't thrown up since . . . he couldn't remember. Still, his mouth had that after-puking taste and smell to it.

Shit. What time is it?

Pat opened his eyes, and he searched the wall for a clock. Nothing.

He tried raising his arm to check his watch, but when he did, a new pain broke surface.

He found a heavy bandage on his upper left arm and a similar one on his right forearm. The palm of his left hand had a heavy bandage on it. O'Connor didn't remember any of it. And, his watch was missing.

The little table to his left with an arm that swung over his bed had a cup with a straw and the remote for the TV that was currently off.

"How are we feeling?" the nurse asked. Evidently, she apparated like in the Harry Potter movies because O'Connor hadn't seen her enter.

"*We* are feeling like shit," O'Connor muttered.

The nurse took his pulse and checked his blood pressure.

"What time is it?" O'Connor asked. "How long have I been here?"

"It's almost two-thirty in the afternoon and you arrived early this morning."

"I need my phone," O'Connor said with a grimace.

"Because of your concussion, you need to stay away from electronics like your cell phone. No TV. Would you like to listen to music?" this last a question, not a command.

O'Connor wasn't arguing with her. It wouldn't do any good.

"Is there someone outside the room? A cop or someone?"

The nurse, a middle-aged lady with a serious attitude, smiled and said, "Yes. Two, actually. The Navajo policeman arrived when you did, and the younger gentleman in a sport coat arrived an hour or so ago."

"The guy in the sport coat. He a cop?"

The nurse finished writing her notes on the clipboard at the foot of Pat's bed, and said, "He looks and acts like one."

"You know cops?"

She smiled wryly and said, "I was married to one," and she left. "I didn't know you were a cop until I read your chart."

"Mostly undercover."

"Looks like it."

O'Connor shut his eyes to gather what scrambled wits he could, and shouted, "Hey, cop outside the room!"

He waited a beat or two and his patience was rewarded when a heavy, bronze-skinned Navajo cop carrying a folded newspaper strolled into the room. He was followed by a young guy dressed in a tan sports coat and jeans with boots. The Navajo cop stood at the side of the bed, while the other, obviously FBI, stood at the foot of the bed.

"I need my cell phone."

"Um . . . the nurse just told us you're not supposed to have any electronics," Young FBI Guy said.

O'Connor grit his teeth and said, "Things are happening. There are four boys I'm responsible for and I need to get ahold of them."

The Navajo Cop shuffled his feet and fiddled with the newspaper with his head down. FBI Guy frowned at O'Connor, clearly weighing what O'Connor had said.

"What four boys?" he asked.

O'Connor shut his eyes, took a deep breath, and began yanking the electrodes off of him.

"Shit, Dude! What the hell are you doing?"

"I'm getting my cell. I'm guessing it's in the closet in a bag with my other shit."

"Jesus! Just stay there," FBI guy said holding his hands out in a stop-right-there fashion. "I'll get it. Just get back in bed and put those damn things back on."

Two nurses came charging into the room. The one that had just been in the room pushed the Navajo cop aside and said, "Both of you leave. Now!"

"No!" O'Connor said. "I want them to stay."

"You're not ready to have any visitors," she said to O'Connor as she began reattaching the wires. She turned her head to the cops and said, "I told you to leave!"

They started out of the room, but O'Connor stopped them.

"Ma'am, I want you to leave and take your friend with you. We were in the middle of something important."

"You're not ready for visitors. You are in concussion protocol."

"I don't give a shit. Get out!"

"Do I need to call the doctor?"

"Listen Nurse Ratched," a reference to the movie from a hundred years ago, "I'm leaving. You can call whoever the hell you want. I'm signing myself out and you can't stop me!"

A middle-aged man in a white coat with a stethoscope draped around his neck stepped into the room and said, "You must be doing better."

"I want to leave."

The two nurses scattered backwards out of the way. One nurse smirked, but O'Connor didn't know if it was because the doc was in the room or from what he had said to Nurse Ratched, who threw him daggers.

"Before you leave, mind if I give you a once over?"

Without waiting for an answer, the doctor took out a penlight and said, "Look straight ahead and shut your left eye."

O'Connor played along.

The doc shone the light in Pat's eye and it was all O'Connor could do to keep from screaming.

"Okay, the other eye."

Pat took a deep breath and opened his left eye while shutting his right. He balled his hands into fists, as the doc shone the light into it.

"Okay, shut both eyes. Breathe and relax."

O'Connor did just that, though his hands were still in fists.

"You're one tough son of a bitch!"

O'Connor snorted, not expecting this from the doc.

"What would it take for me to get you to spend the night?"

O'Connor sighed. Deep down he knew was in no shape to go anywhere. He would be no good to anyone.

"There are four boys out there. I'm responsible for them. I need to find out where they are and get them to safety."

The doc glanced at the Navajo cop and the young FBI guy and then turned back to O'Connor.

"What do you need?"

"My cellphone."

Nurse Ratched stepped forward and said, "Doctor, he's not ready for that."

The doctor waved her off and said to the FBI guy, "In the closet there is a clear bag on a hanger. Inside would be his personal items. Can you get his cellphone?"

Sport Coat Guy retrieved the bag from the closet, looked through it, and found the cell. He stood for a minute as he considered whether to bring the whole bag over, thought better of it, and put the bag back in the closet on the shelf.

"I can read it if you want me to," he said.

O'Connor shook his head once, stopped because it brought on a wave of nausea- noticed by the doc- and said, "I can do it."

The doc snorted, but covered it with a slight cough. O'Connor smiled at him.

Pat thumbed it on, waited, and was rewarded with several messages from Brett, Michael, his partner back in Wisconsin, Paul Eiselmann, and one from Pete Kelliher, an FBI friend.

He opened the email from Brett, read it once, shut his eyes, and read it again. He opened the attached pictures and then brought the cell down to his lap and shut his eyes. The pictures of the truck brought back pieces of the memory of the accident. Not in total, but vague vapors like one has when waking from a dream.

"These are pictures of the truck that ran me off the road. I think. It looks like the truck ... what I remember, anyway. The same guys are after the boys."

Sport Coat Guy stepped around to the side of the bed and took it from O'Connor who gave it up without a fight.

Sport Coat Guy frowned as he read the email and viewed the pictures.

"Mind if I forward these to Agent Reyna? He'll want to see these."

Without waiting for an answer, he did just that. Then without asking, he handed the cell to the Navajo cop and said, "You should put out a bolo on this truck. Suspects or persons of interest."

The Navajo cop read the email, viewed the pictures, and called it in.

O'Connor stared at the wall beyond the bed, then shut his eyes. He'd only be in the way. He would have to trust Michael's skills, Brian's and Brett's intelligence and instinct, George's knowledge of the land, and Graff's and Reyna's ability as cops.

"We need to find the boys," O'Connor said tiredly with his eyes closed. "They're in danger."

The Navajo cop asked, "Would you have an idea where to look?"

O'Connor thought for a moment. He remembered the boys were camping ... somewhere. A lake or pond or ... something. The base of the whatchamacallit mountains.

With his eyes still shut he told the cop, who nodded, clicked his radio, and relayed O'Connor's message, though it was more specific. Evidently, he knew the place O'Connor tried to convey.

The response to the cop was quick, "This is Mills. I'm on it."

O'Connor tried to relax, but couldn't. Part of it was his need to protect the boys ... his boys. The other part? He wasn't sure.

CHAPTER SIXTY-FIVE

"Jesus! They're moving fast!" Brett breathed.

"We've got to go! Now!" Michael said.

The only one who remained calm was Brian. Using his binoculars, he alternately stared down at the oncoming black truck, the same truck carrying the same guys from the trading post earlier that morning, and at the top of the ridge on the other side of the valley. He thought he recognized who was up there, and that puzzled him.

He dropped to a knee and swung his rifle from his back to his shoulder.

"Give me a distance," he said calmly as he flicked off the safety and peered through the scope.

"I don't know. Four hundred yards give or take. We gotta go!" Brett said.

Michael danced from one foot to the other. His voice had risen an octave as he urged, "Guys, we gotta go now!"

"Give me distance," Brian said just above a whisper. "Keep giving me distance."

He was steady, calm. It was the same way he approached shooting a technical foul in basketball or a PK in soccer.

It only took a second for Brett to figure out what Brian was doing.

"Three-fifty . . . three . . . two-fifty . . . two, *Jesus, Brian! You gotta do something!*"

As he did when he hunted, he silently counted *three . . . two . . . one*, exhaled, and pulled the trigger, and then shifted slightly and pulled it again. He kept his eye on the scope just in case, but like in basketball shooting the last-second shot or in soccer shooting the must-have goal, he didn't miss. Not with the two elk earlier that morning, and not with the metallic beast charging at him and his brothers. Not with the first shot, and not with the second.

Brian thought the truck would stop in its tracks unable to advance. What he didn't expect was what actually happened. From Brett's and Michael's reaction, neither did they.

Upon the impact of the first bullet on the front left tire, the truck veered sharply left. Upon the impact of the second bullet on the front right tire, the truck spun tail over nose in an ugly cartwheel once, then twice, finally landing with a crash of bent metal and broken glass upside-down, rocking back and forth like a see-saw before coming to a rest amid a swirl of red dirt.

"*Holy Fuck*!" Brett said. "*Jesus*, Bri!"

At last, Brian took his eye away from the scope and used his binoculars to see if there was any movement from inside the truck. He didn't see any, and a lump grew in his throat. Even though the day was beyond hot, a cold finger of fear traced his spine and a wave of guilt swept over him.

"We should go see if they're okay."

"*Hell, No!* They weren't coming to throw us a party!"

Michael placed a hand on Brian's shoulder and said, "We need to leave. Right now."

"Let's go, Bri," Brett said as he tugged Brian's arm.

Reluctantly, Brian stood up. He took off his hat, ran a hand through his hair, and then set it back down, brim low. He turned and followed the two boys. At first, he walked, but then he broke into a run like Brett and Michael ahead of him.

"We leave everything. We travel light," Michael said. "We can always come back for it."

"All our stuff?" Brett said. "Nothing will be left."

"Yeah, well, mine too," Michael said as he threw a blanket and cinched the saddle on his horse. "I'll come back later to get what I can."

Michael didn't have much to begin with and now he'd have even less. There would be nothing left.

Brian saddled up Brett's horse, threw a blanket on his, and jumped on. He took a last look at the camp site. He couldn't get over the feeling that they were making a mistake. They should be taking more with them. They were forgetting something . . . something important. Maybe several things. The trouble is, they didn't have time, and Brian didn't have time to think it through. Michael was right. They needed to get away while they could. If any of those men survived, they would surely hunt Brett, Michael, and him down. If they were caught, they would die.

Vaguely, between the guilt and the rush to get away, he wondered about the guy with the binoculars up on the rim on the other side of the valley.

CHAPTER SIXTY-SIX

George and Rebecca watched from the hills above Ngo's ranch. They hadn't been the only ones watching.

There were two others, older men, grizzled by age, wind, and sun.

While Rebecca kept a rifle trained on the younger of the two, George double-backed up the trail on foot and came around behind them. When he wanted and needed to be, George could be silent as a ghost in fog. The two were so intent on Ngo's ranch, they hadn't seen or heard him until George clubbed both over the head with a large stone. Hard enough to cause unconsciousness and a low-grade concussion, but nothing lethal. He stripped them of all their weapons and scattered them in different directions. He tied their hands behind their back with the rope the two men had carried with them. As an extra precaution, he gagged them both using strips of cloth from their own shirts.

That done, he and Rebecca waited until Graff and Reyna drove down the driveway and out of sight. They waited long enough to make sure the two lawmen didn't come back. George knew Graff well enough to know that one of his favorite tactics was to double-back to catch a query off-guard.

Finally, George and Rebecca rode side by side down the driveway. George had Charles' horse trailing his. About half-way there and within sight of the house, George yelled, "Hello, *Hosteen* Ngo!"

A minute or two later, Ngo stood in the doorway of his hogan, one hand on the pipe in his mouth, the other relaxed at his side with a thumb tucked in his front jeans pocket. George didn't think he was surprised to see them. In fact, it looked as if he was expecting them.

"*Yá'át'ééh*," George said with a nod.

"*Yá'át'ééh*," Ngo repeated.

He looked past George and Rebecca and asked, "Where are the others who were watching me?"

George answered in Navajo, "Up the hill... resting. I hid their weapons, so they shouldn't be able to harm you or your wife."

"Much has changed since you went to live with the *Biligaana*."

Not sure if it was a rebuke or a warning, George remained silent. He loved *Diné Bikéyah* and even though he loved his family and was happy living with them, he wasn't sure where his heart wanted to reside.

Ngo considered the struggle that seemed to take hold of George, nodded and said in English, "You've ridden a long way. You need something to eat and drink."

George wondered if this might be a test. If he answered yes, Ngo might see him as weak. If he answered no, Ngo might see him as ungrateful.

Rebecca spoke up and said, "If you don't mind, Father, we can drink from your pump. It has been a long day and I am thirsty."

Ngo surprised George by smiling. He answered, "I will get us some fry bread."

Rebecca hopped off her horse, stretched, and walked to the pump. George followed.

Rebecca took off her hat, undid the top two buttons of her shirt, and put her head under the pump. George worked the handle while she first washed off her face and wet her long black hair. She washed the dirt and grime from her hands. Then she took a long drink, cupping her hands to drink from them.

It was cold and smelled of sulfur, but she was used to it. All pumps and wells on the Navajo reservation were like this. However, Rebecca also knew that if they had time and a container, she would fill it, leave the cover or cap off, and an hour or two later, the smell and taste of sulfur would disappear and the water would be clear and cool.

After Rebecca was finished, George took his turn while Rebecca returned the favor for him. By the time they were finished, Ngo was sitting on his chair by the door with a plate of fry bread and a container of honey.

George led the three horses to the trough. He wished he had more to give them.

Rebecca walked up to Ngo, while George squatted down across from the Navajo elder. He and she were patient. They would wait until the appropriate time to discuss the reason they had come for a visit.

"Thank you, Father," Rebecca said as she took a piece of bread, dipped it in honey, and sat down on the rock. Some honey dripped down her chin, and she wiped it off with a finger and licked it off. She smiled shyly.

Ngo held the plate out to George. He nodded encouragement, and George smiled, took a piece, dipped it in honey, and squatted back down. They ate in silence while Ngo puffed on his pipe and stared up at the hills.

In Navajo, George said, "Father, those two men, why were they watching you? Are you and your wife safe?"

Ngo's eyes twinkled. He smiled, and said, "It is kind of you to ask. Your *Biligaana* friend asked the same question. Perhaps you are rubbing off on him."

George smiled, knowing Ngo was teasing him.

"I think when two people are friends, they rub off on each other."

"Only the good qualities, I hope," Ngo said, frowning playfully.

George laughed and said, "I choose carefully."

With that, Ngo laughed. "Like your grandfather."

George couldn't remember Ngo ever smiling or laughing. His demeanor was quite different from the conversation at the trading post in Teec Nos Pos.

"Your two brothers . . . where are they?"

"They have been camping at the pond. Rebecca and I will meet up with them."

"Some *Dine'* come to visit me seeking advice. Others come for healing. There are those who come to threaten or persuade. I do not get many visitors, yet today, I get four."

This was the cue, the opening George had been expecting or at least, hoping for.

In Navajo, George said, "We have been looking for Charles Morning Star, Rebecca's brother. We found the Yazzie family murdered, but Charles' horse was in their barn. We followed Charles' trail here."

Ngo said nothing.

"We are hoping you would know where Charles is. Or where he had gone," Rebecca said hopefully.

Neither George nor Rebecca had talked about how to approach Ngo. But it was so natural between the two of them. It was honest and sincere, and that was not lost on the elder.

"The two of you," Ngo said. He didn't add anything. He didn't finish the sentence, because that was his sentence.

George lifted his head and without looking at Rebecca, said, "I love Rebecca." He looked over at Rebecca and added, "I believe she loves me."

"We have been friends a long time. Our love came slowly," Rebecca added, "and grew."

"Even after all this time away," Ngo said.

"Yes, Father. Even after all this time," George said.

"What would *Hosteen* Tokay say about that?"

George glanced at Rebecca. She was blushing slightly, but her chin had lifted and her eyes held Ngo.

George said, "My grandfather would say that if one heart is meant to find another, it will."

Ngo smiled, nodded, and said, "Then it shall be so."

Rebecca turned to George and said calmly and evenly, "Yes, it shall be so."

George's response was to nod at her. He couldn't help smiling at her.

"You came seeking your brother," Ngo said.

"Yes, Father," George said.

"He is here."

CHAPTER SIXTY-SEVEN

"Kelliher called," Graff said. "Desert Security was hired by a mining firm. There is interest in a spot up in or just east of the Chuska Mountains. Henry Stone didn't know anything about any of his men involved in or causing O'Connor's accident."

Reyna frowned. "That's Navajo Reservation. It's sacred land."

"Sacred, how?"

"In 1868, a treaty was signed between our Navajo Nation and the United States Government. It's called, *Naaltsoos Sání*. This treaty returned our ancestors to our tribal homelands between the Four Sacred Mountains of *Tsisnaajini, Tsoodzil, Dook'o'oosliid, and Dibé Nitsaa*. The treaty ended the war between the Navajo Nation and United States, but more importantly, it established our Sovereignty."

"So, if a mining company wants to come in and start drilling . . ." Graff started.

Reyna finished, "There would be pressure on the tribal council, on the elders to grant access."

"What's the likelihood of that happening?"

"Not very with Ngo on the council. Yes, it might bring jobs and money to the reservation, but like I said, it's sacred land. It would be like," Reyna stopped, puffed out his cheeks and shook his head as he searched for the right words.

"Okay, this is a stretch, but go with it," he said.

The truck hit a bump, and both bounced. Graff took hold of the Jesus Handle above his door for support.

Reyna continued, "Imagine some big CEO comes in and asks the Catholic church permission to bulldoze a cathedral in New York or D.C. so he can put up a corporate headquarters or something."

"It would never happen," Graff said.

"Right. But, if the CEO had power, money, and the shithead in the White House who would turn his head while something like that took place, and, have a security force to muzzle those who might protest . . ."

Graff shook his head, "It still wouldn't happen. There would be public outrage."

Reyna snorted. "Now imagine the Navajo, who have no power, no money, and that same shithead is in the White House who doesn't give a shit about anyone unless a person is white, rich, and a male."

Graff slouched back in his seat. "Fuck me!"

"No, fuck the Navajo."

"Okay, suppose that's true. Why massacre the Yazzie family? Why is a sixteen-year-old kid on the run? Why are sheep dead, and why are ranchers scared?"

Reyna shook his head and said, "My best guess, and it's only a guess, is that whatever is happening to the sheep and the ranchers is separate from the mining thing. How Charles Morning Star fits in is anyone's guess."

"Say you're right. Two different groups moving in two different directions." Graff shook his head and then said, "I can picture the mining thing. That's happening more and more. But seriously, I can't picture Archer Goodnight trying to build a resort here." Graff shook his head again. "Good hunting or not. No offense, but there are parts of this reservation that Satan would feel comfortable in. To be sure, we need to pay him a visit."

"Agreed," Reyna said nodding his head. "Not necessarily about the Satan part, but we need to talk to Goodnight."

"Can you call someone and have him check out the mining in the mountains?"

"Yeah," Reyna said as he pulled out his phone. "I'll get someone on it."

"Better make it a small team. One or two guys might not stand a chance if it's the same outfit that put O'Connor in the hospital."

"Good point."

"I forgot to mention. Kelliher has a computer guy looking into Desert Security financials and phone records."

Graff said, "You said Stone knew nothing about the three or four goons who crashed O'Connor off the road?"

"He claimed to not know anything about that. He said they don't operate that way."

Graff gave Reyna a look of disbelief and said, "He's covering his ass, that's all." He stared out the side window and said, "I'll call Mills, tell him what we've found out, and tell him we're heading to visit Goodnight. I want to hear from him that those boys are safe."

CHAPTER SIXTY-EIGHT

"They're not at the pond. They're gone."

Scared as much as he was angry, Graff asked, "Does it look like there was a struggle? Did you look for a blood-trail? What direction were the footprints? Do you have any idea where they went?"

Mills sat in his jeep on the opposite side of the valley with the binoculars in one hand and the cell in his other and listened to Graff's barrage of questions. He said, "No, it didn't look like a struggle and I didn't see any sign of blood. I have no clue where they might be."

"Fuck!" Graff shut his eyes and pounded the dashboard. "Is there any indication that they are okay? Unharmed?"

"Just a hunch, but I think they're okay. It looks like the three boys are together, though. I didn't see any sign that anyone else was with them."

"Okay, think. Where might they have gone?" Graff couldn't keep the desperation out of his voice.

Mills shook his head and said, "My best guess is up in the mountains. You said the Navajo kid was with them? If so, he'd know the area. He's from the east side of the Chuskas, so if I had to guess, they would go to someplace he was familiar with."

"I'll call O'Connor. In the meantime, Reyna and I will interview Goodnight. Our working theory is that he's behind the dead sheep and the disappearance of Charles Morning Star."

"Could be, I guess, but I doubt it."

"Why?" Graff asked.

"Just a hunch. I could be wrong."

"Whatever. We're interviewing him. Those boys need to be found before something happens to them. If they're riding up in the mountains, I don't want them running into anyone from Desert Security."

Mills nodded and said, "I'm on it. I'll call Shiprock and have them send a deputy out."

"Thanks. I need to have those boys brought in before things go sideways."

Mills ended the call. He didn't actually lie to Graff. He just didn't tell him everything.

Though he hadn't been to the pond yet, there was no way in hell he would drive down into the valley and face those goons by himself. Besides, he watched everything from his vantage point on the far rim.

The fact that the kid in the white cowboy hat had shot the tires out from that distance was damned remarkable. Mills couldn't name more than two guys who could make those same shots.

There was still no movement from anyone in the truck, so he kept his eye on the boys at the pond. He watched them saddle up and ride off up into the mountains. For now, they were safe. Mills smiled. He knew where the boys were headed.

Mills searched the mountainside for any trace of them, but didn't see anything. He lowered his sight back to the truck. Four men crawled out and lay in the grass or dirt as they took stock of themselves. They stood up, staggered over to the truck and inspected it.

It was totaled. The front driver's side tire bent inward at an angle that proclaimed the axle was broken. The cab of the truck was crushed, and it was a miracle that anyone walked away from that wreck.

Mills smiled. They got what they deserved, the arrogant pricks. The kid in the white cowboy hat deserved a medal.

He lowered the binoculars to his chest, pulled out his cell and dialed a number.

"We might have a problem."

CHAPTER SIXTY-NINE

The trail was steep, winding, and rocky. The horses had been ridden too long and too hard. The only critter that didn't seem worse for the wear was Papa, the big wolf-dog, who sometimes ran ahead, sometimes trailed behind, while most of the time, stayed with Brian. The horses were no longer skittish of him.

When Michael reached the waterfall, he brought them to a halt.

"We'll stop here to rest."

It was Brett who spoke, "What if those assholes are on our tail?"

Michael pushed his hat back on his head, and said, "It's a hard ride. It would be a much harder walk, and those guys are in no shape to climb up here."

Brett turned to Brian who appeared ashen. Brian's shoulders were hunched and his head was down.

"Brian, are you okay?"

It didn't appear that Brian had heard him. Brian shoved his hands into his front pockets, turned, and stared back down the trail. Papa hovered at Brian's feet, leaning into his leg as he, too, stared down the trail.

"Brian?" Michael called again.

Brett waved him off and walked up next to Brian and slung an arm around his shoulders. He didn't say anything at first, but let him weep.

"You saved our lives. That counts for something."

Brian took his right hand out of his pocket and swiped at first one eye and then the other.

"Hey," Brett turned to face Brian. "Look at me," he said.

He took Brian by the shoulders and as they did so often, they rested their foreheads together, knocking Brian's cowboy hat and Brett's Badger snapback off in the process. Neither boy bothered to pick them up.

"What's going on? What are you thinking?"

Fresh tears fell. "What if I killed someone?"

Brett kissed Brian's forehead and then hugged him fiercely. He placed both hands gently on the side of Brian's dirt-streaked face. He thumbed tears out of Brian's eyes.

"Bri, those guys were looking to hurt us. You saw them at the trading post, right?"

Brian said nothing.

"Right?" he repeated.

"But they didn't actually do anything to us."

"You know deep down that if the cop and Michael hadn't showed up, something was going to happen, and it wasn't going to be good."

Brian tried to lower his head, but Brett forced him to look into his eyes.

"Brian, you saved our lives. First with the psycho in the woods last winter. Then at George's ranch, and now at the pond."

Brian shrugged.

"Seriously, Bri."

Michael watched the two of them and the big wolf, and a wave of sadness washed over him. Watching Brett and Brian made him feel hollow, empty. He had no one who cared about him. There was no one he could talk to. There was no one who would comfort him. There was no one who would hold him. That sum total brought tears to his eyes.

He turned away and busied himself with the horses, stripping them of their saddles and blankets. He led them to the pool at the base of the waterfall and let them drink. Papa joined them.

Michael took off his boots, his socks, and his jeans and waded in and used his hands to pour cold water onto the horses' necks and backs in an effort to cool them down. He frowned, because he didn't have much to feed them.

That done, Michael sat down on a rock with his feet and legs dangling in the cool water.

Brett left Brian, walked over to Michael and stripped out of his shoes, socks, and jeans, wincing at the blisters on his inner thighs. He picked up the boxers to take a closer look. Both had bled and the blisters that hadn't were raised, red, and angry.

"Michael, do you have Vaseline or something?" Brian asked as he bent down to take a closer look at Brett's legs.

He had followed Brett to the small pool after he had gathered himself. Brian rolled up his sleeves and used the cool water to rinse off Brett's left leg and then did the same to the right leg.

"We've got to get something to cover these." He looked up at Brett and said, "Take off your shorts and walk in there."

Brett did as he was told, sucking in his breath at the cold water. "*Je-sus!*"

"Cold?" Michael asked.

"My balls are in my throat!"

"The cold water will reduce the swelling," Brian said.

Michael walked over with Vaseline, some gauze, and some first aid tape. He took a look at Brett and said, "Is your father a horse or something?"

"Don't get him started," Brian said.

"I'm Italian."

Michael shook his head. "And half-horse," he said as he pulled off his shirt and his boxers. He stepped into the pond. "Feels good, huh?"

"It's freezing cold!" Brett said.

Brian wanted to join them. The day was hot and the ride up the mountain made him sweaty. Riding last, dirt, dust, and grime covered him.

"I will keep watch." He said as he looked back down the trail.

"Bri, they're far off, and we won't be here that long."

Brian shrugged and stripped down. He stepped into the pool of water at the base of the waterfall.

Brett slung his arms across Michael's and Brian's shoulders and hugged them. "I love you guys. You too, Michael. You saved our butts at the trading post."

Michael almost told them about the promise he made to O'Connor.

"Where are we going?" he asked Michael.

Michael said as he leaned back into the waterfall to wet down his long hair. He smoothed his hair down and said, "There's a place I know. It's a little bar and diner not far from here. I work there . . . or used to. We can go there, get something to eat, and sleep a little. Rest the horses."

Michael didn't tell them that O'Connor had forbidden him to return. However, it was the only home he had. He had clothes and supplies there that he needed to pick up, since whatever was left at the pond would be gone or ruined by pissed off creeps.

"What about Chinle?" Brett said as he put his arm back across Michael's shoulder.

Michael pursed his lips and shook his head. "I don't think that's a good idea. I think we can hide out at the diner, rest up, and have O'Connor come get us. Might be safer that way."

"What about the horses?" Brian asked.

"We have a garage. We can keep them there and then come back for them. Besides, Brett isn't in shape to ride much further."

"It's not that bad," Brett said.

In unison, both Brian and Michael said, "It's bad," and then the three of them laughed, the first laugh in a long time.

CHAPTER SEVENTY

Archer Goodnight wore dark clothes like the ones he wore at George's ranch, minus the black Stetson. The black sport coat couldn't hide his shoulder holster. His hands were small and soft suggesting his days of working for a living were beyond him.

The house was expansive, like something Graff might see in a fancy magazine. All brick and glass. The house suggested that he had paid others to work for him. Graff wondered about what kind of work the others did after receiving the pictures O'Connor had sent him, forwarded to Pat by Brett.

Two men hovered nearby. Positioned purposely, Graff thought.

The taller of the two, slender but solid, with dark bronze skin that was lined and weathered, stood at an angle away from them. He carried a shotgun. Though his hair was mostly black and wavy, it showed gray at the temples. Graff got a glimpse of it as he took off his hat and readjusted it several times. The sun beat down on him, but he was not invited up on the porch in the shade.

The shorter, older man had a large bandage on his right hand. He sat on a chair in the sun, but opposite the taller man. He also carried a shotgun, though he didn't look comfortable with it.

Graff sensed that Goodnight and his two men had triangulated him and Reyna. Graff kept his hands tented under his chin so the .45 in his shoulder holster would be handy. Reyna had to have noticed the positions of the three men, but didn't show it.

Reyna handed Goodnight his cell and showed him the pictures that were sent.

"This looks a lot like you and your two men."

Goodnight shrugged and handed the cell back as he said, "Hard to say."

Reyna smiled his big toothy grin, his dimple showing, and said, "You think so?" He thumbed to the next picture that showed a closeup of Goodnight. "This is you."

He turned the cell towards Goodnight, who took a sip from his iced tea instead.

"This is your big Caddy. Same license plate as the one sitting over there," Reyna continued. "Same bullet holes described in the email."

"So?"

Reyna leaned back in his chair.

"Why were you on George's property and why did you draw on three fifteen-year-olds?"

Goodnight said nothing.

Reyna tipped his head in the old man's direction, the one seated with the bandage on his hand. Doing so, he never took his eyes off Goodnight when he said, "Your man over there had a pistol shot out of his hand. I think you lost a cowboy hat."

Goodnight sipped his tea.

"We have reports of you bothering several ranchers. Sheep were found shot to death. A sixteen-year-old boy is missing, and the Yazzie family was found dead. Murdered."

A tic, small but noticeable appeared at the corner of Goodnight's left eye. When he reached for the glass of tea, his hand wasn't as steady.

"What do you know about the disappearance of Charles Morning Star and the dead sheep?"

Goodnight stared at Reyna. It wasn't fear, exactly. It seemed to Graff that Goodnight was calculating what and how much to tell the FBI agent.

"The sheep were killed with a shotgun," Graff said. "Like the one your friend is holding. Like the one that was destroyed at George's ranch."

"I'm a businessman. I offered a fair price for their land. A better than fair price, above what those ranches are worth."

"And when the ranchers didn't accept, you tried to motivate them by threatening them and killing their sheep," Graff said.

"And now, Charles Morning Star is missing, and the Yazzie family is dead. Old man Yazzie, his wife, and his two kids," Reyna added.

"We had nothing to do with that!" Goodnight said leaning forward and raising his voice. "Nothing!"

"And Charles Morning Star?" Graff said.

"Nothing to do with that, either. We were looking for him." As he said it, his eyes shifted to his iced tea.

"Why?" Reyna said.

Goodnight shook his head and clammed up.

Graff leaned forward and said in a loud enough voice so that the other two men would hear, "If you ever go onto George Tokay's land again, there will be a lawsuit slapped on you and your company, courtesy of the FBI. If something happens to Charles Morning Star or to George or to any of the other kids, I will personally hunt your ass down." Graff looked pointedly at both men and said, "And that goes for these two idiots as well."

"You can't come here and threaten me like that!"

"I'm not threatening you," Graff said. "I'm making you a promise."

The two men faced off. Reyna was temporarily forgotten, as Goodnight sized up Graff, wondering who he was. He didn't look or act like FBI. Reyna never introduced him, and Graff never introduced himself. It was all prearranged on the ride to Goodnight's ranch.

"Here is my card," Reyna said pushing his card towards Goodnight. "If you ... *recall* something you ... *forgot* to mention, call me. Either way, I'll have other agents stop by to get a statement from you and your two friends."

Reyna and Graff pushed themselves up from their chairs and started down the steps when Reyna turned back around and asked, "Say, I forgot to ask. What do you know about Desert Security and what they might be doing on Navajoland?"

"That's who you should be looking for," Goodnight said as he sat deeper into his chair. "I'm a businessman. They aren't."

"And how would you know that?" Graff asked.

Goodnight smiled and said, "Which part, that I'm a businessman or that they aren't?" He took a sip of tea and inspected his immaculate nails.

Graff and Reyna got into the truck, turned around, and drove off.

"He's a piece of shit," Graff muttered.

"A piece of shit who knows more than he shared," Reyna said as he used the side mirror and then the rearview mirror to watch Goodnight's reaction. "Like everyone else we spoke to."

Graff said, "Seems like he didn't like his iced tea. He threw it at us."

Reyna glanced back using his side mirror.

Graff said, "We might have gotten to him."

Graff let silence linger. He wondered if he and Reyna put George, Rebecca, Brett, Brian, and Michael deeper into his crosshairs.

CHAPTER SEVENTY-ONE

Rebecca sat on the edge of the bed and held her brother's hand. He was asleep, though fitfully, moaning as if possessed by a demon. Maybe he was unconscious and fighting his way up from the depths, she did not know.

Someone, probably Mrs. Ngo, had dressed Charles' upper arm and shoulder in a heavy bandage. It was pink from blood. His forehead glistened in sweat, as did his chest and stomach.

"Fever?" George asked *Hosteen* Ngo.

He nodded. "Mai has been sponging him with water from the well to cool him down."

George smiled. Mai meant 'Bright Flower' in Navajo. Mrs. Ngo was just that. Always smiling, eyes disappearing behind wrinkles, one or two teeth missing, little and round.

"How bad is his arm?"

Ngo pursed his lips, and said, "He needs a doctor. More than Mai or I can do for him. And the fever." This last he said shaking his head.

Rebecca wiped off Charles' forehead with the sponge that Mai had given her, and then she turned around and stared at George. It was a silent plea that George had come to know through the years of her friendship. *We need to do something!*

Ngo picked up on it and said, "He is not ready to travel. Perhaps later tonight."

Rebecca focused back on her brother. Ngo touched George's arm and led him outside.

They stood in silence with Ngo staring up at the hills. George was patient. He would wait until Ngo spoke. However, he wondered if the tribal elder was worried about the two men George had left trussed up.

That thought led him to say, "Those two men will not bother you, Father."

Ngo sighed and said, "They will go back to where they came from and others will come." He turned to George and said, "I think you need to take Charles tonight after dark."

George nodded and said, "We have his horse. We will go to the Morning Star ranch and use a truck to get him to the hospital in Chinle."

"They are watching Franklin and Rosetta."

George squatted down and lowered his head. The smartest thing would be to call Graff or O'Connor. However, he did not know who he was up against or how many. He did not know the reason anyone was being watched. If someone watched Ngo, then there was a distinct possibility that someone would be watching Graff and O'Connor. They would lead whoever it was to George, Rebecca, and Charles.

Still staring at the ground, George asked, "Who is watching Rebecca's parents?"

Ngo stuffed his hands into his front pockets, shrugged and said, "One group or the other."

George stood up and said, "Did Charles say anything about why he left or who had shot him?"

Ngo shook his head. "We found him lying near our pump. He was unconscious."

George frowned and asked, "Father, what is happening in *Diné Bikéyah*? There were three men at my family's ranch. First, the man told us to leave because we were trespassing, but then he told me he wanted to buy the ranch from me."

"Archer Goodnight. *Dine'*, but more like *Biligaana*."

George knew the Navajo taboo of mentioning the dead, so he said, "Rebecca and I came across a Navajo family who had been murdered, but I do not think it was this Goodnight. The weapons were different."

Ngo turned around and stared up at the Chuskas that loomed off in the distance. Still facing the mountains, he said, "*Biligaana* want to drill on our land. Pollute our water. Kill our deer and elk. They say it will bring us jobs and money. These *Biligaana* have other *Biligaana* who do their dirty work with guns and fists. All of them share a dark heart filled with greed."

"If you and the elders refuse to let them . . ." George let the statement trail off.

"I wish *Hosteen* Tokay stood with me. The *Dine'* need to hear his voice." He turned around, frowned at George, and said, "The *Dine'* call you *Hosteen* Tokay now. Perhaps our people need to hear your voice."

Surprised, George fell silent. A thousand and one thoughts raced through his mind. He was as much humbled as frightened.

He saw himself as a boy, as *Dine'*, then as a grandson to *Hosteen* Tokay, then as son to Jeremy and Vicky Evans, and then as brother of the twins, Randy and Billy, brother of Brett and Bobby, and Brian. A boy, *Dine'*, grandson, son, and brother. This was how he had defined himself. He had never pictured himself in the same light or even the shadow of the light as his grandfather. He did not see himself as *Hosteen Anything*.

The other surprise was that George had held to the belief that Ngo did not like his grandfather. Respect, if indeed there was respect, was bestowed begrudgingly. With these last words Ngo spoke, George had to reevaluate this belief.

In Navajo, George said, "Father, I am a boy."

Ngo smiled at George and placed a hand on his shoulder and said, "It is common that a boy becomes a man. Perhaps that time has come."

Ngo let that sit between them for a moment, and then he said, "Come, let us eat and rest before you leave."

George followed him back into the house with new eyes and a new focus.

CHAPTER SEVENTY-TWO

They had decided to check out the pond where the boys were camping to see if they could round them up and get them to safety. They hadn't heard from Mills and that concerned them both.

Their focus was Desert Security and who they were working for. Their suspicion was that they, or at least some members, were working off book and unknown to the Phoenix office, though Graff was not as convinced as Reyna.

Reyna called the FBI office in Albuquerque requesting any information on where the drilling might be taking place and what they were mining. If the mining was taking place in the area near Brett's, Brian's and Michael's campsite, they would be in danger, though the pond was at the base of the Chuskas. Even so, it was near enough to concern Graff.

"And if possible, have someone find out how many Desert Security personnel are actually on the reservation," Graff asked with his head turned out the side window.

"Did you get that?" Reyna asked.

Graff never heard the answer, but he did hear the report of a rifle as a bullet slammed through the windshield and into Reyna's right shoulder.

Reyna's foot stomped down on the accelerator and both hands came off the wheel.

"*Jesus! Fuck!*" Reyna screamed.

Blood poured down his arm and between the fingers of his left hand as he gripped his throbbing shoulder. He slumped toward Graff.

Graff reacted quickly. He gripped the wheel, kicked Reyna's foot off the gas pedal, and slammed on the brakes in one motion. He wrenched the gearshift into park and pulled Reyna down onto the seat. Graff lay over him as two more bullets slammed into the windshield inches from his head and back.

Jamie grabbed Reyna's cell off the floor. The agent on the other end peppered Reyna/Graff with, *"What's happening? Ron? Are you there? Ron?"*

"We're under fire! Reyna's hit!"

The voice on the other end said, *"Where are you?"*

"Shit, I don't know!"

Graff got an idea. "Can you ping Reyna's cell to determine our location?"

Silence, and then, *"I can't, but I can get someone who can."*

"Do it. I'll keep it on, but I'm getting us the fuck out of here. Pass the location on to the Navajo Nation Police out of Shiprock. There's an officer there . . . Thompson. Get him the information. He'll know what to do."

Graff knelt down on the shotgun side floor, yanked Reyna into the shotgun seat, but kept him lower than the dashboard. He climbed over the top of the injured agent and into the driver's side.

Graff slammed the gearshift into reverse, adjusted the rearview mirror and the side mirror so he could drive backwards without running into anything. He bounced off a boulder, zig-zagged down the road, and backed behind an outcropping of rock. For the time-being, they were safe, unless the assailant shifted his or their position.

He pulled out his clean hanky and stuffed it into the hole in Reyna's arm. The wound looked like a through and through. He turned around and found a bullet hole in the driver's seat.

"You need to hold this tight! How do I get to Chinle from here?"

Even though Reyna had dark bronze skin, he looked ashen. He licked his lips and said, "Back where we came from. Kind of. Head East and then South. Use the Nav system for our hotel."

He leaned his head against the armrest and shut his eyes.

Two thoughts ran through Graff's mind. He had to get to Chinle in a hurry or Reyna might bleed to death. The second thought was, who was shooting at them and why?

The last thought sent chills down Graff's spine. They had not gotten to the pond. Where were the boys?

CHAPTER SEVENTY-THREE

Nearly asleep in the saddle, backs and legs stiff, and bellies clamoring to be filled, it was dusk when the boys stopped in the turnout a mile from Red Rock, the same turnout where O'Connor hired Michael.

"I'm going ahead and take a look around. I want to make sure it's safe," Michael said as he leaned on the horn of the saddle. "Take care of my pack horse and rest. We're almost there."

"You sure you want to go by yourself?" Brett asked. "I can go with you if you want."

"I'll be okay. It will be safer if I go alone. Just watch and listen for anything unusual."

"Like what?" Brian asked.

Michael thought for a minute. Once again it occurred to Brett that Michael could have been a younger, smaller version of George. Same expression. Same thoughtfulness. Same blend of seriousness and playfulness.

"The road beyond this hill isn't traveled on much. If you hear a car or truck slow down and stop, get on the horses and ride East," he pointed the direction he intended to go. "You'll come to a little town. Don't go in right away. Stay back. I'll find you."

"We should all go together," Brian said. He made a promise to Vicky to keep Brett and George safe. Brian extended that promise to include Michael.

Michael smiled at him and said, "I'll be okay. You will too. Just stay alert."

With a quiet *"Haw"* and a gentle nudge of his heels into his horse's ribs, he took off on a cantor. As he did, he pulled his rifle out of the scabbard and held it across his lap.

Brett and Brian watched him until he was obscured by pine and scrub.

"I can't get over how much he looks and acts like George," Brett said.

"Michael is more talkative. George is quieter and more serious."

Brett stretched and said, "My ass hurts and so do my legs. I think my balls melted into the crack of my ass."

"That's disgusting! Let me see your legs," Brian said. "I want to change your bandages."

He dug around in Michael's packhorse and found gauze, tape, and Vaseline. He turned back around and found Brett with his jeans and boxers down at his ankles.

"If someone comes up on us, they will wonder," he said.

"You're a dork," Brian said dryly.

He peeled off the tape anchoring the gauze that showed some blood. The tape pulled on little brown hairs on Brett's inner thigh. His legs, like his face, chest, back and arms, were deeply tanned. His legs toned and muscular.

"Pull it fast," Brett said.

"I don't want to hurt you," Brian said.

"Just do it. If you're that concerned, you can always kiss it."

"Maybe I will," Brian said as he glanced up at him as he yanked off the tape.

"Damn!" Brett hissed.

Brian smiled as he showed the tape to Brett. It had brown hair stuck to it.

"I'll get some water and wash it off before I put Vaseline on it."

Brian walked back to Michael's packhorse and pulled out a bottle of water. He knelt down in front of Brett and poured some water into his hand, some onto Brett's leg, and cleaned off the wound.

"It doesn't look as bad as it did," Brian said.

"Yeah, well, football starts next week, so it has to heal fast."

Brian applied the Vaseline in a thick layer. He took out the gauze and taped it down. He repeated the process to Brett's right leg and then examined his work.

"You forgot to kiss it," Brett said with a chuckle. "I'm disappointed."

Brian said, "When you least expect it."

Brett pulled his boxers and jeans up, and said, "I can't wait."

Brian sat down against a rock, took off his cowboy hat and fanned himself. He sniffed one armpit, and then the other. "I stink." Papa, the big wolf-dog lay down next to him with his big head in Brian's lap. Brian scratched the big dog behind the ear with his free hand.

"I don't smell so good either," Brett answered as he sat down next to Brian, leaning into him. He adjusted his Badger snapback, ran a hand through his hair, and then set it back on.

He asked, "Are you doing okay, Bri? I mean, about everything?"

Brian nodded, but looked away as he did. He fiddled with his cowboy hat, but had stopped fanning himself.

Brett slung his arm around Brian's shoulder, gave him a one-armed hug, and kissed the side of his head near the temple.

"I love you, Bri. Sometimes I think you and Randy are better than the rest of us."

Brian turned to look at him. "I don't feel better. I might have killed those guys back there. What if I did, Brett?" He paused and whispered, "I think I screwed up. Twice."

Papa, sensing Brian's mood, lifted his head and gave Brian a doggie kiss. Brian didn't mind. He hugged Papa and buried his face into its fur.

Brian wanted to add that what was really weighing on his heart was that he was afraid that he had screwed up the family, his friendship with Bobby, and his friendship with George. He was afraid that Jeremy and Vicky wouldn't trust him alone around Bobby any longer, or not trust him alone with any of the guys. Hell, Bobby might not trust him by himself either. Each of those fears- all of them- had been growing like a raging beast since the morning they left for the trip. He believed he had lost Bobby forever.

Just as big a fear was that by shooting the wheels of the truck and causing the accident, instead of protecting Brett and George, he had made things worse. For Michael, too. Somebody would want revenge.

"Bri, you worry too much," Brett said as if he had read Brian's thoughts.

Brian's only response was to shrug and look away.

"Bri, you know I love you, right? No matter what," Brett said giving Brian's shoulder a squeeze. "Mom and dad, the guys- all of us- love you."

Brian shrugged.

"Things will be okay. You'll see."

They sat in the dirt against the big boulder. Weird that they hadn't seen any birds or other wildlife. Papa lifted his head expectantly. So wrapped up in their own thoughts, neither boy had noticed what the big dog had done.

"You guys ready?" Michael asked leaning over the rock they had their backs against.

Both boys jumped. Brian barrel-rolled and came up with his rifle aimed at Michael. He had even thumbed the safety off. Papa lay in the dirt with what looked like a grin on its big head.

"*Je-sus!* Stop sneaking up like that!" Brett said.

Michael dissolved in laughter, but managed, "Gotcha!"

Brett said as he scrambled up. "You are a little shit, you know that, right?"

"If you say so," Michael said laughing.

"But I kinda like you anyway," Brett laughed.

Brian thumbed the safety back on and slung the rifle on his back.

"Everything okay? No problems?"

Michael said, "I think all's good. Let's go."

As they mounted up once again, Brian heard a familiar, unmistakable voice. He alone heard it. The voice was meant for him, and it was a warning.

CHAPTER SEVENTY-FOUR

Sutured and wearing a sling, Reyna waved away any of the pain meds the emergency doctor offered him with the explanation, "I need to think clearly."

"I'm sure you're in a great deal of pain, but if not, you will be. You will need these meds."

Reyna slipped his arm out of the sling and buttoned up his bloody shirt using his one good hand. He fumbled badly and got buttons linked to the wrong holes. He tucked in the front half of his shirt, but the back hung out. Reyna slipped his arm back into his sling and tried to smile at Graff, but failed. His dimple didn't show. He listed to the side and steadied himself on the hospital bed. He fought off a wave of nausea, but regained his balance.

A young nurse holding a clipboard and pen opened the curtain, stepped around it, and closed the curtain behind her.

"Because it was a gunshot, there are a few questions to ask."

"I gave you everything you need." He nodded at Graff and said, "My partner and I need to go. We don't have time."

"Sir," the nurse said as she stood in front of him.

Graff cleared his throat and said, "Ron, answer the questions. I'll go up and see Pat. When you're done, meet me up there."

Reyna sighed, and to the nurse said, "What do you need?"

Graff turned around and left. The emergency doc was waiting for him beyond the curtain and motioned him away towards the nurse's station.

"Here are pain meds. I know neither you nor I can force feed him these, but you know him better than I do. If he needs something, here they are," he said handing them a small plastic bottle with ten pills. "Whether or not he admits it, he's in a great deal of pain."

Graff smiled, took the bottle and shoved it into his front shirt pocket. "He's a tad bullheaded, but I'll see what I can do."

Graff went off in search of his friend and sometime partner. The room wasn't hard to find because two men, a chubby, stocky Navajo cop, and a young guy with a haircut that screamed '*Fed!* sat outside the door. Both stood as Graff approached.

"I'm Jamie Graff, a detective from Waukesha, Wisconsin. Pat O'Connor is my friend. He's a sheriff detective from Waukesha County. We've worked together, and both of us came out here to help George Tokay and Rebecca Morning Star find Charles, Rebecca's brother and George's friend."

Neither of them moved.

Graff tried again. "Could one of you check with Pat and let him know I'm here?"

"Jamie, come in," O'Connor said loudly enough for the bookends to hear.

"Excuse me," Graff said. Neither moved, so he slid between them.

He spied O'Connor and chuckled. "You look like shit."

"I feel like shit."

Graff sat down in an uncomfortable chair at the side of the bed, stared at his friend, and said, "Seriously, how do you feel?"

"I seriously feel like shit."

"What's hurting?"

O'Connor slid a finger under the sunglasses he wore, rubbed first one eye and then the other and said, "Easier to tell you what doesn't. I hurt all over. I think my head was run over. My back is killing me. I don't know what the hell happened to my arms or hand, but they hurt when I move them."

"At least you have good-looking sunglasses," Graff smirked.

"Yeah, well . . ."

"I think the military calls them B.C.Gs."

"What's that mean?"

Graff smiled and said, "Birth Control Glasses, because anyone who wears them won't get anything from anyone."

O'Connor glared at him and said, "Besides giving me a hard time, is there a reason you came up here?"

Graff looked down at the floor, then leaned forward and spoke quietly.

"Something's bothering me, Pat. Something's not right about any of this."

O'Connor waited.

"I get that Goodnight would check George's land to see if anyone was on it. Reyna mentioned that word travels fast around here, so he might have picked up that George and the boys were there."

"And?"

"That might explain Goodnight. He wants to build a resort, so he scares ranchers by killing their sheep to intimidate them."

"He's stupid, but not really a criminal, if you know what I mean."

Graff nodded, "Agreed!"

"So," O'Connor prompted.

"We also know that Desert Security is on the reservation ostensibly to protect some mining company who wants to do some drilling."

O'Connor almost nodded, but thought better of it and sat still.

"But there's something bothering me about all of this. How did they know you were a cop? How did they know where you were staying? How did they know what road you were on?"

"I found a GPS tracker on my car, remember?"

Graff nodded and said, "Yeah, I remember. But how did they know to put it on your car? How did they know you were dangerous to them?"

O'Connor looked towards the door as Reyna strolled in.

"What the hell happened to you?" O'Connor asked.

"Someone shot at us. We left Goodnight and were headed to the pond to check on the boys," Reyna said.

"What the fuck is going on?" O'Connor asked.

"That's only part of what bothers me," Graff said.

"What?" Reyna asked.

"Here's the thing," Graff said. "According to Brett's email and the pictures he sent to you, three guys just happened to show up at the Trading Post. According to Brett, who is perceptive about this shit- way more than any fifteen-year-old should be- they came looking for them. One of them said something like, 'I thought you'd be bigger!' when Michael came through the backdoor."

"He thought Michael was George?" O'Connor said.

Reyna sat down on the side of the bed. He said, "Why would they be after the boys?"

"That's one question. The other would be, how did they know the boys would be at the trading post?" Graff said.

The three men sat quietly. Finally, Reyna said, "They knew the boys would be there."

O'Connor sat up straighter. He said, "Who told them the boys would show up there and at that time?"

"Why would someone tell them?" Reyna asked. "What could they possibly want with the boys? For all they or anyone knows, they're camping and hunting. Dozens of tourists do that."

"None of this makes sense. In any crime, pieces fall into place," O'Connor said. Then he added, "This is doing nothing for my headache."

Graff stood up, looked out the window, and then stepped quietly to O'Connor's bed. He leaned over and whispered, "I don't know the answers to your questions. I don't know how the boys fit into this. Maybe just collateral. You're right, nothing fits. Two seemingly separate groups of bad guys both wanting something that seems to be unrelated. But I'm wondering." He paused, sat back down in the chair and leaned forward. He had whispered before, but he spoke even more softly. "I wonder if the same guy who shot at Ron and me tipped off the three guys about the boys being at the trading post."

He let that sit there like an unexploded grenade.

It was Reyna who first registered the magnitude of Graff's suggestion. Though aching and suffering from a major concussion, O'Connor wasn't far behind.

"That makes sense in a weird way. What would he hope to gain?" Reyna asked as he squinted at the window beyond Graff.

"And why?" Graff added.

"We need to warn the boys," Pat said.

CHAPTER SEVENTY-FIVE

They rode towards the town single-file. The goal was to arrive in the dark. Michael stayed in the front with his packhorse trailing behind him, while Brian brought up the rear. Papa would race ahead, though he didn't stray too far, then he'd double back.

Brian kept turning around to watch the trail behind them wondering and worrying. He felt uneasy, like they were being watched. Perhaps it was the voice he had recognized. Despite the heat, he shivered.

When they reached the town, Michael brought them to a halt and then jumped off his horse. Brett and Brian did the same. Brian stretched and walked stiff-legged. Brett winced with each step. Brian knew the blisters hurt him more than he let on.

Michael led them down a narrow passageway to the side of a rickety wooden building, smaller and in worse shape than the taller, newer-looking building standing next to it. There weren't any lights in town except for one or two cook fires or lanterns in windows. Several porches showed cigarette tips burning reddish-orange.

At a diagonal across the street, a few young kids played some game in the dirt road. They either didn't see the three boys or if they did, they paid no attention. One dog barked, and it was answered by another. The town smelled of wood smoke, and that reminded the three boys just how hungry they were.

Barely above a whisper, Brett asked, "Where are we?"

"Red Rock. I live above the diner," he said jerking his head that direction. He jerked his head in the other direction and said, "This is the garage. Lou keeps his truck in there."

"Will he mind us coming over?" Brian asked.

"He's not around."

Curious in the way he said it, Brett asked, "Where is he?"

Michael shrugged and said, "Not sure, but he's not around. I don't think he will be for a while."

"Is he your dad?" Brian asked.

"He's just a guy," was all Michael said. His tone was low. Neither Brett nor Brian could tell if his voice had a hint of anger or sadness. Perhaps both.

Michael led his horses towards the large swinging garage door so the questions would end, and he expected the two boys to follow him.

"Stay quiet," Michael cautioned. "I don't want people to know we're here."

Brett glanced at Brian. Brian's only response was to purse his lips and glance around in all directions. He tugged on his rifle strap.

They operated in the dark, but the three boys managed to strip off saddles, blankets, and bridles. They led the horses into a small corral. Not too big, but big enough for the four horses. Michael rummaged through the pack that had been carried on one of the horses and frowned at his meager belongings. Most of his stuff was at the pond . . . or was. No telling where it was now or in what shape.

Without being asked, Brian found a pitchfork and fed the four horses hay from the stacked bales against one of the walls. Michael fed them buckets of water from a pump in back of the garage, and some oats from a barrel in the corner. Brett didn't know what he should do, so he sat down on one of the bales of hay, out of their way. He stretched his legs and thought about stripping out of his jeans. Papa kept him company, but the big dog watched Brian.

Both Brian and Michael knew they should wash down the horses and pick gravel from their hooves, but without light and without making noise, it wasn't possible. Maybe later or in the morning. However, Brian didn't know because the plans were unclear.

The truck off to one side was a middle-aged black Chevy Silverado. A dent or two, but no rust. From the outside at least, Brett thought it looked to be in good condition.

"Does the truck run?" Brett asked. He didn't want to get back on a horse anytime soon.

"Yup."

Michael and Brian stood side by side watching the horses eat and drink.

Michael elbowed him and asked, "How do you know so much about horses? You handle the chores well, and you rode bareback like a pro."

"George taught me. I like horses and I don't mind the work."

Michael nodded and said, "We might have to make you an honorary Navajo."

Brian smiled at him and impulsively slung an arm across Michael's shoulders.

"You said you live above a diner. Do you think we could get something to eat? We can pay," Brett said.

"Come on," Michael said leading them out of the garage. "We'll go in the side door."

He peered out the door of the barn at the street, didn't see anything unusual, so he gestured to Brett and Brian to follow him. Michael knelt down, lifted a loose board in the walkway and searched for a key. It was there. He stood up and showed the key to the two boys.

There was yellow and black crime scene tape blocking the door along with a post warning anyone who entered that they would be trespassing.

"Wait!" Brett said. "I don't think we can go in there."

"It's where I live," Michael said.

"Yeah, but if we go in there, we're breaking the law," Brett said.

Michael sighed. He flapped his arms at his side and said, "Look, my stuff is in there. I need it. I don't have any other place to go, so I'm going in. If you want to stay out here, fine."

He turned around, stuck the key into the lock, and pushed open the door. He turned around once more, shrugged, and entered, but left the door open for them.

Both Brian and Brett hesitated, but followed.

"Come in and shut the door. Wait here. I'll get flashlights."

Michael wasn't gone more than a minute or two and when he returned, he had two flashlights. He used one and gave the other to Brett.

"Keep the light low. I don't want to let anyone know we're inside."

"Michael, where is the guy you live with?" Brian asked.

"It's complicated," was the only response Michael gave as he walked deeper into the bar. "You guys have your cell phones? If you do, plug them in and charge them."

"I'll get them," Brian said. "You, get out of those jeans. I want to change your bandages. When I'm done, I'll help you."

If he kept the phones off, they'd charge faster, so that's what Brian did. He searched for outlets in the logical places, found them behind the bar and

243

plugged them in. They needed the cell phones charged, but he was in no hurry to get any of the texts and phone messages waiting for them.

The bar smelled of bacon, grease, and stale cigarettes. Brian wrinkled up his nose. He walked to the back where the storeroom was and found Michael hunched over loose floorboards. He was placing money in two stacks.

"Whose is that?"

Without looking up, Michael said, "Mine and Lou's. He gets more than I do, but he told me about a third of it is mine. That's what I'm taking. I'll put the rest back."

Brian watched him, and then asked, "Where's Brett?"

"Upstairs. There's a bedroom, a bathroom, and an office. He's up there somewhere."

Brian took the stairs carefully, relying on his feet and sense of touch. He turned on his flashlight, cupped his hand over the lighted end and kept it aimed at the floor.

"Brett?"

"In here."

Brian followed the voice to the bedroom and found Brett examining the nightstand on one side of the bed. He'd lift something up, look at it, and then put it back down. He did that with each item. When he finished looking at each item, he went through the two drawers.

That done, Brett turned around and said, "This reminds me of the room I was locked in when I was in Chicago."

Brian thought he knew what he meant, but said, "What do you mean?"

"You know what I mean," Brett said quietly. "I think it explains the crime scene tape."

CHAPTER SEVENTY-SIX

They had to prevent Charles from gulping down water.

"Slow down, Charles," Rebecca cautioned. "Small sips."

Charles nodded, but still tried to drink faster than he should. To prevent this, Rebecca would snatch the glass and hold it away from him, and only after waiting a minute or two did she bring it back to his lips.

He was slick with sweat. His fever might have broken or it could have been the heat of the night and the back room of the hogan they were in, she wasn't sure.

George entered and sat down on the opposite side of the bed from Rebecca.

"Do you feel well enough to travel?"

Charles licked his lips and said, "I think so."

"Your ranch is a fair distance."

"I can do it."

Rebecca shot George a worried glance, and Charles picked up on it.

To Rebecca he said, "I can do it."

"I would like to leave after midnight. Get some sleep."

"Why that late?" Rebecca asked.

Charles studied George and said to Rebecca without taking his eyes off his best friend, "Safer that way."

George smiled, nodded and said, "Eat a little. Drink a lot. And sleep. I need you to be stronger."

Charles licked his lips, nodded, and reached for more water.

"Who shot you?" Rebecca asked.

"Goodnight and the two others showed up wanting to buy the sheep and our land. I told them no. They left. Then someone shot me. I think from the ridge above George's ranch."

"You didn't see anything?" Rebecca asked.

Charles shook his head. "Nothing."

"You don't know who it was?" George asked.

Charles shook his head again. "No. Whoever it was, had to be up in the tree line above your land. After I was shot, the horse took off. I had to hold on. There was another shot, but it went wide. I kept going. I ended up in the Chuskas beyond the pond, near the waterfall. I think I passed out. When I came to, I knew I had to hole up. I lost a lot of blood. My arm went to shit." He saw Ngo standing in the doorway and said, "I'm sorry, Father. My arm was useless. I still can't move it."

Ngo showed no reaction.

"Why didn't you come home?" Rebecca asked.

"Becca, you, mom, and dad would have been in danger."

"But you could have died," Rebecca said.

George could not tell if Rebecca was angry, sad, or scared.

Charles smiled at her and said, "But I didn't."

When Charles finished, Ngo said, "Charles, rest now. I want to speak with your sister and *Hosteen* Tokay." He turned and left the room.

George followed immediately, while Rebecca used a towel to dry off Charles' face, neck and chest.

"Do you need to go to the outhouse?"

"No. I'll call you or George if I do."

Reluctantly, she stood and left the room in search of Ngo and George. Mai Ngo sat in a comfortable chair near a lantern sewing a patch on a pair of jeans. She smiled at Rebecca and nodded towards the door. Rebecca smiled back and walked that direction.

She found both in the front yard facing the Chuskas.

"Father, do you know who might have shot him?" George asked.

"I have my suspicions, but I am not sure."

"We need to warn your brothers," Rebecca said.

George frowned. "Warn them of what? We do not know who shot Charles. We know it has something to do with Goodnight, but that is all we know."

Both George and Rebecca looked to Ngo for guidance. His face was a cloud. Now and then, he would nod, then squint up at the Chuskas, and then nod again.

"Tell your brothers that they cannot trust anyone. Those who seek to help might do so only to harm."

George nodded. He had to warn not only Brian, Brett, and Michael but also Graff, O'Connor, and Reyna.

"Tell them things are not what they seem."

"I will call Brian and let them know."

Ngo cocked his head and squinted at George. George understood the look. His grandfather had a similar one. George wondered if all old *Dine'* had similar looks born of old age and the knowledge that comes with it.

"I will first warn my brothers. After we begin our journey, I will let Detective Jamie and Detective Pat know."

Ngo regarded him silently.

"We need to get Charles to Chinle." George added, "That is our first priority."

Rebecca shuffled her feet, placed her hands on her hips, and stared at George. She had no idea why George did not want to call his cop friends. It did not make sense.

"I think this is the best way," George said meeting and keeping her eye contact.

Ngo folded his arms across his chest. George did not know if he was in favor of it or not.

CHAPTER SEVENTY-SEVEN

"Any luck getting a hold of the boys?" Reyna asked.

Graff shook his head. He wanted to throw his cell phone against the wall. Anger, frustration, fear- he felt it all.

"Pat, do you know where they might go?" Jamie asked.

Pat wasn't up to thinking deeply or quickly. His head ached. Simple things he couldn't remember. He had trouble thinking of his partner's name. Graff had to prompt him, before O'Connor snapped his fingers and said, "Paul Eiselmann."

Graff knew the head trauma was profound. O'Connor and Eiselmann were childhood friends. O'Connor had lived with Paul much like Brian lived with Jeremy and boys before Jeremy had adopted him.

In the end and in answer to Graff's question as to where the boys might be, Pat said, "I have no idea."

Graff looked to Reyna for help, but Reyna raised his hands, shook his head, and said, "No clue. But they are smart guys, right?"

Graff nodded.

Reyna tried to offer up encouragement when he said, "They might not know the area, but they have good instincts."

Graff stood up and paced the small hospital room, his left hand on his hip and the other on top of his head. Reyna and O'Connor watched him, but said nothing.

"Is it possible for you to get agents to look for them?"

Reyna puffed up his cheeks and then blew the air out.

Graff explained, "I mean, you have Goodnight and his two goons. At least two goons, but could be more. Then you have the three or four assholes who threatened the boys at the trading post. The same assholes who ran Pat off the road and put him in the hospital. Almost killed him."

Reyna looked doubtful, shrugged and said, "We already have agents out here. We have a bunch looking into Desert Security. We have one outside Pat's room."

"But we don't have any agents looking for the boys. Those boys mean everything to Pat and me, and we don't know where they are! We can't get in touch with them for whatever reason, and that's not like them. Pat gets a text or two a day from both Brett and Brian. George texts me at least once a day. That's their normal."

"What are you saying?" Reyna asked.

"We told them they needed to check in with us each day, once or twice a day, and definitely when there was trouble. We heard from George once and Brett twice. That's it. They never told us where they were. They never told us they were safe. Just the opposite. George sent us pictures of the Yazzie family. Brett sends us an email and pictures of the assholes who are after them for whatever the hell reason. But not once did they tell us they are safe."

"It could be their phones being dead," Reyna said.

"Mills was supposed to find them and get them to Chinle. That hasn't happened. Hell, he said he didn't know where they were," Graff said.

O'Connor first raised a hand and then waved it. "The boys are with Michael. He knows this land. He knows where to go, where to hide if they are in trouble. Brett or Brian will contact us if they need to. It pisses me off that they haven't, but their cells might be dead or they are in an area where there is no reception. They know to reach out if the need us."

Graff snapped his fingers and said, "Remember on the plane . . . George said something about going to the mesa if they were in trouble."

Reyna sat up straight and said, "*Chaha'oh* Mesa. Shadow Mesa, named after George."

"Yes, that's the one," Graff said. "What if that's where the boys are? Mills wouldn't know to look there. He wasn't a part of the conversation." Graff scrunched up his face and said, "Do you remember mentioning it to him? Either of you?"

Reyna thought for a moment and then shook his head.

"I can't remember a fucking thing." O'Connor sunk back into his bed, shut his eyes, and put an arm over his sunglasses. He said, "My fucking head is killing me. Jesus!"

Graff and Reyna looked at O'Connor, and then at each other. Graff wasn't as confident as O'Connor was that the boys were safe. They might be at the mesa waiting for O'Connor, Reyna, and Graff to come get them.

He walked to the door of O'Connor's room, stuck his head out and asked the chunky Navajo cop to step inside. The cop obeyed and stood quietly at the foot of O'Connor's bed.

"Is there anyway, short of calling Mills, to find out where he might be?" Graff asked.

The Navajo cop thought for a minute, pursed his lips and said, "Not really. It's a big reservation and not too many of us. He could be anywhere."

"But he's assigned to an area, right?" Reyna asked.

"Yes, that's right."

"Where exactly is his area?" Graff asked.

"From the Chuskas to the valley below, as far as Round Rock."

Graff had an idea. He walked down the hallway away from the Navajo cop and FBI agent, and away from O'Connor's room. He pulled out his cell and using speed dial, punched a call to a friend.

"Eiselmann."

For a second, Graff wondered if this was such a good idea.

"Paul, this is Graff. I need a favor and I need it kept quiet."

"What's up? Everything okay? Are the boys okay?"

Graff heard the panic in his voice. He hesitated. He didn't want to share too much because it would cause a domino effect. If Eiselmann knew about O'Connor, he'd be on a plane in a heartbeat. So would Albrecht, along with Jorgenson and Kaupert. It was a tight group. They had each other's backs, and it didn't matter what shit show it was.

At the same time, Graff knew better than to lie to Eiselmann. Lies break trust, and a lack of trust ruins friendships.

"We believe so. That's the best I can say, which is why I'm calling."

"What do you need?"

"Paul, I need you to contact Morgan Billias. I need him to ping a cell phone and pinpoint its location."

No one actually knew who Morgan Billias was. No one knew where he lived. No one knew what his job was. No one knew if that was his real name. All anyone knew, at least all that law enforcement knew, was that he was a tech wizard who helped good guys beat bad guys. It was suspected that Billias worked at one of the alphabet agencies in D.C., but that was only a guess.

Eiselmann met him online through Chet Walker, an FBI agent who met him at a tech convention. At that time, Walker was a hacker. The FBI made him one of theirs and from time to time, Walker reached out to Billias whenever there was a need or when Walker couldn't figure something out on his own. Trouble was, Walker died during the summer of death. Fortunately, before he had died, he had passed Billias' name and number to Eiselmann.

Paul hesitated and then said, "I have no problem doing that, but as you may recall, Summer and Kelliher had a problem the last time I contacted him without asking their permission. They consider him to be their asset."

"I know that, but I need you to contact him without anyone knowing it."

"It's that important?" Eiselmann asked, already knowing the answer.

Graff pictured Eiselmann already firing up his laptop.

"I wouldn't be calling if it wasn't."

"Okay, give me the number."

It didn't take more than ten minutes.

"Morgan says hello," Eiselmann said when Graff answered on the first buzz.

"That was quick."

"Yeah, well..."

"He has a location?"

"Yes. He pinged the number. It was on. He used Google Earth and pinpointed the location. The cell is in the Chuska mountains, heading East. He's moving faster than he would be if he was on foot, so he's thinking he's in a vehicle. The location is above a pond and near a waterfall." He paused and said, "Does any of that make sense?"

"Yes, it does. Please thank him for me."

"He wanted to know if you wanted him to continue to track it for you?"

"If it wouldn't be too much trouble."

"He already said he would, but he just wanted confirmation you wanted him to."

Graff smiled and said, "Thank him for me."

He had another idea.

"Paul, could you also ask him to track Brett's, Brian's, and George's numbers? Chances are their phones are off or dead, but it would be nice to know where they are when they come on."

"I'll ask him, but I'm sure he will."

"Paul, thanks for your help. Please keep me posted."

The call ended and for the first time in a while, Graff's nerves settled.

CHAPTER SEVENTY-EIGHT

A sliver of a moon and surrounding stars showed through a patchwork of clouds. A cool breeze, not uncomfortable, had picked up from the Northwest. Coyotes howled off in the distance. They shared the valley with grazing elk and deer who seemed to either not notice or not care the interlopers moved on their perimeter.

Charles listed first to one side and then the other. His heavily bandaged arm fit in a sling, and his chin rested on his chest with a grimace shown on his face. His eyes were shut, and he had a lean to him that indicated that he might be asleep or unconscious. Rebecca rode next to him and would hold on to his good arm or shoulder if he leaned too far.

George led Charles' horse by the bridle. His eyes watchful, scanning the horizon near and far for anything out of the ordinary. Ngo's words that there were eyes watching had George on alert.

He had called and left voice messages for both Brian and Brett to meet them at the Morning Star ranch. Deciding that wasn't good enough and wanting to be sure, he texted them the same message. He hoped they would receive them and be at the ranch well before sunrise.

George glanced back at Charles and then over at Rebecca. He couldn't tell what the message was in her eyes. He imagined it was fear. Knowing her, a dose of determination as well.

They had a long way to go. At the pace they traveled, it would take well into the night and early morning. George hoped that Charles would survive the trek. He gave little thought to himself, knowing that he'd sacrifice himself to ensure Charles' and Rebecca's safety.

CHAPTER SEVENTY-NINE

Michael had wept when Brett asked him about the man. Brett understood Michael's shame and embarrassment. Michael had described Lou as *'a guy'* who had offered him a job, food, and a place to stay. However, all of it came with expectations. Brett knew all about expectations.

Brian volunteered for the first watch, so he hadn't heard Michael's story.

Brian had rummaged around in the makeshift office, found a pen, two envelopes, two stamps, and lined paper, similar to the type he had used to take notes on at school. The office wasn't neat or orderly like Jeremy's office at home. Rather, this office was a hodge-podge of stacks of papers and folders and bills in haphazard piles.

He had tried to push away the voice he had heard, though the voice was urgent and cautionary. He needed to think clearly to undertake what he needed to do. Besides, Brian didn't need to be told what kind of situation he, Brett, and Michael were in.

Brian chose a booth in the back of the bar where he could see both the front entrance and the hallway that led to the backdoor. Those were the only two entrances, not counting the windows. Papa, the big wolf-dog barely fit under the table. Its head rested on Brian's boots.

He built a contraption using two smelly and stained bar towels that tented over the flashlight in an effort to mute the light. He had rehearsed what he had wanted to say, but was still uncertain how to say it. He began with his letter to Bobby.

Bobby,
There are a lot of things I want to say, but I'm not sure how I want to say them, so this might ramble.
I love you. I love you more than I've ever loved anyone. More than Mom and Dad. More than any of the guys. Maybe more than Brad, though I'm not sure about that. A lot more than Cat. You are the first person I think of when I wake up and the last person I think of before I fall asleep.

Even now, and even though we haven't done anything in a while, I can still feel the muscles in your back, your legs, and your stomach on my fingertips. I still taste your kiss. Kissing you and holding your hand are my two favorite things. I know the spot on your neck just below your ear that tickles you when I kiss you there. I know the spot on your side just below your waist that tickles you. I don't think anyone else knows about those spots. I discovered them and I'm happy about that.

I know I already said this, but I love you. I'm not embarrassed to say that, and I'm not ashamed about anything you and I did together. Anything someone does out of love is good and pure, and I can honestly say that everything I did with you was because I love you. That makes it good and pure no matter what anyone else thinks, and it's good and pure no matter what you think. I will always love you, no matter what you or Mom or Dad or anyone else thinks. I don't give a shit anymore. I love you and because of that, I have no regrets.

The thing is, Bobby, I don't know if I will make it back home. There is some bad shit happening here, and Brett and George and I are in the middle of it. We don't know how we got there, but that's where we are. I think I screwed up a couple of times. Big screw ups. Brett doesn't think so, but I do.

I promised Mom that I would do my best to take care of Brett and George, so if that means that I might not make it home if I can keep them safe, I'm okay with that. It's not that I want to die. It's just that if I have a choice between Brett and George, or me, I'll choose me if that means Brett and George can get back home.

I pray a lot, but you already know that. I'm like Dad that way. I've prayed about you and me, and I've prayed for Brad. He's trying to talk to me, but I want to write this letter first. Then I'll talk with Brad and see what he needs to say. I already know it's something important. But you had to come first. You, and then Mom and Dad. I'll write to them next.

I'll go now. Hopefully, I'll be back. I've made a decision that I think is best for you, for me, and for the family. I will ask Mom and Dad to let me live with Big Gav and his mom. I don't know that I can be around you. It would hurt too much to not touch you when I want to, to not give you that look you and I share.

I would always have to watch what I say. I would have to worry about what Mom or Dad or you are thinking. Even if we're all together in the family room watching TV or something, I'd have to worry about being too close to you. I can't live like that, Bobby. I love you too much and it would hurt too much being around you knowing that you might not love me anymore, or don't want to do anything with me ever again. The thing is, I still love you and I always will. I guess I already wrote that. Sorry.

Better go. It's late.

Love,

Bri

Brian read and then reread his letter. It wasn't perfect, but it was honest. He brushed some tears off his face with his shirt sleeve. His hands and fingers were dirty and grimy and smelled of horse. He hated having dirty hands and dirty fingers. That was his thing.

He sighed. He hoped that Bobby wouldn't think this letter was a guilt trip. He wanted to be as sincere and as honest as he could be. That's how he and Bobby were with each other. He shrugged to no one and decided the letter was the best he could do.

With a sigh, he folded it, placed it in the envelope, and sealed it. He wrote Bobby's name and their address on it. He wrinkled a brow about what to put for the return address and decided to put his name along with Red Rock, AZ, and leave it at that. Finally, he put the stamp on it and set it aside.

He took another sheet of paper, sighed, and began writing.

Mom and Dad:

I needed to write this letter to you because I don't know if Brett or George or I will make it back home. There is some serious stuff happening here. None of us know exactly what it is, but we're in the middle of it. Mom, I told you that I would look out for Brett and George. We haven't seen or talked to George since the day we got here. It's just Brett and me and this kid, Michael Two Feathers. He's a year younger than Bobby, and he's cool. The thing is, he has nowhere to go. He doesn't have a family or a mom and a dad or anyone. So, I'm hoping that he can come home with us. If we're able to get back home.

There are things I want to say if I don't make it. I already wrote to Bobby, but I know I need to write to you too. I will do my best and be as honest as I can. I'm not angry, just sad. Well, a little angry. I can't help it.

I love Bobby. I always have and I always will. I'm not ashamed about anything he and I did together, and I have no regrets. As I said to Bobby, I don't care what anyone else thinks or who else knows, but I love him. Whatever I did with Bobby was out of love, and because it was out of love, there is nothing wrong with that.

The thing is, Bobby told me that he doesn't want to do anything with me anymore. I'm not sure if that is because you talked to him and convinced him of that or if it's his own idea. It doesn't matter. But because of that, I'm asking for your permission to live with Big Gav and his mom, Ellie. I know they will let me. No, I've never done anything with him if that's what you're thinking. I've never done anything with any guy except for Bobby. I never thought about doing anything with any guy until Bobby. That's the truth.

I don't want to have to worry about what you're thinking. I don't want to worry about Bobby and me ending up by ourselves and worrying about what you're thinking. It's been hard enough ever since you made us sleep in different rooms. It's like you don't trust us. Maybe you don't trust me.

Remember that psycho dude that came after George and me? That night, he said that George and I ruined our family by being adopted into it.

Ever since that night, and ever since you made Bobby and me sleep in different rooms, I've been thinking that he's right. I ruined our family by being adopted. Maybe I ruined the family because Bobby and I fell in love. We started out as friends, but little by little, it became way more than that.

The thing is, I don't feel bad about Bobby's and my relationship, at least the relationship we did have. But I do feel bad about making the two of you worry about us. I know you're just being parents. And you're great parents! The best! But I can't live in that house anymore knowing that I somehow messed things up and hurt the family. I don't want to worry about what you think or talk about. And I don't want you to worry about me or Bobby. I don't want Bobby to worry. I think it might be better if I go live with Big Gav and Ellie.

I will visit and sleep over now and then like I used to before my mom and dad died. That is, if you're okay with that. But I think you might be happier if I don't live with you and the guys anymore. I never meant to make you unhappy. Honestly, I love both of you. I love the guys. And I love Bobby, but that's the problem, I think.

So, if by some chance I do make it back home, I hope you will let me move out.

Mom, I want you to know that I will do everything I can to make sure Brett and George are safe. I know Brett means more to you than George or me, and Dad, I know George means more to you than me. After all, he was adopted way before I was. So, if I have to make a choice about whether it's them or me who might die, I will try to make sure they live. I'm okay with that. I've prayed about it. I've accepted it. It's okay.

Brad has been trying to talk to me. I've held him off because I had to write these two letters. But after I mail them, he and I will talk. Maybe he has something to say that might keep us alive. We'll see.

At any rate, please know I love you. I never meant to mess up our family. I never meant to hurt Bobby. I love him too much to do that. I'm sorry!

Love,
Bri

Brian put his head down on his arms and wept. There was so much more he had wanted to write. In the end, as he sealed and addressed the letter. He did the best he could.

At last, he turned off the flashlight. He had noticed the blue mailbox outside of a store across the street when they had first arrived into town. He wanted to mail the letters before he got cold feet. He motioned to Papa to stay where he was. Papa did so reluctantly, pouting as any dog might.

Brian stepped out the backdoor, locked it using the key Michael had used. He replaced the yellow police tape as perfectly as he could. He inspected his work. In the dark, it looked as if it was never broken and that no one had entered the bar.

He reached the corner of the building and peered carefully around the corner. The kids had all gone inside their homes. There were no telltale cigarette or pipe glows from front porches. Adults had vanished inside their homes, too. That was good.

Staying in the shadows, he was able to remain invisible. The hard part was crossing the street out in the open without cover.

Brian looked both ways, took a deep breath, sprinted to the blue mailbox, and dropped both letters into the slot. He was about to sprint back to the bar, but something prevented him from doing so.

It wasn't a voice as much as it was a feeling.

So, instead of running back, he sunk into the doorway of the building and squatted down making himself as small as possible.

A set of headlights appeared over a little hill coming from the direction they had traveled from. It pulled to a stop a block away from the bar. No one got out at first.

Jeremy had an axiom he had mentioned many times in the days and months Brian had lived with them. *If you have a hunch, bet a bunch because your gut doesn't lie.*

Brian swung his rifle from his back, got on one knee and held his rifle at the ready.

It was a jeep, and Brian knew who it was. He didn't know what had prevented him from walking into the street to meet him, but he remained in a shooter's stance.

The deputy didn't even look in Brian's direction. He was intent on the bar. The deputy pulled his revolver from his holster and walked straight towards the building.

He stopped at the front door, tried it, but didn't break the police tape. Satisfied that it was still locked, he went around the side towards the backdoor.

Brian's first thought was that he needed to protect Brett and Michael. He broke away and ran down the other side of the building. It was chancy, in that if the deputy went around the building, Brian would be exposed. He looked for any place to hide.

On the other side of the bar was an outhouse. Brian ran for it. At first, he hid on the side of it, then moved to the back. He stayed low and watched for the deputy.

Sure enough, the deputy crossed the back of the bar peering into the windows. Finally, without looking over at the outhouse, the deputy rounded the side of the building Brian had just run down, and walked towards the front. Brian watched him go.

Only when the deputy disappeared from sight, did Brian run to the back of the building. He crept to the narrow passageway between the garage and the building. Again, staying low, Brian waited until the deputy walked back down the street towards the jeep.

Brian tip-toed up the side of the building, remained in the shadow, and lay down in the dirt with his rifle at the ready. He watched the jeep drive down the street past him and the diner.

Brian didn't move right away. He remained where he was just in case the deputy circled back.

At last, Brian stood up, walked back to the backdoor, used the key to open it, and entered. Papa greeted him, tail wagging.

The first thing he did was go to his cell phone, which was now fully charged. He turned it on and within a minute or two, text message and voicemail icons appeared, each with a buzz and vibration. It might have been his imagination, but the buzzes seemed angry. While he was tempted to check out the five from Bobby, the two from Mom and the two from Dad, and six or so from Graff and O'Connor, the only one he needed to check was the one from George.

He read it twice and then ran up the stairs to wake up Brett and Michael.

CHAPTER EIGHTY

"Billias called. The first number is somebody named Mills. He's a Navajo Sheriff. He was in Red Rock. He didn't stay long. Twenty minutes. Now, it looks like he's on his way to Shiprock, wherever the hell that is."

Graff remained silent.

"Funny thing. Brian turned on his cell. He's in Red Rock. Still is, or was. He's turned off his cell. Maybe Mills was checking on the boys?"

"Thanks, Paul. Appreciate it. Thank Morgan for me," he said as he made his way towards O'Connor's room. He didn't bother to speculate on Mills' intentions. "Keep me posted if anything changes."

The ward was quiet. Two or three nurses or orderlies or aides worked behind the nurses' station counter. Now and again, one would get up and check on a patient. None of them had ventured towards Pat's room. Graff hadn't seen any doctors on call.

The first Navajo cop who had been posted outside O'Connor's room had been changed out for an older one. He had dozed off with a folded day-old newspaper at his feet. The FBI guy was still awake, but blinking himself to death. The remains of three empty paper cups, presumably coffee, Graff thought, stood at the side of his chair.

Graff entered O'Connor's room.

It looked as though O'Connor was asleep. Reyna too, in the uncomfortable chair.

He shook Reyna gently, who snapped to and began to stand. Jamie motioned for him to quiet down and relax.

"You up for a road trip?" Graff asked quietly.

"Where are we going?" O'Connor asked.

"Ron and I are heading to Red Rock. I'm guessing Lou Feldcamp's diner and bar. That's where Brian is. If Brian is there, Brett and Michael are there. I doubt George is anywhere near there. Also, according to Paul Eiselmann and Morgan Billias, Mills was there."

"Was?"

"He's heading towards Shiprock."

O'Connor sat up and said, "I specifically told Michael he could never go back there. I remember telling him that."

Graff smiled and said, "Which is precisely why they're there. It's a place Michael knows. Besides the desert or mountains, that's the place he's safe."

"Damn kids," O'Connor muttered.

Graff turned to Reyna and said, "You up for a road trip?"

"Sure," Reyna said as he stood and stretched his good arm and his back.

"Let's go," O'Connor said.

He swung his long legs over the side of the bed. He hesitated as he tested his equilibrium. Reasonably satisfied, only then did he stand. He yanked off the monitors and shuffled to the closet.

"Where do you think you're going?" Graff asked.

"Try to stop me," Pat said as he began dressing.

A nurse entered his room, took a look, shook her head, and walked out.

"I don't think she approves," Reyna said with a laugh.

"Tough," O'Connor said as he buckled his belt.

"Hoss, you sure you're up for this?" Graff asked.

"Better than sitting in bed. Besides, I need to yell at them," Pat said. "Not much, but a little."

CHAPTER EIGHTY-ONE

George pulled on the reins and brought the three-horse parade to a halt. They had been traveling for at least two hours. While the darkness was comforting, it was also suffocating. City or suburban darkness, even out in the country where he lived, had a different feel and tone to it.

"Why are we stopping?" Rebecca asked.

"I want Charles to rest. He needs his bandages changed."

"We're only five or six miles from home. Can't it wait?"

George looked off in the horizon towards the ranch. He couldn't see very far, but didn't see anything unusual in the distance. That is what bothered him.

"I want to ride ahead and look around." He turned back and met Rebecca's eyes, and said, "To be safe."

Rebecca bit her lip.

"Just to be safe," George said.

Rebecca regained her composure, nodded, and helped Charles off the horse.

George rode off with his rifle across his lap, eyes alert.

CHAPTER EIGHTY-TWO

"Before we go, I want to look at your blisters," Brian said.

"Michael and I changed them already," Brett protested. He didn't want to be back in the saddle anytime in the next century.

Ignoring him, Brian said, "Pull down your boxers."

Brett sighed and did as he was told.

Brian pulled the tape and gauze off carefully.

"Just yank it off! What you're doing is torture."

Brian shook his head and said, "I don't want to use another bandage if I don't have to."

"Will I have any hair on my legs after you're done?"

"I don't think so," Brian said with a laugh. He looked up at Brett, and said, "If you'd rather, I could put some of this tape up there," he said glancing Brett's balls, "and then yank the tape off."

"No, thank you."

He ran his fingertips gently up and down the inside of Brett's leg. Vaseline was still sticky, but there were no signs of bleeding. He nodded.

He replaced the gauze and tape and did the same inspection on the inside of Brett's other leg. Satisfied, he replaced the gauze and tape.

"Not as bad as they were earlier," he said with a smile.

"It would have been better if you had kissed it," Brett said as he pulled up his boxers.

"I told you, when you least expect it," Brian said with a smile.

When Brian stood up, Brett placed his hands on either side of Brian's face, and said, "Are you and I okay? I mean, *really* okay?"

Brian smiled at him and said, "Right now, you and Billy are the only two I'm sure about. Yeah, we're good."

"But you and I . . ."

Brian smiled and said, "We're fine."

He began to walk out of the bedroom, stopped, and turned around. "I'll talk Michael into using the truck. We can come back for the horses later."

Brett said. "My legs and my ass appreciate it."

Brian smiled and said, "We need to get there in a hurry. I don't want George waiting for us. Just in case."

He walked back down the stairs and found Michael checking the lock on the front door and then the windows. Papa stood in the middle of the diner watching him, but when Brian entered the room, Papa walked over to him expecting to be petted.

"Do you think we could borrow the truck?"

Michael thought about it, shrugged, and said, "He's not around, anyway. I'll leave a note for him. You know, in case he comes back."

"Good. We'll leave the horses in the garage and come back for them. I don't think they're ready to ride yet. If we use the truck, we can meet up with George and then get back here by the end of the day."

Michael took his hat off, ran his hand through his long black hair, and repositioned his hat on his head.

"I've never driven it. He said I could if I wanted to, but I never did."

Brian said, "I don't mind driving. Is it stick or automatic?"

"Automatic."

Brian nodded and said, "That makes it easier. Let's get going."

Brett joined them in the back of the bar.

"You guys ready?"

"Yeah," Brian said. "We'll leave everything here except the guns. Make sure they're loaded and bring extra shells."

"Let's roll!" Brett said.

CHAPTER EIGHTY-THREE

George rode in from the north rather than due east where the Ngo hogan sat hunched up against the northern edge of the Chuskas. If anyone had been or was watching the Morning Star family, they might know that Charles had been hiding in Ngo's home. He didn't want to take the chance of riding into a bullet.

The closer George got to the ranch, the slower he rode. As he drew within two hundred yards, he thought he detected the glow of a cigarette near the back of the barn and then another near the outhouse.

Two for sure. George figured that one or two might be in the ranch house keeping an eye on Franklin and Rosetta. He also thought there might be one or two up in the hills overlooking the ranch. He thought there might be one close to the dirt road that led to the ranch.

That left him and his brothers to deal with potentially seven armed men. George didn't like the odds. He pulled out his cell and sent a text to Brian and Brett, hoping they would read it before they drove into a storm.

CHAPTER EIGHTY-FOUR

Graff threw a blanket over the back of the driver's seat because it was still tacky with Reyna's blood. Earlier that day, he had dug out the bullets and sent them to the FBI office in Albuquerque. The windshield had spider-webbed because of the bullets, and that made it difficult to see through.

Reyna rode in the middle on the bench seat, his feet tucked under the front console. O'Connor's long legs folded uncomfortably in the well of the passenger seat, his hand gripping the Jesus handle above his door, and his head leaning back into the headrest. His eyes were closed, and he wore the ugly sunglasses.

"You two doing okay?" Graff asked.

Reyna grunted. O'Connor didn't answer.

If there was to be any fighting, Graff didn't know how effective either would be. Reyna had his good arm in a sling. Potentially, he could still shoot with his left, but not accurately. As for O'Connor, any bright light or any loud noise might send him over the edge.

Graff looked around Reyna at his friend and sometime partner. Even in the dark of the night and in the glow of the dashboard, Pat looked gray.

"I'm hoping we can collect those three kids and get back to Chinle in one piece."

Reyna set his jaw and kept his eyes straight ahead.

O'Connor muttered, "Never that simple. You know that."

"I said I'm hoping."

CHAPTER EIGHTY-FIVE

Michael sat in the bed of the truck, his back up against the cab and his legs stretched out in front of him. He used the little window into the cab to relay directions to Brian. His rifle lay across his lap and his knife sat in its sheath on his hip. Papa lay down next to him with his head resting on its front paws.

All three boys had their cell phones off. They didn't want to risk the chance of them losing charge. Brian said he would turn his on when they was close.

Brett sat in the passenger seat and leaned his rifle between his legs with the barrel leaning against the door. The safety was on and his hands were nowhere near the trigger. His eyes scanned all directions.

He glanced over at Brian. Brian's chin stuck out a little, his eyes narrow. Both hands gripped the wheel in a nine and three position. He seemed so grown up as he drove. Like he had aged five years since they landed in New Mexico.

Without taking his eyes off the road, Brian said, "What?"

"Nothin'. Just thinking."

"About what?"

Brett said, "I've seen that look on your face before. Against Brookfield East when you drilled the last shot. When you kicked a PK against Brookfield Central. You have that same look now."

"Don't know what we're driving into."

"Well, I'm glad you're next to me."

Brian took his eyes off the road briefly, smiled at him, and then snapped his head back, the smile gone, the focus on.

Over his shoulder, Brian said, "Michael, we're coming up to a T intersection. I'm going left?"

Michael stuck his head into the little window so he could see the road.

"No, go right. We're taking a little longer route and come in from the northeast. That's what George wanted us to do," reminding them of George's text.

Brett glanced back at him.

"To be safe," Michael said, and then he turned around and resumed his watch on their tail.

"That's taking us away from where we want to go," Brian said.

Besides George, Brian knew his directions. Out in the woods hunting or on the lake fishing, it was Brian or George who got everyone straightened out.

"We won't be going that direction for long. In about a mile, you'll turn west."

Sure enough, the turn came up and Brian asked, "Here?"

"Yup. Turn here, stay on this road for about three miles, and you'll come to a dirt track. Make another left, and travel south. When you make that turn, we'll need to call George to see what he wants us to do."

"Shit, this is hardly a road," Brian said.

"Wait 'til you see the next one," Michael said over his shoulder.

CHAPTER EIGHTY-SIX

"How do we know our mother and father are safe? We don't even know if they're alive!" Rebecca cried.

Her face was tear stained and dirt smudged. Yet, her beauty was breathtaking. George loved her. Yes, they were the best of friends, but there was more to it than that. There was something electric between them. George felt it each time he looked at her, when he thought about her, and most certainly when he touched her.

He took a deep breath and reached out to hold her, but she pulled away.

He sighed and said, "Becca, we need to believe they are."

She shook her head and jabbed a finger into his chest. "You saw what happened to the Yazzie family," she hissed. "How do we know they didn't do that to my family?"

She had a point. There was no way to know for sure.

He had noticed over time that the longer he had lived with Jeremy, the more optimistic he had become. It was Jeremy's belief that hope bred optimism. Jeremy believed that those two qualities, along with love, were needed to live life. George believed that, too.

"You are right, Becca. We do not know for sure. We will not know until we get to your ranch. If we do not believe they are safe, we have no purpose in going there. In order to keep your mother and father and us safe, we need to wait for my brothers."

"Becca, George is right," Charles said quietly. "There is no way to know for sure. To be safe, we need to wait."

Thankful for Charles' intervention, George picked it up from there.

"With my brothers and Michael, we have three extra rifles. We will come up with a plan and then go to your ranch, get your mother and father, and go to Chinle."

Rebecca regained her composure. She lifted her chin, nodded slightly, and turned her back on him to tend to Charles.

George may have won a battle, but lost a war if Franklin and Rosetta were already dead.

CHAPTER EIGHTY-SEVEN

Mills turned his jeep around. He was exhausted and trying to tie up far too many loose ends. The trouble was, the more he tried to tie them together, the more there were.

He stopped in the middle of the road. At this late hour, or early hour depending upon how you looked at it, there was no traffic anyway.

Mills checked the bar, and it was locked up tight. What he couldn't remember was whether he had checked the garage. Feldcamp was in jail. He was handcuffed and placed in the back of an FBI cruiser. Theoretically, his truck should be in the garage.

What if the boys never entered the bar? What if they were sound asleep in the garage?

"Fuck!"

He needed to check it out.

CHAPTER EIGHTY-EIGHT

They arrived in Red Rock in the dead of night. The town was eerily still. No sounds and no lights.

Graff pulled to a stop in front of the diner. The three of them sat in the truck, not bothering to move.

"You guys ever watch the series, *Stranger Things?*"

Reyna shook his head. O'Connor grunted.

"This town has that same look and feel."

The three cops stared up at the bar. Graff shook his head.

"Looks dark," Reyna said.

"Sleeping?" Graff said.

"They're not here," O'Connor mumbled.

Graff sighed. That was more likely.

"We need to check it out."

The three of them climbed out of the truck. O'Connor took a step back to allow Reyna to get out. Pat turned away from the building and scrutinized the street in both directions, and then the houses across the street.

At last, he glanced at the little trading post where he had purchased the cell phone, the water, and the jerky for Michael. O'Connor considered walking over and knocking on the door, but because it was the middle of the night, he'd be met with hostility at the least and a loaded shotgun at worst.

Instead of following Graff and Reyna to the bar, O'Connor wandered to the garage. He opened the door and was slapped in the face with the smell of horse, hay, and shit. A nauseating cocktail in the condition he was in.

"Damn," O'Connor muttered as he backed away.

Pat leaned against the open door and sucked in fresh air. He waited until the nausea subsided, and then he took off his sunglasses and entered the garage. He brought out his cell and used the flashlight app.

Horses in a stable. Supplies in a pile in a corner, saddles and bridles on a fence or hung up on pegs on the wall. What puzzled O'Connor was the emptiness. Something was missing.

To O'Connor, it looked like a garage, but then space was carved out to make it a makeshift barn.

"Hoss, what are you up to?" Graff said as he walked in. Reyna trailed behind him.

"Did... who's that guy?"

"Feldcamp," Reyna said.

"Yeah, that's right. Feldcamp. Did Feldcamp have a vehicle? A truck or something?"

Graff looked at Reyna, who shrugged ignorance. "I'll call and check."

O'Connor squatted down and shown his cell on the dirty cement floor. He saw a dark stain, ran his fingers across it, and lifted his fingers to his nose.

"Oil."

O'Connor got up and Graff walked over and took an elbow to help stabilize him.

Pat said, "They weren't in the bar, were they?"

"Nope."

"They left the horses and took the truck." He turned to Graff and said, "It has to be a truck. Who in their right mind would drive anything but a truck out here?"

"Where did they go?" Graff asked.

"Somewhere close by or at least a short drive away. Their horses and their supplies are here. They're planning on returning."

"That fits. The bed looks slept in, but that's about it. But..."

"But, what?" O'Connor said.

"We saw bandages in the bedroom wastebasket. Some blood on them. Not much, but still."

Reyna ended his call and said, "Lou Feldcamp drives a 2015 black Chevy Silverado."

"Fuck!" O'Connor muttered.

CHAPTER EIGHTY-NINE

"Find anything?"

O'Connor was slow to react, but he stopped in mid-stride. Reyna jumped and his arm throbbed with the jolt. He bent over and held it.

Graff was the only one who didn't show any emotion, though he was certainly startled. He was the first to notice the police officer standing there. What was curious to him was that he hadn't heard the jeep. He looked further down the street and there it sat, a half-block away on the other side of the street, not quite in front of the trading post.

Mills stood at an angle at the corner of the bar and caught them as they rounded the opposite corner.

Mills smiled and said, "Sorry for the scare. I checked the house and didn't see anything. I was about to check the garage."

Graff remembered the phone call from Eiselmann. Allegedly, Mills was on his way to Shiprock. Jamie decided to keep that in his pocket.

"We had been here for about a half an hour and didn't see you," O'Connor said.

O'Connor had picked up on it too.

Mills smiled and shrugged and said, "We must have crossed each other. You know, me on one side, you on the other."

Graff said, "Something like that."

"Have you been in the garage? Was just about to go check it myself."

"Nothing out of the ordinary. A black Chevy Silverado. Some hay. Nothing special," Graff answered.

"Well, I guess that's that then," Mills said with a smile. "I'll head home, catch a bite, sleep a little, and begin again."

"Sounds like a plan," Reyna said.

Mills offered them a little wave, turned, and headed back across the street.

"You never asked about our truck," Graff said. "Or Ron's arm."

Mills stopped in his tracks. He had a decision to make. He stood out in the open without cover. Graff was the only opponent to worry about. Reyna was winged and O'Connor was wobbly. However, his days of quick-drawing were past him.

He turned around palms up, and said, "Damn, I'm sorry. It's dark and late, and I'm exhausted. Just missed it. Ron, are you okay?"

Reyna gave a sort of head nod, and said, "Mostly."

"I didn't notice the truck. What happened?"

Mills didn't bother to move into a better position to get a look at it.

"We think a rock or rocks were kicked up by a truck. Truck's okay, except for the windshield," Graff said.

"Well, that's something that can be replaced. Fortunately, you didn't get run off the road like O'Connor."

"Yeah, fortunately," O'Connor said.

"Well, it's late. I'll check with you guys in the morning."

Mills walked to his jeep knowing he had more loose ends.

CHAPTER NINETY

"I see you coming. You are a mile away. Turn off your lights and keep coming in the same direction."

Brian said, "You want me to drive without lights?"

George smiled. Of the brothers, Randy and Brian were the cautious ones.

"Drive slowly and straight. You will be fine."

Both boys turned off their cellphones. Reluctantly, Brian turned off the truck lights.

Brett licked his lips and glanced at Brian before leaning forward to help navigate the darkness ahead of them.

Brian glanced into the rearview mirror. If Michael was nervous, he didn't show it. He was in the same position, watching their tail. Papa was only mildly interested in what was happening.

"What's that? Ahead," Brett said pointing. "There."

Brian leaned forward and slowed down to a crawl.

"It's them."

Brian drew up alongside of George who stood in the middle of the dirt track, his rifle cradled in his arms. Brian was beyond tired and still wasn't much interested in talking to either George or Rebecca. He would let Brett and Michael do most of the talking.

He turned around and rapped a knuckle on the back window. To Michael he said, "We're here."

Michael was already moving. Papa stood up, sniffed the air, and waited.

"You coming?" Brett asked.

Brian sighed and said, "Yeah."

Both boys got out and shut their doors softly. Papa jumped out of the truck bed and brushed up against Brian's leg. Rather than face George or Rebecca, Brian got down on one knee to scratch Papa behind his ear.

"Thanks for coming," George said.

"How is Charles?" Brett asked.

George turned around to make sure Rebecca and Charles were still a distance off.

"Charles needs to get to a hospital."

Brett whispered, "Bad?"

Before George could answer, Rebecca walked up.

"Thank you for coming. We need your help."

Michael stepped up on the other side of Papa and said, "What do you want us to do?"

"There are men at the Morning Star ranch. I saw at least two, there could be more." George explained their positioning.

"And your mother and father are there," Brett said to Rebecca.

She bit her lip and nodded.

Brian stood up and said, "What do you want us to do?"

George was grateful and relieved. However, he still didn't know where he stood with Brian.

"We need to get Father and Mother Morning Star out of the house. We need to get Charles to the hospital."

"Any ideas?" Michael asked.

The three brothers looked at one another. Each had their thoughts. Michael looked from one to the other. Rebecca waited with her arms folded across her chest.

Brett finally said, "Rebecca, you wait here with Charles. George, Brian, Michael, and I will go get your parents."

She was about to protest when Brian said, "No."

All eyes shifted towards him.

"Rebecca needs to go with us. She goes into the house with Brett, gets her parents and we get back here in a hurry. George, you watch the guy by the barn. They'll expect us to use the Avalanche. They don't know we have this truck. Michael, you'll go to the far side of the house, further south towards their driveway. I'll keep watch on the hill. In and out fast."

"Why does Brett go into the house?" Michael asked.

"Because he's the best with a handgun. You and George are better with a knife than either Brett or me. Rebecca's parents will trust Rebecca, and not us so much," Brian said.

"We can't fuck this up," Brett said.

"How far is it?" Michael asked.

"Close to three miles," George said.

"Let's go."

George and Rebecca explained the plan to a semi-conscious Charles. They gave him a Brett's rifle, and the five of them set off on foot.

George took point. Brett took up the right flank, with Michael on the left. Rebecca stayed close to George, but kept looking back at Brian, who brought up the rear. Brian kept his head on a swivel, sometimes walking backwards to watch their backside. Papa jogged off in a big circle around them, never actually leaving their sight.

Rebecca dropped back next to him.

"Thank you for coming."

Brian nodded, his eyes moving.

"I'm sorry for what I said. It was wrong of me, Brian."

"It's forgotten."

Rebecca bit her lip and said, "If only that were true."

She sped up and almost caught up to George.

Before long, George lifted a hand and stopped the little patrol. He squatted down, and the group gathered around him. Papa, his head low nestled under Brian's arm.

George whispered, "You can see the outline of the ranch about two hundred yards ahead." He pointed to the far right and said, "Watch. Near the barn. You will see a cigarette." And sure enough, there was a red glow.

"Keep watching towards the back of the hogan, you will see another." Just like that, another red glow in the distance.

"Did you see anything up in the hills?" Brian asked.

George shook his head and said, "No, but they are there. At least one, perhaps two."

Brian squinted up at the hills searching for any telltale signs of someone's presence. He didn't see anything, but he trusted George's judgment.

"George, go off to the right and take care of that guy. Don't kill him if you can help it, but make sure he can't hurt Brett or Rebecca or her parents," Brian said. "Michael, you go left. If no one is there, cover Brett and Rebecca. If someone is there, try not to kill him, but make sure he can't hurt anyone. Do it quietly."

Both George and Michael nodded.

"Rebecca, besides George, you know your ranch better than anyone. Brett, you're there to make sure she and her parents are safe."

"I think there will be at least one or two men in the house," George said. "I will help when I am . . . done."

"Me, too," Michael said.

"Where will you be?" Brett asked.

Brian had never taken his eyes off the hills. He thought he saw movement, but it could have been the night, the darkness, whatever.

"I'll be nearby. I got your back." He finally glanced at all of them, George the longest. "All of you."

CHAPTER NINETY-ONE

George and Michael took off in different directions. Brian sent Papa with Michael, and while he wanted to remain with Brian, the big dog obeyed. Brett, Rebecca, and Brian waited for what seemed like a week, but was only two minutes by Brian's watch.

"Brett, be careful," Brian whispered. *'I love you'* was on the tip of his tongue.

Brett smiled at him said, "Always."

The three of them hunched over and walked almost straight at the house. Rebecca in the middle, Brian on her left, and Brett on her right. As they got to within twenty yards, they heard someone weeping.

Brian gripped Rebecca's elbow, and whispered, "Focus. Keep your head."

Brett waved at them to get down. All three dropped to the dirt.

A shadow crossed the yard, the barest of outlines. Still smoking a cigarette. He stuck his head into the doorway, mumbled something to someone, but the three of them couldn't make out what was said.

As the silhouette moved out of the doorway and into the yard, another smaller silhouette moved towards the man. There was a thud, a groan, and the silhouette fell.

"Move, now," Brian whispered.

Rebecca and Brett took off. As they neared the doorway, Brett held Rebecca back. They pressed themselves against the side of the house. A man walked out, stood just outside of the doorway, stretched, and walked towards the outhouse.

Brett motioned for Rebecca to move into the house, while he kept his eye on the man who had entered the crumbling, smelly structure.

Silently and out of nowhere, George appeared at his side.

He whispered, "Go, I'll keep watch."

Brett entered the house low and fast.

"What the fuck?"

An older, short man had a shotgun pointed at Rebecca. He was shocked and stunned when Brett entered. Franklin held a terrified Rosetta in a corner of the room.

"Who the hell are you?"

Brett pointed his Glock at the man. "Put it down now before anyone gets hurt."

The man pulled the hammer back.

"Don't do it," Brett warned.

The man licked his lips, his eyes darting from Rebecca to Brett.

"Don't," Brett warned.

Rose tried to break away from Franklin and that distracted the man just long enough. Brett rushed him, pushed the shotgun up in the air, but it went off, both barrels. Dust and dirt fell from the thatched and tin ceiling. Brett smashed the Glock into the man's face, knocking him backward to the floor. Rebecca grabbed the shotgun and slammed the butt into the man's head, rendering him unconscious. He might have lost an eye.

"Go!" Brett hissed. "Now!"

Rebecca guided Rose and Franklin to the door as a shot rang out, spitting into the doorframe.

They ducked back inside. Rebecca shielded her parents.

Brett ran to the front of the house.

"Back!" George yelled.

Another shot, then another, but not into the doorway.

Brian had seen muzzle flashes and fired in that direction. He didn't know if he had hit anyone, but for the time being, the shooting had stopped.

He saw four figures running towards him.

Another shot rang out, and Brian answered it with two of his own. No return fire after that.

Papa and Michael appeared on his flank, and Brian swung his rifle on them.

"Dude! It's me, Michael! Don't shoot!"

Brian's heart stopped and then started.

Michael lay down next to Brian, his rifle trained on the area behind Rebecca, Brett, and her parents.

"Where's George?" Brian asked.

"Dunno," Michael whispered.

Brett had Rose by the shoulders, Rebecca had her father by the arm. They didn't stop at Michael and Brian, but kept running past them.

"Papa, go!" Brian hissed.

Papa whined, but took off with them.

"You, too, Mike. Go now!"

"What about you?"

Brian said, "I'll wait for George. Go!"

"You should come too," Michael said.

"Don't argue! Go! Now!"

Michael backed away slowly at first, but then turned and ran after Brett, Rebecca, and her parents, looking back over his shoulder as he did. His promise to O'Connor an alarm in the back of his mind.

Brian felt small and alone, but not scared. Brad was nearby. Brian could feel his presence. Besides, he knew where the others had run to and he would follow. However, he needed to wait for George and make certain no one was following them.

They came at him at a run.

Brian saw one, then two, and then two more. He opened fire, knowing that by doing so, he was giving up his position. After two shots, he had to reload. He rolled to his right so the shooters would shoot where the muzzle flash was and not where he had rolled.

Bullets zinged past him. Each shot a high-pitched whine like bees. He pressed himself into the earth, face into the sand, holding his breath and hoping he wouldn't get hit. When the shooting stopped, Brian pushed five more shells into his rifle and took aim.

He fired and saw one man drop to the ground screaming. He didn't think it was a lethal shot, but it was too dark to tell. Brian fired again and again. Each time he did, he rolled away from his firing position.

It must have been George who covered for him. He had flanked them and shot from the side of the house.

Thankfully, the men backed off.

Brian heard the sound of an engine starting up and he braced himself, waiting to be run over.

It didn't happen. He saw tail lights.

"George, now! I have you covered!"

George darted from the corner of the house and threw himself down next to Brian.

"We need to get out of here before they come back," George said in a whisper.

Brian couldn't take his eyes from the tail lights in the distance. Sure enough, it looked as though it was turning around.

"Go! Go!" Brian yelled.

"You, too!"

Both boys took off, zig-zagging randomly. While George was an all-state runner in both cross country and track, Brian wasn't. He was fast and quick for short distances. Their goal was close to three miles away. They would either be run over or shot. At least he would, probably not George.

"Stop!" Brian said. "Call Brett. Tell him to get back here. Tell Rebecca and Michael to get her parents and Charles to Chinle. We'll hold them off."

George hesitated. Brian's plan was brave, but foolish. They would be over-matched and out-gunned.

"Do it!" Brian yelled as he got down in the dirt. He lay facing the direction the men would come from.

Behind him, he heard the sound of another truck.

No lights. It stopped thirty or forty yards away.

"George! Brian! Come on!" Brett yelled.

"Change of plans," Brian said as he sprinted in that direction. George met him at the truck.

"Rebecca, you and Michael get Charles and your parents to Chinle. Don't go by any normal route. Take a round-about way, but get there. Brett, George and I will cover you for as long as we can."

"I'll stay, too!" Michael said.

"No, Michael," George said. "Rebecca will need someone to guard them while she drives."

"But..."

"No buts! You need to get out of here now! They're turning around!" Brian said.

"Come with us! All of you!" Rebecca pleaded.

"We don't have time! You don't have any time! You have to go!"

George nodded at Rebecca. "Brian is right. Go. Save your family."

"Michael, don't let anything happen to them," Brett added.

"Keep your lights off for as long as you can," Brian said.

He ran around to the back of the truck and smashed both tail lights. He ran back to George and Brett, and said, "Now they can't follow you."

"Go!" Brett said. "Michael, call O'Connor and tell them what happened."

Brian added, "Tell them we'll try to get to the truck at Rebecca's. If we can, we'll head to Chinle."

"If you can't get to the truck?" Rebecca asked.

"Then tell him we'll be up on the mesa waiting for them. It's high ground," George said.

Rebecca sped away.

It looked like Michael's hands were shaking as he pulled out his cell phone.

CHAPTER NINETY-TWO

The boys sprinted at a ninety-degree angle towards the back of the ranch. As they neared it, George held up a hand.

"I will check out the barn and yard. If it is clear, I will whistle. Two quick calls."

"We have to hurry. The night is getting shorter, I think," Brett said.

"Still time. We will be okay," George answered.

As George took off, Brian shifted his position staring off into the darkness where he last saw the men and the truck.

"Do you think they're still around?" Brett whispered.

Brian nodded, but never took his eyes off the road. There wasn't any sound. It was still, quiet.

They heard George whistle once, then a second call.

"That's George," Brett whispered. "Let's go."

"Go," Brian said. He hadn't moved. "I'll cover you."

Brett took off. Brian counted to fifteen and then sprinted in the direction Brett and George had run to. He rounded the back fence and came up on the Avalanche from side. Brett and George were on the other side.

"We can't use the truck," Brett said. "We can't use the Morning Star family's truck either."

"They flattened the tires on both," George added.

Brian sighed. Of course, it wouldn't be that easy.

"What now?" Brett asked.

George looked off towards the hills. He pointed towards a mesa off in the distance.

"We need to get there before sunrise."

Brett shook his head. "Do we have enough supplies? Water? Food? Ammo?"

He already knew the answers to those questions.

CHAPTER NINETY-THREE

O'Connor's cell vibrated. It kept vibrating, indicating it was a call. But with Mills standing in the street facing the three of them, O'Connor didn't want to make any move that could be mistaken as reaching for a gun. He let it go to voicemail.

After Mills got in his jeep and did a U-Turn to head off to wherever, O'Connor reached for the cell in his back pocket and listened.

"That was Michael," O'Connor said. "There was a shootout at the Morning Star ranch. He, Rebecca, Charles, and their parents are heading to the hospital in Chinle."

"They found Charles?" Reyna asked.

"Must have," O'Connor.

"Is everyone okay? Where are they?"

"Still at the Morning Star ranch. They plan to get the Avalanche and head to Chinle. If for some reason they can't, they will be on the mesa."

"*Chaha'oh* Mesa?" Reyna asked.

O'Connor shrugged and said, "Hell, I don't know a mesa from a hill. I guess so."

A shot rang out.

It spit between Graff and Reyna, and into the front of the bar.

The three dove for cover behind the truck.

Three more shots. One into the driver's side window, one into the front tire and one into the back tire. Then all was silent except for barking dogs.

First one light, like a lantern, went on in a shack across the street. Then another in the shack next to the first shack.

"Stay inside. We're FBI!" Reyna called out.

A light went on in the upper level of the trading post. It looked like a regular light, not a lantern. *Must have propane*, Graff thought.

No one came out of any houses, but a voice called out from the trading post upstairs window.

"You okay over there? Anybody hurt?"

"We're good. For now. We think he's gone," Graff yelled. "To be safe, stay indoors."

The three men stood hunched over the hood and back of the truck.

"See anything?" Graff asked.

"Too fuckin' dark," O'Connor said.

"I'm going around the back of the bar. I'll parallel the street and come out on the other side," Reyna said.

"Can you shoot with that arm?" Graff asked.

"No, but I can shoot with my left. Not as well, but good enough."

He didn't wait for an argument, but took off down the side of the bar next to the garage.

"Pat, stay here. I'm crossing the street."

"Better let Reyna know. You don't want to get shot."

Graff nodded. He should have thought of that. He pulled out his cell and told Ron what he was doing.

"Meet you at the end of the street," was all Reyna said.

"And don't get shot by any of the locals," O'Connor muttered.

It took twenty minutes to check the backs of houses, between the houses, and to reach the end of the street. Graff ended his search in less time, because there were fewer houses on his side.

When he saw Reyna, he whistled. Reyna waved and crossed the street, looking off in the direction Mills drove off in.

"Nothing. You?" Reyna said.

Graff shook his head and said, "Long gone."

"Any doubt about who that was?"

Graff grunted. "It was Mills, and I don't think he gives a shit that we know."

A light came on in the trading post and the front door opened. An older man wearing only jeans with suspenders stepped out holding a shotgun.

"Don't shoot me. My wife might be happy if you did, but I won't be."

CHAPTER NINETY-FOUR

"Stop the truck, Rebecca," Michael yelled, beating on the back of the cab for emphasis. "Stop."

Bewildered, Rebecca gawked at him through the rearview mirror, but kept driving.

"Stop! Now!" Michael yelled.

Papa stood up and barked.

Michael gripped the sidewall of the truck bed, threatening to jump.

Rebecca eased the truck to a stop, and Michael hopped over the side. Papa followed him. Franklin sat up in the truck bed. He had been tending to Charles, who had been resting with his eyes shut. Rosetta rode in the passenger seat in the cab. Both he and she were alarmed.

"I promised a cop that I'd watch over Brett and Brian."

Rebecca shook her head.

"Go to Chinle. Charles needs a doctor. Papa and I'll go back. I know where they're going."

Rebecca shook her head again, her mouth opening and closing.

"I'll be okay. Go." When she still hesitated, he said quietly, "Go."

She did.

With Papa running just ahead of him, and with one hand holding onto his cowboy hat, and the other holding his rifle, Michael took off in the direction from which they had come. He hoped he wasn't too late.

CHAPTER NINETY-FIVE

It was that in-between time, not quite night and not quite morning, with more shadows than light. Brett and Brian alternately dozed off fitfully while George watched and waited. He had not shut his eyes but would walk from one trail to the other, and then to the back cliff only to repeat the process. All three were exhausted, hungry, and thirsty. The long walk to the mesa, and then the long, hard climb up the backside in the dark took everything out of them.

All was quiet, but it would not be for long.

Brian stirred and rubbed his face. He sniffed his armpit and winced. They had no food and only one bottle of water left to share, and that would not be enough once the hot desert sun rose overhead.

Brian sat up fighting stiffness and soreness and glanced at George. George had been watching the main path, listening for any signs of approach.

George would crane his neck around a boulder carefully not to show too much of himself, and then he would walk back, and do the same on the main path. Watching, waiting, and worrying about his two brothers more than himself. He had been responsible for them coming on this trip.

Brett had slept next to Brian on the hard-packed red sandy soil, sometimes using Brian's shoulder or chest as a pillow. When Brian sat up, Brett did too.

Brett yawned and looked over at his brother. Dirt streaks and smudges covered most of the sprinkling of smallish freckles under his hazel-green eyes and on the bridge of his nose. His cheeks were red from the heat and from the lack of water. His lips were cracked, his dark wavy hair, was mussed and dirty, and his shirt showed more of the red dirt and sweat than its true color.

Concerned, Brett said, "When was the last time you drank water?"

Brian shrugged and said, "I'm okay."

"You're not okay. When was the last time you drank water?"

"I'm fine, Brett. Honest."

Brian's eyes shifted away from Brett's scrutiny.

"When we took turns with the water, you skipped yours, didn't you?"

Brian looked away.

"Why would you do that? You know how important it is to stay hydrated in the desert and in this heat."

Brian shifted uncomfortably.

"You're our best chance because you're the best shot. Why would you do that?" Brett paused and added, "The truth."

George stopped traipsing from one path to the other to listen.

Brian did not want to answer, but telling the truth was important to him.

"I wanted you and George to have most of the water."

"Why?"

Brian glanced at Brett and then looked away just as quickly.

"Because I promised Mom I'd take care of you." He looked up at George and said, "Both of you." He shrugged, and said, "I fucked everything up though."

Brett shook his head, grabbed the bottle of water, held it out to Brian and said, "Drink some before I smack you."

Knowing he was good with Brett, Brian smiled, and took a swallow.

"One more swallow."

Reluctantly, Brian took a small drink, and then held it out to George who waved it off. Brian handed it back to Brett.

Brett smiled at him, and said, "You have the best heart. You always had the best heart. Even facing this shit."

Brian wiped his lips with the back of his hand, caught another whiff of his underarm and winced.

To lighten the mood, Brett said, "I don't smell like a garden either." Brett yawned, stretched.

George saw the sun winking over the Chuskas. No time for his prayers to Father Sun.

He said, "Two vehicles and six men, but there might be more. They have semi-automatic weapons and they will come any moment."

"Hopefully Rebecca, Michael, and her family got to Chinle last night," Brian said. "They'll send help."

It was the faintest of hope, but Brett said, "Hopefully, Michael was able to get in touch with O'Connor."

Brian checked his 30-06. Three shells. Brett had four and George had two. Each boy had a knife but neither he nor Brett were as skilled with it as George, except when it came to field dressing game. The three of them were the game this early morning.

"Brett, give me two of your bullets. Just in case," Brian said.

Brett unloaded two, leaving him two. Reluctantly, he handed them to Brian, who loaded them into his rifle.

"I want you to stay behind that boulder until I yell for you."

"Why?" Brett asked.

"Because I want to use you to surprise them."

George placed his hands on his brother's shoulders and said, "My grandfather told me that when the warrior within you awakens, you will no longer fear death. You'll realize that a person can kill your body, but they can never kill your soul. My grandfather told me that even though our bodies die, our spirits will live forever." He had meant this as a comfort to them.

Brian believed that too.

Brett said, "Knock that shit off. No one is dying. Not now and not for a long time. We either surrender and die, or we fight this out and live!"

George stood up and took one more trip to the obscure path.

Brett knew Brian still had not gotten over the death of his twin brother. He braved a smile and said, "We aren't dying." He slung an arm around Brian, pulled him close, and kissed the side of his head near the temple.

George walked back from the main trail, squatted down in front of them, and said, "They are coming. Four up the main trail. That means one or two will come up the side trail if they know about it. If no one comes up the side trail, at least two will be watching the trailhead."

Brett was scary calm. He nodded and said, "Let's do this."

George had to keep them safe until help arrived. That is, if help arrived.

There were only three ways to get to the top. No matter who was placed where, each would be in danger, and if one of them was overrun, then all three would die.

Brian was the best shot. Brett wasn't bad, but he was more skilled with handguns. However, Brett had given his Glock to Michael for Rebecca to use. The boys each had one rifle with whatever ammunition was in them. Certainly not enough if they faced the kind of weapons George knew they were carrying. His brothers knew that too.

"I will take the trail on the left. They will try to surprise us. If I get past them, I will make my way around and come up behind whoever comes up the main trail."

Brian said, "Brett, take the back cliff. Stay behind that boulder until I call for you. I'll take the main trail."

George said, "The main trail is the easiest and fastest way up, and more than likely, they will use it to set up an ambush from my trail. That is what I would do. Just keep them pinned down long enough for me to get behind them."

Brian did not say it but with only five bullets, there was no way he could hold them off for long. With Brett, that would make seven bullets between them.

George licked his lips, ran a hand through his long black hair. As if he had read Brian's mind, he said, "If we can get our hands on their weapons, we can make it a fair fight."

Brian and Brett nodded solemnly but did not comment because the chances of that happening were less than slim.

The three boys stood and stared at each other.

"I am sorry. I have not been a good friend or brother to you on this trip." George said.

"You've been an ass but so have I," Brett said. This last he said to Brian. He put both arms around the shoulders of his two brothers, and added, "But we're brothers and friends, and we've all been like that once in a while."

"We're okay," Brian added with a shrug looking off towards the horizon.

Brett said, "We are not going to die! We will survive!" He paused and said in a quieter, calmer voice, "We just need to live long enough until help gets here."

He turned to Brian and said, "Stay focused. No hesitation. Shoot like you mean it."

Brian nodded.

They remained silent, each not wanting to break it, and each not wanting to leave one another.

The three boys looked at each other one last time, and as they turned to guard their assigned trails, George said, *"Yá'át'ééh abiní."*

Brett knew only a few Navajo words and phrases, and he knew this one. Without smiling, Brett answered as he walked off, "No, the morning is not good. In fact, it sucks."

CHAPTER NINETY-SIX

"Fuck!" Graff yelled. "Dammit!"

Both trucks, the Avalanche and the one belonging to the Morning Star family were parked in back of the barn. Both had flattened tires rendering them undrivable.

O'Connor, who either seemed to be rallying to his normal self or was putting on a brave front, inspected the yard using the flashlight app on his cell. He had come across what looked like a pool of blood, still warm to the touch. In the Morning Star home, he found an overturned chair and table, blood on the dirt floor, and in the doorframe, what looked like bullet holes.

"Graff!" he called.

Both Graff and Reyna stepped into the house.

"There was a fight," O'Connor said matter-of-factly. He didn't bother with emotion. He couldn't. The kids were too close to him. He was all cop. "I found a pool of blood in the yard. Bullet holes in the door frame."

Reyna walked through the house and found nothing and no bodies.

The three men left the home and stared up at the mesa looming off in the distance.

"That's where they went?" O'Connor said from behind him.

"Shadow Mesa," Reyna answered. "*Chaha'oh* Mesa."

Graff heard a noise in the dark just beyond the yard. Reyna flinched. O'Connor never let on one way or the other.

"I'm hitting the outhouse," O'Connor said loudly. "Then, we need to get going." He walked the short distance. "Smells. I'll take a leak behind it."

"I'll check out the barn," Reyna said loudly. "The boys could have taken horses." He took off at a quick pace not looking in any other direction but straight ahead.

"O'Connor, you about done?" Graff called.

Jamie had his back to the house so no one could take him from behind. He reached into the shoulder holster and withdrew his .45, but held it across his chest away from where he thought the noise had come from.

A voice called out.

"O'Connor! It's me, Michael Two Feathers!"

"I know," O'Connor said to his side. He had circled around the outhouse and had come at the boy from an angle.

Papa dipped his head and growled, his teeth bared. Michael spun around and jumped backwards. He swung his rifle up at the ready.

"Whoa, Buddy! Take it easy," O'Connor said holding his hands out, his palms up.

Reyna stepped up behind Michael and snatched the rifle away from him. Michael spun at him, dropped in a crouch with his knife drawn. Papa growled at the two of them. It looked as though he was deciding which one he would take a bite out of.

"Michael, stop! Please," O'Connor pleaded. "We don't have time. We need to get to the boys before something happens to them."

Michael relaxed, the fright, and the tension gone.

"Papa, it's okay," Michael urged as he reached out and pet the top of Papa's head. Papa didn't back down. He kept his eyes on both Reyna and O'Connor.

To O'Connor, Michael said, "You scared me." To Reyna he said, "Can I have my rifle back?"

"Will you shoot us?" Reyna asked.

"Of course not! We have to get moving."

Graff had joined the little party. "You must be Michael. Where'd you find the wolf?"

"Papa is Brian's dog."

Jamie shook his head. If the boys made it out of Arizona, Jeremy would get a fourth dog and another kid. He smiled.

"Let's go," Graff said as he walked past the three of them. He continued to walk quickly, but over his shoulder, he said, "You already know Pat. I'm Jamie Graff, and this is Ron Reyna. Ron is FBI. I'm a police detective, and Pat is a sheriff detective."

295

Michael said nothing, but followed him towards the truck walking between Reyna and O'Connor with Papa at his side. For the time being, Papa had stopped growling.

"How far behind them are we?" O'Connor asked.

"They should be there by now," Michael said, hoping they weren't too late.

That was when they heard gunfire. Not single shots, but semi-automatic bursts.

"Fuck! Move it!" O'Connor yelled as he broke into a run.

CHAPTER NINETY-SEVEN

The burst of fire was sprayed in Brian's general direction. Bullets buzzed past him. They sounded like angry hornets bursting from a hive.

Brian burrowed into the earth. He craned his head around to check on Brett, but he didn't see him. That was good. He was tucked away safely behind a boulder out of harm's way.

Another burst of gunfire followed by the sound of running feet.

Brian took aim partially hidden behind a boulder. He saw two men crouched low like fullbacks running through the line.

Brian fired two shots. One at the lead man, the second at the one following.

The first man fell to the ground clutching his stomach, blood pooling on the red earth. The second man spun backwards, the round catching him in the upper chest.

Brian had only shot one man before, wounding him twice on purpose. This was entirely different.

The lead man lay still. No sound. No breathing that Brian could detect. Body curled up in a ball. Hands clutching his stomach. The second man gasped for breath, wheezing, panting, moaning. Tilted to one side either unable or unwilling to move for cover.

Brian watched it all, shocked at what his bullets had done. He rolled for cover too late.

CHAPTER NINETY-EIGHT

George moved quickly. His feet nimble in his moccasins, easily stepping over smaller boulders, climbing bigger ones. He had used the path during the summer of death. That time, he protected Jeremy. This time, his brothers.

He set his rifle behind a rock wall and decided only to use his knife. He had used it several times. Each time causing death.

George heard someone coming. The footfalls unsteady, unsure. The feet belonging to someone who didn't think anyone else was on the path.

"*We need to move faster,*" one man said.

"*Can't. It's too fucking rocky!*" another man said.

"*Just like that mountain we climbed in Afghanistan,*" the first man said.

The first man was one boulder away. George had the element of surprise, but that would only work on the first man. The second man wouldn't be surprised at all.

George had to decide whether to stick with his knife or go back for his rifle.

He waited too long to decide.

CHAPTER NINETY-NINE

"It's a fucking war!" O'Connor said, willing the truck to move faster. "We have to get there, Jamie!"

Michael knelt in the truck bed. Papa stood beside him.

"Stop!" Michael yelled. "Stop here!"

Graff slammed on the brakes and red dust swirled around them.

Michael rocked forward and then back. He jumped down and ran to the driver's side, Graff's side.

"I'm going up the back way. Follow this road. It will take you to the front of the mesa."

O'Connor craned his neck out of the side window and up at the mesa. Yes, potentially it was climbable, but barely. In shadows? Damn near impossible.

"You'll get yourself killed. Get back in the truck," Pat said.

Michael didn't stop running. Papa stood between the truck and Michael, preventing anyone from following him.

"Goddammit, Michael!" O'Connor yelled. "No one fucking listens! Go, Jamie, go!"

Jamie stepped on it, but as he neared the front side of the mesa, he slowed and eventually stopped, not liking what he saw.

CHAPTER ONE HUNDRED

At first, he didn't feel anything. His shirt sleeve tugged and ripped. Then, his shoulder stung, the side of his head, his forehead. He couldn't see out of his right eye.

Brian rolled behind the boulder; his rifle forgotten.

He tried to lift his right hand to his face, but struggled to do so. His shaking hands coming up bloody. His right hand and arm throbbed. He used his left to try to clear his right eye. It stung. His hand bloody.

Blood dripped down the front of his shirt, from . . . where? His arm? His shoulder? His head and face?

"Brett, I'm hit."

He didn't know how loud he said it. It was as if he had looked down from above and watched himself struggle. And bleed.

"Brett!"

He must have said it louder.

More gunfire. Angry hornets filled the air, bouncing off rocks, the ground.

Brian curled up in a ball, holding his head with his left arm and hand, his right arm throbbing and useless.

"Jesus! Brian!"

Gentle hands and arms held him, cradling him.

"Please don't die, Brian. God, please no!" Brett didn't say it as much as it came out in a sob.

Brett pressed Brian's head against his chest and rocked him. "Please, Bri. Please . . ."

CHAPTER ONE HUNDRED AND ONE

The first thing George saw was the barrel of a semi-automatic rifle. Then a hand.

He pressed himself against a rock wall. At the last second, George lunged at the man.

George's knife found the man's soft belly. He plunged it in and sliced it from side to side. With his free hand, he grabbed the barrel of the rifle and wrenched it away from the man.

The man's eyes bulged. Blood gurgled out of his mouth and dripped down his chin and neck.

"What are you . . ." the question was finished by a burst of fire from the dying man's rifle.

Using the first man as a shield, George pulled the trigger once, then twice. The second burst sent the man over the side of the mesa. Whether he died on the way down or when he hit the rocky bottom, no one would know.

The first man reached out and tried to grasp George's shirt for balance. George danced backwards, and the man fell on his face.

George didn't waste any time. He hopped over the man and ran down the path to get to the trailhead. He had to get to Brett and Brian.

CHAPTER ONE HUNDRED AND TWO

Graff wanted Reyna and O'Connor to hang back by the truck. They weren't having it. It seemed no one listened to anyone.

"Two men." To Reyna he said, "The two hired hands at Goodnight's ranch. They're focused on what's going on up there," he said jerking his head towards the mesa.

"Can you hit them from here?" Reyna asked.

Graff shook his head and said, "I have to get closer."

Staying low and using what little cover there was, he was able to get within twenty-five yards.

"Fuck it," Jamie muttered.

He charged them. Reyna and O'Connor followed, but on either side.

Neither of the men noticed them at first. When they did, they pivoted around and crouched in a shooting stance.

Graff opened fire and kept squeezing the trigger. The first shots went wide and high. O'Connor fired from Graff's right. Reyna fired from Graff's left.

Guns clicked on empty chambers, but it didn't matter. Both men guarding the trailhead had died. Graff ran up on them. Bullets had peppered them. Face, chest, stomach, legs, and arms. Neither man got off a shot.

Graff snatched up one of the semi-automatic rifles and took off up the trail, hoping he wasn't too late.

CHAPTER ONE HUNDRED AND THREE

Brett cradled Brian and never heard the man approach.

"They're kids!" he called to someone down the trail.

Brett pushed Brian behind him, using himself as a shield.

"Don't kill him. Please. Kill me instead," he sobbed.

The man hesitated. He licked his lips and glanced back at his partner. He repeated, "They're just kids."

He never saw Michael, who had climbed over the back wall and crept out from behind the boulder.

Michael fired one shot hitting the man in the neck. The second shot hit him between the shoulders, sending him into his partner.

Papa raced from behind Michael and leaped at the second man, his big jaw tearing into the man's arm, his teeth ripping skin off bone. The man screamed and yelled, but Papa had rendered that arm useless and attacked the other arm, the arm that held the rifle.

The man pulled the trigger. Bullets bounced into the dirt, off rock, or sailed harmlessly over the mesa wall.

Michael dove for the ground. He brought his rifle up, but couldn't take a shot for fear of hitting Papa.

No matter.

Papa's sharp teeth sunk into the man's neck, ripping it in half.

The man fell backward, dead before he hit the ground.

"Papa! Come!" Michael yelled.

Papa backed away from his victim, growling and snarling. He turned and found Brian. He licked his face, whined, and nuzzled his neck.

"We have to get Brian to a hospital!" Brett cried. "Brian, please don't die! Please, God! Don't let him die!"

Strong arms reached for Brian, and Brett tried to fight him off, swinging roundhouses.

"Brett, stop! It's me, Graff!"

Another pair of arms hugged Brett from behind. Strong at first, gentle at last.

"Brett, it's okay. Let's get Brian to the hospital," George said.

Graff scooped Brian up in his arms. Brian's head lolled back, so Graff cradled it with his arms.

"Hang in there, Bri. It's over."

CHAPTER ONE HUNDRED AND FOUR

"Am I dead?"

A chuckle. "No."

"I wasn't sure. It hurts."

"I know."

"Remember when we were little, we used to feel each other's pain?"

Another chuckle. "Like the time I sprained my ankle, and you limped around the house."

He smiled. "I miss you, Brad."

He reached out to touch Brian's hand, though it didn't feel like a hand. Just warmth. Comforting.

"I was thinking of killing myself."

"I know."

"But I didn't."

Brad sighed. "You're not ready to die. Not for a long time."

"I miss you, Brad," he said again.

Brad smiled. He bent down to kiss Brian's forehead and said, "I'm always with you, Bri. Always."

Brian didn't feel the kiss, but a moment of warmth, of comfort. "But it isn't the same."

"I know."

Brian paused and frowned at his twin. "Are you happy?"

"Yeah, actually, I am. I'm happy."

Brian began to weep. "I'm not."

Brad smiled and cocked his head like he did for as long as Brian remembered.

"You have a mom and a dad who love you. You have brothers who would kill for you. You have a brother who loves you so much, he's confused and scared."

Brian didn't know if he meant Bobby or Brett. He didn't ask, because he wasn't sure he wanted to know.

"You need to live, Bri. Take it easy. Quit worrying so much."

"I..."

Brad touched his hand, smiled and said, "I'm always with you."

He vanished.

Brian opened his left eye. He couldn't open his right. It was bandaged, covered with something thick and soft.

"Sleeping beauty awakes," O'Connor said with a smile.

On the other side of the bed was Brett. Behind him, George. Brett wiped away tears. George was stoic, but Brian knew he was shaken.

"I'm okay. Honest."

Brett nodded and wiped tears off his face and out of his eyes. George gripped Brett's shoulder reassuringly.

"Where's Michael?" Brian asked.

"Here," Michael said from the doorway. Papa was by his side.

The big dog broke away and almost leaped onto Brian's bed. His back paws remained on the floor, but his front paws landed on the bed. He gave Brian doggie kisses until O'Connor pulled him off.

"He's been by your side the whole time," George said.

"I took him outside to pee," Michael explained.

Brian smiled and called, "Here, Papa!"

Again, Papa's front paws landed on Brian's bed.

Brian couldn't pet him. His right arm was heavily bandaged. An IV ran into the back of Brian's left hand. His arm and shoulder ached.

"What's wrong with my eye?" Brian said. He panicked, worrying about soccer and football, and in late fall and winter, basketball.

"You had some dirt chips fly into it. There is a scrape or two, but no lasting damage that the doc could tell. The bandage is for precaution," O'Connor said.

"He wants you to wear a patch like a pirate," George said.

"For how long?" Brian asked.

From the doorway, a doctor wearing a blue smock said, "A week. Like he said, for precaution."

"What about my arm and shoulder? My hand?"

The doc came over, listened to Brian's heart, took his blood pressure and checked his left eye.

"Some stitches. Four in your shoulder. Five in your upper arm. Three on your hand and on the side of your head along with some staples. Three in your eyebrow. Three just below your eye."

"Will I look like Frankenstein?" Brian asked in panic.

Everyone laughed.

"They shaved the side of your head," Brett said.

"You won't be any uglier than you already are," Graff said from the doorway.

The doc stood up and said, "All in all, you're in good shape. No lasting damage. We'd like to keep you here overnight because of dehydration, but you don't have to if you don't want to."

"I don't want to."

The doctor laughed and said, "I figured. The nurse will be in to get you ready to leave."

He walked out of the room and shut the curtain behind him. Before he did, Reyna joined them.

"Something we have to talk about, guys," Graff said. His tone was quiet and ominous.

Graff sat on the foot of the bed, and said, "Michael, sit here." He patted the bed where he wanted Michael to sit. Michael obeyed.

"Boys, we told you that we needed you to check in three times a day. Morning, afternoon and evening. You didn't do that. We specifically told you to let us know if there was any trouble." He paused and met and held their eyes. "Didn't we?"

"Yes," Brian answered. Brett and George nodded.

"Pat ended up in the hospital and could have been killed. Ron took a bullet in the shoulder. And Brian here," Graff took hold of Brian's toes, "is in the hospital as a result of a fire fight."

The boys nodded.

Brett said, "Brian wanted us to call you. We didn't let him. George needed to find Charles first. So, it wasn't Brian's fault."

"Yes, it was," Brian said quietly. "I should have stood up to you, but I didn't." He looked at Graff, then O'Connor, then Reyna and said, "I'm sorry."

"The thing is, guys," O'Connor said, "we were partners. We had to rely on each other, like Eiselmann and I do out in the field, or like Jamie and I do when we're working together. Partners don't abandon each other. There is trust. If there isn't any trust, the partnership doesn't work."

"I'm sorry," Brett said. George and Brian repeated it.

"Will this happen again?" Graff asked. "Because if it does, we're done. If there isn't any trust, there isn't any friendship. None."

"It won't," Brian said. Brett and George shook their head.

Michael sat through it all, not sure how he fit in. In his mind, he did all he was supposed to do. He was supposed to protect Brian and Brett.

O'Connor turned to Michael and said, "I told you that if there was any trouble, you were to call me. I specifically told you not to go back to Red Rock and that bar. Correct?"

"Yes, Sir."

O'Connor waited, as he and Michael had a stare down.

"I'm sorry," Michael finally said.

"Will it happen again?" Pat asked him.

Michael didn't know how to answer him. On one hand, he didn't think he'd ever see O'Connor or the others again. On the other, to be polite, he thought he should answer him with a 'no' which is what he did.

"So, we understand each other?" Graff asked.

The boys nodded.

"I didn't hear you," Jamie said.

"Yes, we understand," Brett said. Brian, George, and even Michael said they did, too.

No one said anything for a long time. The boys studied their hands and glanced surreptitiously at the three cops.

Brian asked, "Why were they after us? Those men, I mean? What did we do?"

Graff and Reyna tag-teamed the story.

Archer Goodnight wanted to build a resort, but the ranchers wouldn't sell. Deputy Mills was getting paid on the side, and it was he who had shot Charles in the shoulder.

"Why did he shoot Charles?" George asked.

Graff shook his head and said, "If Charles would have told Goodnight that he was calling the police, nothing would have happened. Mills would have been the investigating officer, and nothing would have come from the investigation. But Charles told Goodnight he would go to the Navajo elders.

Goodnight couldn't have that, since his resort idea would be sunk. So, he called Mills, and told him to shoot Charles."

Reyna picked it up from there. He told the boys that Desert Security had been hired by a mining firm who had wanted to mine ore in the Chuskas. There wasn't anything of value, so the mining company pulled out.

But Goodnight wanted more muscle, so he hired several men. The three who went after O'Connor, and some others. Those men served together in the Middle East and had been hired by Desert Security.

It was true that Desert Security knew nothing about their activity on behalf of Goodnight. They were acting as free agents. All six died on the mesa at the hands of Brian, George, and Michael. Brett hadn't killed anyone. He hadn't even fired a shot.

"What happened to Mills?" Brian asked.

"When we went to arrest him, there was a fire fight. He shot himself and died," Reyna said. "We matched ballistics to the shots at Pat and the shots at Jamie and me."

"Goodnight confessed and was arrested," Graff said. "The two guys who were with him at George's ranch died at the mesa."

"There were others who were wounded at the Morning Star ranch," Graff said.

Brian and Graff made eye contact, but it was Brian who broke it and turned his head away.

"Bri, you saved their lives," Pat said.

"Michael and Brett told us about the shots you made at the pond," Jamie said.

"I'm sorry. I only wanted to stop them. I didn't think . . ."

O'Connor reached out and took hold of Brian's left hand, and said, "You had no way of knowing if they intended to harm you or not. You acted to protect your brothers."

Tears fell from Brian's good eye. Probably the one under the bandage, too, though no one knew for sure.

"You protected your brothers, Brian," Graff repeated. "That counts for something."

"One last thing," Reyna said. "George, I know you were friends with Jonathon Laidley. He stood to gain if Goodnight was able to build his resort. After all, his trading post was the closest. He was looking at a windfall."

"He was in on it?" George asked almost in a whisper.

"The intimidation, but not the killing."

"Well, he was the one who told Goodnight about the mesa," Graff said. "He has since closed up his place and moved away. He hopes to sell it."

George had considered him a friend. Laidley had known his family. The betrayal stung.

There was a knock on the door.

Rebecca, Franklin, and Rosetta stood there.

"Can we come in?" Rebecca asked.

"Sure," Graff said as he stood up.

Brian tried to sit up a little straighter, but it hurt too much to move. Michael got up from the bed and stood in the corner near George, behind Brett.

"We want to thank you for all you did for us," Rebecca said.

Franklin held his cowboy hat in his hands, playing with the brim. Rosetta smiled and hung in the background. O'Connor offered her his chair, but she smiled and shook her head.

"The doctor said that if Charles hadn't gotten to the hospital when he did, he would have died," Rebecca said.

Franklin and Rosetta smiled. Franklin stepped forward and shook the boys' hands, then Graff's, O'Connor's, and Reyna's.

Rosetta hugged and kissed the boys and hugged the men. Then her parents left.

"How is Charles?" Brian asked.

Rebecca smiled and said, "He is fine." She thought that over and said, "He will be fine. Thank you for asking."

She turned to the cops in the room and said, "May I speak to them privately?"

Graff, O'Connor, and Reyna pulled the curtain, left the room, and shut the door.

When the door was shut, Rebecca turned to Brian and said, "Brian, I want to apologize for what I said to you."

Brian started to object, but Rebecca said, "Please, let me finish."

Brian nodded, but couldn't make eye contact with her. If he could have left the room, he would have.

"I asked George who was coming. I teased him by saying something like, are they cute? George can get jealous. He said, that yes, both of you are handsome, but you were involved in a relationship. I asked if she was cute, and he said, yes, Caitlyn is cute, but you also were in a relationship with Bobby, Brett's brother.

"So, I said what I said without thinking. I was worried about Charles and my parents. I am sorry. I didn't mean anything by it. I'm not like that, and neither is George. He just gets jealous."

Brian said, "It's okay."

The way he said it, Rebecca couldn't tell if it was okay or not.

Brett knew Brian's meaning from his tone. It wasn't about Rebecca, it was about Bobby, Jeremy and Vicky. Him, too. Probably George.

Brett's cell buzzed. He pulled it out of his pocket and saw it was Jeremy. "Hi, Dad!"

"Everyone safe and sound? Is Brian okay?"

"Yup, everyone's good."

"May I speak with Michael?"

Brett smiled at Michael and said, "Dad would like to talk to you."

Michael's eyes grew large, and he pulled away.

"Here, talk to him."

Both Brett and George were smiling. So was Rebecca.

Michael took the cell and said, "Hello?"

"Hi, Michael. I'm Jeremy, the boys' dad. I'm putting you on speaker so Vicky can talk, too."

There was some noise on the other end.

"Can you hear us okay?"

"Yes, Sir."

"Hi, Michael. I'm Vicky. I'm the boys' mother. Jeremy and I would like to ask you something."

Michael waited.

Jeremy said, *"We wanted to know if you would like to come to Wisconsin and live with us for a month or two."*

"Longer, if you'd like," Vicky said. *"We understand from Pat O'Connor that you don't have any parents or family, is that right?"*

"Yes, I mean, no, Ma'am."

"Well, you could come to Wisconsin and see if you like living with us. If you do, we would like to have you stay with us," Vicky said.

"We would like that very much," Jeremy said.

"I . . . I . . ."

Brett took the phone from Michael, pushed the speaker icon on the screen and said, "I put him on speaker. You asked him?"

"Yes."

"Good, because we would like that, too."

George and Brian smiled. "We would," Brian added.

There was a knock on the door and Ngo entered.

"Yá'át'ééh" he said.

"Dad, we have a visitor," Brett said with a smile.

Ngo bent over the phone and said, "Hello?"

"Hello, Hosteen Ngo. I am Jeremy Evans, and I am with my wife, Vicky. We are the boys' parents."

Ngo smiled and said, "I remember you from when you spoke to the council requesting permission for George to live with you."

"Yes, Sir, that is correct."

Ngo smiled and said, "I was told you wanted to ask me something."

"Yes, Sir. We invited Michael to spend some time with us here. We invited him to live with us to see if he wanted to be a part of our family," Vicky said.

Michael brushed tears out of his eyes.

Ngo smiled and said, "It seems George's half-brother is either sad or happy. I cannot tell."

"Wait, what did you say?" Brett asked.

Ngo smiled, and said, "Michael is George's half-brother. Different mothers, same father. They are what you would call, step-brothers."

George and Michael stared at each other. It seemed neither knew. How could they?

"Michael was born into the *Tséikeeheé* clan."

"The Two Rocks-Sit clan," George said.

Ngo said. "*Hosteen* Tokay is a member of the *'Azee'tsoh dine'é*."

"The Big Medicine People clan," George said. "We are brothers," he said to Michael.

"That explains why you look alike," Brett said.

George shook his head and said, "Father, I did not know."

Michael said, "I didn't either."

"It would be wrong to separate brothers," Ngo said.

"It would be like separating Bobby and me, or Randy and Billy," Brett said. "That does it then. Michael is coming home with us."

"Michael, is that okay with you?" Vicky asked.

"I . . . I . . ."

"It is," Brett said. "He'll be on the plane with us."

"What about my horses? What will happen to them?"

Brian said, "We have room for them."

"I'm sure Jeff and Danny won't mind," Jeremy said. *"When we hang up, I'll give Jeff a call and ask."*

"I had my horses transported to Wisconsin. We can do the same for you," George said.

"Michael, would you be willing to try living with us?" Vicky asked.

"You said you don't have anywhere else to go," Brett said.

Michael and George locked eyes. George smiled, and said, "I would like my brother, Michael, to come home with me."

Michael was overwhelmed. A little scared. Perhaps a lot scared. He only knew the mountains and desert, hunting and horses. He wasn't even sure where Wisconsin was. He didn't know what to say or how to say it, but he found himself nodding and smiling. First at George, then at Brett, and then at Brian. He smiled at Ngo.

"Yes, I would like that."

"We have a new brother!" Brett said.

"And another dog," George said with a laugh.

"What?" Jeremy said.

"Papa! He's Brian's dog. He looks like Jasper, only bigger," Brett said.

"He might be from the same family," George said.

"Okay then. I guess we're adding a boy and another dog," Vicky said with a laugh.

EPILOGUE

The boys, Graff, O'Connor, and Reyna stayed in Arizona an extra two days to finish out the week. They took in ruins, and George and Reyna played guide. They visited the Grand Canyon, and they hunted, though Brian didn't take part. He used his right eye for sighting and his right hand for shooting. Neither worked very well.

They lost a great deal of their equipment and supplies, though one of the dead men on the mesa had the other Glock in his waistband. It was retrieved. The metal case and the rifle cases were gone. Fortunately, the trading post at Teec Nos Pos had replacements.

After a good amount of debate and promises, the boys and Rebecca spent a night camping at the pond. Brian wasn't allowed to get in the water past his chest because of the stitches. He waded in, but couldn't take part in the horse fights or the dunking. That made him sad.

That night, Brett found him weeping as he sat on the rock looking out across the valley with Papa at his feet. Brett sat with an arm around his shoulders and finally got him to the blanket he shared with him where he held him until morning.

On the morning of their last day, Reyna dropped them off at the airport. He told them that Kelliher and Storm were already working on sealing up their records due to their age and the fact that they were defending themselves. Brian was relieved, though he felt both guilt and shame.

Brett and George recognized that Brian grew quieter, more inward. He had always been quiet, but even more so since the fight on the mesa. No amount of coaxing or joking could snap him out of it.

They landed in Milwaukee. Because of the extra body and the extra bag Michael had brought with him, Eiselmann met them at the airport. As if it were prearranged, O'Connor drove Brian, Brett, and Papa, while the others drove to Jeremy's in Eiselmann's car.

O'Connor didn't talk much. Brett didn't bother with the radio. Brian dozed off with Papa's head in his lap. By the time he woke up, they had pulled to a stop in the driveway.

Jeremy, Vicky, and the twins came out of the house to greet them, curious to meet Michael, anxious to assess Brian's injuries. Bobby hung back on the porch with his hands in his pockets.

Handshakes and hugs for Michael. Lots of *"Happy to meet you!"* and *"You look just like George!"*

Papa, Momma, Jasmine, and Jasper wrestled on the lawn like they had known each other forever. Perhaps they did.

While it made Brian happy, it also made him sad. He didn't feel like he belonged.

Billy was the first to speak to him.

"Rrrrr, where's the treasure, Mate?" he said in his best pirate's voice.

Brian smiled.

"You okay?" Randy asked.

Brian shrugged and said, "Just sore and tired."

"Will your eye be okay?" Billy asked. "I mean, for football and soccer?"

Brian shrugged and said, "The doctor thinks so. I'm supposed to wear the patch for a couple more days."

"Let me take a look, Bri," Vicky said after a big hug and a kiss on each cheek. Brian didn't hug her back, but held onto his duffle and his backpack.

She lifted off the patch and gasped.

He had a shiner, and blood had seeped into the white of his eye. His brow and the area below his eye were an ugly blue-black and badly swollen.

"Oh, Honey!" She turned to Jeremy and said, "We need to get him in tomorrow."

"Gees, Brian!" Jeremy said. "I'll call first thing in the morning."

"It's not that bad," Brian said.

"Yeah, it's bad," Randy said.

Brian saw the shock on Randy's face.

"How are you feeling?" Vicky asked.

"Tired and sore." Because he didn't want to talk to them much, he said, "I want to go lay down. I'll take care of the rifles and Glocks later, if that's okay."

"Michael and I will take care of them," George said.

Brian didn't argue. He picked up his bags, climbed the two steps, and without making any eye contact with Bobby, walked into the house.

He walked up the stairs, entered his room, and shut the door. He tossed his bags on the floor by the side of the bed, kicked off his shoes, and plopped down on his back.

He wept. He had never felt this alone. Lost. At some point, he fell asleep, but the tears still fell.

He woke with a start. The window showed a late afternoon sun. He checked the clock on his nightstand. Not quite dinner time, but close.

Sitting at the foot of his bed was Vicky. Standing behind her was Jeremy. The door was shut.

He braced himself.

Vicky handed Brian three Motrin and a glass of water, saying, "This should help with the swelling. Brett said you hadn't taken anything today."

Brian took them from her, popped them into his mouth, and took a long sip of water.

"Thank you."

Jeremy sat down on one side, and Vicky moved up across from him, effectively sandwiching Brian between them.

"We received your letter yesterday," Vicky said. "Bobby received his."

"He didn't share it with us," Jeremy said.

Vicky's face crumbled, and she said, "I promised myself I wouldn't cry. I can't help it."

Brian joined her. Even Jeremy wiped tears from his eyes.

"We've never judged you, Bri. We never worried about you. You've always had good judgment," Jeremy said.

Vicky struggled and said, "I know it's hard for you to understand, but I've tried to love you boys equally. I tried to be impartial. It hasn't been easy, because I gave birth to Brett and Bobby. I'm their mom, but I'm mom to all of you guys. Brian, I have never loved you less than them or anyone." This last she said with a sob.

It broke his heart. He couldn't make eye contact with her. Fortunately, one eye was covered. He focused his other eye on the ceiling.

"Bri, I always thought you and I had a close relationship. We talk about everything. Was I wrong?"

Brian shook his head, still unable to make eye contact.

"Way back before I . . . we adopted you, one night you and I watched a movie while the other guys were off doing something. You asked me if I loved one of the twins more than the other. Do you remember that?"

Brian nodded.

"I said that love isn't a cake. It's not cut up in pieces only to disappear when you give it away. I told you that love is magical. The more you love, the more love you have to give."

Vicky gathered herself as best she could, but wilted under a storm. She held up a hand, shut her eyes, and tried again.

"Brian, when I asked you to watch over Brett and George, I never meant for you to put yourself in harm's way. I never, ever, meant for you to sacrifice yourself for them. I would never do that."

She held both hands to her face and cried. She couldn't stop.

Brian sat up, reached out and hugged her.

"I would never do that, Brian. Never."

Brian nodded.

"And, I don't love you any less than Brett or Bobby. I don't worry about you and Bobby. We asked you guys to sleep in different rooms because you're brothers. Adopted, yes, but you're still brothers. Beyond that, I never wanted the two of you to . . . to . . ." she shook her head and said, "I never intended for the two of you to stop being friends or loving each other, to stop being together. It was about sex and the fact that you're brothers."

"The friendship the two of you have is beautiful, Bri," Jeremy said. "I understand the fact that sometimes you can't control love or the expression of love. Both of us, your mom and I understand that. It's just that as brothers, we thought it best to try to take away any sort of temptation the two of you might have. We didn't want you in that situation. It wasn't punishment."

Brian finally said, "I don't want to talk about this."

"Bri, we have to. You have to understand where your mom and I are coming from."

"Brian, you should never be ashamed of loving someone," Vicky said. "You were right when you said that love is pure. There is nothing wrong with love. There is nothing wrong with the friendship or the love you and Bobby have for one another."

Brian couldn't help but feel anger and frustration.

Jeremy took hold of Brian's hand, and said, "The thing is, Bri, we're family. There will always be disagreements. Sometimes, there are angry words, and things said that can't be pulled back. But we're family. We work through them. We don't run from them."

"We don't want you to move out," Vicky said. "You're a part of this family just as the twins or George or Brett or Bobby are. Now, as much as Michael is. We're family. Our family would be less without you."

She began to sob again, "It would break my heart if you left us. If something would have happened to you up on that hill, it would have broken my heart. Even now, looking at your bruises, your stitches, your eye, and knowing that you felt you had to sacrifice yourself for George or Brett because of something I said, I can't forgive myself. I can't." Both hands went to her face, and she shook her head and rocked herself back and forth.

Brian reached out to hold her and both of them cried into each other's arms.

"I'm sorry," Brian said.

"You're sorry?" Vicky said with a sad laugh. "I'm the one who is sorry, Brian. I'm so sorry."

Brian managed to say, though it came out in snatches and gasps, "I didn't write that letter to make you feel guilty. I wanted to explain myself."

"We know that, Bri," Jeremy said. "We know that."

"I love Bobby." Brian shook his head and said, "I don't know if I can be in the same room with him. I don't know if I can eat next to him. Ride in a car with him. Each time we're in the bathroom getting ready for school or to go to bed . . ."

"Brian, your mom and I aren't worried about that. We never worried about that," Jeremy said.

"But . . ."

"No buts, Bri. We love the two of you. We love you. The friendship, the relationship you have with Bobby is beautiful. We never meant to take that away from you. I know Bobby doesn't want it to end. He's hurting, Brian. He's shattered."

"So am I!" Brian said defiantly. "He drops that on me out of nowhere when we can't even talk it out!"

"Now you have the chance to talk it over with him," Vicky said. "Bobby loves you. He desperately wants your friendship. He never wanted that to end."

Brian shook his head. Neither Jeremy nor Vicky understood what it meant. Even he didn't know if it was his unwillingness to mend the friendship with Bobby, if the friendship was beyond repair, or whether he wanted to give up and walk away from it. From them.

"What are you thinking?" Jeremy asked.

Brian shook his head again.

Jeremy and Vicky waited.

"I love Bobby. I never meant to hurt him. I never meant to hurt you. I never meant anything. I love Bobby. I still love him. It. Just. Hurts. So. Much." He broke down and sobbed.

Vicky reached for him first. Jeremy was content to grab a handful of Brian's hair and then rub Brian's neck.

"I can't be in the same house with him. I can't be in the same room with him. It hurts too much. It's all fucked up! I'm fucked up."

Vicky rocked him and kissed his forehead and his cheek.

Jeremy said, his voice catching, "Bri, we're your mom and dad. Bobby is your brother. We're in this for the long haul. We won't give up on you, and you can't give up on us. You can't give up on Bobby."

Brian didn't know how to respond or if he could respond.

"We're family," Jeremy said. "You're my son. I've always loved you. Even before . . . your parents . . . I loved you. I always thought of you as my son long before I . . . we adopted you. I'm proud to be your dad. Nothing has changed that."

Brian wiggled free from Vicky and latched onto Jeremy. He buried his face in Jeremy's chest and cried.

"I love you."

"Bri, I know that. I love you, too."

"And I love you, Bri. Can you forgive me?" Vicky asked.

After Brett and George told them about what happened on the trip and what went happened on the reservation, she knew it would be a long time before she would forgive herself, if she ever could forgive herself. After reading Brian's letter, both Jeremy and Vicky knew it would be a long time before Brian trusted them again.

The three of them hugged each other and cried into each other's arms.

"I'll always worry about what you think of me," Brian sobbed. "Always. I can't live like that."

Jeremy wiped tears from his eyes, took both of Brian's hands and said, "I know it will take time for you to believe us, but Bri, we love you. We don't think any less of you. We don't, and we won't, worry about you. You have to believe that. Please let us try to get back to the way we were before any of this happened."

Brian didn't know if he could. He couldn't even look them in the eye.

Eventually, Jeremy said, "Bri, why don't you take some time and gather yourself, and then come down to get something to eat. Brett said you haven't eaten anything all day."

Brian sighed and then nodded. He knew deep down they wouldn't let him move out. He didn't even know if he could.

"I know it will take time, but are we good? You, mom, and me?"

Brian nodded, though he kept his eyes downcast.

Vicky gave him one last kiss on his forehead. Jeremy rubbed his nose with Brian's and kissed his cheek.

"I love you, Bri. Always have, always will."

Brian nodded. His smile failed, though.

They got up from the bed and left Brian's room, shutting the door behind them.

He swung his feet over the side of the bed and sat there. He didn't know for how long. Whether he was gathering his thoughts or his courage, he didn't know.

He had to go downstairs and into the kitchen where everyone was. Where Bobby was. Where Brett was. All eyes would be on him. Each of them would have their thoughts. Each of them would watch his and Bobby's reaction.

Brian shrugged to no one.

He took a deep breath, stood up, and stretched. He wiped his good eye one more time and made sure the patch covered the other. And then he left the room, leaving his door open behind him.

ABOUT THE AUTHOR

Joseph Lewis has been in education for forty-four years as a teacher, coach, counselor and administrator. He is retiring this year. He has taken creative writing and screen writing courses at UCLA and USC. Lewis has published six books. *Taking Lives, Stolen Lives, Shattered Lives, Splintered Lives, Caught in a Web,* and *Spiral Into Darkness.*

Born and raised in Wisconsin, Lewis has been happily married for twenty-eight years and counting to his wife, Kim. Together they have three wonderful children: Wil (deceased July 2014), Hannah, and Emily, and they reside in Virginia.

NOTE FROM THE AUTHOR

Word-of-mouth is crucial for any author to succeed. If you enjoyed *Betrayed*, please leave a review online—anywhere you are able. Even if it's just a sentence or two. It would make all the difference and would be very much appreciated.

    Thanks!
    Joseph

Thank you so much for reading one of our **Crime Fiction** novels.
If you enjoyed the experience, please check out our recommended
title for your next great read!

Caught in a Web by Joseph Lewis

"This important, nail-biting crime thriller about MS-13 sets the
bar very high. One of the year's best thrillers."
-BEST THRILLERS

View other Black Rose Writing titles at
www.blackrosewriting.com/books and use promo code
PRINT to receive a **20% discount** when purchasing.

BLACK ROSE
writing